ACROSS THE SEA OF DESIRE

A Novel

MELODY SUE NEFF

FALLON & VICTORIA PUBLISHING

Fallon & Victoria Publishing/Across the Sea of Desire
Printed in the United States of America

Cover design by Josh Alfaro

Across the Sea of Desire/ Melody Sue Neff -- 1st ed.

Hardback ISBN: 979-8-9949377-0-9
Paperback ISBN: 979-8-9949377-1-6
ebook ISBN: 979-8-9949377-2-3

For my sister Patty, who always amazes me with her adventures and inspires me with her courage. May the bond never be broken. For Lisa, thank you for helping me find my smile again. For the band U2 and their ability to make me search for love and truth. For all my friends and family, too numerous to name, who saw only the writer all along.

Also, for Ray, my very own knight in shining armor . . . my husband, my love.

PREFACE

The Promise

It was 1995, and my mother had just become something new: divorced, unmoored, and quietly determined to find herself again. I was ten years old, old enough to understand that something had ended, but not old enough to know what comes after.

She decided a summer in Ireland would be her cure. While she was gone, postcards arrived like small lifelines—green hills, stone cottages, looping handwriting that always ended with *I miss you.* I missed her too, in that deep, childlike way where absence feels permanent even when it isn't. When she returned, our house was filled with new music—Old Blind Dogs, Enya, and Loreena McKennitt drifting through the rooms, songs that sounded ancient and aching and full of longing. She would often sing along, her voice clear and strong, carrying the melodies as if she had brought a piece of Ireland back with her.

When she came home, she wasn't the same woman who had left. She had fallen in love—with Celtic music, with Irish history, with Renaissance fairs and tartans and ancient stories. Ireland had seeped into her bones. She dragged my sister and me to Highland Games all over the Southwest, determined that we would know where we came from, that our roots mattered. A year or so later, she even met her favorite author, Diana Gabaldon, at the Tucson Highland Games—an encounter she spoke about with reverence, as if it were proof that dreams were closer than they seemed.

But what I remember most from that time wasn't the festivals or the music. It was the sound of keys clicking late into the night.

Our family computer sat in the living room of our small apartment, and my mother spent hours there, shoulders slightly hunched, completely absorbed. She was writing a romance novel. I didn't understand it then, only that this story mattered deeply to her.

Years passed. She mentioned the book now and then, always with a mixture of pride and fear. She wanted to send it to publishers—but never quite did. Eventually, she stopped bringing it up, and I stopped asking. Life moved on, as it always does.

Then, in 2011, everything stopped.

My mother was diagnosed with stage IV cancer. Within eighteen months, she was gone. My last conversation with her took place in a hospice bed set up in her living room. It was summer again. She couldn't leave the bed, but she was sitting upright, alert, almost luminous with a sudden burst of energy. I sat beside her, and we talked about the things that matter when time is short.

She told me she didn't want my five-year-old son or my two-year-old daughter at her funeral. She wanted their memories of her to be warm, not heavy. She loved them fiercely.

Then she looked at me, serious in a way that made my chest tighten, and she brought up her book. The romance novel from my childhood, I hadn't thought about in over a decade.

"Promise me," she said, "that you'll publish it."

She told me where to find the thumb drive. Had me retrieve it. There wasn't room for hesitation. All I could say was yes.

I don't know how many deathbed promises people receive from their mothers, but this one lodged itself into me. It would haunt me for the next ten years.

She passed away a few days later. I was twenty-seven, with two small children, trying to understand how to live in a world without my mother. After her funeral, my own marriage began to unravel. I tucked the thumb drive carefully into an important drawer. With every move, every new chapter of my life, I packed it with intention—always knowing where it was, always not quite ready to open it.

I went back to school. I raised my children. Time passed. In 2021—almost ten years after her death—I finally plugged the thumb drive into my laptop and read her novel for the first time. Only half of it was there. The drive had glitched. The second half was gone.

Heartbroken, I called my stepfather. We searched for backups, old computers, anything. Too much time had passed. But he did find something: her original typed manuscript from the 1990s. So I did the only thing I could. I retyped the second half of her book by hand. I'll never know what she may have changed in later years, what edits lived only in her mind. To honor her, I published the novel under her maiden name—Neff—the name she had when the story was first born in 1995.

I think everyone should be so lucky to have their mother leave behind a piece of herself in a love story.

Caroline was based on my mother. And reading her words now brings happy tears—because through this book, I found another piece of her, long after she was gone.

Thank you for being part of the promise I made to her.

—Amanda, in memory of Mom

PROLOGUE

America, Christmas Eve, 1995

She closed her eyes tightly, feeling the dampness of her tear-soaked lashes resting cool against her skin. The warmth of them faded instantly in the cool air. She was shivering violently and colder than she had ever felt. Another tremor shook her body, the tight waves making her insides ache; she grew weary from the constant strain. The involuntary motions weakened her as she fought to maintain her body's heat against the freezing temperatures in the mine shaft.

Attempting once again to shift and pull closer into herself, she immediately felt the ropes that bound her wrists and ankles bite painfully into her swollen, raw flesh. New waves of pain coursed through her entire being. Her thoughts pulsed through her head with the slow thud of her heartbeat against the unyielding tightness of her restraints. This was all so unfair! It was a reminder of lost freedom, of lost life, and of a lost love. Without love, her life seemed lost indeed. This dark place was a testimony to the emptiness without him.

But she had to survive. She *had* to, especially after all she had been through. After all *they* had been through. It didn't seem right it should end now, end this way. She knew she would need the sheer will of her love to get through this, for the time for survival had passed into a calm. The storm's strength waned for a moment, leaving her swirling in the midst of the eye. She felt alone and separated, without anyone or anything except that will.

She could feel the dirt wall behind her. It had long ago numbed her back with its tomblike coldness. She leaned wearily against it with her knees drawn up to her chest, finding it harder and harder to distinguish between the wall and herself. They seemed to become one.

Laying her cheek on top of her knees, she let her aching muscles rest for a moment. She was so tired, and it was so blissful to release the battle for even a brief moment. The events that had surrounded the previous months had taken a toll on her physically, and in this weakened state, she was quickly betrayed by her body's needs. If she closed her eyes, she might be able to forget what was happening. Forget the insane situation in which she found herself, forget her sadistic kidnapper, let the peaceful darkness of sleep take her away. Perhaps if she could close her eyes for one brief moment, the one she loved would come to her mind's eye, where he was never far from her, never out of reach. Just for a moment—just for . . . a . . . second. The promise of his image was so peaceful. She tried to reach out to him and draw on the strength he had so often given her in the past. If only . . .

"Wake up!" the man growled, his voice low and tainted with resigned anger.

She slowly, painfully opened her eyes, feeling the threat of tears lingering in them. She would not give in. She would not let him see her pain, her fear. He didn't deserve it, and as she looked up at him hovering over her, she could sense his own fear just barely hidden beneath the surface. She felt a surge of hope at seeing him trying so hard to conceal it from her. It empowered her to know that he now felt fear, and she almost smiled at the irony.

He placed his hands on his hips, a display of childish domination as he gloated down at her. She saw the muscles in his jaw working. He knew it would soon be over for him—and he was aware that she knew it too.

"Give up; it's over," she said softly, the way a mother might try to explain to a small child that he must accept the punishment for his bad actions. "They know you have me now, and there is no way out."

His mind seemed to work on her last statement. Denial, she thought. He is standing there with his hand in the cookie jar, crumbs stuck to his face, and still, he will deny it. She felt the hope of a smile fighting for release again.

"Shut up!" he yelled down at her. The stomping of his foot sent a small dust cloud swirling about her ankles. "Shut your damned mouth!"

She felt slightly taken aback by the force behind his voice. She closed her eyes, anticipating his actions and praying silently that he would not strike her again. Her jaw still throbbed from his earlier blow at her attempted escape, and she had no desire to feel his wrath again.

As she opened her eyes, she realized he must have noticed her wince. He was smiling ruefully down at her. His eyebrows raised in what appeared to be amusement, and a chuckle escaped his twisted grin. "I'm getting out of here alive, but we both know that's not the plan for you, don't we?" He was sneering now, his eyes dark and glassy. She thought him mad beyond help.

She could feel the chill of his lingering grin as she realized he still meant to go through with his plan to kill her. He turned, his back to her as he occupied himself with something she could not see. She licked her lips, tasting the metallic sweetness of her own blood on her tongue. It sickened her and brought an immediate vision from the past. Blood, rich and thick, coursed through her, and now he meant to steal her life from her, meant to stop the flow forever. He would still kill her, even though he knew he had no means of escape, and it was finally over for him. She had to think fast; the time for mistakes was over. She literally had to take her life in her own hands.

"You could still use me," she said, trying to restrain the hopefulness in her voice.

"What?" he said quietly, his back still to her. He was bending now, going through the brown backpack he had brought with him.

"I said you could use me to make your escape, like a shield or something. Listen, they would never shoot at you with me in front of you blocking their aim; they wouldn't risk it." She watched as he stood, turning and closing the short distance between them. She could see her words registering on his face. He knelt when he reached her, his face close to hers. She could smell his rancid breath—hot, though not from any heat . . . from hate, raw and pure coming from deep inside.

"You would say anything to get out of this alive, wouldn't you?" he asked with a mocking tone, narrowing his eyes at her.

"Yes," Caroline answered truthfully. "But I know you. You do not want to die in here with me, no matter how much you say you hate me now."

He leaned in closer. "It doesn't matter. Nothing matters now. I thought you were special. I thought you were different, but you are just like all the rest. You are going to die, my pet, and that is all that really matters now. Death, Caroline—death is standing right next to me. Smile. He is."

Caroline believed him then, knowing where the hate came from. She let out her breath when he turned from her to continue with his busy work. Closing her eyes once again, she leaned, defeated for now, against the hardness of the cold rock behind her. It sent another chill through her as the dampness seeped through her shirt. It was useless, this bargaining for her life with him. His hatred for her seemed to be the one thought that propelled his actions, driving him on with a relentless passion toward his goal. She knew about that kind of all-consuming passion firsthand, and the knowing did not ease her mind. He would drive on, helpless against the rage eating at his heart. He would make her pay for her love for another, and he intended to make her pay with her life. It seemed nothing else would satisfy him now. She began to drift again.

Her dreams quickly engulfed her, taking her on wings to her true love. Caroline could hear his voice, calming and reassuring in her mind. His presence was so strong she could almost feel him nearby. *I love you*, she thought. *No matter what has happened between us, I will always love you.* She pressed into her thoughts harder, trying to span the thousands of miles that separated them. She hoped to mentally transmit her message to him, as she had been unable to tell him that no matter what, she had forgiven him and would not forget the love she felt for him.

Caroline winced at a surge of new pain when his foot slammed into her thigh, quickly waking her with a start. The stench coming from the darkened corridor was overwhelming.

"Get up; it's time!" The man's voice was demanding, making it impossible for her to stay asleep and safe. "Now!" He had seemingly lost all patience.

She frowned in her mind, wondering if the frown registered on her mouth. "Are we leaving?" she asked hopefully. *Maybe he has decided to take me up on my advice to use me as a shield.* Her eyes widened at the thought.

"*I* am leaving," he said coldly, bringing the shiny barrel of a gun into her line of view. It was level, pointing directly at her heart, his fingers gripping the handle tightly. She noted his hand shaking in the dim lamplight.

"No!" she cried as he gripped her upper arm and jerked her to a standing position with more force than was necessary. "Wait!" she screamed, finally feeling the desperation take hold. Her breath was coming in short, quick gasps. Her head was spinning from the panic that seized her heart. This is it! The realization that she would die at the hands of this madman took her breath away.

She squared her shoulders and lifted her chin defiantly. She heard his voice, but couldn't hear what he said as her blood pounded loudly in her ears. As she watched him lift the barrel of the gun to her head, she closed her eyes and heard the immediate roar of the shot.

Caroline found out then that death had no sting. The darkness was indeed peaceful.

PART ONE
AMERICA

"Be cautious then, young ladies; be wary how you engage."
—William Makepeace Thackeray, *Vanity Fair*, 1811–1863

1.

UNAWARE

Four Months Earlier

"I need an adventure," Caroline said in more of a sigh than a voice. Sitting there staring into her drink, she vaguely noticed the glass had begun to sweat, leaving beads of water condensing on the outside. With one slim finger, she traced tiny circles in the moisture, feeling the coolness of the droplets as her mind wandered back to her one nagging thought.

"Not just any adventure, but a really exciting one, with one of those gorgeous romance novel heroes protecting me from the bad guys in it," she said aloud, lifting the glass to her mouth for a sip. Instead of enjoying cool refreshment, she practically choked on the liquid that had long ago separated. "I think it's time to go," she said, coughing and looking up in search of her friend.

The club was dark, the music was loud, and Caroline's only desire was to find her friend and go home. She really had not wanted to come tonight, but the promise of a good time from her friend Vanessa was something she thought she might be up for. A night out with her best friend should have done the trick, but now, it only served to feed the intense headache she had been nursing over the last hour.

"Where are you?" she said, narrowing her eyes and straining to see through the crowd, hazy smoke, and darkness of the trendy nightclub. As a converted warehouse, the place held a certain charm all its own. In a town full of cowboys, monster trucks, and country-western music blaring in every store, this club, with its slightly punk edge and neon everything, was an oasis to a select group of partiers. Caroline well appreciated it for both the music and the people. It was a loud reminder of home in some way, though nothing compared to the bright lights of Chicago. This indeed was the best this western town had to offer.

Lately, however, this fast-paced nightlife had begun to wane on her nerves just a bit. She felt bored, even drained, with the empty lifestyle in which she found herself. She was torn between the faces of the people around her and the real feelings she harbored behind her own forced smile. She was tired—tired of the shallowness of the people, tired of the lounge lizards who stuffed their wedding rings deep into their pockets when they came through the door. Caroline was tired most of all of the loneliness she was feeling every night as she crawled under her covers alone. Not that she had ever needed to be alone. On the contrary, men abounded at every corner. But their offers of love soon tarnished when she would not give in to their sexual advances. Having been involved in a few relationships as a young adult, she soon decided to forgo that unfulfilling part of her life, and in an almost shameful decision, had decided the next man she would give herself to completely would be her husband. She was completely committed to this promise she had made to herself and her future husband. Besides, in times as dangerous as these, one could never be too careful or too sure.

Tossing her long, black curls over her shoulder, she could not help but notice how warm the place was. Even in the light, cotton, summer dress she had chosen, the temperature was becoming unbearable. "Vanessa," she said, frowning, "I want to go, now." Looking at her watch, she raised her eyebrows in disbelief. "One o'clock!" No wonder her legs and hips were beginning to feel numb. She had been sitting for more than three hours!

Lifting herself off the stool, she smoothed out the wrinkles of her long skirt, adjusted the belt around her small waist, and felt the popcorn crunching beneath the soles of her sandals. The stiffness in her joints made her almost sorry she had turned down every offer to dance during the evening.

Looking out onto the dance floor, she quickly spotted Vanessa dancing with a rather short man who was smiling brightly up at her friend in obvious adoration. Caroline smiled and shook her head at her friend, giving a quick wave in her direction at the same time. Vanessa was never at a loss for admirers, and it was apparent from the short man's expression that he was in total awe of her. Vanessa's tall, thin frame attracted men like flies. The long lushness of her natural, bright-blonde hair served as the honey to which they came. Together, she and Vanessa could turn the heads of every hot-blooded male in the place. In college, they had become known as the "Bobbsi twins," one hardly seen without the other. In fact, Caroline had never known such a close relationship with another woman in her life. She often became close, but they soon became jealous and abandoned her. Vanessa had been blessed with her own abundant charms and natural, all-American California-girl looks. Fate seemed to intervene, and the two became fast friends from the start. The fact that one was outgoing and the other slightly shy had only managed to enhance the relationship. They were kindred spirits, she was sure.

"You know my motto," Vanessa stated, shrugging helplessly and walking toward Caroline after abandoning her temporary dance partner. Caroline immediately knew what her friend was referring to, having stated on occasion she would never turn down an invitation for a dance. *If they get up the nerve to ask you, the least you can do is oblige.* Vanessa lived by that motto and did a lot of obliging. Her easy way surprised most men, who instinctively thought her unapproachable due to her stunning looks. It was a small man's way of excusing his own shortcomings. But Vanessa had a big heart to go with her big, seductive smile.

"You ready?" Caroline asked hopefully, raising her eyebrows to emphasize her desire to leave.

"Yeah, it's a little warm in here for me anyway," her friend answered with a quick fan of her hand at the front of her low-cut dress. Caroline was at once relieved. Vanessa's comment was the understatement of the year.

He watched her walk toward the exit with her friend. She was so beautiful, and it had been all he could do not to approach her, to get closer to her. She was mesmerizing. He had chosen instead to wait in the shadows and watch her from a distance. Her long, dark hair shimmered under the lights; her pale, creamy, white skin almost glowed in the darkness; and those emerald-green eyes were like jewels framed by the lushness of her thick lashes. He grinned at having seen her turn down every offer to dance, refusing even the most handsome of men all night. *She must be pure*, he thought. *Why else would she fend them off so easily? She must be saving it. Saving it for the right man—saving it for me*. He followed the two women toward the door and immediately made his decision. She was the perfect one for him. She was going to make the perfect pet, and when his palms began to sweat, he knew she would make the best pet yet.

Getting into his car, he waited for the red Jeep to pull out of the parking lot. It was one of those high models with a black roll bar and big spotlights on top. The roof was off due to the pleasant temperature of the night air, and he watched her hair blow freely as she drove into the starlit night.

He followed, watching and staying carefully hidden several cars behind her. Because of the height of her vehicle, she was easy to spot, and he drank in her features with each streetlight she passed under. The lights temporarily bathed her in an iridescent glow and made her pale skin look like that of an angel.

His breathing was hard, his heart pounding in his chest. He had come often to the club, and now it seemed all his efforts would pay off. He squirmed in his seat, the sweat dripping down his back causing it to itch. She turned into a dimly lit apartment complex. He slowed, pulling off to the side of the road to watch her. When he saw the blonde get out of the vehicle, he realized it must be her friend's home and not hers. He knew his suspicions were right when the blonde made her way into the brightly lit building and the red Jeep pulled off into the night again. *Home*, he thought. *She is on her way home now*.

She finally pulled into a parking lot some ten minutes later; it was also poorly lit, and Vince easily pulled unnoticed into a vacant spot to continue spying on her. He noted the numbers painted above the spot where she parked and instantly figured out her home address. *This is too easy,* he thought. *Way too easy and too perfect.*

He waited. She walked alone and unprotected to her door, opened it, and went inside, seemingly unaware of his presence. *She needs me,* he thought. *She needs me to be her master and protector.* His mouth curled slightly at one corner. "I'll be kind, I promise," he said softly, turning the key in the ignition. Putting the car into gear with a jerk, he pulled out of the parking lot with his lights still off.

The drive home was filled with many visions, visions of her and all her glory. She was the most exquisite thing he had ever seen, and just thinking of her brought an intense, familiar heat to him, warming his insides. He leaned back against the seat, the wetness of his sweat-soaked shirt annoying him. He reached up, pushed a wayward strand of hair out of his face, and wiped the sticky wetness from his forehead onto his pants, feeling the tiny polyester lint balls of fabric. The motion of his wiping was so close to his point of arousal that it nearly sent him over the edge. He shivered with desire.

She would be different, not like the others. She was older and bigger than the little ones he was used to. *She will be harder to control,* he thought. *Harder but better.* He had grown tired of the small ones. They were getting harder to get, and she represented a new challenge that piqued his interest. Sure, the little ones were beautiful, but this held a new promise. If he could get this one, he could keep her longer, use her harder. The little ones with their tiny bodies wore out so quickly, and to tell the truth, it was boring him now. It was always the same with them. First, they screamed a lot, and then they fought him, but eventually they wore out, and he had to quickly discard their little bodies in the mine shaft. *She will last a lot longer*, he thought. He could feel it.

2.

LIFETIMES PAST

Caroline felt relieved beyond words to be home at last. She quickly rid herself of her dress, the stench of the smoke-filled club still clinging heavily to it. She wondered if this was all there was to her life. A few nights out with Vanessa was about all she could stand. The singles scene had left her cold long ago, and she wanted—no, she needed—more.

Wandering over to her stereo, she picked out her favorite CD. It was an Irish group with a female lead who sang haunting, ethereal songs in both English and Gaelic. Though Caroline did not know the interpretations of the Gaelic, she was sure they were beautiful. Probably love songs, heartfelt and full of emotion, be it for lost loves or a country as beautiful as Ireland. The songs only served to enhance the interest she had recently begun to cultivate for the Emerald Isle.

Working at the bookstore, she often found herself deep into romance novels set in Ireland and Scotland. Their descriptions of the land and the people made her feel a certain kinship with the characters who shared her ancestral bloodline, no matter how diluted it had become throughout the centuries. She wasn't even sure she could claim a great-great-grandfather twice removed as Irish kin. It didn't matter; she was a would-be Celt, if only at heart.

"This music could soothe the savage beast," she said aloud to her cat, who was sitting on the couch next to her. His long, front legs stretched as he purred loudly under her stroking. "It sure seems to work on you, my friend. Did you have a good night?" she asked, as the huge fluff of black fur rolled over for her to scratch his stomach, letting out a faint meow for an answer. "Bet you had more fun than I did," she said softly, frowning as she remembered her wasted evening.

Turning off the light, she headed to the bedroom in search of her journal. Sam followed his mistress, close at her heels, jumping up in front of her onto the bed.

"I am not quite ready for bed yet, you silly," she laughed, pulling her journal out from its hiding place under a stack of letters that were bound with a pink ribbon. It was an organized way of retaining the years of correspondence that started with a weekend camping trip with a high school boyfriend years ago.

She ran her fingers lightly over the bundle in remembrance as foggy visions of her time in an abandoned farmhouse, and it filled her with a sort of melancholy. It was true when women say they never forget their first love. Even after all these years, Caroline could recall the clear vision of the young, fresh-faced boy who stole her innocence before its time, swearing eternal love and devotion to her. Yes, it had been a mistake, but one made in the sincerest form of young love.

She remembered the event as clearly as if it had happened only yesterday. The two of them were on their way to meet friends at the local campground. The car ran out of gas within walking distance of an abandoned farmhouse in the country. And then it started to rain. She could smell the wet farmlands now, the cornfields washed fresh with the dampness, the sweet smell of the corn still on the stalk.

Letting their natural curiosity take over, the two of them quickly found themselves enchanted by the relics of the past contained in the forgotten items left over from the previous owners. Dodging floor-to-ceiling cobwebs, they rummaged as brown dust puffed up under their feet like tiny clouds.

Caroline shivered unconsciously, rethinking how dangerous it could have been if anyone had actually still been living there. Dark forms of killers in those late-night B-movies came to light now, but then, in youthful ignorance, it never would have dawned on them to think of anything except the moment.

The light rain had quickly turned into an all-out summer storm, sending crashing thunder and bright flashes of lightning all around them. They built a fire in the fireplace, and a cozy seduction scene developed as they went through the box of old letters they found hidden in a room upstairs. They were postmarked during World War II. Dozens of letters, carefully bound with faded ribbons, had been lovingly saved, a testimony to the real love shared by two young lovers separated by the war.

Caroline's thoughts of that stormy night in the old house tugged at her heartstrings, and she absently sniffled as memories of the smells of old dust and sweet rain gave her an imaginary tickle. Being a hopeless romantic ever since she could remember, she often found herself back there on that fateful night. After they finished reading the last letter, she sobbed into that boy's chest as they sat on the floor in front of the warm glow of the fire. Her heart was broken for the young lovers from the letters who never saw each other again, for bound within the last pile was the telegram informing the woman of the sudden but heroic death of her young husband. He had served his country well and was a credit to the war effort and the people with whom he served.

Caroline took that night. Took the comfort offered at the unskilled but loving hands of her own young man. Her heart open, raw and vulnerable, she needed and wanted to feel love through the storm raging outside and the one within her own soul. And in the midst of the abandoned farmhouse, she let the innocence of her youth go, and the two became one, blending and merging with the house that was once a home.

Sighing, Caroline pushed the memories of that night back into their hiding place deep within her heart. The memories of her youth and mistakes were still too painful. Oh, she knew it really didn't matter; after all, it's the twenty-first century. Still, she wished with all her heart to have the special gift of herself to give to a husband one day. It would have been something special. Something just between the two of them that no other could lay claim to. She supposed she would have to find just the right man to make her feel whole again, and she crawled into bed next to Sam. His furry body and small amount of heat paled in comparison to the cold void in her heart.

She would pray tonight, like she had all the previous nights of her life. She would send her thoughts toward God and elicit His help in finding her soulmate. She had done this every night since she was ten years old and heard the Baptist pastor say, "If you ask God for anything, He will deliver." As a child, she had asked Him to take her mother then. To take the source of her tormented and abused lifestyle from her and let her begin life anew. It wasn't easy then, and it wasn't easy now. Life as a child in her mother's home was full of hurt, both physical and mental. Her mother, a single parent, was a classic undiagnosed paranoid schizophrenic who drank bottles of Vodka and spent her life drowning in her own hurtful past, blaming Caroline and everyone else for her own shortcomings. Caroline was determined not to turn out the way her own mother did.

It would be a cold day in Hell before she ever laid a hand on her own child, she had vowed. It had taken Caroline all the years of her life until now to learn how to live and be herself, to feel safe within her own skin, and to let her own feelings take hold and dwell within herself. She was free now. The death of her mother two years ago had freed her in many ways save one. Even though she liked being alone in the world, liked being free, she immensely disliked being lonely. So, she prayed and hoped God would hear her this time and send the man who would be her husband and life partner to her post haste.

Until now, her life had remained pretty lonely. She reached for her pen and the journal into which she poured her life's thoughts, and she began. Her pen flowed, thoughts coming quicker than she could write. "Oh, to sit in front of a knight on horseback." She leaned into the thought and gave herself over to it. "To feel his strong, hard thighs guiding the horse." She continued, "Where are the real men of our times? The would-be heroes who would fight for honor and love? In times such as these, women are alone with their fatherless children, unprotected and unloved. In their cold beds of independence, they long for strong arms to warm them in the night." She rolled from her stomach to her back, staring at the ceiling and chewing on the pen as she tossed the thought over and over in her mind. She sighed then, thinking she had written the analogy for the twenty-first century. She knew men's strengths had been weakened along with their intellect, and the computer age had seen to the very last remnants of their ability to outdo women in physical strength, leaving only their minds in direct competition with a woman's.

"How sad it is for us," she whispered to Sam, lying content within arm's reach for a scratch. Petting the cat and feeling the softness of his fur, she thought to herself how women had taken every last resource of men in their quest for equality. Perhaps, in some distant link, that was why crime had so escalated. Was there some connection to the idea that men were just lashing out at society with violence to prove a manhood of greater strength lost?

"Hum?" she groaned, making a mental note to perhaps bring up the question at the next literary meeting at the bookstore where she worked. It was so nice to be in such a peaceful place. Working at the Curl Up and Sit a While was a dream come true for her. She loved everything about the place. The soft lighting reminded her of the candles in her apartment. The dark smells of leather and new, untouched pages. The low, spirit-cleansing music. It didn't matter how hard or fast life was on the outside; people visibly relaxed the moment they walked through the doors. The rich aromas of cinnamon, nutmeg, and coffee drifted from the gourmet coffee bar at the back of the store. That had been her idea—to install a place to curl up with a book and sip on something hot was a given, and besides, all the giant bookstores had them. The Curl Up and Sit a While might not be a giant, megabook outlet, but they knew how to please and what made common sense. Caroline had been there for five years, and she still enjoyed going to work—something not too many people she knew could actually say with a straight face. Her favorite chore was to arrange the display cases and tables. She especially liked that job, as it gave her creative side an outlet. It was the Celtic blood in her that enhanced her ability to set up the displays with a European flair, arranging books amidst the Irish trinkets and Gaelic crosses from her own collection. It made her smile to think how fun her job was.

With a quick toss of the journal on her nightstand, she turned out the light, scooted under the covers, and settled in. With her hand resting lightly on Sam's back, she closed her eyes and fell into a familiar dream she always looked forward to.

He came to her then, just as he often did at night in her dreams. This man of hers had no face, shape, or form, only his mere presence available to her for but a moment.

Each time the same thing happened. She could see herself ballet dancing alone on a deserted stage. A free-flowing, chiffon dress in the palest pink billowed, rose, and fell like dainty pink clouds of smoke against her skin as she pirouetted across the floor. She sensed him near, felt him watching her, but all the time was powerless to stop herself dancing to the beat of the music in her heart. With each turn, she could make out the form of a man, dressed in black and blending into the shadows. She danced closer, willing her body to seek him out. His hand reached out of the darkness as if nobody were attached that she could see, welcoming her, beckoning her to have this dance with him. She wanted to, felt no fear or sense of evil at drawing nearer to him. Just as she reached out to take his open invitation, she awoke, breathless and laden with sweat. A bitter longing lingered in her being. It was something she couldn't quite grasp in the real world. Something perfect, awaiting her just . . . out . . . of . . . reach.

3.

SOMETHING TO BELIEVE IN

"Meow!"

Caroline was awakened to the very loud sound of her cat in the kitchen. He could be quite vocal when faced with starvation at the prospect of an empty bowl first thing in the morning. "Meeeeeow!" He was relentless this morning.

"All right, all right. I'm coming," she groaned. Last night's little outing with Vanessa still beat a slow drum in her head, making her movements slow and deliberate.

After saving Sam from a most horrible death by starvation, Caroline headed for the shower and the sweet release of tension the warm water would bring to her stiff muscles. *I am never going to make it to thirty*, she thought while letting the water soothe her tired body. She took extra care to rinse her hair in the coldest water possible—a trick to bring out the shine she learned from a hairdresser she dated briefly in college. She turned off the water, dried, and headed for her stereo.

Reaching to turn the volume up, she heard the ring. Grumbling, she reached for the phone.

"Hello?"

"Hey, girl, whatcha up to today?" Caroline frowned at hearing an all-too-awake Vanessa bubbling on the other end while her own voice was only now becoming somewhat recognizable.

"I'm off to this Irish Imports store, a customer told me about yesterday at work. It's supposed to have some great, authentic Irish things in it." She was beginning to perk up just thinking about the possibilities.

"You mean, it might have an authentic Irishman in it, don't you?" Vanessa teased.

"Well, that too." They were both giggling like schoolgirls.

"Caroline, I just can't believe how fanatical you've become about anything Irish since you learned about that great-great-something-or-other, on your mom's side, wasn't it?"

"Great-great-grandfather twice removed," Caroline corrected. Her mother would never fill her in on any family history, save for the pieces she chose to endlessly repeat. That usually came when she was in a drunken state and feeling sorry for herself. Caroline had searched high and low for any information on her past as if she were possessed by the thought. She had finally come to understand that for her, it was all about belonging, a sense of being a part of something bigger than just her small, unhappy life with her mother. She had always wanted to be a part of a real family and enjoy the warmth of brothers and sisters, a normal mother and father. Caroline felt that not having a father figure in your life was to miss out on something really special, and Caroline needed to know that somewhere down the line, her family had been normal.

"Right, whatever. I swear, Caroline, you would think you had green blood in your veins to hear you talk." Vanessa's sarcasm jarred Caroline from her thoughts.

She laughed at her friend's remark with a slight smile creeping back to her lips. "You want to go with?" she asked out of politeness. She really had hoped to go on this particular adventure alone. Seeking out one's history was a very personal thing for her, and the sour thought of a giggling Vanessa coming along didn't seem right somehow, especially since her friend couldn't understand her motives.

"No, thanks, I'm off to beat the heat and get all my errands done before noon, if you know what I mean."

Caroline knew exactly what Vanessa meant, knowing the temperature would again reach the hundred-degree mark well before noon. It was the reality of typical summer weather in southern Arizona, a bitter reality Caroline hated every day during the long, unbearable summers. It was a tradeoff, though. There weren't any distinct seasons to speak of, but the rest of the year was pure heaven. In Chicago, with its freezing ice- and snowstorms, Caroline and Vanessa would still be playing their usual weekly game of tennis in seventy degrees and sun. Besides, if she wanted snow, she could always drive up to Mount Lemmon when the roads were clear. Her Jeep could get through almost anything, and it was worth the trip just to taste a steaming-hot bowl of chili from the local cafe up there. She and Vanessa often hiked on the mountain in the summer. It was always thirty degrees cooler in the summer, and the trees reminded them both of home.

Caroline painfully endured the drawback of the intense heat and moving from Chicago to attend the University of Arizona because she valued her friendship with Vanessa, the sun worshipper. Plus, the offer to manage the bookstore was too good to pass up. Where else was she going to use her minor in Elizabethan literature? Still,

Chicago had her heart with its white winters and four seasons. Even the very coldest of seasons.

"Want to meet for lunch?" Vanessa asked, bringing Caroline's thoughts back to earth.

"Sure, how about noon at that soup-and-salad place you love so much—you know, the one with all the hunky waiters?" Caroline teased.

"Oooh, I love that place!" Vanessa sounded thrilled at the suggestion.

"The food or the atmosphere?" Caroline half-teased.

"Yum, both!" Vanessa was incorrigible.

Reaching for her favorite cotton summer dress, Caroline was reminded of her mother once again. The guilt had never left throughout the two years since her death. She should have spent more time with her, should have been a more devoted daughter. It pained her to remember the phone call from the Chicago police.

It had been seven days before anyone found the body, and even then, it was a fluke. A maintenance man found her on a routine check of the apartments. It was an apparent heart attack. She had been found alone in her bed, staring at the ceiling, a slight grin on her face. The man who found her said it looked as though she had been happy. Caroline knew without even seeing the body that she was happy. For the first time in all her life, her mother was happy and finally at peace. Caroline had flown home, the first time in seven years, and found herself not at home, but a stranger in a strange land. Everything had changed. Streets she once knew with her eyes closed were now nothing more than faint memories that needed jarring. Home wasn't home anymore, and it had hit her pretty hard. They say at the end of every road is home, but in this case, Caroline didn't know where her home was. But she knew it definitely was not Chicago anymore. Caroline was alone now. More alone than just two thousand miles from her hometown and her mother. No, she was totally and completely on her own now, and it scared her to think of it for too long. Vanessa helped more than she knew, but Caroline was searching for something more. Even she did not know what it was exactly, only that she still had not found what she was looking for and probably would know it somehow when she tripped over it.

Caroline shrugged as she finished tying her long curls into a loose ponytail secured halfway down with a pretty, light-green clasp. She turned in the full-length mirror in the hall, visually checking herself over. At first, she thought, *Why bother?* By noon, she would melt anyway, and the wind in the Jeep would toss her hair about wildly, leaving her a modern-day Medusa. *So why the fuss? Why not? You never know*, she thought. *You just never know.*

"OH!" she gasped at the sudden rush of hot air and blinding brightness of the sun that forced her to quickly reach for her sunglasses. Caroline kept her apartment cool, and the sudden change in temperature left her at a disadvantage. She had never acclimated very well, and she was already too hot for comfort. Heading for her Jeep, she climbed in and popped in the CD of the Irish group she had fallen asleep listening to last night, backing out of her parking space. With the music playing, she didn't even remember her wish for a real adventure last night, nor was she aware that it had already begun.

The morning sun was blinding, so bright that it hurt her eyes. Caroline had always preferred the quiet softness of low-watt bulbs and candles to the harshness of the blinding sun. Today, it just reinforced her suspicion that she was probably a vampire in her previous life. That and the fact that she preferred the night. She looked around the inside of her Jeep. Her sunglasses slipped a little as the wetness on her brow slid onto the bridge of her nose. It was so hard to keep things clean in the desert. Everything was always dirty, and her Jeep was no exception, with its fine lines of dust always present on the seats, floor, and dash. She liked the full top off, preferring the bikini top for when she drove to and from work in the late evenings. The night air was so much cooler than the blistering sun of the summer days.

"Ouch!" Caroline said aloud as she ejected the CD from the Jeep's stereo. It landed on the seat with a silent thud. Her fingers went to her lips as she frowned at being burned by the disc.

Caroline pulled into a vacant spot directly in front of the store, noting that since there was no shade to be had anywhere, she might as well park close. It was always the goal of every Southwestern person to find a spot of shade in which to park, no matter how insignificant that spot might be. Caroline turned off the engine, grabbed her purse, picked the still-warm CD off the seat, and climbed out. Now standing, she lifted her eyes upward, looking more closely at the sign above her. The Gothic-style green letters were trimmed in gold and read, *Irish Imports*. Just reading the sign made Caroline smile.

"Wow," she breathed as she opened the door to the store. As she stepped through the threshold, the gust of ice-cold air hit her like a brick, immediately sending a wave of cold chills tingling up her arms. The sweat on her neck seemed cleaner somehow at being chilled; it immediately lost its stickiness and felt only slightly damp. She closed her eyes for a split second and breathed deep and strong, filling her lungs and trying to cool her insides. Her face felt flushed from the heat, and she lingered in the small doorway for a moment.

Opening her eyes, she smiled quickly and soaked in all the store had to offer. Caroline's green eyes sparkled brightly, growing deeper in color as they scanned the room. Never had she seen so many Irish things in one place before. Books, tapes, mugs, crystal, jewelry, and clothing abounded. Caroline felt completely at home and could have stood there in the narrow doorway holding the door open all day just admiring the sights, mesmerized, if that deep voice of his had not shaken her from her trance. "Whoa now, Miss, do ya not know you're lettin me air out?"

She hadn't known her mouth was open until she closed it and looked up into the light-green eyes of the most gorgeous man she had ever seen in her entire life. He was standing—no, towering—just inches away from her. She immediately felt herself grow weak. There was no way around him, as he stood in front of her, and the displays on either side of her blocked her escape. He had come around from behind the counter to close the door behind her.

"Raised in a barn, were ya?"

"Uh . . . no." She felt utterly stupid now and more than a little surprised that she had not even noticed him approaching her. He had the stealth of a panther and the looks to match.

She couldn't move; she was frozen by his presence and his arm snaking around her. She didn't even flinch when he placed his other hand on her lower back to keep her from falling over and leaned carefully over her. She melted. He had pressed her into him slightly when he reached around her. Caroline could feel the hardness of the muscles in his arms, and there was something else: she also felt the heat of him, though he managed not to allow their bodies to actually touch. How did he do that?

He stepped back, grinning at the crimson color that flooded her cheeks. She could feel the heat from that too. "It tends ta stick sometimes."

"I am so sorry," she said softly, still looking up into his eyes. She felt warm again despite the coolness of the air.

His eyes roamed from hers to slowly wander across her entire body. She should have been outraged at his rude display, but instead, found herself liking his gaze. She could still feel the heat from his hand against her back where he had placed his hand and touched her.

"Is there sometin you'll be needin?" he asked softly, slowly drawing out the sweetness of his accent.

She swallowed, thinking to herself that his deep voice would make him a great bass vocalist in a church choir, if she knew a church choir, if he would sing for her, to her. Her mind was racing out of control. What was she doing? God, he was just so fantastic! You see these big guys on the cover of books all the time, but you never really ever see one in person or up close. She barely found her voice as she finally said, "Oh, I just came in for a look around." She concentrated on sounding matter-of-fact.

"Right, just let me know if you'll be needin anyting . . . anyting at all."

She smiled and turned as he walked back to his place behind the counter, where he continued to do some paperwork he had abandoned.

He watched her with his head lowered, unable to erase the grin on his face. She was so beautiful. Her long, dark hair hung down her back in a cascade of messy curls. Little wisps had broken free of the clasp and framed her face and slender neck. Emerald-green eyes sparkled against flawless, milky white skin. *Her skin is pale*, he thought to himself. *She isn't from here and definitely not of Hispanic origin. Her speech gives her away, but the paleness of her perfect skin proves it.*

He was surprised to feel so utterly attracted to her so quickly, but glancing up again, he realized this was no ordinary beauty before him. She was soft and smelled nice; he had detected a faint aroma of cinnamon and vanilla lingering in her hair, and those lips—God, a man could spend days ravishing them. Long, long legs and a slim waist complemented her height. His mind was wandering pointlessly when he remembered he was blatantly staring at her, and she was returning the gaze without fear.

"Do ya see sometim' ya want?" he asked boldly.

She almost fainted. *See something I want?* She thought. *Is he kidding? His body, his mind, his children!* She merely looked quickly away, shaking her head so as not to appear too eager. "Not yet," she said teasingly. *Not too fast.*

There were no other customers in the shop, and Caroline continued to browse freely, picking up a box of scone mix, something she had been wanting to try. She also picked up a small handbook of beginning Gaelic, an impulse purchase in hopes she could decode some of those Irish lyrics on her CDs at home.

Normally, she could have shopped for hours without coming up for air, but there was nothing normal about this shop or the man who kept stealing glances at her from behind his pile of paperwork. He was everything she could want in a man—well, his looks were, anyway. He was taller than she, which in itself was a plus. His build was large, but not frightening, and his hair, a deep-midnight-black, was slightly long and held back in a pirate's ponytail with a strip of brown leather. No woman's hair ties for this man. The thought made her chuckle slightly, and she daydreamed, *Just like one of those heroes on a romance novel cover.* She blinked, listening to her own words echo repeatedly in her ears, shaking her head, and thinking how ridiculous she was feeling.

She stole another glance at him from under her lashes and was very much beginning to feel like a stalker now. He was beautifully made, much like human art, and it was very hard not to look at him. *Probably gay*, she thought. All those beautiful men were. *And full of himself too, I bet.* No, something about him made her reconsider all the negative things going on in her head. He was just a nice, big, beautiful guy who probably had a nice, little, petite, blonde wife somewhere. She decided to let it go at that and continue enjoying the store while she was there.

She couldn't help taking just one more quick look. He had become a car wreck then, and she found it harder than ever to commit to her task of exploring the store and not the storekeeper. All she really wanted to do was look over every inch of him, and she suddenly felt very stupid and very childish. *Uh huh, human art, all right—get a grip!*

Caroline watched him covertly. His starched, white shirt was tucked into snug-fitting black jeans, and she reddened at remembering how taut his rear seemed while he walked away from her. She finally found something on one of the display shelves that piqued her interest, and she reached for it. She felt his eyes on her this time, and the stalker became the stalked. She continued to roam about, hoping he liked what he saw, that he was not married, and that he didn't think she was a shoplifter.

She was not aware when she started softly humming a tune from the CD she still held in her hand, but apparently, he was.

"Ya sure I can't help ya, Missy?" he asked, lifting from his seat.

Caroline's pulse picked up speed again as she looked over at his strong face.

"Well, I am looking for some more music by this group, if you have any?" She concentrated on not sounding as stupid as she felt, holding the CD up for him to see.

He was at her side in a flash, taking the CD she offered him. Their fingers brushed for an instant, and Caroline noticed how big his hands were compared to hers, and how rough. He was standing very close to her, seeming to be easy with himself and her. His closeness calmed her now, and she noticed she didn't have to work so hard at keeping control this time.

"Aye, they're the best group out of Ireland for sure. You've a good ear."

She smiled at his compliment and tried hard not to stare at his lips, full and utterly kissable as they were. His presence was commanding, though, and it was nice just to stand there and listen to him speak. He continued; his voice was deep but soft and sure, and she took the opportunity to study him more closely, nodding occasionally and trying to seem interested in his words and not his very intensely masculine presence.

He looked to be in his early thirties, and now that she was so close to him, she noticed a few gray hairs blending among the rich darkness of the rest of his hair right at his temples. He was fresh-shaven. His nose might have been broken at one time, but otherwise it was straight and strong. His jaw was square, Roman, and he smelled like soap and woods. Odd, she thought, since they were in the middle of the desert. It was nice, though, and she unconsciously inhaled deeper, filling her lungs with him and knowing she would never forget this moment. Something to tell the grandchildren.

"Ah, here is me personal favorite." He shifted slightly on one leg, closing the short distance between them and causing their upper arms to touch. He held out the CD to her, and she placed her hands on it, but he did not let go. She looked up, and they both smiled before he released it. "If ya truly like them, ya will love this one. They have more, too; problem is, it's me last one." He actually seemed disappointed for her. "Ya sure there is nothing else?" he asked, sounding hopeful.

She just smiled, shaking her head and turning away. "This is great, thank you." Standing behind him, she suddenly frowned when he turned to lead her to the cash register.

"You know," she started, hesitantly.

"Yea?" he asked, leaning closer to her from behind the counter, a half smile creeping to his lips.

"I . . ." A small lump formed in her throat. "I just thought if you get some more music in by this group, you could call me and let me know?" She couldn't believe how forward she was sounding. *He's going to think I'm really desperate.*

"The number is on the check," she stated as her fingers tore it from her checkbook and handed it to him. When she realized her fingers were shaking, she quickly pulled her hand back.

"I'll be sure ta do just that, ah, Caroline?" he asked, glancing at her name on the check. "By the way, Missy, should I leave a message with yer husband if yer not at home?"

"Oh, I'm not married, but you can leave a message on my machine if you like." She was screaming on the inside; he was obviously fishing!

Caroline headed for the door, bag in hand. When she put her hand on the knob, she suddenly stopped without opening the door. She slowly turned and gave a quick glance backward, wanting to get in one last look at him before she left. He was watching, just as she hoped he would be. Watching and grinning.

Caroline couldn't stop smiling. Every time she tried to put on a straight face, she'd just grin hopelessly and shake her head, trying to clear his image. Paying with a check instead of her debit card was a stroke of genius!

Driving home, her thoughts were centered on one thing . . . him. His face before her each time she closed her eyes, his smell lingering about the bag she had her hand resting on, and that devil grin he gave so easily. It was making concentrating on driving a slow torture. Never had a man affected her so. It was a little frightening in a way and more exciting in so many others. She liked everything about him—his smile, his hair, his great body, and the way he said her name. His accent was musical, and she found herself wishing he would read sonnets to her. She felt something back at that shop, and the feeling remained with her still, just as powerful and just as strong. She hoped he would call her, and she prayed it would be soon.

Caroline dreamed of him all the while she made her way downtown to meet Vanessa for lunch. Her excitement mounted with each block she drove, anticipating the telling of him to her closest friend. She was so engrossed in thought that she never saw the missing child poster tacked to the utility pole at the stoplight or the light-blue Pontiac following her exactly four cars behind—its position never faltering once, its driver wearing a demonic grin.

4.

LOYALTIES

Patrick McNally spent an entire hour on the phone with his merchandising contact in Ireland, his younger brother Sean. When he had decided two years ago to leave his homeland to start a new life in America, escaping the economic hardships and troubles of his country, it was Sean who had offered to be the merchandising contact. Patrick had been thrilled to hire him.

It had been a monumental breakthrough for the strained relationship between the two of them, and it served as a binding tie that most often kept the peace between the two within the family. Their opposing political views and opinions had wedged a thorn in the side of their family for too many years now, and this forced alliance of business had at least put some of that to rest. What it failed to do, however, was relieve some of the guilt Patrick still felt for filling the young lad's head full of the false glory he was so obsessed with now. The glory that threatened his younger brother's life and that of his entire family on a daily basis. For that guilt, there would be no relief.

As Patrick listened to his younger brother's voice coming through clear on the other end of the phone, the distance between them seemed merely a few feet, not the great vastness of an entire ocean, a continent, or even the space they had created within their own hearts. His friendliness seemed to close the thousands of miles between them, and it felt good to be so free in their conversation. It was a luxury still foreign to many of his countrymen.

"Patrick, have ye gone mad, brother?" Sean teased him from the safety of the miles.

"If I didn't know ya better, I'd swear ya gone and lost your heart!"

"Now don't prick me temper, ya wee bastard, just get me the things I'm askin ya for, and be quick about it."

"But can ya not wait until the regular shipment arrives in two weeks? It's gonna cost a leg ta get it to ya so fast." The conversation was quickly losing its fun. Patrick wanted those CDs, and he wanted them yesterday!

"She must be a real looker, 'ey, big brother?" Sean was relentless.

"More beautiful than you'll see the likes of, ya bugger." Patrick smiled with the thought of her.

"Does she know who ya are?" Sean asked quietly, without warning.

"She'll know when the time is right, lad, when the time is right." Patrick's smile turned into a frown then, his thoughts turning dark with his brother's question. "I best be on me way now. Give Ma, Robbie, and Claire a hug fer me . . . and Sean . . ." He hesitated; the visions clouding his mind were choking his efforts to speak.

"I will, don't worry," Sean finished his sentence for him, reading the thoughts his older brother couldn't voice. "Ya too, 'ey?"

Patrick hung up the phone. A chill permeated his thoughts. Would she, could she want him as the man he is now, once she knew the truth of his ugly past? With all the thoughts racing through his head, he knew one thing was for certain. He was at least willing to try to make this one understand, and that in itself was something he had never been willing to even try before. Could Sean be right? Could he really be in love? Lust for sure—just remembering the way she smelled made him ache with want—but love? That was definitely a new consideration for him.

He rubbed the bridge of his nose between his eyes, remembering the strain of past relationships. Women were not apt to dive into them beyond bed after they found out about his past, and he so wanted more. He longed for a family, children to hold, and a wife to adore. Someone to spend time with, go out with, do things with. Arizona was a lonely place, and though he had always been on his own, it was beginning to feel even lonelier as he got older. He just wanted more than one-night stands could fulfill. He wanted a life and someone to share it with. He came to this country to begin anew and find out what kind of man he could be without his past haunting him. Maybe it was time to let someone in and take a chance. Maybe, just maybe, this time he could actually belong and feel something more than hate and fear. At least he was ready to try.

Leaning back against the wall on his stool behind the counter, Patrick gazed mindlessly out of the huge picture window of his shop, silently staring at the world going by and successfully blocking out the few browsing customers who were lingering around the store. She entered his thoughts like a breath of summer rain, chasing away the dark clouds in his mind and replacing them with her warmth. Her eyes sparkled up at him, and he was amazed to discover he couldn't remember wanting a woman as much as he wanted this one, the last time a woman piqued his interest as this one had, or the last time he couldn't think for the want of one.

Three long days later, the package he had been painfully waiting for arrived. Patrick felt his heart skip a beat as he glanced at the Irish postage in the upper right-hand corner of the small box. The Irish harp on the stamp seemed to calm him slightly in the way little reminders of home can sometimes do. He knew without opening it that it was what he had asked of Sean. "God love ya, lad," he muttered under his breath while quickly tearing the package open and taking out its contents. He was careful not to damage any of the items lest he should have to wait out another moment of the torture before calling her.

He held the CDs, feeling the weight of the three of them in his hand. His mind summoned her memory to his thoughts again. He would make no mistake this time and take no chances on letting her get away. The last few days had not pressed her from his thoughts, though he had tried; instead, she was more vivid than ever. That seemed right somehow, and he gave himself over to it. Patrick felt determined to make her his, to get to know her thoughts and fears. God, I am headed for bedlam, he thought, but the smile nevertheless surfaced again.

He had placed the discarded package on the countertop when he heard the faint rustle of something still inside. Turning it upside down, he was surprised by the little clank of the object in question sliding from its hiding place and bouncing noisily across the glass counter. "Ey now, what's this?" he asked himself aloud as he picked the object up with his thumb and forefinger. He held it up and turned it over in a streak of the morning light streaming brightly through the window and instantly recognized it, having seen it in his mother's keepsake box as a lad. He held it suspended in the air, examining the delicately carved metalwork. It was his mother's engagement ring. He was sure of it, and as the light bounced off the silver inlay in a woven ancient Celtic pattern, Patrick smiled, knowing it was a lover's knot. Sean must have heard more than he thought in his voice on the phone when they last spoke, and Patrick shook his head at the gesture Sean had made in sending the ring on to him without his needing to ask. It showed great insight into the feeling the two of them could still share despite their distance in miles. It also proved that though their political opinions clashed and had pitted them against each other, he knew the rich, red blood of brotherhood was stronger than the spilt blood in the name of politics or of opinions, be they right or wrong.

His smile widened as he took Caroline's folded check from his pocket and reached for the phone. He bit the inside of his cheek as he began to dial her number. Holding his breath, he slid the tiny ring over the tip of his little finger; it rested snugly, barely under his nail, as he waited for the sweetness of her voice to ring in his ears. This is it; no turning back now.

5.

TWO HEARTS

Caroline twirled around and around. Her hands painted invisible pictures with graceful movements onto a canvas of air. The emptiness of the darkened theater was everywhere. Black and so cold as it was, she could see her breath bathed in the blue glow of the spotlight that was her only companion. Music, soft and compelling, drove her on in an endless search for elusive fulfillment. On and on she danced, never losing her breath or her footing, as if she were not a body but a spirit.

He came then. She could sense his presence in the shadows, beckoning her to come to him. With a single outstretched hand, he called to her without making a sound. Ending her dance, she stood a few feet away from his form, outlined in black against the curtains of the stage. She went closer slowly, with deliberate steps, having no will of her own, only feeling the need to be with him.

She lifted her own hand to place it in his waiting one. She could feel the heat of him even before their palms met. Placing hers at last to rest in his, she nearly jumped as the electricity of him shot through her as if she were struck by lightning. Her knees went weak, and she almost fainted from the sheer, overwhelming power coming from him. They had never touched before. Caroline tilted her head back, closing her eyes and feeling her long hair sway heavily against her back. She was becoming dizzy with the effects. This intimacy felt as if they had joined as lovers, the effect of his touch having forced her into a sort of frail state of rapture from this simple union of souls. Her senses reeled. His hold steady, and she was not afraid. She never was.

Caroline recovered her own strength and opened her eyes, seeking his face in the darkness. Narrowing her eyes and tilting her head slightly, she struggled to make out his features and began slowly pulling him toward the center of the stage and into the light. A slight resistance forced her to give a gentle tug. A second seemed an eternity as they stood alone in a battle of wills. Then, as if she won by a greater desire of her heart, she began to feel his resistance lessen. Her heart leaped in her chest, picking up speed with the victory. He was coming with her! Trying to coax him further, her eyes widened as she saw his darkened form start to lighten. His face! She was going to see his face!

Caroline tore her eyes away from him, annoyed at the ringing sound coming from nowhere and everywhere.

Again, the ring sounded, louder this time. She frowned, closing her eyes to block out the sound.

When she opened her eyes again, she was not on the stage anymore. Not holding his warm, strong hand in hers, but in her own room, in her own bed. Alone.

Blinking the sleep from her eyes and the haziness of disappointed thoughts, she reached with shaky fingers for the phone on her nightstand. Her heart was still pounding loudly in her chest from the reality of the dream.

"Um, hello?" she asked quietly, her voice still not her own.

"Is Caroline there?"

She almost dropped the phone as her eyes bolted open at the deep Irish brogue of his voice on the other end. "Ah, this is her, I mean me." She felt awkward and fuzzy.

"This is Patrick McNally from the Irish Imports store. I didn't wake ya now, did I, Missy?"

"Oh no, I was just getting up," she lied.

Relieved, he continued, "I just called ta let ya know I got in some more of that music you were askin about. Ya did say ta call, 'ey?"

"Yes, yes, I did. How nice of you to remember and call to let me know like this." She was feeling more confident hearing her own voice take on some semblance of its normal tone. "Can I come and pick them up today? I could be there around noon."

"Sure, Miss, I'll hold 'em fer ya." It seemed as if Caroline could hear a smile in Patrick's voice.

"I'll see you then," Caroline said as she held the phone to her ear, listening for the click and the steady drone of the dial tone. She didn't want to break the connection with him so soon, and she waited a moment longer before she reluctantly returned it to its base on the nightstand.

She was already bounding off the bed and yelling, "Ya-hoo!" before she thought to look at the clock.

"Oh, my God!" she gasped, blinking in disbelief at the time. It was nearly eleven o'clock! She had given herself less than an hour to get ready and get across town!

Rushing around the room, she nearly tore her nightgown in an attempt to get it off quickly. Racing to the living room, she went directly for the CD player. She would need the fast-paced sound of some kind of loud music to make it on time, and an Irish reel would be perfect.

Sam, tired after a long night of stalking nonexistent mice in the apartment, lay on the foot of the bed and watched his mistress racing around. He didn't bother to lift his head but instead gave a long purr and closed his eyes to the fury.

Across town, Patrick hummed for the first time in a long while, his own excitement building with each tick of the clock. This stranger had made his heart sing with a strange kind of anticipation, and hearing her voice again just a few seconds ago left him sighing like a lad after his first kiss. Sean would goad him good if he knew what a lovesick pup he'd become over a lass he'd met only once. That thought of his brother quickly brought more pressing thoughts of home. He missed Ireland. Missed all the natural beauty and life there, his friends and his family. It seemed a lifetime since he had rested his eyes on his home and family, and he was not surprised to realize how it affected him.

America was indeed a great land, but for all its pluses—which were too numerous to name, as far as he was concerned—there still lurked an underlying complacency to the people here. A dormant state of mind from being lulled to death by the modern media, to which young and old alike submitted on a daily basis. It often left them with a sad sense of ignorance as to what was really happening to the rest of the world. If you didn't see it on television, then it must not be happening—or even true, for that matter. He sighed, shaking his head slowly with the thought that it took that monumental occasion to wake them up. Until then, it had been an escape living here, a vacation for his mind from the stark realities of the rest of the planet and its problems. It was a vacation he had lately grown weary of. That was, until Caroline walked into his shop and into his life. She gave him a new sense of himself, and his alertness was at an all-time high. She was already proving herself to be a great asset in his life, making him feel alive again for the first time in years, and they hadn't even had their first date yet.

He glanced up at the clock on the wall again, his eyes seeing but not registering the silly leprechaun chasing the tiny pot of gold around the rainbow.

Patrick watched her pull her red Jeep into the parking lot, smiling wide when she took the empty spot right next to his own black Jeep. "Imagine that," he thought, noting the irony of them sharing the same taste in vehicles. If his heart was pounding in anticipation before, it was nothing in contrast to what he was feeling the moment she stepped out of her vehicle and into his direct line of vision. With the noonday brightness of the sun at her back, he was immediately treated to the best set of slim, long legs he had ever seen, as it gave way to the fact that she wasn't wearing a slip under her long skirt. He couldn't tear his eyes away as he watched her come through the door. "Holy Jesus and Mary," he breathed as the room began to spin. God, but the weather was unusually hot today. His white, linen shirt felt more like a burlap bag as it suddenly began sticking to him, despite the air conditioner blowing cool air from the vent directly above his head.

"Hi, ah, Patrick?" she smiled, flashing a set of perfect white teeth and holding her hand out for him to shake. He immediately shook his head to clear the sudden unwanted memory of his last blind date, and the words *horse-mouthed* came along with the vision. Caroline knew his name now, and hearing it come across her lips made for a whole new set of visions coming to mind, bringing a rush of heat with them that had nothing to do with the weather.

"I'm Caroline; we spoke earlier on the phone." She waited, but he gave no response. "You were holding some CDs for me, remember?"

"Oh, aye," he said dryly. A sudden lump had lodged itself in his throat. He reached out and took her small hand in his; it was soft as velvet. Her hand was flushed warm from the sun. He noted how she quickly closed her eyes for a second when their hands touched. Did she feel it too? It was written all over her face! He felt the muscles in his face relax as a half-grin took hold. A brief chuckle escaped as he noticed her regain her composure and pull her hand out of his with a blush.

He covered his laugh under the disguise of a short cough. He liked this about her—liked it a lot. She wasn't very good at hiding emotions, and for him, that was a welcome blessing. It proved an inner honesty she'd never be able to hide, and that in itself was an endearing quality lacking in so many of the women he had met. They all seemed to want to play games with him one way or another. He hated that with a passion, and now he stood in the presence of a real woman, one who blushed at his touch and showed her feelings on her face. My God, he thought, what great force of luck brought her to him at this point in his life?

Caroline stood looking up at him. At five-foot-eight, she had to tilt her chin up quite a bit to meet his eyes. She found herself mesmerized by his green eyes that were so like her own. It was a stunning contrast to the fair shade of his Celtic skin and black hair. He wore a white, cotton shirt again today, tucked neatly into snug-fitting black jeans that had her wondering how he ever got them up over those thickly muscled thighs. He wore his hair loose around the tops of his shoulders. Thick waves of it splashed against his shirt, and when he reached up with one hand and tucked one side behind his ear, she thought she'd die. A single, tiny gold loop earring peeked out at her. She at once thought it charming in a pirate sort of way, and he smiled at seeing her apparent approval.

His eyes sparkled as they stood there for what seemed like eons, merely gazing, drinking in every feature of each other and totally unaware of the time as they were so engrossed in the moment of relaxed intimacy with each other. She wanted to kiss him then and there, with no regard to the time or place. It all seemed unreal, and she was at once frightened and entranced. This couldn't be happening. She couldn't be in love with a stranger she'd met only once. It was absurd, and yet, here she was, and there he was. He was staring back at her, and she couldn't take her eyes off him. It was real. Everything anyone had ever said about love at first sight was true.

Caroline felt the bond of those first few moments like nothing she had ever felt before—thick and strong between them, like they were linked together in a past life, perhaps two great lovers in another time. It would have frightened her more if it had occurred with any other human being other than the one standing in front of her, if it had been any other man than Patrick sending those waves of intense emotions sweeping her off her feet. And that was exactly what he was doing—sweeping the very earth out from under her.

6.

TIME

Caroline could have stood there all day just looking up at him, and since he hadn't made a move either, she supposed he could have too. "I think you have a customer," she said, noticing the woman standing at the counter in front of the register. The woman was looking around for someone to help her, rolling her eyes and impatiently tapping on the glass countertop with her long, painted, acrylic nails.

"Oh?" He moved his eyes enough for Caroline to realize he was now staring at her mouth, but she figured he probably hadn't heard a word she had said. She bit her lip nervously. She really wanted to lick her lips, which were now dry, but his eyes were revealing a depth of emotion that thrilled her. What sort of man is this?

He suddenly spoke. "Don't go away," he said, turning and abandoning her with all her emotions swirling about her. The request was made with a slight tone of authority, leaving no doubt it was meant as a demand, not a request. She nodded; no way was she going anywhere.

She raised one eyebrow slightly as she watched him walk behind the counter and ring up the waiting customer's purchases, all the while noting the way his eyes kept coming back to her. For reassurance, she supposed. To see if she was still there. It seemed he didn't want to break the bond either, and Caroline noticed his smile never faded. She also noticed the effect that smile had on the woman at the counter. It amused her to see the older woman blush and fumble with her purse in his presence.

"I've got a daughter, you know; lovely girl, really." The woman was leaning on the counter now, looking up at him, batting her eyes and smiling big enough for Caroline to see the woman's lipstick smudges on her teeth. Patrick simply smiled, nodded, and bagged her purchases. "She's a great cook, too," the woman continued. "Big, strong fellow like you should have a nice girl to cook for you."

"I don't really . . ." Patrick couldn't finish his sentence before the woman interrupted him, her New York accent high and whiny.

"You're not gay, are you?" the woman asked suspiciously. "Not that there's anything wrong with that, of course, but I want grandchildren soon. So many men are that way now, it's hard to tell." She lifted her hand to her chest and made a sour face as her ringed fingers rested against her wrinkled, aged, unnaturally tanned skin.

Caroline hated the way the woman whispered the words *gay* and *that way*. It made her angry to think people still condemned what they didn't understand. She narrowed her eyes in disgust and listened to what Patrick would say.

"Well now, ya know what they say about us Irish?" He grinned, drawing out his accent, and the woman had to lean in closer as if he were going to tell her a secret.

"No, what?"

"Get a few pints in us, and we'll bugger anytin tats not nailed down!"

Caroline chuckled as the woman feigned insult and outrage. *What a rogue*, she thought, and she remembered to lick her lips.

The loud crash that erupted behind the counter brought everyone in the store to a sudden stop as they all turned toward a rather red-faced Patrick apologizing for his clumsiness. He looked directly at Caroline and shrugged in mock bewilderment.

Caroline had to turn away then. She squeezed her lips tight to keep the laugh from escaping and embarrassing him further. He had character, she thought, and he was funny too. Funny and quite charming in every way. Her mind drifted beyond the item she gently ran her fingers over. The cool crystal beneath her fingertips warmed as she saw his chiseled features in the brilliance of the cut. Angles took on new dimensions, and the colors sparkled in the shimmering sun coming through the large windows of the store.

"Beautiful," she heard his voice behind her. It was deeper now and utterly masculine, surprising her that he moved so fast.

"Yes, yes they are," she whispered, suddenly feeling very small and feminine with his presence so close behind her. She knew if she took a step backward, she would be against his chest. Immediately, the heat in her cheeks matched the heat of her backside. Didn't this man know anything about personal space? And didn't he know he was standing right in the middle of hers? Didn't he know what it was doing to her, being so close?

"This is me favorite," he said, reaching around from behind her, his large hand cupping a tiny, delicate, crystal bird. It was beautiful. She couldn't tell which moved her more, the way his large, powerful hand held the fragile crystal like a real bird, or the rich Irish accent that sounded so musical in her ears.

"T'ean," he said softly as his large hand engulfed the tiny piece of crystal, lifting it with amazing gentleness from its resting place.

"Tea ann?" she asked, turning slowly around to face him.

"Aye, that's what they're called in Irish."

She looked past the tiny piece of crystal he held up to the light to look into his eyes. They were magnetic, drawing her like a moth to a flame.

"Beag t'ean," he said, lifting his deep-green eyes off the item and meeting hers. "Like you, small bird." Caroline saw the corner of his mouth twitch slightly, and she smiled with the growing redness in her cheeks.

He put the item back on the shelf and turned toward her. "I'll be gettin those CDs ya wanted," he said with a hand gesture toward the counter. "I held them over here for ya."

"Great," she said, reluctant to end their meeting so soon. A wave of disappointment came over her as he led the way across the room. He went ahead of her, around to the other side of the counter, bending low to retrieve the items from a shelf underneath. She waited as he placed them on the glass in front of him. Caroline shifted her weight so she was leaning closer to his side of the counter and reached for them.

"Have you heard these also?" she asked, trying to nonchalantly make conversation.

"Aye. They're all the same—beautiful." He was bending over close to her now. Something the way the word *beautiful* ran off his lips made her breath catch enough for her to part her lips ever so slightly just to breathe.

Leaning on his elbow and meeting her at eye level, he asked quietly, as if not wanting to ask at all, "Does yer boyfriend like their music as well, then?"

"No boyfriend," she stated in a matter-of-fact way, trying to keep those magnetic eyes from locking hold on her once again. If she looked up, she might jump over the counter and kiss him, something she very much wanted to do right then, and yes, that would look a little desperate. She busied herself fumbling for her wallet.

"Pretty little missy like you?" he asked skeptically. "I can't believe it."

She noticed his look of genuine surprise. "No, really. Just me and Sam," she said, putting the tape back on the counter and finally pulling her wallet out of her purse.

"Weel now, would that be yer son then? Oh, forgive me, I am being rude and busy in yer business." It was a natural guess; many women had children from previous relationships. It would only be natural in this day and age for someone as beautiful as Caroline to have been involved before.

"Son, Sam? Oh no, Sam's my kitty." She smiled wide at his error.

"A puss, then?" he asked, and when he saw her eyes grow larger, he seemed to immediately realize his blunder and quickly corrected himself. "Sam would be yer kitty then and not a son?"

"Yes, Patrick. Sam is my kitty. I have no children . . . yet," she said, mocking his Irish lilt and laughing. He, too, could turn various shades of red, a fact she was amused to discover.

With that little embarrassing moment behind them, they settled into the peace that had become their own. "Would ya consider, I mean, if yer of a mind. Would ya consider lettin me take ya ta dinner tonight? I know this is short notice, but I'd love ta see ya again, Caroline."

Caroline almost fell over right then. Here was this big, beautiful guy laughing and sharing something special with her and then this, a date? Of course!

Patrick just stared at her for a long moment, and then his eyebrows lifted in question.

She looked back at him, and then it dawned on her, "Of course!" she said aloud this time.

He looked startled. "Okay then," he said, with as much enthusiasm. "Where would ya like to meet?"

She cleared her throat. "You can come by my apartment if you like." She thought she was still sounding too excited.

"Okay then," he smiled and put her CDs in a bag.

"Okay then," she countered as her insides were screaming *Oh, my God!*

Patrick couldn't believe she had agreed to go to dinner with him tonight on such short notice. He was still grateful she followed her own set of rules instead of worrying about other women's ideas of relationships. Another plus for her, and they were adding up quickly. Too quickly?

He practically shoved the customers out of his shop at closing time and raced across town to his home to shower, shave, and change. He hadn't bothered to press the button on his answering machine when he saw the light steadily blinking as he entered his bedroom. His excitement was too high, and he didn't want anything to ruin tonight.

He smiled as he stood in his bedroom, his mind still on her. He was nervous, and it pleased him to be so. The life he knew before would never have allowed such an extravagant emotion as foolish as this. No, there had been no place in his life for that emotion before.

"It's all different now, Caroline, you'll see," he said aloud at his reflection, running a large hand through his still-wet hair and remembering what Sean had said on the phone when last they spoke. "Does she know who ya are, brother?" Sean had said, and Patrick shook his head to clear the lad and his dark foreshadowing from his thoughts.

Loose or tied? He forced his mind onto the current matter at hand, his hair. Loose, he concluded; there would be nothing uptight about tonight. As he grabbed his car keys and headed out the door, the light glowing red on his answering machine was left neglected. No news is good news, or so he thought.

7.

STARRY STARRY NIGHT

Caroline heard the knock at the door and looked over at her vanity where her clock sat. Exactly seven o'clock; good punctuality. Her pulse was racing so fast she almost dropped the bottle of her favorite perfume she was holding. She closed her eyes, took a deep, cleansing breath, and then said aloud, "Okay, get hold of yourself." As she placed the nearly full bottle back on the shelf, she spoke to her reflection in the mirror one last time. "There is no reason to be so nervous. He is just a man. A gorgeous man, but just a man," and then winked. She took another deep breath, waved the air about her, hoping her perfume was not too strong, and headed to the door. Patrick thought he had died and gone to heaven when she opened the door. His senses were reeling at the sight of her. She wore a short dress this time, made of a lightweight, baby-blue material that floated around her slim thighs, hinting that it might reveal more at the slightest breeze. It had short, peasant sleeves and a tiny bow that gathered the material under her full breasts, showing just the tip of her cleavage and nothing more. Her skin was a healthy pink, and she wore her hair in dark ringlets, loose about her shoulders and cascading down her back. She wore little makeup, and her full lips showed only the slightest hint of pink. She was a vision the likes of which he had never seen before.

"Hi," he choked, clearing his throat, but made no move toward her.

"Hi, you," she said with a grin. "Please come in."

As she stepped back and gestured for him to come in, he caught a glimpse of her sandals. Her dainty feet were crisscrossed with straps the same color as her dress, and for the slightest moment, he wanted to touch those same feet to see if they would feel as tiny in his hand as they looked.

Caroline wondered as he walked past her and into her home if this man could get any better. He smelled clean, like fresh soap and aftershave. His hair was loose and still damp from his recent shower, and her mind lingered for a moment, wondering what it would be like to run her hands through it.

"You've a lovely place, Caroline," he said, surveying the room with great interest. He meant it. Her taste in decorating made him at once feel at home with the cozy feel it inspired. Dark woods and rich, earth tones blended together with an antique quality he liked. Crystal lamps adorned lace-covered tables, and overstuffed tapestry pillows of the deepest maroons and hunter greens beckoned one to their softness.

"Thank you, Sir," she said, closing the door behind him. Patrick slowly turned to face her, and then he took a single step in her direction and stopped. She immediately felt it then, hitting her hard and without warning. His masculine presence filled her home, his large frame conveying a silent plea for her to draw nearer. She stepped back, not from fear of him, but from fear of herself as the faceless man in her dreams came to mind. Patrick was dangerous, and well she knew to keep her distance unless she was willing to lose more than her heart this night.

"I would think you would find my home a bit, well, feminine for you," she stated nervously, wanting to ease the electric tension between them. He was doing nothing to her, and yet she was feeling more passion in the last few seconds than she had felt in her entire life.

"Aye, it's a woman's home ta be sure, but it invites ya ta come and sit a while and rest."

She thought she caught the giggle before it escaped.

"Someting funny?" he looked confused.

"What you said—it's where I work." When he still looked confused, she went on. "The name of the bookstore where I work is called the Curl Up and Sit a While," she explained, walking toward him. She was surprised to hear a man with such obvious brawn make a statement so sensitive. Her interest was piqued by his ability to see beyond the ordinary.

Feeling warmer all of a sudden, she suggested that they best be on their way.

"Is something wrong?" Caroline asked, surprised to see him leaning next to her against the wall as she locked her door. He was making no inclination to move as she stepped back and slid her key into the little beaded purse she carried. He was staring at her with a frown. Caroline looked down at her dress, thinking something was amiss. He lifted his hands out to her, and she stepped toward him without hesitation, lifting her own and placing them in his bigger ones. She looked up, surprised at herself with the display of intimacy with a stranger. Patrick's dark-green eyes were filled with questions, and she realized he was just as confused by their mutual attraction as she was.

"It's just that . . ." he trailed off, shaking his head.

"Yes?"

"It's just that ya take me breath away, you're so lovely. I am sure to be the envy of every man tonight, and I wanted ta thank ya now for giving me the honor of escorting ya ta dinner."

Caroline's eyes grew wide in wonder. No man had ever spoken to her in this way before. She smiled and squeezed his hands in response. He looked down at their joined hands and closed his eyes with a single nod. Her hands seemed so little in his.

"You're fine with me, 'ey? Not too scared?"

"Oh, I am fine with you, Patrick, and yes, I am a little scared, but I do have a question for you." She swallowed her fear and asked him, "Patrick, are you for real?"

"Umm," he said, lifting his eyes to hers and giving her hand a gentle squeeze back. "Probably more real than you're ready for, but I'll tell ya this, Missy. I am real. Flesh and blood, body and soul. And if you'll have me, I am yours for the askin, yours for the takin."

Caroline asked herself again and again that same question and a thousand others before the night was over. *Is he for real?* She really didn't know the answer. Oh, he was flesh and blood, all right; there was no mistaking that. His masculine presence was both commanding and intoxicating to her, and he carried himself with a leadership quality. He seemed to give the air about him a certain amount of authority. He had treated her with the utmost care all evening. Her every wish his command. Her every whim was his sole mission to fulfill. Yet she still asked herself how he could be real.

Later that night, she stood barely a few feet away from him on the shore of the small pond that shimmered under the moonlight of the deserted Reid Park. They had decided on a walk after dinner, both wanting to linger in each other's company without the world interfering. She was not interested in the normal routine of a movie date, and he was in full agreement. There was something special happening here, and both of them could easily sense it. This thing between them was quietly intimate, a substance so thick it was almost tangible. It was fragile and yet strong at the same time. For Caroline, it seemed to all be happening so fast, and all the while it seemed right, seemed safe, and seemed perfect.

She studied him much as she had all evening; so entranced by him, she found it hard to take her eyes off him for a moment. His hair, long and sleek and dark as midnight, was blowing gently around the tops of his shoulders, framing his face. It made his skin appear to be glowing with the stark contradiction of light from the moon and the sleek blackness of his hair against it. He had an inner glow, she thought, feeling a bit of its warmth radiating off him. He was strong-muscled, well-built, and disciplined with his body, a fact she discovered during their meal when he told her he was a vegetarian. It had taken her by surprise at first. She had earlier envisioned him with all his muscles ripping the leg off some great beast at the dinner table of some medieval castle, devouring it like she had seen in those old movies, with juices running down his chin as he banged on the table, bellowing, "More ale, wench!"

She had a chance to study him more closely now, noticing that his features seemed relaxed but void of any emotion that she could read. No telltale signs of his thoughts were discernible in his eyes. His hands were clasped behind his back, and his face was lifted slightly, studying the brightness of the full moon. Caroline thought he was truly magnificent, and she found her body responding to the mere sight of him and tingling in all the right places. She needed no words of encouragement from him to answer as she found herself drawn to his side, seeking him, wanting him. It would be hard, this fight she had taken on. How would she ever resist him? He was overwhelming to her senses, and she knew it would take real restraint on her part not to give in to the desires he had awakened, ones that had been asleep for so long now, dormant within the confines of her heart.

The gentle breeze blew in the trees around them. The rustling of the leaves made for a relaxing musical backdrop. He turned and looked over at her, as if hearing her thoughts, and she could smell him again. His wonderful masculine scent drifted to her on the warmth of the air. He reached for her, and she suddenly found herself molded tightly against his strong body. She didn't care if he thought her lascivious as she slipped her arms around him, pressing her palms to his back, drawing him in even nearer.

Patrick smiled at her gesture, pleased that she wanted this as much as he did. Her eyes were large and revealing as she blinked up at him, trusting and accepting of his hold.

Their bodies fitted together perfectly, each nook and cranny, each curve and valley touching and blending into each other. *God, she feels good, this feels so right.* He began to feel his own body responding to hers. She was so soft, and it had been a long time since he held a woman in his arms. *It's more than just the holding of her*, he thought. *More than just the feel of her breasts firm against my chest, the feeling of her soft skin against me. No, there is more, much more. There's a rightfulness, a certain kind of easiness free of any guilt or shame.* He gazed down at her with new emotions clouding his eyes. Not moving, he just held her.

She saw it there, his love, and her lips parted for him with the escape of her breath at the sight. Patrick kissed her. His acceptance of the emotion filled him with renewed vigor as he bent and brushed his own lips over hers. He began to whisper incoherent words as his mouth lay claim to hers again and again, each time becoming stronger and demanding more of her. She responded, and he took what she offered freely, giving back double as they stood like lovers learning each other with the intimacy of the kissing. His hands were never roaming, never freeing her from his embrace, but only tightening more with the wanting of more closeness.

Caroline was so lost in their first kiss, lost in the swelling emotions she had seen in his eyes, that she whimpered slightly at feeling his lips pull from her. She opened her own eyes dreamily and gazed up at him, almost stunned. He still held her. It was a good thing, as she was weakened by the kiss and sharing of emotions. He was staring down at her with a look she could only describe as pain. His eyes were dark, his lids heavy. What had she done, allowing him such free rein with her senses like that? Yes, she had felt powerless to his touch, but that kiss he had just bestowed on her felt as if they had made love right there on the shore. She was weakened and lacking in her normal resistance when she saw the look in his eyes a moment ago, a look she thought was love. Now, seeing him with new eyes, she had a frightening thought that she might have misjudged him.

He was torn, his insides on fire from her touch. He had almost lost all self-control and would have forgotten they were in a public place, forgotten she was a lady worthy of treasuring, forgotten he was wooing her for greater things. If his mind had not been stronger than his desires just then, he might not have waited until she knew the truth of him and his past. He now knew he was in love and also knew this love was all-consuming. He would make her his, yes, but he would make it right for her. Make it right for him to claim her as his own forever. If Caroline would still have him after she knew the whole truth, then he would make sure she would want to stay with him forever. Neither one of them would ever have to be alone again.

He watched the play of emotions on her face and the way his kiss had caused her full lips to become swollen and more inviting. He would have her, and his lips spoke the words his heart wanted to say.

"Oh, Caroline," he sighed, and he tightened his hold on her, wanting to reassure her of his love, of the emotions he was feeling. He pulled her close, resting his chin on the top of her head, brushing back and forth, feeling the faint tickling of her silky curls against his skin. The familiar spiciness of her scent rose to greet him. "I . . . I have never felt like this before."

She felt the deepness of his voice as it vibrated through her entire body from the top of her head to the very tips of her toes. She pressed herself closer into him, her body telling him it was all right, that she understood, and that she was feeling it too. She couldn't bring the words to the surface.

"Aye, it's true, then," he answered her silent pleas. "I can weel feel ya know what I mean, Missy. This thing, this happening between us is special, and ya know it is too."

"Patrick?" she finally managed to whisper faintly into his chest.

"No, let me speak me mind before the sound of yer sweet voice has me at yer lips again."

She closed her eyes, letting him continue, letting him say all the things she was feeling herself. She never wanted this moment to end. She wanted to listen to his voice forever.

"Caroline, I am no saint, and, weel, there are things ya don't know about me. Things that may frighten ye if I spoke of them. Things in me past I can neither change nor have power over now." He felt her stiffen in his arms for a brief second. He lowered his lips to her hair and placed a single kiss atop her head for comfort, his own as well as hers. He didn't want to frighten her, but he would never let this get any further if he didn't at least try to let her know the way of things. He smiled when he realized she wasn't pulling away. She may have been a little frightened, but she was still there. Still holding on to him as tightly as he held on to her.

"I'd hope ta have ya love me knowin all there might be of me and I'd have honesty between us from the start. There are things I will tell ya in time, when the time is right, and I'll not let ya worry that yer mixed up with a man who would lie to ya just ta bed ya. Do ya understand?"

Caroline didn't know why she did, but she did. It had never dawned on her that he could be anything other than just a wonderful man.

It didn't scare her now to think of him in any other way. What really *did* scare her was the thought of what he might be going through or had gone through and that she was powerless to help him with it. She thought she should be running as far as she could from this man. He could be any number of things. Could have done any number of things. And as she stood there in the stillness of the now-deserted park in the arms of a stranger, listening to his words of endearment, she could hear only the soft, sloshing sounds of the water lapping gently against the shore and the faint rustle of the leaves in the trees.

With his large arms around her, holding her with extreme tenderness, she knew it would be all right. She knew without a doubt that no matter what he would confess to her, she would forgive him, knowing it had to be some sort of injustice. Was she a fool? Probably. And yet, in the embrace of his arms, she let her fears go on the wind.

Caroline had known from the first time she saw him that he was going to be a great power in her life, a force and maybe even a part of her destiny. Now she also knew she was willing to at least find out why her heart was so open to this man. Why her body responded to him like they had always known each other. Why she was willing to risk whatever fate might bring her with him at her side. Caroline had always believed in love at first sight, and standing there, she knew her own heart had at last discovered it too.

"Patrick?" she asked, waiting a second and expecting him to stop her again. When he didn't, she continued. "I don't know what this is between us, either. Maybe we knew each other in a past life." She hesitated, never before having said or heard words like they were sharing and finding it a little hard to believe herself. After all, she remembered, it was their first date.

"I only know that it feels right, and that is all that matters now," she said. She was surprised by his sharp intake of breath and the sudden feeling that her bones were going to be crushed as his hug on her increased tenfold. He picked her up and swung her around, making her dizzy as she heard his deep laughter echoing across the pond.

"God, Caroline," she heard him say as he finally set her down, letting go of her for a moment before gripping her shoulders gently. "Marry me!"

She heard him say the words, but she didn't trust her own ears. She must have been mistaken.

"What did you just say to me?" she asked, laughing.

Suddenly, they were both laughing. "I said . . ."

Caroline watched, her eyes wide, as he dropped to one knee in front of her, his large hand reaching out and taking one of hers in it. He brushed a slight kiss over the knuckles and then held it against his cheek. She could feel the rough bristles of his beard starting to grow back. He lowered her hand with great tenderness to his heart. His own hand covered hers, and Caroline realized he felt overly warm as he pressed her palm slightly against him. "I said, Caroline, will ya marry me?"

"Patrick McNally, do you always go around asking women to marry you on the first date?" she cried, pulling her hand from his and placing her fists on her hips. "Is this what you want to confess to me, that you're a . . . a serial marriage proposer?" She jumped as he lunged for her and wrapped his strong, muscled arms around her waist, burying his head against her skirt. Caroline was surprised, to say the least, but found her hands going quickly for his hair, something she had been wanting to do from the moment she first saw him. It was soft—coarse and thick, but utterly soft.

"I'm sorry," he said into her skirt. "And no, I have never before asked anyone to marry me."

"I just meant that, well, we should get to know each other a bit more before we start planning a wedding, don't you think?" She couldn't believe he had asked her. More than that, she couldn't believe that she had almost said yes!

He rose slowly, knowing she had a valid point. His hands followed the curves of her hips and came to rest on her waist. She reluctantly moved her hands from his hair and followed the strong lines of his neck and shoulders until they came to rest on his thick forearms.

"Aye, I know you're right. It's just that I want ya like none other, and I'd make ya mine in the eyes of God and man before I . . . before we . . ." He stood and looked down at her. She was shaking her head no, and he gave her a puzzled look.

"You can't know what that means to me, Patrick. I really thought I would have to fight you off like all the others. I thought—well, never mind what I thought. Are you really saying you want to get married before we . . ." She wasn't sure he would be able to wait, despite all her own convictions—convictions that sounded rather lame at the moment. She could easily feel his intent as he held her close.

"Yes. Do ya think ya will want ta wait long before ya decide on a date?"

He did look a little anxious. "Well, I don't really even know you," she said, pulling back a step. "Look here, mister. I really think this is a bit fast, and I think—"

"Ya think too much," he interrupted, leaning down for a missed kiss.

She pushed him back a little more, finding a little self-restraint. He retaliated by quickly pulling her close again.

"Caroline, I love how yer mind works. Weel go slow or fast, whatever ya want. Take yer time or not, I'll wait. There is nothing more I want than to feel ya against me but getting ta know me is going to take some time, Missy. Are ya sure you're willing ta wait?" He asked the question with the emphasis on *you're.*

Before she could answer, he lowered his lips and found hers. She moaned against him and gave herself over to the feeling. He was a great kisser, and his lips were so soft. She never kissed like this, and it occurred to her that this was how soulmates must kiss. When she finally parted her lips and his tongue found hers, she could not believe the way it felt.

He wasn't real—that much Caroline knew for sure. No man had ever said the honeyed words that pierced her heart as his had. How did he possess the knowledge to know her so well? Maybe his secret was that he could read minds. He certainly seemed to know her inner desires, and as they walked back through the park toward his Jeep, she realized he must be a product of her imagination. She would wake up tomorrow and be sad that he was just a wonderful dream. When she looked over at him walking next to her along the path, she noticed a smile on his lips. His hand had never let go of hers for a moment. Caroline's thoughts raced. *I'm going to pray hard tonight. Pray and hope this perfect man will still be in my life when the dawn comes instead of disappearing like the man in my dreams always does. I will pray that he stays just the way he says he will, flesh and blood, warm and real. Mine for the asking, mine for the taking.*

8.

A DISTANT STORM

"Shit!" He swore at the mess of secret sauce now dripping down the front of his T-shirt. They always did that, put too much sauce on when you need to eat in the car, and they never seem to give you enough fries—and on the rare occasion when they did, the fries were never hot. *Soon I won't have to eat like this.* He reached for the single, white paper napkin in the bag.

He had been watching her again tonight, and even though the store owner had left some time ago, having kissed her goodnight at the door, the man continued to watch her lighted window from the safety of the shadows where he parked his massive black Jeep.

His anger had flared briefly when he had seen the store owner pull her into his embrace and kiss her full on the mouth a short time ago. The man had gotten over it, though, when he heard her say her goodnight and close the door without inviting the guy in. He would have to do something about that guy, he supposed. What to do?

Every night for the past two weeks, he had come to watch, and every night that bastard was already with her. It was always the same thing, time and again. He pulled into her apartment complex and caught sight of the big black Jeep already parked, and the man with the long, black hair was already inside with her. They would go out, the man and she. A concert, the park, a horseback ride, dinner, or just a walk. He followed them, watching their hands locked together more often than not. The sight of them together sent waves of jealousy coursing through his veins like hot lava. *She is mine, not his!*

He had been furious with her at first, but soon he focused his anger on the man. He was a sly one, with his wavy, perfect, dark hair and his tall, muscled body. And his money. An endless supply, so it seemed—he noticed her with roses in her hands on several occasions, a small gift box here and there. No, he was not angry with her. It was the man he felt he needed to deal with now, and he sighed at the realization. It simply had to be done, but he knew it would be no small feat. This was not a child to be grabbed off the street with a quick hand over its mouth and some duct tape. The man with the black hair had an advantage of more than a hundred pounds, and the thought of a physical confrontation and getting his ass kicked was not high on his list of things to do right now.

He reached for his drink, hoping to quench his thirst, though he knew it would take more than a drink of cola to ease the drought that scorched his insides. He had tasted the clear, fresh waters of the spring that was her. He needed more than a mere sip of her; he wanted it all, and if things worked out like he hoped, that's exactly what he would have. Just like the sweet smoothness of the drink he now held, soon he would also know the sweetness of her.

He caught movement out of the corner of his eye. She was turning out her light, and his head jerked abruptly toward the source, his breath catching as he stopped his chewing for a moment. She would sleep now, and he was free to leave again. Soon, my pet, soon. He continued his chewing, the wad of tastelessness mixed with the plan already seeded with the blackness of his heart.

Once home, he fumbled with the lock on the door to his room. He quickly stepped in, anxious to be rid of the prying eyes and ears of his mother. He hated her so, and the insufferable babbling she had succumbed to over the last few years was really grating on his nerves.

His mind envisioned the image from the old photograph she kept of herself on her nightstand in her room. His mother had been beautiful once. She had been a beauty queen and had won the hearts of several suitors, ranging from that of a congressman to that of the janitor of the local library where she worked during the war.

He turned and closed the door behind him, taking great care to bolt the three locks securely. He bit the inside of his cheek as his thoughts drifted to his mother again. She was once vivacious, though no semblance of that woman existed now. No, quite the opposite, in fact. He pitied her, this woman. Her life had been given to a man who thought of her as a possession while she wasted her love pining for another. She had been tortured daily after she married his father. Richard had been a hard man. He was one who demanded perfection from everyone around him, including his wife and son. The bastard. She sobbed quietly at night, as though she was trying to hold it back, to hold it in. She was unable to. She could never please his father, and she submitted to daily and nightly verbal abuse. Oh, he didn't have to raise a hand to her. No, he had a more effective method of destroying her on a daily basis that didn't leave marks for the world to see. He wounded the heart and stole her soul instead. Vince felt a chill at the image of his father.

"Vince?" He heard her yelling up the stairs and closed his eyes tightly, trying to squeeze her voice from his mind. "Vinnie, is that you? I need my medicine. Where have you been? Vince?"

He shook himself free of her. It never lasted long. With her endurance so weakened from the stroke and heavy medications, her pleas never lasted very long. He pulled off his shirt, catching a quick whiff of the sauce stain he'd gotten while eating in his car. He stood, listened at the door, and smiled, knowing that his mother had given up on him again. This was not the first time she'd given up on him, and he knew it was for sure not the last.

He threw the shirt in the corner and swore aloud, "That bastard!" Vince had seen them kissing again. *No, not just kissing*, he thought. *Loving*. That was what it looked like to him as he saw their faces when they pulled apart. She was quickly succumbing to the charms of the Irishman. She was so naïve, her mind so open and vulnerable with that great hulk. Did she really think he would love her? *Not likely*, Vince thought. *More likely, the man just wants her. Wants her like I do.*

Vince grinned; she wasn't letting that happen as far as he knew. Their evenings always ended the same, with a long goodbye kiss and then the closing of her door as the Irishman sulked off. Vince's grin turned downward, a dark scowl replacing it. It couldn't last long, her denying the Irishman. Their kissing lingered longer and longer, and the apparent reluctance of the nightly partings made him think that the man would not be denied much longer. *I'll have to act quickly; there will be no second chances.*

He walked over to his dresser, opened the top drawer, and reached far in the back under his clothes to retrieve the large manila envelope he had hidden there yesterday. He sat on the bed and opened it, spilling the contents out onto the bed. He stood then, looking down at the hundred or so snapshots of Caroline he had taken of her over the last few weeks. He looked at them, studied her mouth and the tiny peaks of her nipples showing through the thin fabric of her shirts. He felt himself growing hard as he looked at her. He liked the position he had taken. Standing there, hovering over her image looking up at him, as she seemed to lie helpless below him. He felt strong, powerful. *It'll be like this when we are together, my pet. I'll stand above you and you'll . . .*

He felt himself jerk as his hands went for his belt. The khaki pants fell to the floor with a clank of the belt buckle hitting against the zipper.

He knelt on top of the photos. A drop of sweat rolled off his neck and dropped onto one picture of her sweeping off her front sidewalk, the salty wetness fading her face. He reached down and grabbed himself. It wouldn't take long; it never did.

He let his breath out and collapsed onto the pile of photos, now slick with the stickiness of his release. He rolled from his stomach to his back, bringing dozens of them with him as they stuck to his skin. Running his fingers over the ones at his sides, he lifted handfuls of them above him and released them in a flutter of paper raining down on him. He picked up one off his chest; a shy look, he thought. He smiled and brought it to his lips for a single kiss against her mouth and fell asleep with it over his heart.

9.

PROMISES

Patrick listened to the woman on the stage, though he could not see her. She sang in Italian of a lost love, and he could hear the orchestra echoing her sorrow with expert timing. The skilled musicians of the Tucson Opera were making everyone breathless in anticipation of the finale. He listened, but his eyes were not on the stage below; they were on Caroline, who was seated next to him. She was beautiful tonight. She was beautiful every night, and he could feel his heart constricting in his chest just by looking at her. Her features were shadows and light. Her coloring was black and white in the darkened theater. He sat next to her, mentally tracing the delicate lines of her jaw, her swan neckline, the glowing alabaster of her perfect skin against the black velvet gown she wore tonight. Patrick wanted to touch her, to reach out and trace the smoothness of her cleavage and breasts with his fingers. She was perfection, and he couldn't take his eyes off her for a moment.

He caught sight of the tears welling in her eyes moments earlier, and now, as he was watching her, a single one escaped and began a slow trail down her cheek. *A diamond,* he thought as it made its way over her delicate, high, porcelain cheekbone and caught the shimmering lights from the stage. She turned slowly to face him.

Caroline caught him staring at her and offered a sad smile as he tightened his comforting hold on her hand. Her emotions showed on her face, as usual, and he felt his own heart break with hers for the tragic tale being played out below. So like her, he thought, feeling so deeply for something like this. He was getting to know her pretty well by now, and the idea of spending the rest of his life getting to know her better brought a sudden thrill to his insides.

She hadn't asked him of his past or of the secret that he carried with him every moment. She hadn't asked him what it was that kept him from really living and letting go. And he never asked her again to marry him after their first date. He held hope she would give her answer any day, though. The quiet gentleness between them made the pair of them extremely comfortable with each other, and both had confessed without words their mutual physical attraction as far as they could without crossing the boundaries. She held this power over him—not in a mean-spirited way, but in a way that commanded respect and kept his thoughts clear when his body cried out for her touch until he thought he might die from the ache.

This much he knew for sure: Caroline had bewitched him, and he couldn't take his eyes off her. She watched him as if sensing his thoughts and locked her emerald eyes with his. Patrick's breath caught in anticipation as she raised his hand to her damp cheek. He felt the smooth velvet of her skin as she tilted her face to allow his large hand to cradle her cheek in his palm.

"Yes," she mouthed, though no sound came forth.

He closed his eyes and let his breath out, knowing she had finally given him her answer. He opened his eyes to her steady gaze. She had made him the happiest man on the face of the earth at that moment, but hidden beneath the surface, mingling with the joy of the present, lay the notion that he would now have to tell her the truth about himself and face her turning from him when he needed her the most.

The drive back to Caroline's apartment was quiet. They needed no words to convey their thoughts to each other and spent the ride bonding closer in the stillness and enjoying just being with each other. Her hand rested on his thigh as he drove, and looking down at her delicate bone structure, he realized again just how fragile this relationship truly was.

Given the late hour, Patrick was surprised when she invited him in this time. They stood in the middle of her living room, holding each other and swaying slowly as they always did whenever they held each other. It was a dance, he supposed, a dance to some music only the two of them could hear. They stood, swaying and embracing the sweetness of the moment. Patrick cleared his throat to begin his confession.

"I love you, Patrick," she said suddenly, beating him with her own confession. "I know it's crazy, given the short time I've known you, but I can't help it. I've been in love with you from the first moment I saw you at your store."

"Caroline," he whispered, wanting to begin his story before he lost his nerve.

"Patrick, you do love me, don't you? I mean, I'm not dreaming, am I? It just seems too good for this to be happening so fast. I've waited a lifetime for you, and now . . ."

She reached slowly up and placed her palm against his cheek, rubbing lightly and feeling the roughness of new beard growth. He saw himself in her eyes, and he was strong and sure, confident and true. It broke his heart to know in a moment's time she might never look upon him with the same devotion as she did at this moment. "Caroline, no one has ever loved you more. No one has ever wanted you more than I do."

"I'm afraid," she confessed into his chest.

He swallowed hard, thinking she must know there was something within him, fighting to get out. "No, love, there is nothing to fear here." He tightened his embrace, and her hands went to the back of his neck, finding his hair at the nape and playing gently there. His confession would wait. Now was not the time. She was too fearful of the unknown between them, and he would not set her on the path of destruction tonight. No, tonight they would be just as they were now, in love and basking in the unknown. The demons would be there tomorrow, and there was time for all things to be brought to light.

His mouth found hers, and their lips met in a fevered kiss. All the emotions of the evening spilled into the onslaught of passion that was now overwhelming them. She was warm and soft in his arms, her mouth giving all he demanded as she leaned into him. This was more than a kiss; this was the seal on the bargain they had made this night, and it served to forge the promises between two people who had all of eternity to love and be loved by each other.

Caroline lowered her hands to his belt. Seeking, she undid the buckle with one hand and fondled him gently with the other, feeling him already hard and wanting through the silky fabric of his slacks. He was lost as his own hands went for her breasts with a certain urgency. Their breathing became loud in his ears as she rubbed the length of him. He knew he would lose control in another moment if he let her continue. Somewhere deep inside, he found the strength to honor her this night in his own way.

"Caroline," he breathed, pulling away and grabbing her hands in a lock. He could feel her trembling, and he forced himself to gain some control. Finally summoning the courage to do what was right, he released her hands and placed his own on her shoulders to distance himself . . . "Caroline, I want ya with every bone in me body. I want ya so much it hurts right now."

She leaned into him, seeking his mouth again. He pulled away with much effort. "Tis true, Missy, I want ya that way and more, but . . ." His eyes widened as she gave him a look that could seduce the devil himself. "But, I'd make ya me wife first, and I'd have our wedding night one ta remember, one ta look back on and treasure. When we join, it will be the start of forever."

She suddenly went stiff and stopped fighting him. He gave her an unsure grin and a raised eyebrow to get his meaning across. She stepped back, frowning, and his heart sank. Had he said the wrong thing? Had it come out wrong? He wanted only to honor her in this. It was true—he did still mean to tell her of his past, but he had been sincere in his desire to take her only after she was fully his.

"If that's the way things are to be, then . . ." She went to the front door and opened it. His blood stopped cold in his veins. She couldn't have taken it that wrong, could she?

"I'm afraid you'll have to leave this minute," she stated coldly, gesturing through the entryway. "If you just stand there with your mouth open, I'll be forced to close this door and throw myself at you until I make you want me so bad you won't be able to leave. After all, you're not the only one who's hurting now." She smiled wickedly, her eyes teasing him.

"You!" he roared. "I thought . . . I thought . . . well, never mind. Meet me tomorrow so we can get the plans underway, so neither of us has ta hurt fer too long." He went to her and leaned an easy kiss to her lips. She resisted the urge to reach for him again.

"How about lunch?" she asked against his mouth.

"Aye, lunch," he answered, pulling away and heading out the door. He was breathing fast, and the noticeable bulge in his pants was proving to be a great distraction and source of discomfort under her direct gaze. Soon, my love, soon. Patrick took a deep breath. The space between them was seemingly vast, but not unattainable. He was content with it for the moment, and so was she.

Caroline had just put her journal down and was reaching for the light when she was startled by the sudden, unexpected ring of the phone. "Hello?"

"Er, is Mrs. Patrick McNally there?"

She immediately smiled broadly at the sound of his thick Irish brogue shining through the attempted American accent.

"Oh, my, David, how did you find out so soon? You and I will not be able to meet so easily now that I'm about to be some boring old housewife," she said, teasing Patrick mercilessly.

"Who the bloody devil is David?!" he roared into the phone so loudly that she had to hold the receiver away for a second to save her eardrum.

"I'm just attempting to tease you, silly. I know it's really you . . . Jim."

"Caroline!" he roared again.

"Calm down, my love. Don't you know you are the only man in my life? The only one I can't wait to get my hands on?" she asked with great tenderness, listening to the sudden stillness on the other end. "Patrick?" she asked.

"Aye," he said hoarsely.

"Are you okay? I'm sorry if my teasing—"

"Caroline, it'll always be so, 'ey?" he said, interrupting her.

"Yes, every moment of every day," she said, choking back the salty tears.

"I'll do my best to make ya happy," he promised, and she remembered how safe she felt in his arms as he held her less than an hour earlier.

"I can't wait," she stated truthfully.

"Nor I. Meet me at the shop for a bit of breakfast around eight, instead of waiting fer lunch, 'ey?"

"Yes, I'd like that. Do you want me to bring something?" she asked.

"No, I'll arrange it. I can't wait fer the sun ta come," he said, getting quiet again.

"I love you," she said, matching his tone.

"I'm wishin ya wer 'ere whi me." She noticed his Irish brogue was getting thicker with his emotions. She could feel the love in his voice.

"Me too."

"I'm countin the 'ours," he said, and she listened as the dial tone signaled his goodbye. She felt a sudden ache in her heart. A longing of sorts, but she chalked it up to bridal nerves. She smiled, liking the thought. *Bridal nerves.*

10.

COMES THE DARKNESS

Patrick arrived at his shop around seven-thirty with a brown paper bag full of bagels, a large chocolate milk for himself, and two little glass bottles of apple juice for Caroline. Putting the bag on the counter by the cash register, he began removing the items from the bag when he realized that there were no napkins to place the bagels on.

Annoyed that he had forgotten to get some at the bagel shop, he walked behind the counter and stooped low in search of something to make do with. "Damn," he said, frowning at not being able to find anything that would work. He raised his eyes, searching the shop for something to use. He hadn't acquired much in the way of a breakfast, and even if she didn't eat much, he would be damned if he let her eat without at least a napkin. He smiled then, her face coming to mind. "Beag T'ean, Caroline," he said aloud, remembering the way her small cheek fit so nicely in the palm of his hand last night. The feel of her velvet skin had matched the softness of the velvet dress she had worn to the opera. He shook his head at her filling his mind so vividly, and in that instant, his eyes locked on the small, crystal bird glimmering brightly on the glass shelves. It sparkled, and light danced from it as it caught the rays of the morning sun coming through the shop windows.

"Aye, little one," he smiled, making his way out from behind the counter toward the object in view. "You'll have a new home tonight, and with any luck, I'll soon join ya there."

Patrick lifted the bird from its place, noting the faint circle left behind in the dust and making a mental note to tell the cleaning lady not to forget the shelves in her duties.

"Not too bloody shabby if I do say so," he grinned, taking a step backward and admiring the newly wrapped package before him. "Just one final touch, 'ey?" he said as he selected a small note card from the assortment behind the counter. Customers always wanted their purchases gift wrapped, so he had made the note cards, bows, and shamrock-laden wrapping paper a free gift with a purchase. It was a stroke of genius he was particularly grateful for today. He leaned on the counter, thinking of just the right words to write, his pen poised and ready.

"Caroline," he began, "Together we will soar the heavens." Perfect!

He signed the card, neatly tucked it in its envelope, and taped it to the top of the package just under the bow. He was smiling with the thought of the thank-you kiss she would soon please him with. His smile faded when he suddenly remembered his need for napkins. He headed off to the stockroom with the gift still in his hand. He whistled with excited anticipation of her arrival and glanced down at the box again. Opening the door to the darkened storeroom, he reached around with one hand, groping quickly in the dark for the light switch. Patrick knew he had some paper towels on supply for the cleaning woman in there somewhere, and they would do better than the toilet paper he was considering as his last option.

The noise that greeted him in that next moment was accompanied by such a powerful thud that he thought there might have been a car crash in the storeroom. A blinding flash of bright light left him with a burning sensation in the middle of his chest. "What the hell?" Patrick swore aloud at the tightness constricting his breathing as his hand went to the source of the pain. His fingers gripped the front of his shirt, and he felt wetness there, warm and slightly sticky. The light in the storeroom suddenly came on, and Patrick slowly lifted his head to come face-to-face with another man. "Who the hell—," Patrick asked, and the face of the stranger darkened as a smile flashed behind the barrel of the small handgun he was lifting, higher now and pointed directly at Patrick.

Patrick's mind was racing out of control, his thoughts fleeing his grasp as he tried to find the strength to think. Another flash. Another jolt, and he felt himself falling backward. The gift for Caroline plummeted from his grasp, and his eyes caught in slow motion as the pretty paper rolled under the shelves next to him, the green ribbon trailing behind it wildly. He had been trained, of course. Trained in the mud-soaked fields of his homeland for just such an assault. But the shock of it finally happening was astonishingly surprising. He smelled the hot metallic odor from the gun as his eyes closed briefly with a new surge of pain. Blood, he thought. His entire mouth tasted of the thickness of it. He licked his lips and painfully opened his eyes to the assault. Confusion set in, and he fell to his knees. This wasn't Belfast. No, he was still in America, all right, and he was still in his storeroom. On the floor, but still in his storeroom. He quickly concluded this man before him was not likely the enemy, but merely a surprised robber.

"Not so tough now, are you, you big piece of Irish shit?"

Patrick blinked in amazement at the lad who stood before him. His attacker appeared to be just out of diapers, and given his slim build, it was obvious why the kid held the gun so tightly. Even though Patrick remained on the floor for now, helpless, he knew the lad felt fear from him still. He had seen it before, this fear, but only on young men with a greater mission in mind, a passion of sorts, one they were willing to risk or give their lives for when the need came.

"I'm no about ta hurt ya now, lad. Put the gun away and let me see the face of me murderer, so I'll know who ta look for when the time's right ta haunt ya with me dying spirit." Patrick choked on the blood in the back of his throat. He had no intention of dying, but the tactic of keep 'em talking seemed the right thing to do.

"Shut up!" the kid yelled, and Patrick coughed at the blood filling his throat, bubbling and rising. He was getting dizzy, fighting back the pull of his body.

"You've done yer damage, now . . . now off whi' ye."

Patrick knew he was fighting now. The pull on his mind was winning. The darkness threatened him, its icy fingers secure in their quest to have him. She was coming. His eyes bolted open, and he was surprised to find his attacker bending over him. He must have blacked out briefly. Patrick had to get rid of him, he thought. Caroline was coming and would be hurt if this murderer were still here when she arrived.

The kid jumped back at seeing Patrick's wide-open eyes.

"No, no, I am sure I won't be seeing your stupid Jeep parked at Caroline's anymore," the kid hissed at him, boldly taking a step toward him at the realization his victim wasn't really going anywhere.

My thoughts must be fuzzier than I guessed. Now the lad is saying her name. "Who . . ." The pain was coursing through his head now, his heartbeat slow in his ears. "Who are ya?" he managed to whisper, the effort draining much-needed strength. He had to protect her!

"I'm the man who's just erased you from her life. How does that feel, huh?"

"Caroline?" The kid wasn't a robber after all; he was after her. Caroline! He had to warn her, but his body wouldn't obey his commands, and the darkness was there again, pulling. He was panicking now. Perspiration rolled down his forehead, sticking to the stray pieces of hair that were strewn across his face. "I'll kill ya . . ." was all he managed to say before the blackness engulfed him. He was losing, and in his last thoughts, he saw her face smiling brightly for him.

"So much for you, Irishman," Vince said, slowly standing. "She's mine now."

11.

FOREVER

"Late as usual!" Caroline frowned as she glanced at her watch. This was one of the thousands of times she wished she had taken Vanessa's advice and purchased a cell phone. Vanessa had always warned her she might need one in an emergency—and even if this did not qualify as one, she still wanted to call Patrick at the store and let him know she was on her way. He would be worried by now, and the thought of her large fiancé hovering by the door waiting for her made her anxious. *Fiancé.*

How perfectly wonderful the word sounded! *Fiancé.* She was going to belong to him forever. She supposed that the idea should have scared her a little, especially given the state of her stomach this morning. But it didn't. She just couldn't think of one good reason not to marry him, not even one. There was that little secret thing of his, but it was probably nothing. This felt right. It *was* right. It was just meant to be.

She smiled, spotting his shop just ahead of her. She consoled herself by thinking, *What's twenty minutes, when we have the rest of our lives?*

Rushing through the front door, she stopped and put her purse down on the counter.

"What a guy," she said aloud, noticing the juices and the bag of bagels.

"Patrick?" she called. The shop was very quiet, maybe a little too quiet. She stood still and listened for any small noise that would lead her to Patrick. "Patrick, I'm here," she yelled, a little louder this time. "Anybody home?"

No spirited Irish tunes or even the haunting Gaelic stuff she liked came from the music system. Maybe he stepped out, leaving the door open for her. She felt a little disappointed that he wasn't there scolding her for making him worry about her.

Then an uneasy feeling crept over her, filling her insides with a sudden stillness. "Patrick?" she whispered to the emptiness surrounding her. Something did not feel right.

Caroline glanced around more intently, looking for clues. Maybe a note? This just wasn't like him to leave her worrying like this, though it did serve her right for being so late. *Wait just a minute*, she thought, a sudden smile replacing the frown. It came to her then. The other day, when she had been in the shop with him, just hanging out and talking, he had asked her to retrieve some extra receipt paper for him from the stock room. He had sneaked in after her, grabbing her from behind and lavishing her neck and shoulder with his warm kisses. "Didn't want tha customers ta see me ravishin ya, my love," he had said. Her smile grew wider now with the memory.

She stepped lightly towards the door, her pulse picking up speed in anticipation of his touch. Her heart quickened as she reached for the doorknob. If he meant to surprise her, two could play at this game.

"Oh, no, you don't, mister, we're not married yet!" she sang happily as she opened the door.

Nothing could have prepared her for what she saw. "Patrick, oh, my God!" she screamed, racing and falling to her knees beside his still form. She slid into his side as her knees hit the pool of bright-red blood around him. "Patrick!" she cried, reaching for the sides of his face with her hands.

He was covered in blood, lying still on the cold, hard floor. He was warm, thank God, and she could feel the slow thump of his pulse beneath her fingertips as she cradled his fresh-shaven face. Caroline gently brushed back the strands of hair across the bridge of his nose and forehead. Her mind was racing in a hundred different directions all at once. Panic seized her heart. She had to get him help, call someone, but the thought of getting up and leaving him alone on the floor evaded her.

"Patrick?" she whispered again, hoping in some way he would awaken and tell her exactly what she should be doing right now. She needed him, needed him to tell her he was going to be all right. Tell her he would still spend the rest of his life with her. Her mind was screaming. *Get a grip, you fool, he needs you!* She gathered all the courage she could and spoke directly to him, inches away from his face. "You fight, do you hear me? You fight for us, and you hang on!" She lifted her palms from his face and firmly squeezed his large, lifeless hand at his side. She felt his blood like a barrier between them. It was so red.

"You stay with me!" she said, turning to get up. She was startled as a weak hand reached for her, grabbing and locking onto her wrist. "Patrick!" she fell back to his side.

"Don't leave me . . . my . . . my love," he said, so softly she barely heard him even as she leaned in close. She leaned in even closer to his face, wanting to feel his breath against her skin for reassurance. "Patrick, I've got to get you some help. You've been hurt, and I need to get you to a hospital."

Her breath came in short, quick gasps, catching in her throat when his eyes opened halfway. They were heavy-lidded, and their normal shade of emerald was so dark that she thought them more black than green.

"Don't leave . . ."

"I promise, I'll come right back." Her heart physically hurt her now, the pain of it all slamming into her chest with each heartbeat.

"Please . . . I've somtin ta tell ya." His voice was still low, but his eyes were now open, and his breath was coming with a sickening gurgling sound. She could not will her body to leave him as his eyes locked her to him. Her heart was aching. *I love you.*

"I know," he said softly, echoing her thoughts. His eyes closed briefly as he licked his lips. Caroline suppressed a gasp as his tongue traced them in blood, staining them crimson.

"Listen ta me," he said. "I want ya ta take me home."

"No!"

"Caroline, I want . . . I want ya ta take me home . . . ta be whi' me family in Ireland."

"No, you're going to be all right! I just have to get you some help. You have to get to a hospital." She refused to even think of what he was telling her. She closed her eyes to the pain he was in.

His grip on her increased, and when she opened her eyes again, his gaze was there, steady and sure, holding her to him with all of his love.

"Promise."

"No!" The tears streaked down her face.

"Promise!" he demanded.

"Yes, yes, all right!" she promised as the knowledge of his leaving filled her with an unprecedented pain the likes of which she had never known. She wiped her tears with the back of her hand, a smear of blood branding her. She knew she would not close her eyes to him again, knowing now this was the last she would see of him. The last time his eyes would lock with hers.

He offered her a faint trace of a smile, the corners of his mouth turning slightly as if he meant to encourage her. "Go to Ireland . . . to Sean."

"Your brother?"

"Aye. Go ta Sean and tell . . . tell him this fer me."

She listened as he said the words in Gaelic. She would remember them. She would commit each one to memory to be pulled from later, like her own name.

When he was through, and she had repeated the words carefully back to him, she felt him shift his arm and saw him wince with the pain of such a small movement. His hand reached shakily into his pocket, coming out with something. A ring!

"Give this ta him . . . when ya say the words," he said, slowly handing her the ring.

"Sean?" she asked, confused.

He placed the ring in her palm and closed her fingers over it, placing his large hand over them and squeezing with only feeble strength. She looked from the ring back to his eyes and saw the pain clouding them, their light slowly beginning to fade.

"He'll know," he said softly, reassured. She felt him relax against her as she shifted to cradle his head in her lap. His hair fell over her thighs, and she stroked it gently, committing its feel to memory.

"I'll love ya for all time," he whispered clearly, and she had the sudden realization he meant to leave her now. Somehow, he knew it was time, and she felt her heart ripping from her chest as he took it with him in his departure.

"Patrick! Please don't leave me!" she cried against him, her tears soaking both their cheeks as she bent over him, pressing herself closer, one hand still being held by his and the other entangled in his thick hair.

"I love ya . . . me beag . . . 'tean . . ."

She moved her mouth to cover his, feeling the last word come out in a tremble. At the touch of her lips to his, he pressed himself roughly against her, and she tasted his blood as she felt the life force drain from his powerful body, leaving him limp and heavy in her arms. "Forever," she whispered, saying it again and again as she sat on the bloody floor of the stock room. Her own crying was the only sound as she rocked him back and forth, unaware of everything except the pain of this moment. Unaware of the nightly cleaning lady, Rosa, tucked neatly away in the closet barely five feet away, her cries silenced for all time.

"Oh, God, NO! . . . Patrick!" Caroline could not stop screaming.

PART TWO

IRELAND

"I love thee with the breath, smiles, tears, of all my life!—
and, if God choose, I shall but love thee better after death."
—Elizabeth Barrett Browning, *Sonnet 43*

12.

FADED EMBERS

"Are we landing?" Caroline asked the pretty, slim flight attendant, who was quickly walking down the aisle of the plane.

"No, Miss, just a bit of turbulence is all. Don't ya go worrin' yer pretty head about it. It'll be over in a moment. Ya did fasin' yer seat-belt though?"

"Um, yes. Thank you," Caroline replied, not really paying attention to the question once she heard the woman's familiar Irish lilt. *It sounds so much like his*, she thought, and it sent new waves of pain gripping at her heart.

Looking around at the other passengers, she tried to fix her attention on something, anything that would free her for a second from the thoughts that had plagued her every waking moment over the last three days. Three days. She was drowning. Patrick was everywhere and nowhere, just like the man in her dreams. She saw his face in the clouds, looming low and dark. She smelled him in the rain, sensed him in the darkness.

She felt she might not be able to survive this. The constant, unrelenting pain drove on and on in its torment. She did know one thing:

if Patrick had not asked this of her, asked her to bring him home to his family, she was sure she would have locked herself away and never seen the light of day again. She would have given herself over to the deep depression pulling at her. As it was, she was practically a zombie. She was here, there, nowhere. Her mind was as dark as the blackness of night outside the small window of the plane.

Caroline stared out into the nothingness, seeing only her reflection blurred by the rain against the window. Her image seemed to mirror her inner self—here for the moment but blurred beyond recognition. A shell of her former self. *I am nothing without you, my love.*

The plane gave a sudden jolt as it hit another air pocket. Other passengers were getting nervous, demanding explanations from the flight attendants and squirming in their seats. Caroline's mind drifted back to Patrick, and she sank lower in her seat, lower into herself.

He was there with her in a way. She sorrowed as she thought of his lifeless body in the darkness of the cargo hold, alone. *I am here, my love.*

She hadn't looked when they loaded his steel-gray casket onto the plane. She couldn't. She knew he was there with her, and she knew no matter how hard this was going to be, she would see it through, see it done as he wished. It was the least she could do.

The detectives had told her she shouldn't leave the country with the ongoing investigation, but she had plans to carry out and promises to keep. She still blamed herself for not getting right up and calling the paramedics when she had the chance. She had beaten herself up with the what-ifs, and the simple truth was that she would always blame herself. The coroner told her he was too far gone by the time she reached him, that he had lost too much blood, and the internal injuries were too severe. Nothing could have been done. Vanessa had put her arm around her and told her she should just cherish the last moments she had with him, and that in some way, God spared her the coldness of the hospital waiting room while the last voices Patrick heard would have been doctors, nurses . . . strangers. Caroline knew all this, yet still the doubts and what-ifs wore her down. She could not remember when she last slept, ate, or smiled, and she had the feeling she wouldn't do any of those things for a long time yet.

The plane lunged again, and she looked around at all the frightened passengers. Their faces showed their fear openly while she simply stared ahead. If this was to be her fate, to plunge into the ocean with him, then let it be so. The thought of being in a watery grave with him dulled her senses, and she realized she might indeed like that. To be forever with him seemed right, even if it meant death. *Oh, God, I am going mad now.*

She tried again to pull out of her thoughts. Vanessa had given her the book *A Hundred Things to Be Happy About* when she stood in line to board the plane, thrusting it into her free hand with a granola bar. She had hugged her and told her she needed to eat something. She reminded Caroline that it had been three days since she had eaten, and she looked pale and weak.

"I can't believe you are actually going; you don't even know these people!"

Caroline knew Vanessa was right, of course. She was off to a foreign country to stay with people she didn't know. But she made a promise, and nothing short of the plane going down was going to keep her from her task. Patrick wanted it, and that was that. Period.

Caroline ran her fingers over the bright-red cover of the small book that was unopened in her lap. She closed her eyes and leaned wearily against the back of the seat. She wanted to die. Wanted the plane to go down. In her dreams, he was waiting with an outstretched hand to take her with him on some great journey. His strong arms surrounded her in a lover's embrace. She would give anything to just lean her head against his chest and smell the musky smell that was his alone.

She thought she was still dreaming for a quick second when she heard the pilot's voice booming over the speakers and shaking her from her sleep. He was telling the passengers that everything was all right and that the worst was over. Sighs of relief were heard from everyone, including the four flight attendants.

Caroline did not open her eyes but could feel the tears again. She just wasn't ready for any sort of happiness right now and wondered if she ever would be again. She fought the tightness in her throat that threatened to unleash another flood of tears and found herself wishing with all her heart that she and Patrick had made love.

"I'm so sorry, Miss. He's not usually so cranky. It's just that he's not used to being so restricted in his movements. At home, he is happiest running and playing like a wild Indian." Caroline watched helplessly as the young mother tried without success to calm the young boy down. "It's okay; I don't mind." She tried to reassure the young woman, who looked a little worse for wear. This was a long flight, and she couldn't imagine what the young mother had done to keep him so entertained for so long.

"I hope you don't mind us moving next to you like this. The man we were sitting next to kept making rude remarks to me."

"How terribly awful." Caroline was disgusted at a man she hadn't even laid eyes on. Who would make rude comments about a toddler?

"I thought it was awful, too. Any other time, my husband would have shown him a thing or two. Anyway, thank you for the seat. He really should be falling asleep any moment now; it's way past his bed-time." Caroline noticed the small child could barely keep his eyes open.

"How old is he?" Caroline was surprised to hear herself asking a question aloud.

"Eighteen months."

"Oh."

"Yes, I know. What on earth is a woman doing taking such a small child on such a long flight anyway?" Before Caroline could deny, the woman went on. "You see, we haven't seen our daddy yet, have we?" She was addressing her son with the comment, and Caroline thought her a bit nervous. "He's with the foreign ministry in Ireland. The peace envoy that the Prime Minister has placed there."

Caroline merely nodded, thankful for the moment to be distract-ed in some way. She noticed the boy had placed his head against his mother's breast, his thumb simultaneously going for his small, cherubic mouth.

"He got assigned there right after we found out I was pregnant. It took us this long to save up for the flight over. He's British, you see, and we met while he was on vacation in the States, and, well, the rest of that is history, as they say. I can't wait to see my husband again." Caroline flinched with her last sentence. *Can't wait to see my husband again.*

"Are you going to live there now?" Caroline asked, wanting to change the direction of the conversation.

"I want to, but John, that's my husband, thinks it's too dangerous."

"Too dangerous? Ireland?"

"The terrorists, you know?"

Caroline gave her a surprised look. She really didn't know much about the country she was on her way to, except for general descriptions Patrick had provided.

"The bombings?"

Caroline still looked lost.

"They're famous for them. The IRA and all that?"

Caroline nodded politely. She wasn't much on world events, and the only things she really knew of the country were the historical things she had read in her romance novels and the great music. She really didn't watch much TV. As a matter of fact, Patrick was always the one bringing up news stories. He had valued her opinions and asked her frequently what she thought of this or that. She was pleased that he liked her mind as well as his obvious attraction to her body. *We would have been great lovers.*

"Anyway, I told him we should at least give it a try."

Caroline snapped back from her memories and wondered if things were really that bad.

"What did he say?"

"Six months."

"I hope it works out for you."

"Thanks. Hey, look, he's out like a light." The woman smiled and put her hand over the little boy's ear to block out any noise that might wake him.

Caroline watched, entranced with the exhausted tot. He was fast asleep, and she let herself smile a small bit as she watched his slow, even breathing. His white-blonde curls were tousled about his head like the angel hair she'd seen as a child on her aunt's Christmas tree. It was longer than acceptable for a boy, but she thought it enchanting. His cheeks were a deep shade of pink in sleep, and she noticed he sucked on his thumb every so often in his dreams. Caroline again found herself wishing she and Patrick had made love. She might be pregnant with his child had they had the time together. She wished she were on her way to tell his family he'd left a piece of himself behind in her. *We would have made beautiful children.*

She turned her back on the mother and child, preferring the coldness of the darkened window glass to the painful thoughts that were surfacing. She also did not want to have to explain herself to the woman for the sudden rush of tears now flowing freely or for the grief she was feeling for children who would never be.

13.

SHADES OF GREEN

Caroline reached high for her carry-on bag, wedged between two others in the overhead compartment. Its cramped position was a direct result of all the jumping and lurching the plane had done earlier.

"Here, let me get mine first," said a low voice coming from behind her. Passengers were already filing off the plane, and the aisle was crowded, giving her a quick feeling of claustrophobia with all the bumping and pushing. She let her hands drop in defeat and immediately felt the warmth of a strong arm coming around her left side, brushing lightly against her shoulder.

"It'll be easier, then I'll get yours fer ya."

Caroline looked past her shoulder, following the direction of the brown leather bag as it came free from where it was lodged. She could only agree and then began to feel herself pushed up tightly against the man. He was tall and had the clearest blue eyes she had ever seen; she likened them to those blue ice pops she loved as a child, the ones that turn your teeth and tongue blue.

"Thank you," she said, offering a scant smile as he handed her bag to her. Someone suddenly bumped him from behind, sending him into her with a thud. "Oh!" she cried.

"I'm sorry, are ya still in one piece?" he asked with a fair amount of concern. She liked his Irish brogue, as it reminded her of Patrick. She nodded up at him in reply.

He surprised her by turning to the man who had bumped them and growling something low and menacing. She noticed the exchange of words left the other man with a look of fear across his face.

"You didn't have to do that. I'm fine, really." *I'm actually never going to be fine again.*

"Aye, may well be, but he was in the need of the reminder of his manners," he said in a matter-of-fact way, and she noticed the way his red curls flopped around as he moved. His hair was long enough to brush the tops of his shoulders, shaggy and unkempt. Boyish.

"Yer American?" he asked. Given their close proximity, she felt him trying to ease the discomfort that must surely be showing on her face. "Yes," she answered, turning away, careful not to meet his eyes again. She turned back to him but looked past him over his shoulder down the aisle for an escape.

"Business or pleasure?"

"What?" She didn't want to meet those eyes again.

"Are ya here fer business or pleasure then?"

She could tell he was staring directly down at her, and she raised her eyes only enough to focus on his beard. She studied it and noticed it was several shades darker than his hair, with streaks of silver and dark cinnamon browns. "Oh, I . . ." She didn't know what to say. She felt guilty. She felt sick.

"Oh, finally!" she said in a rush of relief. The crowd had started moving forward, giving her a way out. "Thank you again for helping me with my bag," she offered weakly as she turned quickly and made her way down the aisle.

"I hope ya enjoy yer stay," she heard him call after her, but she did not turn back. Oh, God!

Emerging from the plane, Caroline noticed one thing right off: she was fast becoming lost among the shuffle. The Shannon Airport was busy, booming with newly arrived passengers, all smiling and being very loud. Feeling alone, she nervously glanced around at the crowd of people hugging and embracing each other. Fear began to rise as she watched men smacking each other on their backs and children running into the arms of elated adults. It was too much—too much and too soon. Her stomach rolled with an uneasy feeling as she realized she was standing in the middle of an airport in Ireland and did not know a single soul. All those smiling faces, and not one of them knew her from Adam.

Alone in the midst of hundreds of strangers, she immediately felt the tears starting to brim. She was tired, scared, and hungry. She was also weakened from all that had happened and was beginning to feel overwhelmed by it all.

She tried to think, to focus. *First things first*, she thought, regaining some sense of balance. Since there was no sight of Patrick's sister Claire or his younger brother Sean, she supposed the best thing to do would be to get her luggage and go through customs. That way, at least she would be ready to go when they did show. If they showed.

No, they said they would come, and if they were anything like Patrick, they would be true to their word. She wouldn't blame them if they did decide to abandon her. After all, they didn't know her any better than she knew them.

She had phoned them, of course, since she was the one who had to tell his family about the tragedy. She had broken down as she cried into the phone to his sister thousands of miles away. It amazed her then how she never once heard any form of emotion from Patrick's sister. She instead answered her in short, to-the-point answers. While Caroline was glad that the ordeal didn't drag out, his sister's response was strange. It was as if his sister knew to be strong, to carry on, and to get things arranged. It was his family who had made all the arrangements for Patrick's body to come home. Caroline would be eternally grateful to them for sparing her that. She supposed Claire must have been in some sort of shock. Different people handled this sort of grieving in their own ways, and after the thorough questioning the police had subjected her to, she needed the strength that this sister of his gave so easily.

Caroline stood in the customs line, lingering in thought, wondering what sort of girl Claire would be and if they could become close through Patrick. She wanted to hear about him, to know everything he was, and lose herself in his home and family. In some way, it might help relieve some of the hurt, might keep him near for a while longer.

"Any firearms or contraband to declare?" the customs officer asked her, shaking her from her thoughts.

"No," she said, softly shaking her head. He was young, but his short-cropped, blonde hair gave his boyish features a quality of authority. How serious he was in his uniform. Not a hint of emotion or thought showed on his face, and she felt a certain chill at watching him go so intently through her bags. With expert fingers, he searched without making a sound. Glancing around, she counted five other men at counters doing the same thing. Passengers waited patiently in lines without grumbling or complaining. Now that the world was not such a safe place, it was something you just did without comment. Like sheep.

"Clear," he said, zipping her bag closed and setting it down on the floor next to the counter. "Next," he yelled after quickly plastering her bag with a red-and-white strip of security tape.

"Thank you," she said, picking up her bag and heading off in the general direction the rest of the cleared passengers were going. He never acknowledged her but continued on with his duties. It was a chilly reception indeed.

I should wait close to the gate I arrived at so they can easily be able to find me, Caroline thought. Despite the temporary attention she had been given at the customs checkpoint, she was fast becoming nervous again. The minutes ticked on, and she kicked absently at her bag at her feet. *They forgot.* She groaned inwardly. *They decided against picking up such a weeping baby.* She put her hand in her pocket, searching for the phone number Claire had given her in case of an emergency. The paper was there, crinkled from repeated checks, but there nevertheless. It felt like the security blanket she used to hang onto as a child. Only now, it was a grownup sense of security she needed.

She spotted the pay phones along the wall. *No, they're coming. I am not going to lose it here in the middle of this airport!* But even as she thought it, the fear was quickly escalating inside her. She was so tired, her body crying out with both emotional and physical needs. The weights of burdens she could not bear much longer seemed to pull at her very soul. She was just about to give up when she suddenly felt a warm, strong hand on her shoulder.

"Caroline, is that you, lass?"

Caroline froze as her handbag fell from her hand. There was no mistaking the deepness of his voice, the strength of his hand, or the richness of his brogue. Whirling around, she threw herself into his arms, burying her face against the softness of his leather coat, feeling his strong arms embracing her. "Patrick!"

"There now, lass, it's gonna be all right. Yea mustn't go on so. I'm here, and no harm will come to ya now." The voice above her head vibrated into her whole being. His arms, strong and sure, held fast as she sobbed uncontrollably into his chest.

"Caroline, are ya all right, girl?" Claire asked as she stood there in disbelief at the distraught girl her brother was holding. Claire watched as his hands stroked her long hair with calming reassurance. Patrick had told them she was lovely, but he must have conveniently forgotten to inform them she was really quite beautiful.

Claire studied Caroline while her brother calmed her by speaking soft words in Gaelic. Caroline was as tall as she was and about the same size—slim with a bit more up top, she thought with a touch of envy. She seemed delicate, almost frail in her beauty. Patrick had obviously picked her for her looks without giving a second thought to her brains, if she had any. All she knew of this American girl so far was that she cried too easily, and it was going to take a great deal of patience to put up with her through all of this over the next few days.

Losing patience with the scene taking place before her, Claire sighed loudly, crossed her arms across her breasts, and asked rudely, "My God, Sean, do ya think she's gone mad?"

Sean looked up and frowned at her abruptness. "Ya do well ta mind yer manners, little one," he threatened. "Have ya not an ounce of pity in that cold heart of yers?"

He continued to stroke Caroline's hair. It was the softest he had ever felt. The silky curls tangled around each of his fingers, teasing and falling with each stroke. She was trembling as she clung to him with a vise grip around his waist. Her sobbing was gentler now, but the feel of her firm breasts against him left him a bit surprised. *What am I thinking? She is practically Patrick's widow.*

He had been prepared to dislike this American woman who knew nothing of their lives or country. Save for the fact she was only one of dozens of girls Patrick had won over with his abundant charms, she would mean little to them. The sooner she was on her way back to the States, the better. She had fulfilled her duty escorting him home, and now she could leave as soon as possible.

Or that *was* the plan, until he saw her standing alone, fearful and quiet in her pain. He saw her eyes only for a second, the green light in them dull. Her sadness engulfed her, and it made him uncomfortable to face his own pain of loss so directly. Finally, he began to feel her pull away, her warmth leaving him and sending a shiver coursing through his insides.

"Sean?" she asked, looking disbelieving up at him. She had only heard his voice, and with the lack of sleep, her constant crying, and the long flight. . . .

She stepped back, finally realizing her mistake. "Oh, I'm . . . I'm so sorry," she said, now looking up, stepping back another small step, and getting a full view of him. "I thought you were . . ." She looked down and then closed her eyes, not able to say Patrick's name aloud.

"Aye, I can see yer mistake. People are always doing that, ya know. No harm done. Are ya all right now?" he asked quickly. She looked slowly up at him as if the sight of him, so much like Patrick, would physically wound her. "Yes, I . . . you look so much like—"

"Only a bit taller, 'ey?" he said with an easy grin that nearly took her breath away. It was Patrick's grin. Given easily and with a hint of mischief. "Yes, taller," she choked out. That was not all, she thought, soaking in his features. Same nose, chin, mouth, and sleek black hair. Only Sean's was longer and a bit messier, and with his two-day-old beard scruff, it gave him a more rugged, dangerous look. The resemblance was uncanny, but the most striking thing about him was his eyes. They were exactly the same shape and were fringed in the same black lashes most women would kill for. They were exactly the same except for one thing: where Patrick's had been warm and friendly, Sean's were distant, like cold, emerald stones. Beautiful, yet empty and hard. He had a small scar too, about an inch under his lower lip. It was barely visible, but she was noticing every difference at this point. They all screamed in her head, *This is not Patrick. Patrick is dead.*

"Ah-hum," Claire coughed. "Ya better be gettin her bags, SEAN!" She uncrossed her arms and placed her hands on her hips, sticking out one foot and tapping it impatiently.

"Hadn't ya better make the introductions first?" he growled.

"I figured she already knows who we are, ya big oaf! She already thinks she's seein double by the way she can't take her eyes off ya!"

"Claire, you'll watch yer wicked tongue!" he spat at her, his eyes darkening even more. Caroline was immediately embarrassed. It was true. She had not, could not take her eyes off him. His presence filled her senses; he was so much like Patrick. How was she ever going to get through this? It was obvious the sister did not care for her, and just looking at the brother filled her heart with a tangible pain.

The brother and sister continued their argument, but Caroline's thoughts drifted inward. Her chest hurt so much it felt like someone was reaching in and tearing her heart out. She was wishing for Patrick's strong arm to hold onto; she felt strangely light with a sense of peace as her legs weakened and the darkness beckoned, promising an escape and bringing relief from the pain in her heart. Her fingers tingled, and she felt a chill as the room began to spin and stars twinkled all around her. . . .

14.

EASY AND SLOW

"Did ya see how pale she went? Do ya think she might be carrin?" Claire asked over Sean's shoulder from the back seat of the car.

"Do ya think she's all right?" she probed again, causing him to glance over at Caroline's sleeping form. She looked so peaceful in her dreams. Her face was relaxed and childlike. He looked into the rear-view mirror at his sister. "Aye, I suspect she'll be fine once this whole bloody business is over." He chose not to answer the first question.

"Aye is right, and I suspect you'll be there ta make sure, 'ey? I saw the way ya seemed so content ta lend yer comfort back at the airport. Do ya have it in mind ta seduce her while she's mournin our brother?"

His anger flared at her snide remarks. He knew all the anger inside wasn't her fault, yet it still managed to send his hands around her neck in his mind quite often.

"Don't," was all he could manage to say while struggling to keep his temper in check. He gave Caroline another quick look. She did go quite pale back in the airport, and his natural instinct had been to comfort her. She seemed to draw that from him without even knowing it. When he had noticed her falling, his hands went right for her, without hesitation, without thinking. That was a strange thing for him, given his suspicious and calculating mind of late.

He let his eyes lower to her stomach area. She was flat as a board, and the blue jeans she had on were snug. No, there was no trace of a babe there . . . yet. His mind began doing the calculations, and he did not like the results. *Patrick, me lad, what have ye sent us?*

He looked back at his sister in the mirror again. She had her head back against the seat, dozing and quiet for now. He gave a quick sigh at the sight of her. She, too, seemed childlike in her sleep. His brow furrowed in remembering his sister's little pink cheeks in her crib when she was small, so innocent and sweet then. He grimaced at the thought of that sweet face with a black knit ski mask pulled down over it. He could see her long, red braid hanging down the middle of her back as she lay in the mud on her stomach, her slim hands grasping her gun, eyes fixed and glowing bright green at her target.

He closed his eyes for a second at the vision, thinking she should be holding babes of her own like so many other young women, not rolling around in the cold mud, training with him and his mates, shooting at cardboard cutouts of the enemy. She should be gentle, not that she ever had been, always following him and Patrick around. She had wanted to play their games and be with their friends. She never did enjoy the girlish pursuits of dolls and playing house. Claire always opted for a game of war or knights. An unconscious chuckle gave rise in the back of his throat. She had been better than most of the lads.

Staring out into the darkness in front of the car as he drove, he was saddened then at the politics of his country. It weighed heavy on his mind to think of a guerrilla group that would accept such fragile creatures like his sister to help in a war for the good of a cause. He had to admit, though, that things would never be right in his country if everyone did not take a stand and fight for what was right—but still, he would prefer to leave the fighting to the men. He was sure Claire would certainly have something to say about *that.*

Sean was mesmerized by the car headlights on the winding road in front of him, and his thoughts returned again to the stranger in the seat next to him. She moaned softly, stirring in her sleep, moving her feet closer to his thigh. Her small boots rubbed gingerly against him, seeking out his warmth. Her head rested against his jacket, which was balled up against the window. Her legs and feet were up on the seat, and she was still making soft, whimpering noises in her sleep, the effects of a lingering nightmare or from so much crying, he thought. Even with her jeans and brown leather boots on, he couldn't help but notice how long and shapely her legs were.

Sean cocked an eyebrow at her, stealing another glance at her face. In the darkness, the glowing lights from the dashboard illuminated her features, and he found it hard to take his eyes off her for the necessary moments it took to keep the car on the road. Her soft, full lips were parted slightly; her dark hair framed her face in a cascade of soft curls. He had felt the softness of that hair already and found himself wanting to reach across the short expanse of their two bodies and know the feel of it again. "Oh, hell," he muttered, scolding himself. He would need to be extra careful when he was around her. She looked so damned vulnerable with those soft, lovely looks, and his brother was not even in the ground yet. God in heaven, what was he thinking? He shook his head to rid his thoughts of her.

"Caroline?" a voice whispered softly in her ear, beckoning her to awake. She was so tired, and it seemed a struggle just to open her eyes. "Caroline, we're home, lass."

"Home?"

Opening her eyes, she smelled him before she actually saw him. His masculine cologne wafted around her, and his breath was warm against her face as he leaned over the small expanse of the seat. She felt like a truck had run her over. Her entire body ached, and she was freezing—except for her feet, which were deliciously warm. She immediately felt a strong, warm hand gently shaking her calf.

It took her eyes a moment to adjust and her brain to start functioning again. "I'm sorry; I must have dozed off. I guess I am more tired than I thought," she said, looking over at him sleepily. "I don't even remember leaving the airport."

He was not making an effort to move his hand from her calf as he sat there with that grin on his face. "Aye, well—"

"Are we at your home?" she interrupted, making a fair effort to straighten up in her seat. She was stiff as she pulled his balled-up coat out from behind her. She looked at it, immediately knowing it was his, and held it out for him. His hand rested a second longer on her calf, and then he reached over for the coat. "Thank you," she offered weakly.

"Don't be afraid," he said, the grin disappearing and his eyes becoming dark.

"I'm trying not to be," she said quietly.

"Good, let us go in, then."

"Should I be?" she asked suddenly as her arm found his forearm and used it for support to steady herself upright in the seat. "Afraid, I mean?"

"Aye, there is much to be afraid of here, Missy, but not in this house and not while I'm around."

Caroline was taken aback by his statement. She tried to smile at him, but it was lost in the darkness of the car. Instead, she just stared after him as he opened his door and went around the front of the car.

Sean opened her door and held out his hand. Caroline took what he offered, thinking he probably didn't offer much more to a woman than his hand now and then.

She looked around, her eyes trying to adjust to the darkness. She made out forms of buildings, and the hint of a faint tree line shone across what appeared to be a meadow of some vast acreage. The stark light from a huge spotlight shone bright against the top of a barn some distance away, lighting the ground around the entrance. The doors were open, and a soft glow spilled out onto the ground from within. Caroline could see stacks of bundled hay and a large piece of iron machinery just inside. It never occurred to her that Sean's family could be farmers.

Emerging from the car, she thanked him as the moon made its way clear from the clouds and his face came into a soft blue glow. It was painful just to look at him, and she quickly glanced away. The moon revealed much of the surrounding area in that instant as the clouds suddenly parted. Caroline turned her thoughts to the house. It was huge and was not at all as Patrick had said it was. She struggled again to remember what it was he had said. Oh, yes, "a wee bit of a cottage in the forest." *Hardly*.

Looming ahead of her was a three-story stone structure whose very presence said *medieval.* "Don't ya be frightened now, it's just a wee house," she heard Sean say over her shoulder. She shivered just the same.

"I can bet he didn't want ya distracted from his charms by the idea of all this," Sean half laughed and cocked his head toward the house.

"Umm," she moaned, feeling at once enchanted and frightened.

The gothicness of the structure made it appear to have grown up naturally from the ground, like a giant boulder planted firmly there for the last thousand years. Though the moonlight bathed everything in an eerie glow of violets, grays, and blues, she was relatively sure the house itself had no color to speak of—merely gray.

From the back of the house, Caroline could see a great many of the tiny windows glowing with a quiet, yellow light from within, their thick glass distorting the views. "It's beautiful," she breathed, gazing up.

"Best we get ya inside before the wind has ya," Sean said softly, indicating his desire to go inside. "Come round the front so me ma sees I have more manners than ta let ya come in through the kitchen like a stray madra."

"Madra?" she asked after him. He was already well ahead of her, his long legs making great strides toward the front of the house, effortlessly carrying her bags with him.

"Oh, ya know, dog?" he answered, turning and cocking his head at her in question. He stopped for a second as she rushed to catch up to him. "I'll try not ta use the Gaelic while yer here then. I don't mean ta be rude."

"Oh no, on the contrary, I want you to," she said softly.

Sean lowered his eyebrows, completely confused by her statement.

"Not to be rude, I mean. I would like to learn some Gaelic while I'm here. Patrick is . . ." She looked up at him helplessly. It was so hard not to think of Patrick as still being alive. His presence was still so much a part of her.

"He was teaching ya Gaelic, then?" Sean asked, his features softening as he looked down at her. She was breathing hard, not from the strain to catch up with him but from the emotions weighing so heavy in her heart. She nodded, looking down, not wanting him to see her eyes. She did not want him to see the fresh tears.

"I'll be proud ta teach ya if that's the desire of yer heart, but for now we best be gettin ya inside before me ma brains me."

Caroline looked up at him, seeing through tear-filled eyes a man who would be her brother even now, and she found herself wondering what kind of man would say something so gentle as to refer to the desires of her heart.

The front of the house was much the same as the back. Two large, stone pillars guarded either side of the enormous, double front doors. They sat on a wide, gray stone porch that spread itself lazily around the entire front of the building. It was surprisingly a lot like a southern mansion, with its large, inviting rocking chairs and overstuffed, cushioned, porch gliders. Plaid throw pillows and thick rugs welcomed a weary traveler.

She was just about to expect Scarlet to come gliding across the porch when the front doors suddenly burst open. Streams of soft, golden, yellow light spilled into the night, and the plump shape of a short woman emerging from within came into her line of sight.

Caroline watched as the woman stopped in the doorway for a moment, and she saw Claire come up behind the woman and whisper something in her ear. The woman nodded slowly, then made her way down the stairs to meet them.

"My dear child, how glad we are ta have ya at our home!" the woman exclaimed. She grabbed and hugged Caroline with great intensity, and Caroline could smell the sweetness of brown sugar, cinnamon, and flour in the woman's hair. "God in heaven, yer nothing but a rail!" Caroline was immediately thrust backward at arm's length and examined.

Caroline took the moments to make some examinations of her own. The woman's eyes! Even in the darkness of the night, she could see him there. The very shade of green glowed with a remembered friendliness that made her breath come thick and heavy in her throat. She opened her mouth slightly to speak but was interrupted by the woman.

"I'm Mary; ya must be our dear Caroline," she stated with a hint of sadness, her eyes—so like his—blinking at the thickening emotions of the thoughts that connected Caroline to their family now.

"I'm so glad ya've come ta stay with us," she said, so slowly and softly that Caroline had the feeling she really meant it, not just the horrid façade of politeness showing through like so many others. Mary's warmth was quickly taking the chill from the night air.

"Thank you, Mrs. McNally."

"Mary, please!" the woman insisted with a genuine smile.

"Mary," Caroline repeated. "But, if it's too much trouble, I mean with everything that's coming, well . . . I could really just stay at a motel or something." Caroline was feeling awkward all of a sudden. She wanted more than anything to stay in Patrick's home with his family, and the thought of being alone through this was simply heart-wrenching.

"Won't hear of it!" the woman stated firmly, and Caroline felt the relief of the demand, smiling at the way her Irish brogue made the word *hear* sound more like "ear."

"We'll be needing each other ta get us through the next few days, 'ey?" Mary said, closing the distance she had made between them, putting a warm arm around Caroline's waist and urging her toward the doors.

Most of Caroline's fears were laid to rest with those few gentle spoken words, and she felt the weight of hours of worry being left behind with the darkness of the night as she stepped through the threshold of the front door and into the peacefulness of the unknown. *Patrick's home.*

15.

QUIET SECRETS

It was the most beautiful home she had ever seen, and as Caroline stood in the entryway, she was overwhelmed. Not from outrageous opulence, but from a magical sense of, well, *home* could be the only word to describe it. It was unlike any other feeling she had ever had toward a place, and she knew once she'd stepped through the threshold that she never wanted to leave.

Dark and light woods came together in an old-world sort of style of mixing battered antiques with well-loved period pieces. A thick, handmade, braided, cream-colored rug lay resting under a beautiful, round, mahogany foyer table with legs of lion's claws and a top that was shined so painstakingly, she could see herself in it as she glanced down. A beautiful crystal vase holding dozens of large field flowers seemed perfect for the centerpiece, and she was relatively sure that was authentic Irish lace under it. The vase was identical to one she had seen in Patrick's store, and she resisted the urge to reach out and touch it. "I've never seen such a beautiful home," she said as Mary took her coat and purse. The little woman uttered a thank-you as she hung up Caroline's coat and purse on the wooden hooks beside the door.

"It's been a long time in tha fixin up, I can tell ya that," she said in a matter-of-fact way, smoothing out her crisp, white apron.

Caroline smiled at the persistence of the woman, supposing she probably spent a great deal of time in the actual cleaning of this huge house herself.

"I've made a stew if ya can stand it; might as well get ta puttin some meat on those sticks ya call arms right now," Mary stated, nodding toward Caroline's upper arms.

Caroline was hungry, her body protesting her forced fast of sorts, and the aromas that greeted her made her mouth water. When was the last time she ate? She couldn't remember at first, and then she did. It was the night of the opera, dinner with Patrick beforehand. They had a nice Chardonnay, some new potatoes, and lamb chops. When was that? Three, four days ago? She found it hard to think now as he began to cloud her mind again. "I really can't right now, Mary."

"Caroline, lass?" she heard Mary's voice somewhere in the midst. "Caroline?"

"I'm sorry, I was just remembering . . ."

"It's all right, dear. Robbie will take ya up to yer room for a wee bit of rest before we sup."

Caroline, so engrossed, had not even seen the young boy enter the room, or had he always been there? She wasn't sure of a great many things lately. "Yes, thank you," she stated, letting Mary's firm hands guide her toward the giant, elegant staircase before her. She stopped and turned to ask a question but was answered before it left her lips.

"Aye, I know. You'll be wonderin why it looks so much like the one in *Titanic*?"

Caroline nodded.

"Yes, well, it was Claire, ya see. She fell so in love with the history of the damned thing. We lost two ancestors, ya see. Third-class passengers. Never had a chance, poor things. Claire thinks it as sort of a memorial, ya see. I love the wood, of course, but it's the clock most people identify with the most."

"It's so authentic," Caroline stated, dumfounded.

"It was the boys who did it fer me. They worked day and night for a month while I was away on holiday to get it ready for me as a birthday surprise. Sean cut his hand, and Patrick had to rush him off to Doc McFinny." Mary chucked and drifted off in her own memories.

The banister felt thick and coldly smooth beneath Caroline's fingers as she obediently followed after young Robbie.

Watching him from behind, Caroline noticed the boy's bright-orange hair hung in a mop of uncontrollable curls about his neck. She smiled as a slim hand came to his forehead to brush back the loose curls again and again, only to have them stubbornly fall back to the exact spot. He wore faded jeans and a blue sweater, looking especially Irish with his fair skin and bright McNally eyes.

Stopping halfway up, she turned to survey the room below her. Sean came through one of the side rooms carrying a small load of firewood in his arms. He sensed her presence there, though she made no sound. He stopped; his eyes looked up and met hers, locking and holding her to him. He had that certain gaze that drew her to him in much the same way Patrick could. She felt uncomfortable at being so near him again. Lowering her eyes quickly, she turned and caught up with Robbie, who was waiting for her at the top of the landing. "There's no need ta fear him, ya know. He'll not hurt ya unless ya rile his temper."

"Oh?" She was at once intrigued by his statement given so honestly. Was it fear she had been feeling? Maybe.

"Oh, aye, he's known over three counties for the fierceness of it!" he said proudly, and Caroline knew this young brother fairly worshipped the older one in that instant.

"I'll be sure to be careful when he's around," she said in all seriousness.

The top of the landing was covered with a thin tapestry rug that gave the appearance of being hand-woven. The colors, rich and deep, seemed to run so smoothly together that they appeared to be more of a painting than fabric. Along the walls of the long hallway hung large portraits of some rather fierce-looking people in some historic period clothing. Kilted men and gowned women adorned the thickly carved, wooden frames, and with the matching eyes of each picture's occupants, she knew them at once to be long-lost McNallys. Ghosts, she was hoping, who were sleeping peacefully somewhere else tonight.

Around one corner and then another, the sights before her gave her heart a quick jump with each new turn. Patrick had played in these halls as a child, had run down the stairs to dinner, and somewhere, she was sure, had slept in his own room in this very house. She felt an overwhelming urge to find it, to seek it out, to seek him out. Caroline wanted to see the things he had seen, touch the things that had been his.

"Here ya be. I hope it's to yer liking?" Robbie said, stopping and opening a door to a room a few feet away. "Me ma had me scrubbin it fer hours so ya'd not choke on the dust from it being tucked under for so long."

"Tucked under?"

"Oh, aye, ya know, closed up?"

"Oh," she acknowledged, guessing she'd say that a lot over the next few days. With everything so new and different, she found herself really feeling like a foreigner, even if they did speak English . . . sort of.

Robbie stepped back, allowing Caroline to enter the room first as he held the door open for her. *How gallant for such a young boy*, she thought before quickly correcting herself. He was closer to a *man*, since he was taller than she and showed the early promise of filling out equal to his two older brothers.

Caroline had to remind herself to close her mouth as she stopped abruptly, causing Robbie to bump her from behind. "Sorry," she apologized without turning. The room was more than she could have ever hoped for, and she felt her body responding immediately to its surroundings, relaxing and calming in such a way that she felt the pull of sleep just looking at the bed. It was quite magnificent in its own right. Four thick mahogany posts stood proudly displaying a lace-covered canopy, and across the bed was a matching quilt and half a dozen pillows. Caroline was sure she could literally spend the rest of her life sleeping right there. She would really like to just never wake up again. Ever.

A small fire flickered gently in the hearth, and two overstuffed chairs sat in front, welcoming one to sink in and gaze for hours. "It's beautiful," she breathed, catching sight of the window seat. That in itself was begging her to climb up on its soft cushions and escape the stark realities of the world she had come to know. Instead, it called to her to immerse herself in a great historical romance. Heathcliff and Catherine would be perfect, and she could have just reason to use them for the tears that were still coming so easily.

"I knew ya'd like it," Robbie said, shaking her back to reality.

"Oh, why is that? You have never even met me before," she said, running her fingers over the skilled craftsmanship of the carvings on the bedposts.

"I knew, cause . . . well, 'cause Patrick said ya were a real lady and that ya blushed all the time."

"He did?" she choked.

"Oh, aye!" he said with great enthusiasm. She looked over at him, feeling the heat rising to her cheeks from his remark. Patrick had said that? *Real lady*. It warmed her deeply in a peaceful way to remember the times he had caused her to blush.

"I do love it. Thank you so much for your thoughtfulness and your hard work." She stepped toward him, noticing his own cheeks pinking as she got closer.

"I hope you and I can become great friends," she said, taking his hand.

"Aye, I'd like that as well. Teagan will be in te check on ya soon," he said shyly, releasing her hand, turning with a smile and closing the door behind him.

She stared at the door for a moment, feeling the spell of the closeness of the moment broken, sending another sudden chill through her arms and straight to her bones.

"She's lovely, that one," Mary McNally said over the shoulder of her large son. He was sitting at the kitchen table, busy spooning great heaps of stew into his mouth without pausing for a breath. She dipped the ladle in the pot she held and poured another helping of the thick stew into his bowl. He grunted in appreciation.

"Sean, are ya plannin on comin up fer air?" Claire asked, squinting her eyes at him from across the table.

He shrugged, reaching for another slice of soda bread, dipping it in the rich, brown gravy. He didn't know why he was so ravenous, only that he needed to somehow satisfy his hunger.

"Yer an animal, Sean," Claire said in disgust. "Mam, can't ya even make him swallow before he takes another bite?" she demanded, shaking her head and pushing her own bowl of half-eaten stew away. "He makes me sick te watch."

"Ya best be mindin yer manners, lad; after all, we've a guest in the house," Mary said, giving him a slight nudge with her hip against his large shoulder. "And I want ta warn the both of ya, I'll have no talk of the business while she's in tha house." She sat the pot of stew back on the stove with a loud clank to get their attention. "I'll not be forced ta explain while the two of ya have gone and lost yer heads, so intent ya are on spendin the rest of yer lives in the Crum." She had their attention now, both of them staring at each other with a mutual understanding across the expanse of the table.

Walking back over to them, Mary sat at the head of the table—a place previously reserved for her husband, now hers by default since his death four years ago. Had it been so long already? The sudden thought struck a familiar chord in her heart, tugging until it brought back hurtful memories she carried with her daily. She missed him, missed him more and more now that her children were involved in the same things he had been. Things that she couldn't understand and was helpless to help them with. "Do ya understand me then?" she said quietly with her hands trembling in her lap.

Sean looked from Claire to his mother. Mary sat still, her eyes holding a slight tinge of pain. He offered her a weak smile, reaching out for her small hand. She nodded at his silent promise, feeling his large, callused thumb, warm and caring, tracing gentle circles on her wrist. Of the three of her sons, this one held a special place in her heart, his looks and build so like his father's at his age. True, Patrick did share the same handsome looks and fierce build, but it was Sean who stole her breath with his unyielding mind and unbridled passion for living. Patrick had always been the peacemaker, Sean the storm.

He watched, reluctantly releasing her hand as she looked after Claire, who had excused herself silently from their company. It hurt him to know she didn't think she pleased their mother. Claire was always thinking her mother wished for a perfect daughter she could dress up and turn into a doll of sorts. The truth of the matter was that Claire was close to what their mother had been like at her age, and it pained Mary to think Claire might make the same mistakes she had in her own youth.

He shrugged again, having long ago given up on trying to bring the two closer. It was something they would have to work out with time, between just the two of them. He could not interfere in this matter.

Sean lowered his head, his appetite sated for the moment. He picked up his spoon, stirring the leftover vegetables in his bowl. It wasn't often he left food uneaten, but his thoughts returned to the one word his mother had said earlier: *Crum*.

It was a hellhole, that place, and her reference to the prison on Crumlin Road in Belfast made his throat feel tight and dry. He swallowed hard, thinking of boyhood friends who now called that place home. He could feel his anger starting to boil at the thought of the R.U.C. and how that particular branch of the British police force could put a body there without any evidence at all, saying whatever they liked and being believed entirely because of their positions of power. The muscles in his jaw clenched tight at Duncan Coogal's face coming to his mind's eye. His childhood friend from school was still there, held without bond for participation in a car bombing more than five years ago. There had been no proof, no evidence. Duncan just had the misfortune of mind to run when he heard the blast. Everyone ran or hit the ground in an attempt to save themselves. It was a way of life here, but Duncan had run directly into a policeman, knocking him down. Suddenly, the police had a suspect, and Duncan had no say.

Sean's absent stirring of his leftovers stopped as he remembered. He closed his eyes briefly in an effort to restrain the fire of anger rising in his blood. Sean knew, all right—knew Duncan was innocent of trumped-up charges . . . knew because it had been someone else's hand on the explosives that night, someone else's hand on the ignition switch, and someone else's mind who made the mistake of not letting the sound reasoning of a friend talk him out of the act that fateful night. He knew, because Sean was the one who had done the bombing that night. Sean had been the guilty party who now caused his friends needless suffering and wasted youth.

Now, like so many others, Duncan spent his time writing letters and speaking out on behalf of the cause. A cause he never meant to join but now rallied behind from his prison cell. It amazed Sean that his friend would not let him take his rightful blame for the crime, instead insisting he be allowed to take the credit for something he did not do. Sean had demanded why he would want it so, knowing deep within himself the real answer. Just as he had guessed, Duncan had wanted the credit along with the blame for the crime for his own reasons. Sean knew before the telling what those reasons were.

It was difficult to become part of such an organization he was so committed to now. They didn't just let anyone join ranks because he claimed to be committed or felt the draw of the fight; instead, they chose to hand-pick certain individuals over a long period of time. The proof of dedication came from the time-tested and tried. Duncan wanted to belong but lacked the physical and mental determination to see it through. The false acceptance of the bombing that night let him into a world he could have only dreamed about, and Sean had reluctantly agreed with his friend's desire to belong. It was hard to imagine Duncan there, but the strong had to look out for the weak, and that was what the whole fight for the cause was really about. Justice for the weak and fighting for what was right for each individual. It was a lesson he would rather not have had to inflict on such a loyal friend, but Duncan was happier now, confined as he was. Sean supposed it was freeing for him somehow, and he understood that freedom came in many different forms. *Aya, Ma, I understand, all right*, he thought and pushed his bowl away as he rose to leave the table.

Mary went upstairs to check on her new guest. *I like this girl*, she thought to herself as she rounded the corner to the girl's room. She seemed sweet and honest in a way that gave Mary a sense of peace in her presence, a knowing, of sorts, of her honor and integrity in their first meeting, brief as it was.

Pausing at the door, she took a deep breath, saddened again that it took such a horrible twist of fate to bring her to them. If only . . . She forced her hand to raise in a soft knock, trying to force Patrick again from her thoughts with the action. He wouldn't want this—wouldn't want her so saddened at his loss. No, he would want her to be strong and take care of her new charge, as if he were there to see to Caroline's comfort himself. And Mary would too, leaving no doubt in her mind he had loved them both. Loved Caroline enough to send her to them now and trusted his family enough to include her and make her feel wanted and a part of things.

Mary knocked again, this time opening the door a crack and peeking her head in to give a word of warning of her entering. She smiled at seeing a sleeping Caroline in one of the chairs in front of the twinkling fire, legs drawn up, head bowed. The tray of stew the maid Teagan brought up was untouched beside her on the table, something that turned Mary's smile into a frown.

The fire was beginning to fade, the room a bit darker than usual. Mary quietly stepped in, tiptoeing on the creaky wooden floorboards until she reached the edge of the thick, braided rug that finally stopped the irritating noise. She had guessed right—the heat in the room was fading with the light of the fire, and she reached over to the bed, where a red, plaid blanket lay at the foot. Shaking it out gently, she walked over and placed it strategically over Caroline, making sure to cover her arms and feet.

Mary stood there a moment, glancing down at Caroline's sleeping form. It was good she slept. Good, she could sleep, something Mary herself wasn't so lucky with lately. *How in the world did this wisp of a girl find the courage to come all the way from America?* she wondered. She must have really loved him to trust in him so much to do as he asked without thought, without question. Mary's eyes misted slightly as she looked down at the girl's closed lids. Thick, black lashes rested spiked and damp against Caroline's pale skin, and Mary realized she must have been crying a short while ago. Maybe she even cried herself to sleep.

Patrick loved this girl. Loved her enough to want to marry her, and it tore at Mary's heart to realize now he would never marry, never have a wife or children of his own. She racked her brain trying to remember his face all of a sudden. It had been so long since she last rested her eyes on him that she swallowed a small cry at realizing it. Then her unshed tears pooled heavy in her eyes, and she knew the slightest movement would send them racing down her cheeks. Her grief was powerful, and now, staring down at the face of one who had almost become her daughter-in-law, she felt a strange kinship to this girl who shared her love of her son. *How long will she stay?* Mary wondered as she glanced toward a crackling noise in the hearth. Tears spilled as she blinked and thought how she would try to figure that puzzle out another time. Tonight, she would pray to God for the strength it would take to see her through tomorrow. Strength needed to see her through the putting of her firstborn into the cold, dark earth, along with another piece of her heart . . . and for the will to survive it.

She turned to leave then, giving Caroline's shoulder a gentle squeeze. His face came to her then, suddenly and without warning, as her hand came into contact with the girl's smooth skin. It wasn't the face of the man she would say goodbye to tomorrow, but the face of a young boy of thirteen or fourteen, fresh and full of life in his newly budding manhood.

She paused, not wanting to break the connection. She saw him smiling and riding Thor, his favorite horse. The corners of Mary's mouth turned up, and she absently wiped with her free hand at the flowing tears dripping down her cheeks. She was remembering the child he was. Patrick always loved legends, and he named everything dear to him after Celtic and Viking folklore.

Thor . . . she watched the image dance before her clouded eyes. That horse had been everything to him, serving him well in mock childhood war battles and letting Patrick dress him up for a game of joust without flinching a muscle. Patrick had spent a long time grieving his beloved horse's death, and she wondered as his image finally faded if they were together now. A boy and his horse, united again at last.

16.

THUNDER SATISFIED

Caroline dreamed the dream of the dead. Her recurring dream had returned to her night visions once more. It left vengeance in its path, causing her to thrash and gasp for air in her sleep, spitting her out and leaving her soaked with sweat amidst a tangle of sheets.

She could see him again, this dream visitor. His hand suspended in time as she again placed hers into it. A shock left her shaken as she felt the coldness of his touch. Where there had been sweet warmth before, now only the coldness of death remained. She pulled quickly away, the sense of wrongness lingering as she held her palm up to her face. "No!" she screamed. "Patrick!"

The dream blood flowed freely down her wrist, thick and red against the paleness of her skin. He stood still, blended into the shadows. His face was still hidden in the darkness. She begged him with her heart to step into the light. She needed to see him. She needed to know it was really him. He stood his ground, refusing her silent pleas. She dropped her hand to her side, turned, and fled the empty stage, crying and running down a never-ending aisle of theater seats. The rich red of the velvet-covered seats became a bloody blur as she raced on and on.

Caroline awoke with a start, panting, tears streaming down her face. Her mind was still fuzzy from sleep that bordered on reality. She remembered somehow getting herself from the chair by the fire to the bed.

Her eyes adjusted to the darkness, and she left the warmth of the bed and headed for the window seat. She grabbed the red plaid throw off the floor and settled into the seat with her legs drawn up under her chin, the throw warming off the chill. She settled with her back against one wall for support and lifted a trembling hand to her heart, feeling the racing beat from the nightmare finally beginning to slow.

Blowing against the windowpane, the hotness of her breath cleared the frost. She lifted a corner of the throw and rubbed in a circular motion until she created a space big enough to see through.

Sitting there in the predawn quietness of the room, she stared out the little viewing circle at the sun barely lighting up the sky over a hill in the far distance. She watched without moving as it slowly turned the sky different colors as it rose to create the day.

Her thoughts were on Patrick, wishing he were there with her, seeing this sight unfolding before her eyes. She wished harder that he was sitting behind her, his strong arms embracing her in their warmth and spreading his love like the plaid around her . . . through her.

Today, she would have to say goodbye to him. She would have to stand and watch as they lowered his once-strong body, lifeless now, into the ground. Death stealing his strength, death stealing her love.

Her heart wrenched in her chest as the tears flowed easily while she stared out at the sky, seeing nothing now beyond the grief in her heart. The pain in her chest was unrelenting.

Sean licked his lips, tasting the saltiness of his own tears mixed with the morning rain that misted from the low, angry, gray clouds.

He stood watching with his arms around both his mother and his sister as his elder brother and friend was laid forever to rest next to his father in the family burial site. With no will behind them, his eyes sought out Caroline. She stood alone, without a caring arm around her for support. She stood straight, strong in her grief as the rain poured from the sky, as if it too were grieving with them this day. The large hood of her black coat enhanced the smallness of her features, shielding her from the drops as she held no umbrella. Her long, dark curls flowed generously down both sides of her face, reaching the curves of her breasts. Tears dripped on them, mixing with the rain.

Sean continued to stare, helpless to pull his eyes away from her. A sudden breeze sent a chill through him, and with a quick shiver, his eyes were drawn to her skirt. The gentle sway of it about her ankles and black leather boots hypnotized him for a moment, freeing his mind from the pain.

"Amen," the crowd said in unison, and Sean's thoughts were interrupted with a tug on his sleeve.

His mother looked up at him with red-rimmed eyes, swollen from crying. She would not stay to watch the earth being thrown over her son.

"Claire can take me home, Sean," she said in a whisper, nodding at the well-wishers as they walked by. "You go and fetch the lass. She shouldna be alone now."

He gave his mother a gentle squeeze in understanding and bent low to hold her close in farewell. "I'll not be long after," he told her as added reassurance. "You stay close ta Claire, 'ey. She needs ya now," he added, nodding quickly for emphasis.

Standing a moment longer, he waited as Claire helped his mother across the lawn to the waiting car. Young Robbie following close behind. Sean lowered his head for a moment. The effects of this day would be remembered long and hard into the future. He could not remember his chest ever aching so.

"Are ya ready ta go?" he asked Caroline hesitantly.

"If you don't mind, Sean, I want to stay just a little longer," Caroline said without emotion, her eyes glued to the silver casket.

"We'll, I'll stay wi' ya then. If ya don't mind me bein here?"

She did not answer but merely stood still, staring down at the casket. He looked down at her. She held a certain amount of frail beauty in her grief. Her nose and cheeks were pinkened from the cold, making her pale skin seem even paler. Lips, full and swollen from biting, mouthed silent words, and he counted his brother lucky to have someone who cared so greatly, grieving so mightily for him.

When they were the last two people left, and it seemed they could indeed be the last two people left on the earth, he placed a hand on her shoulder. His palm felt the small roundness of her through her coat, his fingers gently coming to rest on her prominent collarbones. "It's time we were leavin."

She surprised him by quickly lunging forward, leaving his hand suspended in midair where it had been resting.

"Oh, Sean! I can't go . . . I can't leave him here alone! It's so cold; he hates the cold. That's why he moved to the desert, so he would be warm. Please . . . I can't!" Her voice was two octaves higher in her desperation.

He stared down at her. She had been so calm, so quiet, and now she was on her knees beside the casket, gripping it so hard her black leather gloves were stretched tightly across her knuckles. He did the only thing he could; he knelt on the ground beside her, one arm coming around her side, his other hand resting with gentle pressure atop hers.

"He's not really there, Caroline. I mean, his body is, but he's not."

She looked over at him with liquid green eyes.

"Do ya understand what I'm tellin ya?"

"I can't," she choked out. "He . . ."

"Ya must," he said softly, reaching up and catching a falling tear with his thumb. "He wouldna want ya in so much pain fer him."

Sean saw the meaning of his words taking hold in her mind as she looked again at the casket before them. Caroline leaned forward and, in a heartbreaking gesture, placed a lingering single kiss atop it. "I'll love you forever," she breathed and turned, looking up at Sean again. Their eyes locked, their gaze steady as comfort passed without words between them, creating a bond the likes of which he had never known.

"I just don't want to let him go," she whispered, and he felt like an intruder into her heart.

"Me either, Missy, me either."

They made their way down the hill. The shared grief of the moment between them linked them together in strength. Neither one spoke; neither one needed to.

17.

SOMETHING TO SAY

She saw him there, Sean on the hillside, walking alone with his head slightly bent. He was watching where his feet were slowly leading him, oblivious to his surroundings and looking very deep in thought. His hair was loose and blowing about his face.

Caroline stood at the window a moment longer, watching and buttoning the last two buttons on the front of her shirt. It had been a week since the funeral, and the dawn was just peeking over the horizon of a new day. She had risen early, not being able to sleep again, and she had hopes of just such a walk herself. "Humph, guess I'll just go another direction," she said aloud while straightening up and reaching for a ribbon to tie at the base of her ponytail. Satisfied with the effort, she grabbed her coat off the bed and headed for the door.

Caroline ran a finger along the wall to steady herself while she tried to step light as a feather down the long hall. She did not want to wake anyone who might stop her in her quest to investigate the grounds and forests around the house. This was the first time she had left her room since the funeral, and she still wanted to be alone, without hiding in her room anymore. She needed to breathe, to feel, to be outside with living things. *Death*, she thought, *was a selfish companion*. Eyeing the door to her near right, she could faintly hear a feminine voice coming from the other side.

It was Claire, but no one answered her when she spoke.

"Don't ya be gettin yer dander up wi' me. I said I'd think of somthin, and I will!"

Caroline peeked inside and caught a glimpse of Sean's sister with her back to her, sitting on the foot of her bed, the phone cord stretched long across the room. "I don't care; I'll no be havin our plans for the cause disrupted over this!"

Caroline frowned at the seriousness of the girl's voice, and she slipped past the door undetected, picking up her pace along the way. Though most of the McNally's had treated her with the affections of a long-lost relative, she had no desire to warrant their mistrust should she be caught eavesdropping at bedroom doors.

Reaching the bottom of the stairs, she noticed a pale light coming from the direction of the kitchen. Were they all such early risers?

Caroline suddenly got a whiff of fresh-baked bread and cinnamon emanating in the air as she walked toward the front door. Maybe Teagan would save her some of whatever it was that was making her mouth water.

She suppressed a smile at thinking maybe not . . . if Sean was coming back soon.

Opening the door, she was quickly greeted with a bracing burst of cold air. She quietly closed the door behind her and turned around to take in great gulps of misty fog. Closing her eyes, she smelled the sweetness of wet, green grass and tasted the different varieties of plant life on her tongue. The air was chilly, and new sensations ran over her entire body, washing some of the sorrow from her soul. It was making her feel truly alive for the first time in days. *Welcome back to your life, Caroline.*

Stealing around to the back of the house, she made her way to the barn; its open doors were calling her inside.

The straw smelled sweet as she slowly made her way down the walkway, glancing into stalls on both sides of her. Caroline smiled as the horses came to the front of their stalls to greet her. Their long noses smelled her as she walked up to each one in turn and gave each a little rub, taking in the unbelievable velvety softness of their noses under her fingertips. One in the stall she had not yet reached poked his massive head out and tried to reach her as she lingered with the brown in front of her. She stepped toward the nosy, darker one, reaching out to make sure he was friendly and letting him sniff her extended hand.

He was black as night with a thin white stripe that flowed vertically from the middle of his twitching ears to the tip of his nose. "Yes, you are very pretty too. I bet everyone wants to ride you." She smiled and gently rubbed his ears. He was bobbing his head against her chest, sniffing and nuzzling. "Maybe I could ride you one day; what do you think of that?"

"Not likely he would let ya. He's a devil, and none can ride him but Sean."

Caroline jumped, turning to face young Robbie as he made his way out of one of the stalls.

"Robbie, you scared me," she said with a start. Over the last few days, she had become quite fond of the boy and spent every night indulging him in a fireside game of chess after his chores in the barn.

He always smelled of fresh soap and water before coming to her room. She supposed he was sent up to keep her mind busy, but she suspected more that he really liked the challenge. From what she had heard, no one else in the family could play chess, and he did seem to really enjoy her company and respected her alone time for the better part of the day. At fourteen, she was surprised that this boy had great skill for his lack of partners. "What are you doing up so early?" she asked.

"It's me horse, Meghan. She's due ana time now," he said a bit nervously, and she noticed his hands leave the rake he had been holding as he propped it against the wall and quickly shoved his hands into his front pockets. He stood there looking down now, almost as if in some way he had overstepped his limits of normal conversation. It seemed for now that if she wanted more information, she would have to pry a little. *It had been much the same with all the McNally men*, she thought. *They were vivid in expression but needed the okay to indulge in matters of voice.*

"Meghan?" she asked, nodding over at the small, gray horse in the stall behind him. "Is she yours?"

"Oh, aye!" he exclaimed, pride showing on his face. Caroline smiled. He was so sweet with his unruly red curls and freckles—not too many, but just enough to enhance the fairness of his own skin. They were light liver in color, splaying down his neck and disappearing under his shirt collar.

"She's beautiful," Caroline commented, walking over and resting her elbows on the wooden stall door. "She looks like a Meghan," she said. At least Caroline thought so. The gentle-looking horse gave the impression she would be great with children, and with her giant, swollen belly, she appeared now to closely resemble a short, fat pony, rather than a riding mare. She was trying to get her master's attention by nuzzling him under his arm, almost knocking him off balance more than once. Caroline smiled as she watched Robbie pull a small carrot out of the shirt pocket hidden under his coat. The horse nibbled greedily, and Caroline stood there watching the sweet interaction.

Caroline realized that it was not lonely here; someone was almost always around and offering their support with kind hugs or gestures and smiles. She felt a pang in her stomach as she watched Robbie pick up a leather-handled, wooden brush, and she could swear the horse smiled as Robbie began to make gentle strokes across her back and sides. Caroline was reminded she was in a strange place, and it enhanced everything in her mind. Not being surrounded by things familiar left her with a lost sort of feeling, which was no doubt homesickness.

She continued to watch as she caught Robbie run a slim hand through his wild locks again. As usual, the effort was wasted on curls that seemed to have a mind of their own.

"You must love her a great deal," Caroline said. She meant it as a statement, and she watched as mention of the word *love* caused the tip of his nose to flush pink.

"Aye, weel, ya know . . . I'm all she's got."

Ah, young boys, she thought. *How wonderfully sweet they could be. All raging hormones and newly discovered masculinity.* It sobered her, watching him shift his weight from one foot to the other in uneasiness of being so close to a female, not to mention the word *love* shared between them. Men could be emotional in their own right—Patrick had shown her that. Most women, she supposed, just had to find the real human being underneath all the layers of social pressure and male macho façade so many of them were buried under. *So many layers*, she thought sadly. *It's nice to just stand in the middle of a barn, talking to one who has not quite figured the whole thing out yet.*

It was a short walk to the edge of the forest. The denseness of the trees blocked out some of the light, giving it a sort of eerie, haunting quality, especially with its silence.

The twigs snapped unnaturally loudly under her feet as she walked on, oblivious to her surroundings, as she became lost in her thoughts. She pulled the ring Patrick had given her out of her pocket and fingered it, reciting the Gaelic words he had told her. As she recited them over and over in her mind, the torment began to dwell inside her again. The precious metal, cool against her fingertips, felt strange somehow as she glanced down at it. It seemed to attract the thin beams of hazy sunlight streaming through the treetops, reflecting bright little rainbows in all directions.

The ring was the only tangible piece of Patrick she had, and she had been reluctant to tell Sean the words Patrick had told her, for fear of losing this last piece of him. The passage of time would soon fade his image from her memory, and this last shred of evidence felt right on her wedding finger. It was a link to keep him near her always, and she did not want to part with it so soon.

Walking on, she closed her fingers into a tight fist, as if to forge the metal into her flesh. She wanted it to brand her, to mark her body as he had marked her heart. *Patrick, where are you?*

Sean found her sitting alone on a fallen tree log, her hand in her lap and her face pale in the shadows.

He knew he should make his presence known, but his breath caught as he watched her sitting unaware, his eyes captivated by the sight. She was beautiful in the emptiness of it all, surrounded by beauty and leaving it all dark in comparison. Strands of her dark hair floated freely about her shoulders, having come loose from the ribbon still clinging to the base of her ponytail. The silken strands danced, floating about her face like butterflies in the breeze. Sean watched as slim fingers shooed at the mischievous strands of hair tickling her ears.

She let her hands fall into her lap again with a sigh, giving Sean the impression she was deep in thought. She was thinking about Patrick, he figured, and it angered him on some level that she should still be in so much pain. It had been a week now, and still she failed to reveal the sparkle of the woman he was sure lay hidden under the darkness of the sorrow. He wanted to reach her, reach out to her. Take her in his arms and comfort her, feel for himself the silkiness of the curls that danced about her face. She was real, this one, and Patrick had taken the life out of her with his leaving.

Suddenly, Sean felt the emptiness in his heart at the thought of his brother and his senseless death. The elder McNally had gone on to America to avoid the random violence of his homeland, but he had become just another statistic of violence in the land of the free. Patrick should have stayed and stood his ground beside Claire and Sean and all the others in the real battle that was still waging here.

Instead, Patrick had chosen to run when his back was put to the wall, not being able to stand the constant pressure of his comrades demanding he stay in his place of leadership among the ranks of his true countrymen.

Sean blinked, then, in an effort to hold the threatening tears at bay. *What a waste to die for nothing, to have lived for nothing*, he thought, and the sight of Caroline brought him back to reality. She had been watching him, unaware of the struggle in his heart. He had loved his brother, but he could not forgive Patrick's cowardice—and he wondered then doubted whether Caroline really knew the man who would have been her husband.

Sean coughed to announce his presence, then said, "I'm sorry, Missy; I didn't mean ta frighten ya."

"Sean, will you sit with me for a while?" she asked as she patted the space next to her on the log.

"I didn't mean ta intrude in your thinkin."

"Please," she smiled up at him sweetly enough to send his thoughts in a different direction. He was a man, after all, and no ordinary man could be within twenty feet of her without thinking of her beauty. He immediately felt the rise of familiar emotions. She did it to him, with her shimmering hair catching the light beams and her smooth skin begging for his touch. It had been a long time since he had felt the pull of a man's emotions toward a woman as strongly as he did when she was near. It was no wonder Patrick acted as quickly as he did in asking her to be his wife.

"Yer hair's got a fair amount of red in it," he said, the words already out before he could stop himself.

"It lightens up a bit in the summer," she said, pushing a wayward strand out of her eyes. He smiled at the fluttering of her long, dark lashes. He stood directly in front of her now, causing her to lift her chin to meet his eyes.

She reached up and took his hand, pulling him with gentle effort to sit next to her. His eyes were glued to the flutter of her racing pulse thumping wildly at the base of her neck. Then his gaze traveled upward, catching sight of her generous, full lips.

"Sean, there is something I have to tell you," she started, and he felt an ache beginning to grow in his loins. God be blessed, but she smelled so nice, and being this close waged war on his senses. He needed to remain in control; she was still so vulnerable, and her grief for his brother was strong and real. He couldn't take the risk of her misinterpreting his actions. His body wanted her, all right, but his mind screamed she could never be his, not with Patrick forever between them. His desire had flared for her at the first sight of her at the airport, and as he had held her close to him then, he knew his heart was lost at that meeting too. It did not matter how hard he fought it, she had gotten under his skin with her smile and into his every waking thought with her gentle, childlike spirit.

"I've somtin ta talk ta ya about too," he said with an authoritative tone. His mind recalled his conversation with Robbie about her desire to ride his horse a short while ago.

"Can I go first?" she asked softly. "Before I lose my nerve."

His eyebrows drew downward in confusion. "Yer not afraid of me now, are ya?" he asked, concerned. That was the last thing he wanted her to feel for him.

"No!" she said quickly, shifting in her seat and sitting with her back straighter, her chin lifted slightly higher.

"Good, cause by the blessed and holy iron, I'd never harm one hair on yer head," he said, his tone getting louder.

"Holy iron?" she asked, surprising him and turning on the log toward him, pulling her knees up under her chin like a small child in wonderment.

"Aye, it's what an Irishman says when he really means it," he answered her, the mood lightening between them. The peacefulness of friendship permeated the space around them.

"Oh, like the cross?" she asked with her head cocked like a puppy he once had.

"Weel, no. That would be when he would say, he swears by the crass." Her eyebrows rose slightly, urging him on with the explaining.

"The Irish have always considered iron a sacred metal. Thieves are adverse ta stealin it, thus the horseshoe above the door's fer luck. It's an oath fer us."

"Oh, I see," she said with a tone of understanding, and he caught a faint sparkle in her eyes. She was beginning to relax with him here in the midst of the forest, and it warmed his heart to see it easing her in this way.

"But . . ." he began, feeling a bit like a teacher in the matters of his country. "Should he say, by the Piper O'Moses, weel, that would be the richest lie he could tell ya with a straight face."

"Oh," She breathed, her eyes filling again with emotion. He knew at once the friendly chatter was over. She had something serious to say, and it waged war on his insides to think what could fill her with such emotion so quickly.

"Sean, Patrick wanted me to tell you something. He told me before he . . ." She lowered her head.

"Go ahead, cushlamachree," he urged. He had not meant to call her that, but the stillness of the forest demanded he comfort her. Calling her the pulse of his heart in Gaelic seemed a natural thing, since she had his pulse racing with each rise and fall of her chest. "Go on; say it, Caroline. I can see it is a hard ting fer ya ta do."

"He said . . . right before he . . ." Sean saw the moisture in her eyes and knew she was fighting back tears. He reached out, placing his hands on her shoulders, prepared to draw her near should he need to. "He wanted me to take him home."

"Aye, and well you've done that."

"There was so much blood, see, and he . . ." The tears were flowing now, a steady stream of glistening wetness sliding down her cheeks. He squeezed her gently, seeing the pain in her eyes.

She was openly sobbing. He acted gently, pulling her into his arms and onto his lap. She was curled tight into a ball with her face in her hands, knees still drawn up.

After a while, the pain easing a bit, the memories draining her strength, she looked up at him with swollen, red eyes. "He told me something in Gaelic to tell you."

"Me? In Gaelic? Are ya sure, lass?"

He felt his heart beating so fast that he was sure she must feel it too, as she was so close, still held in his protective embrace. "Caroline, I want ya ta repeat the words ta me very carefully . . . slowly, one . . . at . . . a . . . time."

Caroline swallowed hard, licked her lips, and thought of the cold stockroom floor where she had held Patrick as he died. She did as

Sean coaxed, slowly repeating the words she did not understand, shivering with the unforgettable smell of Patrick's blood fresh in her mind.

18.

MESSAGES FROM THE HEART

Caroline remained seated on the log. The rich smells from the morning fog misted around her as she watched Sean pace back and forth in front of her. Once she had repeated the words Patrick had sent her to say, Sean had jumped, nearly knocking her off the log. He looked as wild as a caged animal with his hair blowing about his face from the increased breeze that chilled her now.

"Sean?"

He paused, met her eyes, shook his head, and then continued pacing.

"What does the message mean?" She had been crazy with the implications of the unknown meaning.

The tension was clearly visible on his face, and it was also clear to her that the message meant something of great importance to him.

He stopped and looked directly down at her, giving her the impression that he was going to tell her something. His face lit up as if some sudden idea had come into his head.

"What?" she asked. Caroline had finally kept her promise to give Sean the message, and now she wondered if she had done the right thing.

"I canna believe it," he muttered quietly, and she noticed his face might have become a shade paler. He was fair-skinned—all the Irish she had met so far were—but this was definitely not a normal pallor, even for him.

"Sean, what did he say?" Caroline was dying inside. *What could Patrick have said to get such a reaction from his brother like this? Oh, God! Maybe I misquoted it or left some word out.* But when she quickly said them again in her mind, she knew she had remembered and repeated them exactly. "Sean!" she yelled, sending a few fluttering of birds to wing.

That did it. He stopped dead in front of her, green eyes meeting green eyes. "It's personal, for me ears only. Don't tell a single other soul."

"Sean," she pleaded, "can't you at least tell *me*? It's practically the last thing he said before he . . ." She still could not bring herself to say the word aloud yet.

"I'm sorry, lass, I canna, but I *will* tell ya one thing."

"Yes?" Her heart leaped.

"You'll not be catchin that plane tomorrow." He said it calmly, putting one large hand out to help her up from the log. He had said it so matter-of-factly, like he would tell her dinner was ready, and she felt her own color fade from her face. A stab of fear penetrated her insides.

She placed her hand into his, accepting his offer. "Sean?" she asked quietly as she stood, her chest meeting his, softness meeting hardness.

His hand still held hers, and he gave a little reassuring squeeze. "Aye?"

"Sean, I have to go home," she said, unmistakable firmness in her voice.

"I'm not about ta argue this with ya." He laced his fingers through hers.

"Sean!" she cried, raising her voice. "Unless you tell me what you mean by that statement, I'm still catching my plane tomorrow!" She tried to jerk her hand out of his. *Who does he think he is, anyway?*

"Caroline!" He grabbed her shoulders, his strong fingers biting into her flesh. She had not seen him so angry, and it instantly reminded her of the conversation she had with Robbie. The boy had said, "He'll no harm ya unless ya rowl his temper. He's known in three counties for the fierceness of it." A red light began to flash in Caroline's mind.

"Sean, you're hurting me," she pleaded. He instantly softened his hold on her but made no move to release her.

"I'm sorry, Missy, it's just I'm worried like nothing has ever worried me before." He spoke softly now with a possessed man's conviction, and she eased out a breath when his hands started absently stroking her upper arms as if to soothe away the hurt that he had inflicted.

"Sean, you must—"

"Caroline," he interrupted, his voice low and husky. He stopped stroking her arms and lowered his head, unable to meet her eyes.

"What?" she asked, noting that he suddenly seemed uncomfortable—even nervous.

She watched, amazed he could change so quickly before her eyes. Gone was the anger of a moment ago; in its place was a boyish uneasiness she'd seen in young Robbie earlier. *What a puzzle he is*. "Sean, what is it?"

"All right, then, here it is. I know no other way than ta ask ya outright."

Caroline was holding her breath again

"Are ya . . . are ya by any small chance perhaps carrin?"

"Carrin?" she asked, surprised. She had a pretty good idea what it meant, and a flood of pain spilled from her heart.

"Could ya be expecting?" he rephrased.

A sudden lump formed in her throat, preventing her from speaking. She lowered her eyes in defeat.

"Caroline, ya fainted at the airport, and ya went pale." She felt his thumb, warm under her chin, as he gently urged her to look up at him. "Tis nothin ta be ashamed of. Ya loved him, I know that. We all know that. You were ta be married, and no one will fault ya fer yer human instincts."

She was so shocked by his statement and the very real pain that filled her womb in place of the baby she longed for more than anything else. She just stood there, frozen, unable to do anything but shake her head in the negative.

"Aye, weel, if you were ta be my wife, I'd not've been able to keep me hands from ya. How could Patrick?" he said, inhaling deeply in defeat.

Caroline let her head fall back and closed her eyes, trying to gather her strength. He has misunderstood her silence—but more than that, the statement he just made sent her blood pumping. "Sean," she finally said. "I'm not pregnant." She realized that it hurt her to say it aloud. The tightness around her heart squeezed a little tighter with the confession.

"Are ya sure?" His eyes brightened.

"I am sure," she stated firmly, getting a small smile from him. She thought for sure he had been hoping she might be pregnant, but the look he had on his face now only served to confuse her. Were the corners of his mouth actually lifting in a slight smile? She thought she had better finish off the line of questioning before he misunderstood something else. "I'm sure, because . . . because Patrick and I never, I mean, he wanted to wait until after we were married before we . . ."

That was it. She couldn't say another word, and her face felt like it was on fire from embarrassment. She suddenly could not breathe without effort. Caroline could not believe she was having this conversation with Sean in the middle of the forest, and why was he so physical with her? He had not taken his hands off her since telling her she would not be flying home tomorrow. She frowned, and when his laughter began to rise, her eyes opened in sheer astonishment. "Sean?"

It was hopeless now. He was laughing so hard, and before she could think twice, he had pulled her into his arms with a bear hug, ignoring her squirms of protest.

When he finally sated his bout of happiness, he held her at arm's length, searching her every feature. His eyes roamed over her every detail as if in some way trying to see into her very soul.

"Caroline, I was just fearful for a moment. That's somethin I'm not accustomed to very often, and when I'm proved wrong, weel, laughing is just a bit o'release is all. I had an idea in me head after ya fainted and again with the tellin of Patrick's message, and weel . . . I suppose I got married ta it, and . . ." He shrugged as his voice trailed off.

"What did he say in the message?"

"It'll do ya no good ta worry over it," he lied, smooth as silk.

"Oh, God!" Her heart slammed against her chest with the very idea. "Sean, what did he say? Was there something else I could have done for him? I mean, did he want something more?" Her eyes filled with tears again as her mind whirled with the implications. If there had been something more she could have or should have done for him and didn't . . .

"No, it's not about what you could have done fer him, but more like what he wanted ta do fer you."

"Me? I don't understand."

He reached for her face, cupping the sides and steadying his gaze into her eyes as he drew closer and whispered within mere inches of her cheek. She could feel his breath hot against her skin as he spoke, and she breathed it in, closing her eyes to him. She became perfectly still and listened with all her might. *Patrick . . .*

"He said . . ." Sean leaned even more into her, and she melted against him, instinctively knowing she would need his support. "He said, you're in grave danger, and I'm ta protect ya with me very life as if ya were me own."

She felt her mouth drop in a gasp, and her eyes flew open as she tried to push away from him. She settled back just far enough to stare unblinking up at him. Caroline then shivered deep and felt a chill in her bones take hold. It would last the rest of the day.

19.

FEAR OF THE UNKNOWN

"Caroline, did Patrick say anythin else ta ya? Anythin that ya might have left out or forgot?" Sean quizzed her from behind, walking slowly around her seat at the kitchen table like a lawyer might do in court. "Do ya ha any reason ta think ya might be in danger, girl?"

"No, I don't think so. Oh, wait; Patrick might have told me I was in danger before he told me the Gaelic stuff. It's so hard to remember; it was so . . . so fast and so . . ." She didn't want to go on remembering.

"Caroline, I'm thinkin tha's why he wanted ya here with us," Claire said from the seat next to her. It was the most Caroline had heard her say at one sitting.

"Yes, yes, of course, my dear," Mary said, carrying a serving tray with steaming mugs of hot cocoa on it. She began to place the cups one by one in front of the three of them.

"But, I thought he wanted me to be with him. I mean . . ." Caroline couldn't finish and lowered her eyes to her cup.

Noticing her distraught features, Sean moved to sit in the chair in front of her.

"Caroline," he said, speaking softly. "Of course, Patrick would have wanted ya ta be with him, but he was fearful for ya too. Maybe it has something ta do w'the murderer? Maybe he meant ta come after you too?"

A collective gasp sounded around the table. Caroline glanced from one set of green eyes to another, all nodding in agreement.

"That settles it!" Mary said with great sternness afforded to one who has raised sons. "You'll stay w'us till we're sure, and that's that." She spoke the last words with a curt nod.

Caroline merely shrugged. Knowing she apparently had no say in the matter, she reached for her cup and reveled in the soothing warmth of it.

Caroline returned to her room and stared into the fire, listening to the small pops and crackles of the exploding embers. She sat and watched the flames jump and thrash about, like some ancient dance before the Gods. Though she loved this room, the coziness of it, the safe feeling she had being in it, she still knew that no matter how enchanting the idea of staying here forever, she was really just a guest. A guest in a foreign country, at that. Oh, she had made great strides with the family and really felt like she belonged, was in some real way becoming a part of the family. But she knew it had to end. *I'm just a guest,* she thought, reminding herself again of the reality of her situation.

She eased back into the chair and thought of Patrick. He would have brought her here as his wife, made her a real member of the family. Now, she was just nothing more than an American visitor in the home of some Irish family she had already grown to love, but to whom she had no real ties.

She was beginning to feel alone again, wishing she had something stronger than cocoa in her, when she heard a slight knock on the door.

"Come in."

The door slowly opened, and Sean tucked his head in. "I just wanted ta check on ya. Ta see if ya might be a bit scairt."

"Oh, my knight in shining armor, are you, stopping by to check on the fair damsel?" She smiled shyly and motioned him to come in and sit at the empty chair beside her.

"Very funny, but a bit true, I'd say."

Caroline wasn't sure if he was teasing her. He was such a mystery with his dark thoughts and absurd business meetings at all hours of the night. *Who does he think he's kidding, anyway? Obviously, he must be attached to some girl or two.*

They remained silent for a while, both lost in their thoughts as they stared into the fire. A comfortable silence settled between them.

Strangely, Caroline thought how she liked being in his presence now. Maybe it was the talk they shared in the forest or the way he made her feel safe when he was around. She just had a sense of closeness to him that was not there before. *It's probably just his resemblance to Patrick.*

"Oh, my, Patrick!" she suddenly gasped aloud.

"Patrick?" Sean was already on his feet when she motioned him to sit and began fumbling in her pocket.

"Patrick, wha the devil?" Sean lowered dark eyebrows at her. She was busy pulling something out of her pocket.

"I almost forgot. Patrick said I should give this to you when I told you the words. He said you would know what it meant."

"Oh, the Gaelic, ya mean?" he asked a little calmer, sitting again. Caroline nodded.

Reaching over, he took the object from her small, outstretched hand. He suddenly felt an instant surge of happiness or fear—he couldn't distinguish which as he recognized his mother's engagement ring. He knew exactly what Patrick had meant by it. He turned it over and over, letting the light of the fire dance across its shiny surface. It was still warm from its hiding place in her pocket.

He realized the instant he saw it, what his brother had meant in making her give the ring to him and the absolute meaning behind the words she was commanded to recite. He knew without a doubt that Patrick had meant to give Caroline to him, not only to protect, but to take as his own . . . and with the giving back of their mother's ring, he also meant for Sean to take her for his wife. In death, Patrick had made the ultimate sacrifice for him, and in giving him his blessing and his most precious gift of Caroline, he had erased the hurt that stood between them.

Patrick could never have known the real gift he had given him. Sean now had his brother's blessing on something he was already quite prepared to take.

Sean glanced over at Caroline.

"Does it make you feel better to have something of his?" she asked quietly, innocently, not turning toward him but continuing to stare into the fire, holding back the overwhelming sadness at its loss.

"Yea, thank ya," he said softly, clasping the ring in his fist and bringing it to rest over his heart.

He watched her for a long time. She just stared, her eyes blinking ever so slowly, heavy in their weariness, her mind too full to shut down yet. *We'll make a McNally of ya yet, and don't ya worry, you'll be gitten this back soon enough, sweet Caroline*, he thought with a slightly upturned grin.

20.

PLAIN SENSE

Caroline awoke to the heavenly scents of baked apples and cinnamon drifting into her room. The air was so thick with their sweetness, she could almost feel her thighs becoming fatter just by simply inhaling the calories that seemed to hang heavy in the air. She fought the urge to grab her robe and race down the stairs in hot pursuit of the villains responsible for such an attack on her senses. Instead, she obeyed her better judgment and, feeling the chill in the air, she decided a hot shower and some proper clothes would be the best idea.

Shower done, she stood braiding her long hair to form a single, thick, damp rope down her back. Looking into the free-standing, wooden mirror, she recalled the outrageous notion Sean had of her not returning to the States today. Had she really agreed with him? Had she really made the decision to stay in Ireland a bit longer? Though the idea of it appealed to her, she really couldn't grasp the notion of someone actually trying to kill her. Surely the person who attacked Patrick was just a desperate burglar caught in the act. Caroline shrugged the thought from her mind, closing her eyes tightly to the unwanted feelings surfacing fresh in her mind. It was all still too painful to think about, even for a second.

She opened her eyes and looked at her reflection staring back. She could see her packed suitcase against the wall. She felt empty, lonely. Her eyes drifted unwittingly down to her flat stomach. It hurt again. The pain in her heart just literally hurt whenever she thought of him too hard. *Patrick . . .*

"Caroline, how nice ta see ya up so early. Are ya hungry, lass?" Mary asked, holding a large, steaming plate of freshly baked muffins right under her nose.

Caroline could feel the heat rising in her cheeks as she glanced from the plate of muffins Mrs. McNally was holding to the array of curious faces staring up at her from the table. Even the reserved Claire managed to roll her eyes, and Caroline assumed that was the best form of friendly emotion she was likely to see from her. For some reason, she felt embarrassed, almost chastised on some level. Maybe tomorrow she might focus on making this girl like her, but for now, there was a muffin with Caroline's name on it, and she was satisfied to feel the warmth of it instead. "Thank you," she managed to say as she took one from the plate.

"Weel now, we're going to make a right fine Irish woman of ya yet." Caroline heard the low voice tinged with a small grunt of approval coming from behind her.

"What?" she asked as she turned around to find Sean's large form looming in the doorway. The corners of his mouth turned up ever so slightly, but Caroline could not mistake the twinkle of tease in his eyes. The large kitchen suddenly became somewhat smaller with his presence, and Caroline found it was hard to manage even the smallest bite with him so near.

"I'll never get the burrrr's though." She tried to exaggerate the *rs*, making them sound more like the letter *L* instead, as her tongue stuck ridiculously to the roof of her mouth whenever she tried. Sean reached past her for a muffin from the plate. The muffins had seemed impossibly huge before they were dwarfed by his large hand.

"Thank ya, Ma," Sean said over his shoulder as he brushed past them and headed for an empty seat at the table. The halted conversation at the table started up again, and the giggling grew a bit louder. Caroline glanced up from her plate to find Robbie smiling with a large mouthful of muffin. She smiled sweetly at him, and he immediately began choking. Mary walked over and put the plate of muffins down next to him, giving him a swift pat on the back to bring him around.

"Thank ya, Ma," Robbie said, wiping the tears in his eyes with the napkin from his lap.

"You're disgusting, ya pig," Claire suddenly spat at Sean. "Ma, make em stop!"

Claire threw her napkin into her plate of half-eaten food in a huff as Mary said, "Leave yer brother alone, girl; he's a growing man, after all."

"All the men in my family eat like Sean," Teagan said with a wink at Sean. "The women keep their fine figures because of it," she said, laughing, with her hands on her slim hips for emphasis.

Sean smiled widely at Claire as he placed a second whole muffin in his mouth all at once.

"Pig!" Claire said, low and dark.

This time, Caroline found herself grinning in Sean's direction. Her grin was more than enough to make him stop chewing, causing him to force down his entire muffin in a dry gulp.

Caroline felt a chill as she glanced over at Claire, who was staring daggers at Sean. She then felt the chill a little deeper as Claire turned and looked directly at her with the same intensity.

"Woa, now, that one's a wee bit of a bugger," Sean said, seeing Caroline heading for the stall that held his own horse. "How about nice little Dove here?" he encouraged while motioning her to the stall closest on his left.

Caroline walked hesitantly over and glanced inside the stall he had motioned her toward. She looked up at Sean and smiled a knowing grin.

"You don't think I can ride, do you?" she asked with her hands on her hips.

"I, ah, um, I just don't want ta see ya get yer pretty little neck broken is all," he said, back-peddling.

Caroline looked inside the stall, where she saw probably the oldest horse in all of Ireland staring back at her with huge, soft, brown eyes and a muzzle full of gray. She looked back over at Sean. His eyes were down in apparent shame, and she raised a single eyebrow at him and waited for him to get the message.

He raised his eyes to meet hers and yelled over her shoulder, "Robbie, me lad, go and fetch the missy here Lillie's saddle and bridle if ya will." Sean never allowed his eyes to leave hers as he spoke. "I'm thinking there will be no pleasin ya until ya do break yer little white neck." His voice held a certain bit of amusement, and Caroline had no doubt he had no intention of giving in. It was much like their other conversations, and she would have to really press her point of going back home—if not today, then by the end of the week at the latest.

In a small sense, Patrick was here, but her attachment to him and all the things they knew together were far away just like he was. A tiny bit of panic welled in her with that single thought, and she made a firm commitment to talk to Sean and make him understand. She simply had to find her own way, intended murderer or not. She had to find her home again and figure out where she belonged on her own.

Caroline turned from the intensity of his familiar eyes. She was sure she was going to need this ride, if nothing else than to just feel like she was actually doing something—anything. The little bit of sanity she felt in control of was quickly losing ground. All things familiar to her were gone, and in this strange place and the close proximity of Patrick's look-alike brother, it was a struggle to keep it all in. She knew she was not very good at hiding her emotions; the freedom of a ride with the wind in her hair would either help her or kill her.

Kill her was more like it. Sean rode beside her quietly as she stole glances at him. He was strong like his brother, brute strength and muscle beneath fair skin and dark hair. The conflicting emotions she had for him were at bay for the moment, and she eased into her thoughts of the area. "I think this must be the most beautiful place on the planet."

"Aye, it could be," Sean said cautiously.

"Could be?" His tone confused her.

"Never mind; aye, it's beautiful, as you say."

Caroline could tell he did not want to elaborate, and with other pressing matters on her own mind, she decided it just was not the time to push him in a direction he did not want to go. That would come soon enough.

"It really is, though; I love all the green and the smell . . ." She inhaled deeply and closed her eyes. She could feel the warmth of gentle Lillie beneath her and silently thanked Sean for picking this horse for her. She had to admit it; she did need to feel safe. "From the airplane, it looked like a giant salad," she commented.

"What?" he looked over at her, not understanding her meaning.

"I said, your country looks like a giant salad with all the different green colors mixed together." She gestured toward the countryside with her free hand.

"Oh, and what would your country look like, then?" he asked, amused.

"Well, my country in general has a lot of different areas, but where I live, it mostly just looks like a big kitty-litter box filled with brown sand." She still did not understand why she actually lived in the desert when she longed for the ocean. The water had always held a certain soulful draw for her. Even as a child, being near the water always felt more like home than anywhere else.

She looked over at him to find him staring at her with a huge grin on his face.

"Why on earth would ya want to live in a pussy box?" he asked, shaking his head.

"I didn't say it was a kitty box, I said it *looked* like one," she corrected, feeling a little insulted at her own foolish comment.

"Right. And would ya say ya love tha heat also? Does it not feel like Hell itself in the summer?" he challenged.

"Well, only for three or four months in the summer. It's like your winter. We stay inside and hibernate with our air conditioners, like you do when you huddle around your heaters when it is too cold. It's just the opposite. The rest of the year is beautiful, and we also get monsoons in July."

"What, rains like in the jungle?" He was really interested now.

"Yup, big thunderstorms and sometimes even hail." She did so love the summer storms and the smell of the desert afterward. The temporary spurt of green that came after the rain and the magnificent rainbows over the Catalina Mountains were really beautiful.

"Rain in the desert; I've heard of everything now," Sean said, shaking his head. "Is that what keeps ya there, rain?" he continued.

"It helps." With that, she was done. It did not matter about the rains, and no rainbow in the world would keep her there like Patrick could have. He was the desert in bloom, and his smell was the only smell she longed for now. How on earth was she ever going to go home? *Home* . . . the word seemed foreign to her now. Suddenly and without warning, the tears welled, and the pain in her chest slammed into her with such force she thought she might fall off the horse. It was too much, unbearable almost, and as she tried to hold back the onslaught of emotions, she managed to spur the horse slightly forward. Caroline wanted nothing more than to go home, but only if it meant going home to Patrick. Home was not home anymore without him, and she suddenly knew in that instant that she didn't belong anywhere. *I have no home.*

21.

HAWKMOON

The moon glowed bright and full in an almost cloudless sky, lighting up the night with a certain brilliance. The leaves on the trees made faint rustlings from the breeze that was carried in from the restless sea below the nearby cliffs. The smell of the sea was wafting through the air with a very fine mist of salt and fish. Sean licked his lips, and despite the chill of the night air, he could feel himself sweating. Tiny drops of perspiration ran from behind his ears, tickling their way down the back of his neck.

Glancing at the moon, he cursed under his breath, slightly shook his head, and rolled his eyes heavenward. This mission was supposed to be an easy one, information-gathering surveillance only. He frowned as his eyes took in the area around him again. How could they get the full moon schedule so wrong? He knew he should have checked and rechecked them, but his mind was elsewhere. It was a mistake that could dearly cost them tonight, and he was solely responsible. He alone would accept the fault and take the consequences. As the captain, he alone bore the blame.

He swore under his breath as he looked over at the isolated cliff house, brightly illuminated under possibly the brightest orb of the year. The clouds had been thick when they set out on the mission; rain was expected to cover any sounds, and a moonless sky was expected to cover their presence. At least they had the sea. It was angry tonight with the promise of a late storm, and the waves crashing against the rocks below would help hide any sound they made. That was something, but he feared it was not enough. The night had become unnecessarily dangerous, and he realized without a doubt that this was not the night to bring Claire along.

All week, she had begged to come along, not an easy thing for her to do given her superiority of mind. He remembered her young face ablaze with excitement and her flaming-red hair shaken loose from its braid from the incessant pleading. He had looked into her glowing, green eyes, knowing if it was not this time, it would be another—perhaps a mission far more dangerous than the simple information-gathering they were supposed to do this night. Sean had reluctantly agreed to take her along, hoping to appease her for a while.

From his position behind the tree, he could see her as clearly as if it were daylight outside. Crouched down in her assigned practiced position behind a bush under the second window of the lower floor of the house, he could easily make out her slim build in her black outfit and her matching ski mask. His eyes were wide in the holes of the mask, but to her credit, she was sleek and stealthy as a panther on the hunt. Unfortunately, if he could see her, so could the enemy.

Sean lifted his own mask, swiping his forehead with the back of his gloved hand. His other hand rested lightly on top of the gun that weighed heavy in his belt holster. He prayed silently that there would be no need to pull it out, but he quickly unfastened the snap with one practiced finger just in case. He hated this mask. Sean would prefer to fight his enemy face to face, but he knew the rules and codes and kept strictly to them. There had to be order in the ranks, or they would lose this fight to utter chaos; rules had to be obeyed at all costs. Rules number two and three were that no man was to be left behind and masks were to be worn at all times. Rule number one was to *never* divulge anything about anything or anyone in the army. This meant that if you were captured, you never spoke a word—ever. Complete silence. The cause was the only one you answered to; everything else was a moot point.

Sighing, Sean pulled the mask back down over his face. The material itched as he pulled it into the proper position, all the holes matching where they should be. Since they had all gathered for this little party, he decided to get this task over with as quickly as possible. He raised a hand in silent command to the other five members of his squad. He could not actually see them but knew precisely where each and every one of his team was located and that they were all watching him for their commands.

Keeping a practiced eye on Claire, he watched her nod and begin to move catlike in the darkness along the ground without making a single sound. He had to admit to himself that she was good; he would have to remember to compliment her later on her stealth. She stopped and waited for his signal. Sean lifted the small pen and aimed. The tiny red light flashed once, twice in succession, and then again . . . *proceed with caution.* She moved toward the back of the house to her preplanned position directly under the kitchen window. It was well lit within, and he held his breath as she lifted the small, retractable periscope pole with a laser camera on the end of it. From the small, black box she held in her palm, she would be able to see what the camera saw. She held up her other hand; three fingers equaled three targets inside the room. Wait; she corrected herself. There were four.

Damn! Sean thought as he bit his lower lip in frustration. He could see her plain as day with the moon shining directly down on her! This was too risky! He turned sharply to the left as a faint sound caught his attention. Anyone walking up the drive would be able to see her if they were looking. He raised his hand silently to get her attention. She had her head down as she watched on her camera the four who were in the kitchen.

Sean thought to run over to her, but that could attract attention. Instead, he pointed the red laser light at her. Startled, Claire at once looked up, and he motioned with a quiet swirl of his finger in the air to wrap it up and get out. She looked for a second longer, then shook her head no. He started to move when all of a sudden, the back door opened, and light spilled onto the back porch. Sean's heart skipped a beat as a man strolled out with a large bag of trash and headed to the garbage can next to the stairs, making quite a bit of noise.

Sean quickly looked for Claire. She was still there, frozen like a statue with one hand poised in the air and the other holding the small camera. With the door open, the men inside could be heard roaring with laughter, a sound that pierced the silence of the vast, deserted area. Even though they had this temporary cover of noise, Sean knew that any movement would be caught immediately, and their cover was still compromised. Sean quickly looked from the man to Claire and back. The man had put the trash in the metal garbage can, but instead of going back into the house right away, he lingered on the porch, lighting a cigarette and leaning against the banister rail.

Sean looked again at Claire. She was barely ten feet away from the man, but still unnoticed for the moment. Sean's fingers instinctively went to his gun and wrapped around the handle of his pistol. He clenched his jaw tightly as he watched and waited. He did not know how long his baby sister would be able to hold her position. Holding one hand high in the air at that degree for an extended period might cause her to flinch or wear out. *What had I been thinking?*

Suddenly, Sean's thoughts were interrupted by a loud voice booming from inside the house, saying, "Thompson, get your ass in here, we need to get this worked out!"

The man outside with the cigarette quickly snuffed it out on the banister, then threw it to the ground, hastily making his way back into the house. Though he knew better, Sean could have sworn that he heard a collective sigh of relief from his entire team waiting in the area. Sean almost fell over from his crouched position and finally let out the breath he had been holding.

Sean looked over at Claire. Her eyes were wide behind her mask as he lifted the penlight to signal her to continue. Claire immediately lowered her arms, and the camera came to rest in her lap with a slight slump forward of her shoulders. He stood and stepped out from behind the tree for her to get a look at him. She immediately held one hand up in protest, signaling him not to advance. She shook her head no and lifted the laser eye of the camera back up to the window to continue what she had started. Sean motioned her to stop and retreat. She just ignored him and continued, surprising him with her stamina and courage. Sean thought to himself how proud he was of her as he returned to his hidden, crouched position. *Ahhh, Claire, ye should have been born a lad!*

Caroline was lying in her bed; the fire in her room was small but still crackling and sending off a small amount of warmth and light. Her light was off, and the soft glow of the fire was holding her attention with its flames licking at the wood and sending a heavenly smell throughout the room. She could not sleep, no matter how hard she tried. The empty teapot Teagan kindly brought her earlier was still sitting on the small, lace-covered table next to her.

She was making mental lists in her head of why she should or shouldn't stay in Ireland a short while longer. She needed to think things through and mentally focus on everything that was involved and happening. It was a subject that was never going to allow her to sleep, no matter how hard she tried. Glancing over at the nightstand and the empty teapot, she decided that some more hot tea might help. It would certainly warm her frozen toes, if nothing else. She sat up in the bed, reached for the extra blanket draped across its foot, and wrapped it around her shoulders. She realized how frigid the air outside her toasty covers was the moment her feet made contact with the icy floorboards. Nights in this country were positively freezing. Later, she was going to have to think of a way to tell Vanessa that she was going to stay a while longer and that, oh, by the way, her life might be in danger, and would she mind watching her cat a while longer? Maybe for now, she would leave out the part about her life being in danger.

Slipping quietly out of her room, she made her way down the hall to the staircase, not an easy task considering how dark this house could become. Everyone else appeared to be asleep. She was relieved to see that the windows in the foyer had enough light coming through them from the moon to provide ample light to keep her from falling down the stairs. The moon was huge, casting a purple glow about the rooms below, stealing the rich colors and making everything a faded, dark purple and white.

Heading to the kitchen, she noticed the door was slightly ajar, cracked enough for some golden light to spill into the adjacent hallway. *Teagan is probably slaving away over some delicious new thing.* The McNally's had some idea that she was not eating enough, and they were probably right; her jeans and shirts had begun to feel a bit loose. She had not had an appetite since Patrick had died.

The thought made her stop, close her eyes, and quickly shake herself back to reality. She did not want to go there now. Patrick was always with her, but she was trying to stay focused, stay awake on some level, and remain among the living. It was painful to think of him, and she knew it would be painful for a long while yet. She was trying very hard to think of him as just being away, not gone forever. In her mind, she practiced a fine art of assuming him as just somewhere waiting for her to join him. *He's just on a trip.* She repeated that fantasy over and over, and in some way, it was helping her just a little.

There was no sound coming from the kitchen, and Caroline soon found out there was no one in there. Slightly disappointed not to see Teagan's smiling face, she was also glad no one else was there. Sean would badger her about facts, Mary would try to feed her, Claire would be nasty, as usual, and dear Robbie would have dropped stuff and made a terrible racket. He was so nervous around her, but she liked the easy smile he gave her when they ran into each other. She liked Patrick's family immensely, but for now, in the stillness of the house asleep, she realized she liked the quiet of it most of all.

Reaching up high into a cupboard for a mug, she happened to glance out the kitchen window into the backyard and over to a light coming from the barn. The door was open, and the brightness of the light spilling into the yard shone like a welcoming beacon in a tempest. Caroline did not make much of it but guessed Sean or Robbie must be checking on the animals and tucking them in for the night. The fact that it did not get dark here until almost 11 p.m. was strange to her, and it was an adjustment to think it was not just early evening when, in fact, it was almost 1 a.m. It was more likely Robbie out there with his horse, Meghan. She was heavy with a foal and ready to deliver any moment. Caroline thought how wonderfully supportive he had been to her when she first arrived, and she decided to turn the favor. He was probably all alone out there and worried sick. Since she could not sleep, she might as well go out and give him some encouragement or at least some company.

Caroline was out the door and running for the barn before she realized she did not have on any shoes or decent clothes! She stopped midway and adjusted the blanket around her; the last thing she wanted to do was scare the poor boy to death by being half-dressed in her nightgown. She shivered; the night air was cold enough for her to see her breath under the bright moon, and she at once took a big gulp of it. The salty sea air was so refreshing; she took two more deep breaths before continuing quickly the rest of the way to the barn.

Caroline stepped through the open door, rubbing the cold from her arms and shivering deeply. "Robbie?" she whispered softly, not wanting to frighten the animals with her sudden appearance. "Robbie, are you here?"

"Where is he?" she asked aloud, peeking into one of the stalls. A sleepy mare answered her with a soft shake of her head up and down. As Caroline walked toward Meghan's stall, Sean's horse gave a loud whinny and kicked the back of his stall. He shook his massive head back and forth, sending his black mane flying from side to side.

"You don't frighten me one bit, you big bully!" Caroline said, shaking her finger at him. He kicked again in protest. Caroline peered around at the next stall, expecting to see Robbie sound asleep, curled up next to Meghan in the fresh hay. She was more than surprised to see the stall completely empty. Sean's horse gave a whinny and curled his lips in protest.

"Hush, you silly!" she scolded. Caroline was beginning to feel like something was not right. Emptiness in her stomach left her with an uneasy feeling that something was wrong. She took a closer look around Meghan's stall and suddenly noticed that the door was not left open by accident; it was actually smashed in at the bottom, and two boards were hanging in pieces. She felt the grip of fear take hold as she ran her fingers along the supporting side beam and noticed the latch to the door had been practically ripped out by some strong force.

Caroline knew something was terribly wrong. Her instincts were screaming at her, and the fine hairs on the back of her neck rose as she took a closer look into the empty stall. The hay in some places was darker than in others. She knelt and looked closer, lifting a handful to get a closer look. *Blood! Oh, my GOD!* Her world started to spin as the image of Patrick lying in his own pool of bright-red blood flooded into her mind. She closed her eyes quickly as the metallic smell of it assaulted her senses. Reaching out with one hand to brace herself, she reached up and placed her free hand over her nose and mouth. *Get a grip!*

Her first thought was to run and find Sean, but she quickly remembered his car had not been outside when she came across to the barn. Of all nights for a hot date! Deciding not to wake Mary until she was sure something was really wrong, Caroline did the next best thing she could think of: she grabbed the large, black, leather bridle off the wall and opened the door of Sean's stall.

22.

SHARP AS ICE

Sean's horse was prancing around wildly beneath Caroline. His strong, muscled neck turned rapidly and pulled hard on the reins in her hand. "That's enough!" she scolded in a stern voice about two octaves lower than her natural one as she yanked hard, jerking him in the direction of the forest. She could easily see tracks in the snow in the bright moonlight. She gave the huge beast a hard kick and was nearly thrown backward with the force of his lunge. He was in a full run, and she hung on for dear life to his thick, coarse mane. She had felt so panicked with the need to find Robbie and Meghan that she did not bother with the oversized saddle; she simply jumped on the monster bareback, a decision she regretted immediately.

The forest was darker than the yard area because the thick trees blocked out the direct beams of the moon. Caroline had to duck several times to prevent herself from being unseated or injured by low-hanging limbs. Sharp branches and twigs pulled at her gown and scraped against her legs and arms.

The horse slowed a bit, and Caroline began to wonder if she had slightly overreacted when she realized she was not wearing any shoes again, and she might actually get lost. That would be her luck—run off half-naked in her nightgown with bare feet and get lost in a freezing forest in Ireland! Her train of thought was suddenly interrupted by a small, frantic sound in the distance, and her instincts jumped back into gear as she kicked the massive beast beneath her and steered him toward the sound. The horse jumped forward again with renewed vigor as Caroline leaned into his neck to dodge the branches.

The trees cleared a bit, and she heard the sounds louder now. As she burst through the tree line, a large, flat meadow came into view. Toward the center of the meadow, she saw Meghan raising and lowering her head, prancing and whinnying loudly. As Caroline's eyes followed the direction in which the little horse was looking, she quickly noticed something about thirty yards farther toward the center of the meadow.

"Oh my God, Robbie!" she screamed as the full force of what she was seeing hit her. This was no meadow—it was an iced-over lake, and Meghan was at its edge. Robbie had fallen through the ice! He was splashing and fighting to stay above the water. "Help, Caroline!" he cried.

Meghan was prancing back and forth along the edge and taking a step or two onto the fragile ice, then stepping backward. Caroline raced to Meghan and quickly slid off her horse as her bare feet sank into ankle-deep ice water. She screamed in Robbie's direction, "Hang on! Oh God, Robbie, I'm c-coming!" Her teeth were chattering, and without the warmth of the big horse, she felt the freezing temperature clear to her bones. Her heart sank as she could clearly see the struggle taking place in the water ahead of her. Without thinking, she began to wade into the ice water until it became thick enough that she could step up onto it.

A hole had broken through the ice toward the middle, and Robbie was splashing about, desperately trying to hold his head above the cold water. Caroline's mind whirred at the sight. Robbie was holding on to Meghan's new foal, trying with all his strength to keep them both above the water. One hand held the foal's head up, and the other was clinging to the solid part of the ice, scraping as the ice broke away in chunks—each time sending them both under again.

"Robbie, hold on!" Caroline yelled. Her voice echoed over the frozen acres.

"Caroline, I can't hold on much longer!" he yelled. "H-hurry!"

Caroline was treading out onto the frozen lake, her bare feet burning as the cold wind tore through her nightgown. She kept inching her way toward him, but she could feel the ice fracturing ever so slightly under her with each step, forcing her to go at an agonizingly slow pace. *Oh, God, help me! Help us,* she silently prayed with each step.

"Caroline, its verra thin; be careful," Robbie whispered, as if any sound might break the ice.

The foal that had been fighting in Robbie's arms suddenly became still, and the splashing ceased. Caroline looked up as she heard Meghan's loud whinny from the shore. She saw Robbie's head slip under for a second, and she screamed, "Robbie!"

She did not know how long they had been in the water, but it was clear he could not hang on much longer. She dropped to her hands and knees to better distribute her weight over the ice. Crawling, she reached the edge of the hole. Lying flat on her stomach, she reached down into the freezing water and felt a thousand tiny knives rip into her flesh as she felt his hair just below the surface. As she grabbed a handful of curls, she jerked him up with all her strength. He came up with a woosh of ice water, coughing and blowing water out of his nose.

"Give me your hand!" Caroline begged.

"No, get tha babe first!" he coughed. Caroline realized that his other arm was still hanging onto the foal.

"No, let me get you out first, then the foal! I don't know how long this ice will hold," she pleaded, noticing that his lips were way too blue.

"The babe canna stay afloat without me holden it!"

Caroline knew she had no choice; he would rather die than let go of that baby. She reluctantly let go of his hair as he went under again. He came up with a heave that pushed the small animal into her lap. A sharp hoof caught her in the forehead, and she winced with the onslaught of new pain. She quickly pushed the lifeless animal toward the mother and turned to reach for Robbie again. The ice was slowly cracking beneath her, and she had to back up a little. She was lying flat on her stomach and reached out with both hands, her arms stretched out straight in front of her, as she waited to feel him come out of the water. When he didn't, she screamed his name, and without a second thought, she jumped in after him.

He was not hard to find in the water, and she felt him as she jumped. Grasping at him, she got herself under him and gave a push with all the strength she had left. The two of them came to the surface, Robbie half out of the water, dead weight in her arms, but lying waist up on the ice. She sucked in her breath and went below the surface once again. With a mighty heave, she pushed the rest of him out of the water and onto the safety of the ice. Faintly, she could hear the horses at the edge of the water and see the lifeless shapes of both the foal and Robbie ahead of her. She had traded places with Robbie and the foal, and now she was the one trapped in the water. She didn't have the strength to pull herself out and would not risk the added weight on the ice for fear of it breaking and drowning all three of them. *I've given them a chance,* she thought as she held on to the edge of the ice with frozen fingers. She closed her eyes, and a few desperate seconds later, she heard Robbie coughing with choked effort. She had an overwhelming urge to keep her eyes closed and just go to sleep. Her lids were so heavy. At some point, she thought to sing to stay awake, and she began a hum in her strangled, raw throat. *Patrick, is this what it is like to die? I'm so cold and tired.*

"Sing, Caroline, sing ta me." She could hear Patrick's whispered voice in the distance.

With her eyes closed, she continued to quietly hum the tune to one of the CDs Patrick had given her from his store. In her mind's eye, she saw him standing before her on the edge, his strong arms outstretched and lifting her out of the water. Horses were screaming in the background.

"It's all right now; I've got ya." He continued to speak soft words in Gaelic that she did not understand as he held her close, warming her body with the heat of his own.

The horses stopped screaming, and she slipped into a dream.

23.

A GENTLE PRESENCE

Caroline could feel the pain in her forehead long before she made the decision to finally try to open her eyes. Its searing force threatened to tear her apart from within. At one point, she actually entertained the idea that she might be dead, but her belief that one should not feel any pain in the afterlife convinced her she was either alive or in Hell.

The memories of Robbie and the foal in the lake invaded her dreams, causing her to finally face waking up or die from her own curiosity, so she began the slow, agonizing effort of opening her eyes. As she pulled herself back into reality, she could see at once through her heavy lids that she was safe in her own room at the McNally's. Though the room was darkened, she could see the familiar surroundings by the soft glow of the fireplace.

Her tongue stuck to the roof of her mouth, and her lips parted with a small pop; she cautiously tried to turn herself toward the nightstand where Teagan often left her glass and water pitcher. The sudden, intense pain tore through her head like an ax, forcing her eyes to close tightly. She put her trembling hand to her head to seek out the source of her agony and immediately felt a bandage taped across her forehead. *Oh, good, someone took care of that*, she thought as shaky fingers lingered over the smooth plastic; for a moment, her hand dropped to her side.

Something pinched at the skin of her inner elbow. Licking her lips, she opened her eyes again and saw Sean sitting slightly slumped over in a chair next to her bed. His head lay cradled in one huge hand, his eyes were closed, and his long, black lashes rested against pale skin. She could make out the thick, blue veins that roped along the back of his hand. *Patrick had those same big veins in his hand too*, she thought, and she closed her eyes with the thought of him. *He's just on a trip; he's just on a trip.*

Caroline opened her eyes again and let her weariness invade her thoughts as she rested them on Sean's strong features. He was a formidable presence when awake and yet so peaceful in his sleep. His hair was unbound, loose around the tops of his shoulders, slightly covering one side of his face. She noticed the small scar across his chin and wondered how he got it. His dark beard growth led her to suspect he had not shaved in a while, and the scar was white against the dark growth. Her eyes roamed downward across his huge chest area; his muscles were tight and corded beneath the wrinkled shirt he had on. It was unbuttoned to the middle of his chest, and she noticed he had little, if any, chest hair. She let her gaze wander still further to his lap and his thighs. His legs were thick and strong, his belly taut and flat. Seeing his build reminded her of a conversation she once had with Vanessa about the qualifications of a date.

Caroline smiled, temporarily forgetting the pain in her head as she remembered Vanessa saying she would never date a man whose waist or thighs were smaller than her own. She found she missed her friend quite a bit.

When Caroline lifted her eyes again to his face, she was startled to see him awake and staring back at her. His eyes were dark green and smoky; his grin turned up one side of his mouth as if he had some humorous secret. She blushed, thinking what he must have thought about her smiling as she looked at his lower body. It was too much effort to explain at this particular moment.

"I'm glad ta finally see ya awake; ye gave us all quite a bit of o'scare," he said softly.

"How's Robbie?" she said, her voice low and throaty. She was more than a little afraid of his answer.

"Oh, himself; he's been up running after that foal of his for two days now," he said with a slight shake of his head. He ran one big hand through his hair with a yawn that was replaced by a smile when the surprise registered on her face. He was pleased she asked about his baby brother right away.

"Two days? How long have I—" She croaked, trying to sit up in bed, and the pain in her head shot through her like a knife.

"Three," he interrupted.

Caroline closed her eyes, squeezing them against the pain.

"The doc left this for ya, for when ya finally woke up. Said it would help with the pain a bit." He lifted a small, brown bottle off the nightstand, opened it, and handed her a tiny, blue pill.

Caroline spotted the water in the pitcher. "Water, please," she managed to ask with a fair amount of begging in her voice. Sean immediately grabbed the water pitcher, poured her a glassful, and held it out for her to take. Caroline struggled for a moment to sit up, but after several days of not using her muscles and not eating, she was just too weak and shaky.

Sean came over to the bed and lifted her head and shoulders while moving her pillows. He slid in behind her, bracing her against his chest and lower body.

"Here, now, let me help ya," he spoke softly above her head into her hair. As he gently held the glass for her to drink, she felt a strong sense of safeness being there so close to him. His broad chest was warm and hard against her back, and she leaned into him with a certain intimacy.

He put the glass down on the nightstand when she was done drinking but made no attempt to move their positions. He let his arms brace her sides, and the fingers of one hand began to absently caress her forearms.

"You said a doctor was here to see me?" she asked softly.

"Oh, aye, good Doc O'Ryan was here ta see ya twice after the ambulance men left. The first time he came after I pulled ya from tha pond looking like a drownd rat, and the second time was only this morning when we all feared ya would not wake." His fingers continued to rub little soft circles around her elbow.

"Did he say everything was all right? No stitches?" She was more than a little scared to think she had not checked to see if she still had any toes after being in the freezing water. It *had* suddenly occurred to her to ask about the bandage on her head, as thoughts of a long, side-to-side, horizontal scar entered her mind.

"No, no sewin; your beautiful face still that . . . he said ya were just in need of rest and some food." He said the word *food* with some emphasis. "He said if ya won't eat in a few days, we're ta bring ya in for an I.V., and he'll force feed ya."

"He did not!" she protested with a frown. *Did he say she had a beautiful face?*

"No, but I told him I'd bring ya in myself if ya didn't eat." He placed his chin lightly on the top of her head with the last statement and let out a sigh. They were quiet for a few moments, and then he spoke quietly. "He's gone, and ya must eat now," he commanded softly. She only nodded her head twice in acknowledgment; tears he could not see burned down her cheeks and fell onto his forearms.

"I'll help ya," he said, lifting his hand to stroke the side of her face. She turned then with her eyes closed and buried her face in his chest. With her knees drawn up in a fetal position, she cried silently as he held her small frame in his arms with his head on top of hers.

Sean held her like that until the drug took effect and her breathing evened out. He kissed her softly on her hair. When he could stand to be parted from her, he slid out from behind her and placed her down under the covers, gently holding a palm against her wet cheek for a moment as she slept. With a side grin, he went back to his chair, stretched out his long legs, and placed his folded hands in his lap. *She will be all right. She just needs some time like the rest of them. Patrick still holds her, but he won't forever,* he thought as his own eyes grew heavy and he too slept, thankful she had not noticed the IV needle mark on her left inner elbow.

24.

THE GIFT OF SONG

Caroline awoke the next morning with a renewed vigor she had not experienced in weeks. Whatever the good Doc O'Ryan had given her, it certainly managed to do the trick. She felt well rested and not too groggy, and her energy seemed to have returned.

Sitting up cautiously in her bed, she glanced over at the clock on the nightstand next to the water pitcher. A wave of dizziness surprised her, and she clung to her sheets and the thick quilt on her bed as she rode out the nausea. "Guess it is still slow going for today," she said aloud to the empty room. As the nausea subsided, she said to herself, "This is always the way; your mind wants to go, and your body cannot keep up."

Wrinkling her nose at a rather putrid smell, she looked down at her wrinkled gown, disgusted when she realized the smell was actually coming from her. *What did Sean say—three days?*

She managed to make it to the bathroom; her legs were weak but moving. She was determined to take a shower if it was the last thing she did.

Looking into the mirror above the sink, she frowned at the sad image that stared back at her. Wild, tangled, Medusa-like hair framed her pale face with hollow cheeks and large, dark circles under her eyes. A large, white piece of gauze was taped over the right side of her forehead. Curiosity got the better of her, and she tentatively started to remove the bandage. The tape came off easily, revealing a small but nasty three-inch slice. Thank God, there were no stitches. *Beautiful face? The man obviously needs glasses.*

The shower was heaven in itself, and when she opened the door, she discovered someone had already put fresh sheets on the bed and laid out another clean, cotton gown for her across the bottom half of the bed. *I wonder if Teagan would like to return with me to Tucson,* Caroline thought as she sat on the edge of the bed. Her thoughts were interrupted by a light knock at the door.

"Come in," Caroline said, and she was surprised when Claire peeked her head inside.

"Oh, yer up, then?" Claire asked.

"Finally; come on in." Caroline did not know what to think as Claire opened the door and stepped inside, obviously hiding something behind her back.

"I'm glad ta see yer up; I've brought ya sometim if ya can stand it," she said almost shyly, causing Caroline some confusion by the sudden interest in her. This girl had managed to be in the same house with her these past weeks and had not spoken more than three sentences to her the entire time.

Claire stepped toward Caroline and produced the hidden item from behind her back. It was a CD.

"Thank you," Caroline said, taking it from her. "Oh, I . . ." she trailed off.

"What, don't ya like it? Sean said ya would." Claire was defensive again.

"No, I love it, thank you. It's just that . . ." Caroline was choking on the explanation and bit her lower lip.

"What is it, then?" Claire asked.

Caroline didn't look up; she couldn't. It was harder and harder to be here sometimes.

"I just wanted ta thank ya for Robbie is all." Claire was mistaking Caroline's emotions.

"It's just that Patrick used to . . . I mean, he always gave me new music from his country, and this was his particular favorite."

"Oh, well, then . . ." Claire was obviously uncomfortable with the heavy emotions in the room, and she turned and started out the door. Caroline spoke as Claire was turning. With Claire's back to her, Caroline managed, "I love them, you know. I loved all the music he gave me." Caroline could feel her eyes welling. Claire stopped, but she did not turn back to face Caroline.

"I loved him more than you could ever imagine," Claire said quietly as she stepped into the hallway and disappeared down the hall.

"Thank you," Caroline said to the empty air. "I loved him more than you will ever know, too," she whispered. She laid back against the pillows, her newfound energy suddenly drained.

25.

CART BEFORE THE HORSE

Sean could hear Caroline's soft voice as he approached the kitchen door. He stood just on the other side and listened to his mother and Caroline talking and laughing. It was good to hear the two of them together and even better to hear them laughing. He closed his eyes and listened some more. Caroline's voice reminded him of the terrible scene he had found at Kellond's Pond just more than a week ago.

His fists balled at his sides as he remembered coming home late from his mission with Claire and his team. That night had scared the hell out of him, as his baby sister had almost been compromised. She could have been caught by the Brits or worse, and it would be a long time before he would take a chance with her like that again. As a matter of fact, it made him realize just how dangerous this whole business of the cause had become for his family.

Before, when Patrick had been in charge, it had just been a few of his friends doing what they thought was in the best interest of Ireland. Joining the cause, taking a stand, and fighting for the good of their country seemed like the only thing they could do to try to right the injustice brought about so long ago. There had always been some amount of danger involved, but now it was hitting too close to home again, and he had begun to think they were going about things backward in getting their point across. This was a new world, and technology—not physical might—was ruling the world now. Sean had seriously begun to rethink his views on the right way to handle things and considered that big brother Patrick might have known what was right all along. At least Patrick had tried for another kind of life, but no one here would admit to admiring him for it, especially now. Troubles of another sort had found him an ocean away.

Sean cleared those thoughts from his mind and returned to thoughts of last week. That night, he and Claire arrived home to find the barn door open, a damaged empty stall, Robbie missing, and his own horse gone. Feeling a deep sense of fear take hold, he and Claire grabbed the emergency kit and jumped into the work truck, following the trail of horse hooves. It led in the direction of the forest.

In the midst of the trees, they lost sight of the trail in the forest, where the moon's brightness was blocked by the canopy of trees. Sean was digging for the flashlight when they both heard a faint sound in the direction of Kellond's Pond. Fearing the worst, he hit the gas pedal as they both held their breath.

"I can hear them!" Claire yelled, waving a hand in the general direction of the water.

Sean was shocked to find his baby brother, half frozen, lying on the ice in the middle of the pond with Meghan's foal next to him, barely alive. Caroline was hanging on for dear life in the freezing water. He quickly grabbed the rope out of the back of the truck, threw it around the trailer hitch, and tied it around his waist as he headed out onto the frozen lake. Getting Robbie was easy; the ice held for both him and the foal.

Caroline was another story. The moment Sean got close to her, the ice gave way and sent him feetfirst into freezing water. Like a madman, he swam quickly toward her, using his fists to break any ice that got in his way. When he finally had her, he yelled, "Go, Claire!" The rope and the truck pulled both of them to safety. She was so cold—in fact, she seemed lifeless—that he feared the worst. He tried talking to her, shouting at her to speak, and when she groaned, he kept her semi-awake by making her sing to him. All she could manage was a pitiful hum, but it was something; it was life, and he was extremely thankful. Claire called Doc O'Ryan on their way back to the house, and he sent an ambulance to meet them there.

The ambulance team worked on Robbie and Caroline while Sean worked on the foal. Lying next to Robbie on the ice, the baby and Robbie shared some body heat, but Caroline was alone in the freezing water. No one expected anything good to come of it all. Hospital personnel said that the freezing temperatures actually aided in their survival, slowing down all body functions and putting them all in a state of suspended animation. Thankfully, no one had internal injuries, and the only other injury was the bad scrape on Caroline's forehead. They all recovered. Caroline drifted in and out of consciousness after the ordeal, but Robbie made a quick, full recovery.

Caroline did not remember anything about the hospital, the ambulance, or anything else involved in her recovery. Doc O'Ryan had a heavy hand with medication, and she slept through the entire ordeal. Sean didn't allow anyone to say anything to her about the whole thing. He knew she would be mortified if she had given his family any cause for concern in any way. All she was to know was that she was brought back to the house, she slept, and she recovered. Period. No fuss, no muss. She did not need any needless guilt encouraging her incessant urge to leave. The fox that had invaded the barn in search of food was dead, stomped to death in Meghan's stall, and life would go on as if nothing had ever happened.

As his attention returned to the present, Sean leaned against the door with one hand, letting the soothing voices of his mother and Caroline put his own mind at ease as a smile grew on his face. His peace was interrupted by the shrill voice of his little sister.

"Just what's got ya looking like you're a naughty boy, Sean McNally?" Claire accused in a sarcastic tone.

Sean groaned, opening his eyes to the sight of his sister with her hands on her hips and her all-knowing expression on her smug, little face.

"Aye, wouldn't ya be wantin ta know that now? It's an evil mind ya have in that pretty head of yers."

"Humph!" she said, lifting one eyebrow at him as she brushed past him and pushed the door open to the kitchen.

"My God, what's this about, then?" Claire asked, seeing her mother and Caroline in the middle of quite a mess. They were both covered in flour, their aprons useless against the fury of the two mad bakers. Though they both had their hair tied back, both women had streaks of white in the strands that had come loose around their faces. Teagan looked over at Claire and simply shrugged her shoulders in mock defeat. "They've been at it all afternoon," she said, sounding defeated.

Caroline looked over at Sean and explained, "Your mother is teaching me to make real scones." She wiped the back of a flour-covered hand across her brow.

"That's good," he said with a grin.

"What? Next, she's teachin me ta make Mexican burritos!" his mother said, laughing and giving Caroline a nod of approval. "She's a natural in the kitchen," she added.

"Burritos?" he asked, shocked. "That would not have anytin ta do whi donkeys, would it?" A look of disgust crossed his face.

All three women looked at each other and then suddenly erupted in laughter all at once. Caroline took pity on him and explained, "No, silly. They are made with beef, no donkeys!"

Sean looked around for the cooking sherry bottle when the women started loudly snorting and mocking him with various versions of "Hee-Haw's." Busy with her task, Mary spoke over her shoulder at Sean, saying, "We're having an Irish-Mexican supper tonight."

"Oh, I . . ." His mind would not work fast enough for him to think of an excuse to bow out of dinner when he noticed Caroline stretch long across the large counter, reaching for something. Her left leg lifted slightly as she stretched, and her bottom jutted out ever so slightly. It was enough to pull her jeans tighter, defining its perfect roundness. His mouth went dry. He turned quickly and began rummaging through the pantry for something to eat.

"You're just like yer da when it comes ta keeping ya full up," his mother said behind him.

The comment made Caroline slow down what she was doing. She did not look up but listened for more elaboration about the father. No one had said anything about him until this moment. Patrick had also been evasive when she brought him up at home. She finally looked up to see Mary with her hand gently on his back. The moment was broken when Teagan dropped a pot onto the floor, causing a loud clang.

At the same moment, Robbie came bursting through the back door, out of breath. "Caroline!" Robbie yelled. "I've got sometim ta show ya outside!"

"Robbie, for Christ's sake, she's not deaf, ya know!" Sean scolded.

"Sorry, I just got something for ya is all."

"Well, then, I guess we'd better go and see what has gotten Robbie into such a huff," Mary said, untying her apron and heading for the door. Caroline rushed after her, throwing her own apron across a nearby chair.

"Oh, Robbie, how wonderful!" Caroline said. Standing before her was her assigned horse, Lillie, hooked up to what appeared to be a small, open, wooden cart of some sort on two large, spoked, wooden wheels. Walking closer for a better look, she peered inside at a bench seat for two.

"How incredibly charming. Will you take me for a ride when you get a chance?"

"Take you for a ride? Why, I mean ta give it to ya for savin me foal and all," he said, looking at his hat in his hands.

"Oh, Robbie, I could never, I mean, you're really giving me this? I love it, but I don't think they'll let me take it home on the plane." Her smile started to fade as she immediately felt staring eyes on her.

Looking around for some hint of understanding, she met Sean's eyes. "Oh, my, you all have to know I have to go soon. It's been a month, and I'm sure you are all growing tired of me by now—and, well, I have a job I have to get back to and all." She swallowed hard.

Now the McNally's were exchanging glances among themselves.

"We thought you liked it here." Robbie looked at her with tears forming in his eyes. Caroline went over to embrace him. Putting her arms around him, she felt his arms come around her in an instant bear hug. For being only fourteen, he had a fair share of strength that promised he'd one day match both his older brothers in size.

Robbie held on to her for a long moment; being as tall as she was, her face was buried in his wild nest of red curls. She closed her eyes, enjoying the clean smell of soap mixed with horses that lingered about him.

When he let her go, she stepped back and watched him push an unruly curl off his forehead with a quick swipe of his hand. She stood smiling at him when it fell back immediately.

"I do love it here, really, but this isn't my life; my life is in Arizona."

"Here, now, we'll just have ta see about changin your mind is all," Mary said, coming over to her and putting an arm around her waist. "Besides, ya won't be leavin before the big party we got planned for ya anway," she said, giving her a slight squeeze.

"Party?" Caroline looked down at her in surprise. *Oh, no.*

"It's a celebration for the safe return of Robbie and you, of course," Clare said, heading back into the house.

"Yes, dear, that's right. A celebration of life." Mary gave her another squeeze. Looking into her eyes, Mary let Caroline know it was more than just Robbie she was grateful for—it was the sheer fact that she'd not be attending a second son's funeral this time around, and she knew it was the mere presence of Caroline Blackwell at her home that she had to thank for that.

Sean watched his mother walk Caroline back into the house. *I'll find a way*, he thought to himself. *I'll find a way to keep you in Ireland and safe with me.* He headed off to the barn with Robbie trailing closely behind him. "We'll find a way, lad."

"Aye," said Robbie, "we'll find a way."

26.

CELEBRATION OF LIFE

"What ya thinkin, Sean? Ya look deep in thought," Claire asked. Sean continued to stare across the crowded room at Caroline.

"What? Oh, just watchin Ma's old cronies going at poor Caroline." He lifted his glass and took a drink of whiskey, closing his eyes and feeling the warmth of the alcohol spread into his body.

"Sean, ya know she's leavin soon," Claire said, looking up at her brother, who had not taken his eyes off Caroline. There was a look on his face she'd never seen before. His features were softer, slightly mellower than before. His eyes almost glowed with a hunger of some kind.

"Aye, I know she thinks she's leavin soon." He turned his head and met his sister's eyes.

"Sean, ya can't force her ta stay. I know ya got ta take into account what Patrick wanted, but she's American. Patrick was a fool ta get involved with her. Now look at you, standin there thinkin with your pants also."

Sean narrowed his eyes at her as he said, "She's stayin if I have any say in the matter."

Claire took a small step backward. She had learned at a young age not to remain too close to any McNally with that kind of look in his eyes. "So, just as I thought." She smiled up at him wickedly. "You've gone and fallen for her then? You're going to protect her for yourself, isn't that right, Brother?"

"Aye, and right now she looks like she needs protectin from those old agers." He put his glass down on a table and walked toward Caroline. Claire watched him place a hand on Caroline's elbow and whisper something to her. "I've come to rescue ya," Sean whispered in her ear. Caroline felt his hot breath in her hair.

"Excuse me, ladies, but I want ta introduce Miss Blackwell to a friend of mine. Besides, I think the good Father Dougall needs some advice about the upcomin fundraiser for the parish."

Sean held Caroline's elbows firm as he led her out of the foyer and into the deserted study. Caroline sat on the leather sofa, leaning back in obvious weariness. "Can I get ya somethin ta drink?" he asked as he closed the door.

"Yes, please." Caroline took off her shoes and bent over her legs to massage her feet and ankles. "Thank you for rescuing me, from those women, I mean. They were sweet, but my cheeks were beginning to hurt from all the smiling."

He looked down at her. Bending over like she was, he had an ample view of her chest, its fullness apparent. He turned quickly, feeling the rush of heat to his face. "I, I could tell ya needed me, I mean, needed my intervention."

"Seems as though you are always there at the right time for me, Sean." She looked over at him as he filled her glass with an amber liquid. She couldn't help noticing how broad his back was, how tight his buttocks seemed, how long his legs were.

"What was it ya called me? Your knight in shining armor, was it?" He handed her the glass and sat down beside her on the sofa.

"Yes, well . . . what is this?" she asked after taking a sip.

"That there's just a bit of the hair of the dog is all," he said, resisting the urge to reach over and touch the creaminess of her shoulders. Her hair was swung over one side of her neck. One thin, black strap of her dress fell over her white shoulder.

"Well, it's wonderful; may I have another, please?" Sean raised his eyebrows at her when she handed him her empty glass.

"Do ya like your party so far?" he asked, going back over to the bar.

"Oh, I love the people here. Everyone is so nice. I've met the most interesting people. Do you know all of them?"

"Aye, they're a good lot for sure," he said, handing her back a full glass of brandy.

"Sean, it must have been wonderful growing up here in Ireland. I really do love it here."

Sean saw his opening at once. He had been waiting for the right moment to spring his idea on her. "You can't really say that, lass. You haven't even seen the whole of Ireland yet; you've only been here on the farm and at the homes of a few of the neighbors with Robbie in his cart. I was thinking I'm going ta be off up the coast on some business this week, and, well, if ya want, you could come with me and get a real look at our country." His pulse was racing.

"Sean, do you think I could? Would it be all right, I mean proper, you and I alone and all?"

He looked at the joy in her eyes. "Oh, aye, I'll arrange separate rooms at the bed-and-breakfast we'll stay in along the way." He reached over and took her small hand in his. When she did not pull away, he rubbed his thumb over her knuckles, gently feeling her delicate bones and smooth skin.

Caroline looked up at him; she was beginning to feel an almost forgotten excitement building inside her. He raised his head and met her eyes. "Caroline, I—"

Just then, the door to the study burst open, spilling loud music and three men into the room. Caroline hastily pulled her hand out of Sean's, feeling a bit embarrassed at the warmness overtaking her body.

"Sean, old man, what's keepin ya from the party?"

"Shut up, Kenny, can't ya see he's entertainin a lady, ya drunk fool?"

Sean rose from the sofa to greet the three staggering men, all of whom seemed to be making a gallant attempt to keep each other from falling down. "Caroline, let me introduce me good friends to ya." He went behind them and stood with his hands on the shoulders of a rather attractive young man with wild, curly, red hair much like Robbie's. "This here is Paul Finners." The man gave an exaggerated bow, making Caroline smile wide. "This here fool is Michael Kenny; he's a wee bit of a troublemaker." Sean winked at Caroline from behind the man's shoulder. "Now this here is Wee Willy Flint." He lowered his head and faked a cough.

"You'll not be tellin the lass that, do ya hear me, ya savage?"

Caroline lowered her head, looking up at him through her lashes. Sean was patting the short man on the back and saying something to him in Gaelic. The other two laughed and snorted.

Caroline studied the four men in front of her. They were all sturdy-looking men with athletic builds; even Wee Willy had thick, strong legs for his height. Sean still towered over his friends by a head, and the way they responded to him, she was sure he was the chosen leader for this group.

"Beautiful Caroline, come and join us for a toast ta Robbie now," Michael said to her as he broke free of the others and came toward her. "Unless ya rather stay with Sean; you two did look somewhat preoccupied when we came in."

"Oh, no, I mean yes, I'd love to go and toast Robbie." The others quickly came to her sides, leaving Sean standing alone. "Won't you come too?" She smiled at Sean, and he opened the door, gesturing them out with a wave of his hand. "After you, m'lady."

He lagged behind, watching his three best friends and comrades escort her out into the hall, frowning and feeling a slight pang of jealousy as he saw their hands about her waist and shoulders.

"Yes, yes, see ya all at church on Sunday." Mary waved the last of her guests on to their cars. "What a party!" she said, closing the door and leaning against it.

"I'm going to help Teagan clean up, Ma," Claire said, heading for the kitchen.

"Don't worry about it, dear, it'll still be here in the morning. Ya best be off ta bed with ya."

Claire stopped on her way, passing the open door to the study. She saw her brother standing above the sofa, Caroline fast asleep, curled into a ball on one end. She quietly entered the room and stood next to him.

"She came in here about an hour ago," he whispered.

"No taste for parties?" she asked a little sarcastically.

"No taste for ale. I'll carry her up and then come back down ta help you and Ma with straightin up." He bent and scooped Caroline effortlessly off the sofa. She gave a little sigh and snuggled into his arms. Claire raised her eyebrow at him.

"I'll be right back," he told Claire when he saw her expression.

"Sure ya will, brother dear," she said, picking up a few of the empty glasses off the table next to her.

Sean carried Caroline up the stairs and into her room. Laying her on the bed, he felt the warmness of her breath against his neck. He was quickly overcome with desire.

He had watched her all night. Watched the way she moved in that tight, black dress, the way her hair fell over her creamy shoulders, her long, slim legs in those tiny high heels she wore, and the way her full, sensuous mouth moved as it smiled and drank.

Now, she was just inches away from him, those very same lips slightly parted and beckoning him to taste their fullness. He hesitated, looking at her dark, lush lashes closed tight against the high arch of her cheekbone. The passion he held in check all night overflowed and spilled into desire.

Soft as a feather, his lips brushed hers. When she did not stir, he tasted her again. This time, he was shocked as she responded, putting her arms around his shoulders and lacing her fingers through the back of his hair.

He started to pull away, but she pushed her neck up, capturing his mouth with her own in a sensuous, searing kiss.

His own need became hard to control, and when he thought he couldn't control himself any longer, her arms went limp, and she stretched like a purring kitten under him, rolled over, and gave a great sigh.

Sean stood for a moment watching her peaceful sleep, his own mouth still tingling with the sweet taste of her kiss, his loins burning with the heat of her touch. Never before had he met such a woman as his Caroline. That was how he was going to refer to her from now on. *His Caroline*. Even if she didn't know it yet.

27.

A JOURNEY OF THE HEART

"Can you smell it?" Sean glanced away from the road long enough to see Caroline rolling down her window.

"Oh, it smells so wonderful! I love the ocean!" He smiled at the road ahead of him. He'd traveled this road many times and knew what lay ahead beyond the next hill.

"How much further, Sean? I can't wait to see it." Caroline was glowing with a childlike excitement, her heart pounding with anticipation.

The trip so far had been wonderful, the scenery spectacular. She was sure Ireland was the most beautiful place on earth. Long, narrow roads carved their way through hills and valleys. Endless rolling acres of the greenest, grass-covered hillsides stretched for miles without end, and Caroline's senses were treated to an explosion of sights and smells.

"Close your eyes, lass."

"What?"

Sean made a small grunt as he said, "I said close your eyes; it's a surprise."

Caroline closed her eyes tightly; her heart picked up speed. Within a few moments, she felt the car turn off in a new direction. "Sean?"

"No peekin' now; keep those lids closed till I say so."

She felt the ground shift under the wheels, and the sound was quieter now; they were not on the road anymore. "Now?"

"A few more seconds is all; hold tight."

She reached out when she felt the car stop. With her hands on the dashboard, she heard him unbuckle his seatbelt.

"Now?"

"No; can ye no stand a little surprise? Do not open till I say."

Caroline groaned in disapproval as she heard him open his door and get out. Dropping her hands into her lap, she was suddenly tempted to sneak a peek when her door abruptly opened, and she felt a rush of cool air fill the car.

"Ye didn't peek, did ya?"

"No. I was a good girl. Now?"

"Just a moment longer; watch ya step now."

She knew from the way he was behaving that she was in for quite a treat. As they had driven through the town of Limerick, he had taken great pains to show her the main points of interest in his hometown. She had listened carefully as he explained in great detail everything that held a story for him and his family. Now she wondered what else he had in store.

Caroline was sure this big hulk of a man did indeed have a very soft heart, as Patrick did, only she was not sure why he tried so hard to hide it. Perhaps this trip would bring out his true colors.

"Okay, lass, ye can open now," he said, letting go of her arm and taking a step back.

Caroline gasped when she took in the sight before her. Nothing she had ever imagined could have been so beautiful.

Her eyes took in the sight of the most gorgeous coastal area she had ever seen. She stood for a second, not being able to breathe.

Before her, for what seemed like infinity, stretched the deep blue of the Atlantic Ocean, its salty air blowing through her hair.

Looking around her, she saw they were standing atop a half-mile-high cliff; the lush green grass under her feet came to a sudden stop at the edge. She took a few steps forward and peered over the cliff.

She gulped at the apparent height of the spot where they stood. The choppy sea drove itself angrily over and over again against the rocks at the bottom, its white, foamy waves etching a line for miles along the base of the cliffs.

Caroline was so enchanted with its beauty as a whole that she did not notice Sean had gone back to the car until he placed her coat around her shoulders. "Well, what do ya think? Magnificent, aye?"

"Oh, Sean, thank you for bringing me to see the rest of your country. I could never have imagined any place to be so beautiful." Caroline shivered against the coolness of the sea mist, but her feet were firmly planted at least for the time being, and her body did not give in to the cold.

"These cliffs are called the ‹Cliffs of Moher.' Magnificent, aye?" He stood close enough now that his arm brushed against hers.

She looked at him then, his face slightly reddened by the cold wind, his eyes deep green in a private thought as he stared out into the vastness of the water.

"*Magnificent* is the perfect word for this." She turned, faced the sea, and joined him in his stare.

She saw the ocean in all its glory then, thinking she'd never forget this sight for the rest of her life. She also thought she would never forget the look in Sean's eyes as he stared with such love at the sea. She closed her eyes, absorbing the smell and feel of the sea breeze.

"Will ya have another, Sir?" As the waitress addressed Sean, Caroline shook her head and gave a slight chuckle under her breath, glancing at her empty plate.

"Aye, I'll have Guinness if ya will, lassie." Sean smiled wide as the waitress bent in front of him to collect his empty plate, simultaneously giving him an ample view of her enormous breasts, squeezed into a shirt that was two sizes too small.

Caroline watched as his eyes followed her backside when she walked away.

"Do all women fall for your irresistible charm, or is it just the ones in this particular restaurant?" She raised her eyebrows at him in question.

"Do they, now? I hadn't noticed." He gave her a wicked grin. Her face reddened with the knowledge he had caught her in what appeared to be a slight state of jealousy.

"I only meant that ever since we came in here, all the women have been looking at you like you were on the menu or something."

"Aye, well, I've no need of becomin' some lass's desert tonight. What say ya we find our lodgings and call it a night? We've a long drive tomorrow."

"Humm, the thought of a nice, warm bath does sound heavenly. I think I have sea salt covering my entire body."

"Wait till you see what I've got ta show ya tomorrow. Guaranteed ta wear ya out."

He watched her eyes grow large with anticipation, and he thanked the good Lord they would not be sharing a room with her tonight, as it took him great effort to control his growing desire and remain at arm's length from her. He had also discovered she was especially attractive with salty-covered skin.

"Which city is it your business is in?"

Sean shifted uncomfortably in his seat. "Belfast."

"Sean, I've been meaning to ask you, what is it exactly that you do?"

"Um, I'm in public relations," he said, swallowing hard.

"Oh, sorta help the public, so to say?"

"So ta say." He was frowning now. Caroline shifted in her seat and looked at him driving, his brow furrowed, a tone in his voice that indicated she should stop asking questions. She remembered the way Patrick had that exact expression on his face when she spoke to him about Sean. He just kept telling her Sean was a bit of a rebel and left it at that.

Looking over at Sean now, Caroline was puzzled by his expression and wondered what kind of *public relations* he meant exactly.

She was staring at him intently when she caught sight through his window of a red flash over his shoulder. "Sean, slow down; what is that?"

Sean pulled off to the side of the road. "Where?"

"There," she said, pointing out his window.

Turning to look out his window, he smiled and started to unbuckle his seatbelt. "Come on," he yelled and was halfway out his door in an instant.

"Oh, Sean, they look so regal in their outfit."

"Aye, that they do."

They stood leaning against his side of the car, watching the graceful riders on horseback in their pursuit of an unseen prey. Each rider wore a red blazer with matching black derby hats, white pants, and shiny black leather riding boots.

"That there would be a Blazer's Hunt," he said without turning from the sight before them. "Doesn't look as though they're having much luck, though." The corner of his mouth turned up slightly.

"Why do you say that?" she asked.

"See there?" he said, pointing at the horses' legs. "The dogs are all underfoot; they've lost the scent."

Caroline looked at the riders. They were definitely groaning about something, waving their hands, pointing, and looking at the ground beneath them as their horses pranced about in tiny circles.

"What are they hunting?" she asked softly.

"Fox for sure," he answered, turning to look at her.

"Oh," she said and nibbled on her lower lip. He watched her teeth rake gently over it again.

"What will they do if they catch one?"

"Weel, if the dogs don't rip it to pieces, the first one who comes upon it will kill it and rub the blood across his face and the face of the newest member of the hunt."

"I hope they don't find one."

"I hope they don't either, lass, I hope they don't either." He swallowed hard and smiled at her. "Let's go, eh?"

Getting back in the car, he glanced one more time across the meadow, thinking to himself of the first hunt he was in and of the strangely sweet metallic taste of the warm fox blood across his face and lips.

A shiver ran through him as he pulled back onto the narrow road and saw through his rearview mirror the barking dogs headed off again into the woods, the riders in hot pursuit. *We Irish have never been known for our kindness to animals.*

"We best be on our way, lass, if we are ta make the next town before nightfall," Sean said.

"I'm coming," Caroline said as she walked across the bridge. The wind whipped through her jacket, and she tucked her hands into her pockets for warmth despite wearing leather gloves. "The fish are so fun."

"Oh, they are, now? You poor lass, we've got ta show ya some real fun if ya think watchin the salmon leap up the Corrib on the Weir bridge is fun for ya." He laughed then as she met him at the end of the bridge.

"Look at ya now. I leave ya to make a phone call, and ya have gone and froze ta death on me." He wrapped one arm around her shoulders and walked her toward the waiting car.

"What town are we in?"

"Galway."

"It's peaceful here, huh?"

"Aye, for what peace can be found in Ireland these days," he said, opening the car door for her.

"What?"

"Oh, nothin, lass," he said, closing her door. The sick feeling in his stomach grew with each mile they drove toward Belfast.

Caroline closed her eyes, trying to will her body to sleep. After a few moments, she sat up in bed and turned the bedside light on. Knowing it was pointless to keep on trying to sleep now, she slipped out of bed and reached for her robe.

Feeling the cool, wooden floorboards beneath her feet, she walked over to the window and pulled back the curtains. The darkness of the yard made her think of the McNally's home in Limerick. The quiet peacefulness of this quaint, country bed-and-breakfast held the same sort of soothing comfort. *I really could live in Ireland the rest of my life*. With that thought came a small smile, and she could see her reflection in the glass.

Standing there a moment longer, she saw the smile slowly fade as the real implications of exactly what she was doing here in an Irish inn in Ireland took over her thoughts. In an instant, all the memories of Patrick and of what had happened in the last few weeks came flowing back to her, bringing with them a familiar ache in her heart.

Caroline sighed as she leaned against the window frame, her face so close to the glass pane she could see her breath beginning to fog its gleam, her cheek cool against its smoothness.

She thought of Patrick, but someone else was also there, forcing his way into her thoughts and bringing new confusion to her heart. *Sean.*

Tightly closing her eyes, she tried to block Patrick from her memories, barring his formidable presence from her mind's eye. He wouldn't leave. His face was there whenever she closed her eyes. A tear slid down her cheek, and she absently traced the outline of her lips, trying to remember Patrick's taste and feel against them, his breath warm and smelling faintly of peppermint. She inhaled deeply as if to conjure it all and somehow make him more tangible.

Why had Patrick's face become so hard to remember lately? She could see him standing before her, but his features were hazy and fog-like. Her heart felt like it was tearing in two. *How can I have loved someone so much one moment and not remember his face the next? What kind of person am I?*

Turning her back to the window, she folded her arms across her chest and walked over to the chair by the door. Slumping down, she felt a longing for the warmness of the fireplace in her room at the McNally home, not so much for the warmth, though her toes *were* cold. No, it was just the calming effect of the flames warming her soul that she needed now. What she needed most was the gentle effect of the colors that held her eyes captive, mesmerizing her thoughts and leaving her deep inside herself.

Looking over at the wall that joined her room with Sean's, she wondered what he was doing now. Was he asleep? Was he blinded by pictures of the day, as she was, and unable to sleep?

What was it she saw when she looked into those liquid, dark-green eyes of his? Compassion? A sense of honor in holding a promise to a dead brother to keep her safe and protected?

Caroline gathered her cold feet under her in the chair.

"Yes, that was it," she said in a whisper. He must feel overwhelmed by her and this unspoken bond that held him prisoner to her.

Caroline closed her eyes, feeling a small bit of relief at the thought that she'd soon free him of his obligation to her and be on her way home. At the same time, she felt a great sadness about leaving a place she had come to love and a brother who showed her there really were gallant men left in the world.

His breathing slowed, and his heart finally began to calm as he lay in the darkness of his room alone, listening to a restless Caroline in the next room.

He wanted to go to her, to gather her in his arms and hold her against the storms of tears that overwhelmed her in the night. He heard her again tonight as she quietly whimpered alone. At one point, when he thought he wouldn't be able to stand it any longer, he almost burst into her room to try to comfort her, but she stopped—just like she always did, falling asleep with her light on, protecting her from the darkness once again.

Sean rolled over and stared at the light streaming under the door from her room into his. His fist gripped the sheets tightly as his body cried for her with a man's need, but also with his heart's need to love her and his very soul's need to protect her.

How could one woman make him so torn inside? He had been with other women before, known them, bedded them, and thought he loved them, but this was different. This overwhelming feeling he had for Caroline was above all else he'd ever known. It was all-consuming, like a fire raging in his very being. It started out as hate—hate for a woman who would keep his brother in America and far from his family. Then it turned into a simple desire for a beautiful woman. But by the time she gave him the ring from Patrick with all its implications, he had already sensed a greater force driving him to her. Now it was a feeling in his whole essence that drew him to her—a need so great it scared him, so powerful it drained him.

He closed his eyes when he was sure she was asleep, his thoughts floating toward tomorrow and his assignment in Belfast. His political views had also undergone a change with his newfound needs. His taste for vengeance was made bitter with the sweetness of Caroline in his life. Before, driving forces led him relentlessly toward violence and hatred; now they drove him toward peace.

He had already made up his mind to end his hatred with this last mission and start anew. Perhaps if he and others turned from violence toward peace with the same convictions, they just might stop blowing each other up and might find some real and lasting solutions to their problems.

His mouth turned up slightly in one corner. *Now I'm sounding just like Patrick.* He drifted off to sleep seeing his brother's face smiling back at him.

28.

BELFAST

"Oh, Sean, what a wonderful day it's been. I've never had so much fun before!" Caroline laughed as she threw her bags down on the bed in her room.

"Aye, weel it's fer sure you know how ta wear a man out, lass. I'm not sure I'll be up for my meeting now." He collapsed into the overstuffed chair next to him, overexaggerating exhaustion by throwing his arms out over the sides and stretching his long legs out far in front of him.

"Meeting?" she asked, going for the water pitcher on the nightstand. "You really have to leave now? What about dinner?"

"Weel, I'll grab a bite after. As fer you," he said, looking at the bed and then at her, "why don't ya order up and rest your bones. I wish I could do the same. I best be on my way now if I'm not ta be too late." He stood and came toward her beside the bed.

Placing his hands on her shoulders, he looked into her eyes and mustered up a serious expression on his face. It was hard; she was so damn beautiful as she looked up at him innocently, eyes big and trusting.

"What?" she asked, looking with a bit of concern at the look on his face.

"I don't want ya ta go out of this room while I'm gone, do ya hear me, lass? It's verra dangerous in this city, especially for a woman alone after dark. I'll have your promise on that."

Caroline was about to give him her women's lib speech she used on macho men before, but his grip on her shoulders tightened slightly; his demanding presence and the serious look in his eyes told her she'd best give in on this one occasion. After all, this was an overprotective man she was dealing with, and to tell the truth, she was surprised to realize she really liked it about him. It sorta gave him a caveman quality in a slightly charming way. "I will," she said with a mischievous look in her eyes.

"I said I'll have your promise, lass." His eyes grew darker.

"Okay, I promise," she said, quickly giving him a peck on the cheek, feeling the day's growth of stubble on his face.

Caroline stepped out into the cool night air. The shower she took had made a tremendous improvement in her outlook and revived her tired body so much that she soon felt claustrophobic in her hotel room and decided a small hop over to the pub she saw on their way to the hotel was just the thing. Maybe after some Irish ale and a few of those wonderful scones, she'd be back in her bed fast asleep without Sean ever knowing she had gone out.

She put on her gloves and looked down the street to her right, then to her left. It was dark. The streetlights shone down on a few couples linked arm in arm, their shoes making loud crunches on the wet leaves and loose stones while walking down the sidewalk.

"*Which way did we come in by?* She squinted and tried to see down both ways. *Oh, well, you can't swing a dead cat without banging on the door of a pub in Ireland.* She grinned at using the phrase she borrowed from Sean, and she started walking down the right side of the street.

Caroline walked for blocks, not paying much attention to how far, but instead gazing at the wonderful rows and rows of houses that stood three and four stories high along the road. *They're so beautiful*, she thought to herself as she pictured them all lit up at Christmas with giant decorated trees in the front windows and big, green wreaths with red, velvet bows adorning the doors.

The section of the street changed, and she soon found herself at a fork in the road. One way headed to what appeared to be a more downtown area of the city, while the other seemed to go off in the direction of a huge, stone bridge and shipyards of some sort.

"Just a quick peek at the water, Sean," she said to herself and arched off toward the bridge.

The bridge itself was mammoth in size, and Caroline soon found herself in the middle, leaning on her elbows and looking over the stone railing. The water was black; seemingly without depth, it stretched on forever in the night, and Caroline felt a chilly wind whip through her jeans. Shivering, she decided to head toward the hotel and take Sean's advice to order room service. Turning to leave, she bumped into a young man with his hands stuffed deeply into the pockets of his pants. "Oh!"

"Sorry, mum, I didn't mean to frighten ya now."

"Oh, no, it's my fault; I wasn't paying much attention," she said, trying to lighten the scared mood she suddenly found herself in.

"Weel now, look what we've got ourselves here, lads—an American lass, and she's all alone."

Caroline turned quickly to see two other young men coming up from behind her from the other side of the bridge. Her heart was racing, beating so fast she thought it might leap out of her chest. She was in serious trouble, and she knew it. "I'd best be on my way, boys, if you will excuse me." She turned toward her right, knowing it was not the way back but not caring to go through the three boys who now blocked her way.

"Did ya hear what the lass said, lads? She's gone and called us, boys. I feel a bit insulted m'self; I'm thinkin we should show this American lass what a real Irish welcome is. What say you?"

Caroline didn't hear the others reply as she broke into a fast sprint that soon became a run for her life. She didn't turn back to see if they were close, but the sound of their boots was echoing in her ears as she headed for an empty building, with a prayer there might be a watchman on duty.

She ran through the darkened parking lot; not a single streetlight was on. Her tennis shoes crackled with the sound of broken glass under her feet.

Oh, God, she thought when she heard their voices rounding the corner of the tall, brick building. Her heart was screaming in her chest as she realized she had turned into a dead-end alley. She could hear Sean's words of warning as she searched desperately for a weapon, as there were no apparent means of escape. If she was going to die, she'd be damned if she let them rape her without a fight.

Caroline swallowed hard when she saw the first one stop at the entrance of the alley. "I've got er, lads," he yelled, and the other two came to his sides.

Walking toward her, the one who was apparently the leader said to the others, "I'll get to poke her first, seein how I found her first."

Caroline felt a wave of nausea as he came close enough for her to get a good whiff of his breath, which stank of strong liquor and cigarettes.

"You'll have to kill me first—that is, if I don't kill you first!" She lunged at him with the sharp piece of broken glass she held hidden behind her back.

"AAAGH!!" The boy stumbled backward, grabbing his cheek, red blood flowing freely through his fingers. "Get her!" he roared to the others as she rushed past him.

"AAAGH!" She screamed as her cheek hit the roughness of the brick wall, and she fought the blackness that threatened her senses. Fingers dug into her arms as one of the other two slammed her up against the wall, pinning her there.

"I'll make her pay with my pleasure before sending her ta meet her maker," he yelled back at his friend, who was still writhing on the ground.

"Aye, and make damn sure ya leave her still screamin for me, eh? I aint about to poke no corpse." The man hissed as he grabbed her hands. Caroline winced at the pain of the deep cut on her palm from holding the broken glass. "Where ya want to do her?"

"Over there," he said as he lifted himself off her, pointing to a ratty old couch next to a trash dumpster.

Caroline struggled between the two as they dragged her over to the couch, kicking and screaming all the way.

"I said I get her first!"

Caroline gasped when she saw the one she cut standing before her with a deep gash along his cheek and halfway down his neck. He had taken off his coat and stood before her with blood staining his shirt and a look of hatred burning in his eyes.

"Yea, yea, do it, and let's be gone. She's made enough screechin ta row the Brits."

He walked closer to her, and suddenly his wet mouth was on hers. She gagged back the bile rising in the back of her throat. Pulling back, he ripped her shirt all the way down to her waist. "No!" She screamed as his hands fondled her breasts. In another instant, he gave a quick jerk as her bra gave way, spilling her breasts into full view.

Caroline heard a united gasp as all three looked at her nakedness, their eyes raking over her. She felt a sick sense of irony in the comment she'd made to Sean about him being some waitress's dessert as she felt hot tears flowing down the sides of her face.

"Round the back, lads," the one with the gash said as his hands went to his belt.

"No! Please!" she screamed as the two holding her arms flung her face-forward over the back of the couch. She knew right at that moment he intended to take her from behind like the rutting dog he was. A wave of shame swept over her as he came up behind her and began to pull her jeans down over her buttocks, exposing them to the bitter night air. With his hands on her hips, she felt him prepare to enter her and wished for death along with the pain that was surely coming.

"Hold it right there, lad, unless ya want me ta shoot yer willy off!"

Caroline heard her attackers collectively gasp as she felt their hands loosen their grip on her arms. She sank to the ground with her back to them; she couldn't see what was happening.

"Sweet Jesus, it's the bloody IRA," one of them growled.

"You lads best be on your way; you've done enough damage here, and I'm in the mood ta shoot some bloody knees off, Brit or no!"

When Caoline heard the sound of their boots running away from her, she grasped at her coat with one hand to hide her nakedness and pulled her pants up with the other.

"Here now, lass, it's all over now; they're gone."

She felt a strong hand helping her up and attempting to shield her from the others at the same time. "Thank you," she managed to whisper, her voice hoarse from screaming.

Caroline took a step back when she finally looked into the face of her reluctant savior. He had no face at all, just a black ski mask. Her free hand went to her mouth when she looked at him and the three others standing a few feet away. All of them were dressed in black, wearing black ski masks with machine guns strapped to their shoulders.

She watched the one who helped her up; his eyes grew large as if he saw something about her that terrified him. She clutched her coat tighter when he turned to the others, and they started conversing in Gaelic.

"Oh, my god!" She gasped loudly as she recognized his voice. "Michael?" she asked.

They all immediately stopped talking. "Aye, it's me, lass," he said guiltily as he raised his ski mask above his eyes and pulled it off. His soft eyes smiled at her.

"Paul and Willy, is that you?" she asked the others.

Both answered, "Aye," and lifted their own masks up. The third lifted his, and Caroline didn't recognize him.

"That there is Wasp, or so he likes to be called," Michael said.

"Michael, what in God's name are you all doing here, and why on earth are you dressed like that?" Caroline was totally in the dark as to why Sean's friends were in Belfast and dressed like a SWAT team.

"Caroline, we might just be askin you that verra same question, lass. What on earth are ya doin in this rundown section with those lads in the middle of the night?" Paul asked her as the others nodded in agreement.

"I, I just went for a walk, and I lost track of how far I was from the hotel," her teeth were chattering now. "I just wanted some fresh air. Sean told me to . . . *Oh, my God.* Sean is going to kill me when he finds out; you have to get me back to the hotel. Does he know you are all here?"

They looked at each other in silence, and then Michael cleared his throat.

"Aye, lass, he knows," Michael said. "Come round with us; our bus is just around the corner. Ya best be gettin out of this night air, and ya've had quite a shock." He put his arm around her, and the five of them left the alley. On her way around the corner of the building, Caroline turned one last time and looked over her shoulder. The black leather jacket of the boy whose face she had slashed lay on the ground, its zipper shimmering in the iridescent moonlight. The sight of it and the thought of what might have happened made her shiver far worse than any chill of the night air.

"Here, lass," Michael said as they paused outside the minivan. He took his own coat off and then proceeded to lift his black sweater over his head, leaving on his matching black turtleneck. "Ya go on in the bus while we wait here for ya ta change." He held the sweater out to her and opened the back door of the van.

"I don't know what I would have done if you hadn't come along when you did," Caroline said. "You know, you really saved my life back there. I don't know if I'll ever be able to repay you." She reached out and took the sweater from him, looking into his gentle eyes. "*Thank you* doesn't seem quite enough for something like this."

"It's more than enough, lass," Michael said softly, and she saw him blush when he took her hand to help her into the van.

When he closed the door, she turned to see that the four men had discreetly turned their backs to the window, and she smiled with the wash of relief that she was in the presence of decent men again, listening to them converse in Gaelic.

Pulling the sweater over her head, she smelled Michael's scent and felt the warmness of his body still lingering on it. Her mind was just now beginning to grasp what had just happened a few short minutes ago.

Did she hear her attackers collectively? *Did they say Michael and Sean's other friends were the IRA? Well, they certainly look the part in their outfits and guns.* Her mind reeled at the implications, and though she knew little of the IRA's activities in Ireland, she did know enough from the Western news reports to figure out that they were no one to be meeting up with in dark alleys.

A quick knock on the van's door ripped her away from her thoughts.

"Caroline, we best be on our way, lass," she heard Michael's voice taking on an air of command in its tone.

"Are you going to take me back to the hotel now?" she asked Michael, opening the door and stepping outside to put her jacket back on.

"Weel, lass, that's what we got ta talk to ya about. Ya see, we don't have the time right now, and we are late for a meetin that we can't miss, ya see, and—"

"Ya've got ta tag along with us for now," Paul interrupted.

"Oh, where is your meeting?" she asked. She knew they were serious, but she couldn't very well say no to the men who had just saved her life a few moments ago.

"Just up the river a bit—and Caroline," Michael said, looking into her eyes and grabbing onto her shoulders with strong hands, "it could prove a bit dangerous for ya."

"Dangerous? You mean more than what just happened to me back there?" She gave him a slight grin, and his mood changed as he let go of her and joined the others in a good laugh. "Ya got spunk, lass, that's fer sure! Come on, then, let's be on our way."

"She'll be needin a bit of this," Wasp said as he held out a small container of blackish substance.

"Oh, aye, thanks," Michael said, taking the jar from him and dipping two fingers in it.

Caroline felt the cool slipperiness of the black oil against her cheeks as he wiped a generous amount across each one, her forehead, nose, and lastly her chin and neck.

"Since we got no mask for ya, this will have to do," he joked.

"Is this meeting we're going to illegal, Michael?" She swallowed hard, waiting for his answer and not so sure she wanted to hear it.

"Weel, that does depend on who's been making the laws in these parts lately. The ones with the most guns rule here, lass." She saw his brow furrow and knew whatever meeting she was about to participate in tonight wasn't going to be held in any boardroom.

"We walk from here, lads and lassie," Paul said, looking over at Caroline as he parked the van along a deserted stretch of the riverbank. "Won't be long now."

Waiting in the darkness, an eerie feeling crept over Caroline as she thought of herself waiting along the still water.

Since she was a slightly reluctant member of this group, they hadn't offered her a gun. She looked over at the men beside her; the impressive weapons that hung on their shoulders gleamed under the light of the moon. She gave a sigh and hoped they were meant for looks only.

"Here they come, lads," Willy whispered next to her. He was slightly out of place among the other three men with his stout little legs and smaller frame, but the way he held his gun suggested one didn't have to be tall for this business.

Caroline froze when she heard the faint sound of a boat engine, its volume growing as it came closer. Within moments, she saw what appeared to be a small ferry boat; an unmarked dark blue van was its only passenger. "Wait here, lass, and don't come out till I call fer ya," Willy hissed. She nodded with her eyes.

Her eyes wide as saucers, she watched as the small ferry glide close to the railing, slipping past them quietly as they stood undetected in the shadows. When the ferry passed them, she saw two armed policemen in the back, one steering and the other looking into the night with his gun ready.

Her heart raced when the ferry stopped along the side of the rail a few yards from where she stood with Sean's friends. She blinked in surprise when she heard a man's voice inside the van yell out to the two policemen on the outside. "What the 'ell you slowin down for? This is not the place ta meet the others!"

Caroline watched in horror as the two policemen in the back pointed their guns at the back door of the van and opened fire. Bright flashes of light bounced off the door as bullets riddled the area around the door handle. There was little sound; the men had obviously placed silencers on their own guns before opening fire.

"Open the door! You've no fightin' chance now, lads!"

"We'll not die for the IRA tonight, lads, we'll be comin out," a man inside the van yelled back. Caroline let her breath out as she watched the door open and two men in police uniforms exit with their hands up in the air in an attitude of surrender.

Just then, the four men she'd been standing with left her side and darted over to the ferry.

"Hand us yer rope, lads." Paul held out his hand to catch the rope thrown to him. Willy and Michael jumped up onto the ferry and raced past the other two men in uniform, who were forcing the real policemen face down to the ground, placing their guns at the base of their necks.

Caroline placed her hand over her mouth when she saw Michael and Willy carrying out a young man, one on each side. He appeared to be extremely weak and had quite a bit of trouble walking on his own. "Come out and give us a hand, lass!" She thought she might faint, but she quickly raced over to where they were placing the young man on his back on firm land at the side of the railing.

She gasped loudly when she caught sight of the young boy who appeared to be nothing more than a teenager; his face was badly bruised, and there was dried blood on one corner of his mouth. She quickly checked for broken bones, relieved to find none.

Smiling at the boy, she softly placed her hand on his cheek. "He's fine so far as I can tell, just a little worse for wear." He smiled shyly back at her.

She stood as Michael and Willy lifted the young boy up and carried him off to their waiting van. She started to follow when she heard Paul loudly arguing with the two fat policemen, their backs to the real ones who were lying on the ground.

Looking over at the ferry, she saw one of the men on the ground reaching into his pocket and pulling something out. She squinted as if to get a better look. "Wasp, look out!" she screamed, catching sight of the barrel of the small gun in the policeman's hand.

She closed her eyes tightly, not wanting to see the sight that might be ahead of her. A few seconds seemed like a week, but when she opened her eyes, she saw the glorious sight of Wasp walking toward her with a wide smile on his face.

She raced over to him and gave him a giant bear hug. "I was afraid I yelled too late."

"I'll thank ya, lass, for savin me life," he said into her hair as she felt him stiffen in her arms. She pulled away, taking a step backward so she could see his face. His features were a mixture of emotions, and Caroline could not make out what they were saying to her, but the rush of redness to his face told her how embarrassed he'd become.

"You'll not want ta see that, lass," he said as he reached out to turn her from the sight of the boat behind him.

"They're not going to—" She couldn't finish the words as she caught sight of the men on board scrambling to subdue the one with the gun.

"Nay, lass, they'll just tie 'em up and set 'em out to float a bit is all. Do not worry your pretty little head about those two."

Caroline tried to smile, but she didn't take much comfort from his words.

On the drive back through town, Caroline looked out her window and frowned as they drove right past her hotel.

"Hey, you passed it!" she said, tapping Paul on the shoulder as he drove on into the night.

"Nay, lass, ya won't be goin back there tonight. We're on our way to a warehouse just out of town," he said, looking at her through the rearview mirror.

"Aye, Caroline, you're one of us now, like it or not."

She felt her heart sink as she looked across the seat at Michael, who was sitting next to her. She felt a sick feeling in her stomach thinking about Sean and knowing it was no use to argue with his friends. She looked out into the darkness as they drove further and further away from the hotel and Sean.

"This 'er is yer room for the night, Missy. There's fresh tow'es and soap in the bath for ya. I'll be up in a few wi' a snack, ya poor dearie; ya look exhausted ya, do."

Caroline smiled and nodded at the plump little lady. Her eyebrows lifted slightly as she gave Caroline a flash of yellow-stained, crooked teeth.

Watching the woman toddling off down the hall, Caroline leaned against the door frame of the room. Her head was spinning, and every bone in her body ached. She closed her eyes, sighing and rolling her head up and around, trying to release some of the tension in her neck and shoulders. Perhaps she would try to call Sean, but first she wanted to take a nice hot bath with a lot of soap.

Caroline scrubbed her skin like a woman possessed. The need to rid herself of the dirt and oil was nothing compared to the need to erase the memory of the attack earlier in the evening.

As she soaped the washcloth again, she wondered how she could have ever been so stupid as to go out alone after dark in a strange city. *Sean is going to kill me; he's going to think I'm the stupidest person in the world!* She let the washcloth fall into her lap and felt the tears beginning to rush down her cheeks as wave after wave of emotion swept over her, leaving her sobbing uncontrollably. Tears dripped into the fragile, white bubbles.

Sitting on the floor in front of the fire, she ran her fingers through her long curls for lack of a brush. The warmth of the flames soothed her worn body, leaving it flushed and hot. Drying her hair there on the floor with a towel wrapped around her, she heard a small knock on the door.

"Come in," she said, absently checking the position of the towel. The clothes she had left on the bed had disappeared during her bath.

"'Er ya go, dearie," the little woman said as she strode into the room with an armful of clothes. "I thought ya might like these, seein 'owl I took ya other ones ta be washed an all—not that the'll be in any too good of shape as torn as they were." She placed the clothes on the bed and glanced down at Caroline with a smile. "It's gonna be all right now, lass; yer safe w'us for the night. No one bothers us out 'er in these parts."

"Thank you, you're very kind . . . Mrs.?" Caroline asked.

"Oh, the lads all call me Lou, dearie. I've never seen you before," she said, narrowing her eyes. "How's a pretty little lassie like you get mixed up w'the likes of those lads?"

"Just luck, I guess." Caroline didn't know how much Lou knew of the group's activities or what they told her about her being with them, and she wasn't about to say more than she should. "Do you have a phone I might use?"

"Sure, lassie, come on don when yer dressed an I'll fix ya up." With that, she was out the door, closing it loudly behind her.

Well, this will have to do, I suppose, Caroline thought as she buttoned up the large man's shirt. It fell well below her knees, and she had to roll the sleeves up several times just to get them above her hands.

She sat on the bed and began to pull on the socks when she was suddenly aware of a loud commotion coming from downstairs. Her heart began to pound when she heard someone bounding up the stairs and down the hallway toward her room.

Oh, my God! she thought as she leapt off the bed. *It's the police! It's the police, and I'm going to spend the rest of my life in an Irish prison.*

For the second time in one night, she looked for an escape and found none. Suddenly, the door burst open. She jumped as a huge man dressed in the same black outfit she'd seen Sean's friends wearing earlier stood in the doorway. She took a step backward, fear rising in the pit of her stomach.

"What the hell are ya doing here and dressed like that, lass?" The deepness of his voice made her legs weaken as she watched his hands go up to take his mask off.

"Sean!" she screamed as she ran into his outstretched arms.

"I did not mean ta frighten ya, lass. It's just yer the last person I meant ta find here. Caroline, can't ya do as yer told?" His hands were stroking her damp hair, bringing the sweet scent wafting up to his nostrils as she sobbed in his arms.

Her body was pressed so tightly against his that her arms clung for dear life the way she had in the airport when she first thought him to be Patrick.

"I, I . . . Oh, Sean, I'm so glad to see you!" She pressed her cheek against his chest, feeling the steely hardness of his muscles beneath his sweater and smelling the mixture of outdoors mingled with his own masculine scent.

"It's all right now, lass, I'm here, I'm here," he whispered with his chin resting on the top of her head.

The flood of emotions finally subsided, clearing the way for a new, more powerful tide of feelings that were spreading through her. She raised her head and looked into his soft, green eyes that held her in their loving gaze. He pulled her closer to him, and in an instant, his mouth was on hers, drinking her in, tasting her lips with such passion she'd never dreamed of.

Her arms went around his neck, her fingers lacing through the thickness of his hair and urging him closer still. She melted into him, not yet being able to let go. His arms suddenly slid down her waist, and she was effortlessly picked up as his mouth never left hers. He finally pulled back, standing perfectly still, his eyes burned into hers for a final approval before kicking the door shut and carrying her over to the bed. He didn't think he would be able to stop now. His body was screaming for her.

He laid her down gently, never allowing their bodies to lose contact as he followed her down, his kisses burning a trail along her neck and shoulders. "I love ya, lass. I've loved ya from the first," he whispered in her ear.

She felt his breath hot and ragged as he pressed himself down on top of her, balancing his weight with his elbows. He stood then, and she closed her eyes while he undressed.

She couldn't believe it. His hands were stroking her, his mouth seeking hers in inflamed passion. His tongue ran along her lips, seeking entrance to mate with hers. When she opened up, giving him access to it, she felt a groan deep in the back of his throat.

His hand reached down and raised her thigh. As he stroked the smooth skin, his touch left a hot trail where his fingers had been. She arched her back slightly, pressing his hardness at the juncture of her most intimate part. He was so gentle, his touch light as a feather.

He heard her let out a quiet moan as he raised up to undo the buttons of her shirt. His hands trembled when they spread apart the shirt, exposing her full breasts to him. He took one hardened nipple in his mouth while his other hand kneaded and toyed with the other.

Caroline wriggled beneath him, her own chest heaving in great sighs as his mouth moved to the other hardened nipple, his hand slowly moving down to her stomach. With his thigh draped over hers, he led his hand to the softness of her, his fingers sliding gently in the wetness he'd created, seeking out the nub of her desire.

She gasped as his fingers drew her close to the edge. She put her hand atop his, lifting herself against him. Sensing her need, he moved, placing himself between her thighs and letting his hardness rest between their moistened skin.

She rose up, her arms grasping his shoulders and feeling the strain of the corded muscles tighten. "Please," she whispered, feeling the dampness of his sweat-soaked hair swaying loose about his shoulders against her cheeks. He rose slightly to position himself. She felt him enter her, bringing fire with him. He hesitated for a moment as he gazed into her eyes. He thrust into her. Then, with their eyes still locked, she opened her mouth to scream with the passion he filled her with, but in the same instant, his mouth was covering hers, his tongue like soft velvet.

Sean. The fullness of him was overwhelming, his desire almost animal-like as he thrust deeper and deeper. She held tight to him, feeling the same need to become one in the night together.

"Say it again, lass," he said breathlessly.

"Sean," she said softly, biting his earlobe.

"Sean, Sean . . . Sean," she whispered again and again as they drove deeper into each other, deeper into the depths of need and deeper into the sea of love until the waves of release brought them safely to shore in an exhausted heap of mingled heat, sweat, and tears.

Not breaking apart, they lay in a tight embrace, their mingled smells of each other drifting in the air.

"Sean?" Caroline asked softly enough not to wake him in case he was asleep.

"Yes, love."

"If those men had . . . would you still have wanted me?" She held her breath with her head resting on his chest in the crook of his shoulder, listening to his heartbeat.

"If those men had . . ." He hesitated, and Caroline closed her eyes tightly. "The only difference is I would have killed them first."

His arms tightened around her, enclosing her within his strength. She knew his words were no threat, and she smiled as she felt the warmness of the safety surrounding her and listened to the slow, even breathing of a man she held deep within her heart.

Caroline found herself dancing on the deserted stage again, only this time she was not alone. She was being swept to the soft music by a man who held her close to him, his strong arms gliding her around and around in his embrace.

She looked straight ahead into his chest, wide and impressive. He wore a black suit with a white shirt and a matching tie. Her eyes lifted to his face. Her heart was beating fast and hard; never before had she seen this face who beckoned her to dance time and time again.

She closed her eyes, half afraid after the last dream that left her with Patrick's blood on her hands. Opening them slowly, she looked up. Green, liquid eyes gazed lovingly down at her, and his mouth held a familiar slight grin. "Sean!" she yelled. "Sean."

"Wake up, lass, wake up. It's Sean; I'm here." He had heard her yell out and came running from the bathroom to find her in the midst of a dream, yelling his name.

"It's you!" she said, raising up to wrap her arms around his neck. "I love you."

"Oh, Caroline, I hadn't dared hope ya would love me. I have loved ya all this time from afar, wantin ta make ya mine, but I never dreamed ya would love me, not in a million years."

His kiss was searing, and she pulled him atop her on the bed.

"No, lass. We can't; we've got ta go now," he said, looking at her apologetically.

"But Sean . . ." she said teasingly as she gently bit his shoulder where she'd pulled down his shirt. She could feel his desire growing against her thigh, and she knew he was putting up a brave fight.

"Why, Caroline, I thought ya were such a proper lady and all," he smiled, reveling in her soft kisses along his neck, "and look at ya, practically raping me." He felt her suddenly stop and immediately knew the error of what he had said.

"Oh, God, Caroline, I never meant . . . I mean, I would never mean to . . ." He pulled her close to him and closed his eyes against the guilt overwhelming him. She lay still against him, feeling the fresh stab of pain that riddled her own heart with guilt.

"Caroline, it's just that when I came here last night, and Michael told me what had happened to ya, well, I was so angry. Angry at myself for leaving ya alone and not bein there ta protect ya. If they would have . . . if they would have hurt ya more than they did . . . if I were ta lose ya—"

"Shhhh," she interrupted, placing her fingers to his lips. He kissed them, and she pulled his head to her breast, gently stroking his hair. "I'll forgive you, if you forgive me?"

"Forgive you?" he asked, surprised.

"For not listening when you warned me to stay put, and for making us go so long without each other. Sean?" she asked as he tightened his hold around her waist.

"Do you think Patrick would mind? I mean about you and me and all."

"Weel, I guess he'd tan me good if he found out I let ya get involved with Michael and the lads and all, but if yer asking if he minds that you and I are now together, no, no, he doesn't mind, lass." He smiled and snuggled against the roundness of her soft breasts with his arms around her tiny waist. His mind savored the feeling of being so close to her now; his body never wanted to be further away from hers than this for the rest of his life.

"Sean, why did those friends of yours take me along with them last night? I'm sure it would have been all right to take me back to the hotel."

"It was their way of checkin ya out is all. Ya see, they wanted ta see where ya loyalties were, and they knew I'd be round here after my meeting anyway."

"Sean?"

"Hmm?"

She already knew the answer to the question she was about to ask, but she needed him to explain it to her anyway.

"Are you, like Michael and the others? Are you in the IRA?"

He turned his body so that he faced her. With his face so close she could feel the warmness of his breath, he answered, "Aye, lass, I am—and so are you, Caroline, like it or not."

He kissed her then as waves of mixed emotions went through her body. This man that she loved was a member of a terrorist group, and he had just told her she was too.

He pulled the covers off her, his hands seeking to fulfill her again as she let him erase the terrible thoughts clouding her mind. She loved him. She loved him no matter what, and as he slipped inside her again, she arched to meet him, her thoughts turning toward the burning desire he had awakened and to the love she was lucky enough to find for the second time in her life.

29.

CASTLES

The long road stretched ahead of him, lined on one side with short, rock walls and the ocean on the other. Sean was feeling anxious.

"Are ya hungry?" Sean asked. He glanced over at Caroline, who was staring out her window. Her long hair tumbled down her back. Memories of the night before and this morning's lovemaking kept invading his thoughts. Her passion for life spilled over into her passion for love. She gave with an open honesty he'd never felt from another woman before. She gave herself to him so completely that it made him take stock and rethink his every action. He vowed he would guard his love for her and protect it and her with his very life.

Looking over at her now, a new sense of pride raked his heart. She was so gentle in spirit, yet so utterly spirited that it caused a slight heaviness in his chest just looking at her and wondering if she could ever love him. It was almost physically painful.

Frowning, Sean noticed she had become increasingly quiet along the drive. He had specifically chosen the Antrim Coast Road for its spectacular scenery along the ocean, but she seemed a little too quiet to just be enjoying the sights.

"Caroline, love?" His chest felt another pang when she turned to him, her green eyes clouded with unspoken emotions.

"Yes?" she said softly through the full lips that had been his just hours ago.

"Is everything all right? You're so quiet?"

"Sean, can we pull over? It's so beautiful here, and I'd like to take a walk with you right down there along the beach," she said, pointing toward the deserted stretch of coastline below them. "Would you mind?"

"How's this?" he asked, stopping the car on the side of the road as he reached over, taking her hand and giving it a gentle squeeze.

She looked down at their locked hands and then up at him, smiling. "Perfect."

"You'll have ta watch your step here; it's a bit tricky."

Caroline held fast to his hand in front of her. She liked the gallant way he insisted on going down first to test the steps and to be there to catch her should she fall. He turned and lifted her off a large rock and onto the sand. His large hands spanned her waist and made her feel extremely feminine and a little flushed with the heat they left behind from his touch.

She stopped and stood facing the ocean with her eyes closed, deeply inhaling the sea air as she said, "I love the ocean."

He took a chance and reached out, pulling her close while tilting her head up with his thumb under her chin. "Is the ocean the only thing ya love?"

She smiled wide, her hair dancing widely around her shoulders and down her back with the breeze from the sea. "I do love you, Sean McNally. I love you like I've never loved anyone before except for . . ."

She hesitated, then suddenly lowered her face and tried to pull away from him.

That only made him want to hold her tighter. He wanted to never let her go. Knowing that it was *Patrick* she had meant to say, his fingers bit into her upper arms. He felt no guilt when it came to taking her love from his brother, and he knew she would have to face her decision to choose to love him straight on, or Patrick would forever remain between them. Sean also knew it was time to tell her about the ring, the meaning of Patrick's Gaelic words. He had never dreaded anything more in his entire life.

She leaned back against him. His arms came instinctively around her, engulfing her in his warmth and protection. They sat in the sun, and she could feel the cool grains of sand under her and Sean's heat radiating from behind her. His arms were around her, and she was surrounded by a blanket of warmth and love.

The Gaelic words he slowly translated for her were simple, but true. Patrick had wanted her to be with Sean, wanted them to love each other. He had known she would need him when Patrick was gone. Hot tears welled in her eyes at the painful vision of Patrick dying on the floor in the stockroom and knowing that, through all the pain he must have felt, with all of the things that might have been racing through his mind as he lay dying, his only thought was for her. Tears coursed down her cheeks and fell onto her lap.

Sean shifted, pulling her even closer and resting his chin on her shoulder. "Do ya believe me when I tell ya it would have made no difference ta me if he had never given ya the ring ta give ta me? I would have loved ya without it."

She nodded but was unable to speak through the lump in her throat. The tears began flowing faster.

"Caroline, when ya come into a room, it's like the room is on fire—or at least I am, anyhow. I canna breathe, and my hands get all sweaty. I thought I knew what real life was before, being in the IRA, but now I know there is a difference between real life and the life that ya come ta know on a daily basis." He swallowed hard, and he placed his forehead against her back.

"I love ya so much it scares me, Caroline, like I can't control myself with the need of wanting ya so much." She turned to face him. It was her turn to lift his head up. Looking up into his face, she cupped it with both hands and kissed him with all the love burning in her heart.

It was the most charming place Caroline had ever seen. It had high, sunny ceilings and thick wooden beams that had darkened with the ages. It smelled of sweet hay, horses, and fresh foods.

"Oh, aye!" he said, "but that is not enough food ta feed even this young lad here." Sean's large hand tousled the bright-red hair of the little boy standing next to them. His mother looked from Sean to Caroline, her eyes lingering just a few seconds longer on Sean.

"Yer on yer honeymoon, ain't ya?" she asked, giving a knowing look back and forth between the two of them and nodding.

Caroline could feel the blood rushing to her face. "Oh . . ." She started to protest, but Sean quickly put his arm around her shoulder.

"Why, yes, ma'am, how'd ya guess?" he asked, goading the woman. He squeezed Caroline close into his side and gave her a little peck on her cheek.

"It's the lassie, the way she looks at ya when ya ain't watchin." She pulled the little boy up from the baskets of fruit. "Come along, lad, this 'ere new bride's best be fillin her man's belly w'more than love if she means ta keep 'im."

When the woman was off amid the other shoppers, Caroline turned and gave Sean a punch in the arm. "You" was all she got out before his mouth came down hard on hers. She sighed as he pulled her closer and reveled in the long, thorough kiss he was giving her.

Suddenly, he pulled away. "I almost forgot, I've something for ya," he said, pulling a key out of his pocket.

"How'd ya like ta stay the night in a real castle?" He gave her a quick wink.

"Really? How . . . when did you . . . Sean, you know I would!"

"Come on, let's eat! I'm starvin, and not for food," he said as he pulled her out the door and toward the main castle.

The room itself was quite beautiful with its four-poster, antique bed, and delicately carved headboard. Thick pillows and rugs were intricately woven with soft tapestries of greens, reds, and browns. A crystal-and-brass lamp adorned the nightstand, and several pieces of dark period furniture sat about the room.

Caroline marveled at the windows, two on either side of the bed that went from floor to ceiling, covered with thick, heavy, woven draperies that fell to the floor in great billows of fabric. Looking out over the massive grounds, she could see the comings and goings of the tourists and the little horse-drawn carts bringing the happy passengers back and forth down a long stretch of driveway leading to the castle from the main road.

She smiled as she tried to see Sean, who was close to the floor in front of the fireplace. All the fireplaces everywhere were probably the best thing about Ireland. She stood watching as he knelt to arrange the logs, his unbound hair falling across his face and swaying with his movements. It was dark and fathomless like him. She felt relief from the guilt that had plagued her after their lovemaking this morning, a happy result of the earlier talk they shared at the beach. Tonight, they would belong to each other free of pain and free of the past. "I'll be back in a little while," she said as he stood from the now-blazing fire.

He gave her a grin she loved so much as he watched her pull something from her suitcase and head off toward the bathroom. He turned to gaze into the fire, his thoughts focused on her soft, full mouth and the gentle sway of her hips as she walked away.

She waited in a chair by the fire, its soft glow lighting the darkened room. *What's the deal? Maybe he changed his mind; no, not with that devilish grin on his face earlier. He left twenty minutes ago on a mysterious errand; what was taking him so long?* Just when her thoughts were trying to betray her again, she looked up to see him coming through the door.

"Sean?" She looked at him with a questioning attitude, her head tilted to one side. In his hands, he held a bottle of wine, two long-stemmed glasses, and a tray with an assortment of cheeses, meats, and fruits. "How do you keep doing that?"

Giving him a hand, she noticed how nice he smelled. A little further investigation revealed that his hair was damp and he was clean-shaven. Narrowing her eyes at him, she asked in a teasing tone, "Where have you been?"

"There's a nice lad just down the hall a bit, seemed more than happy to accommodate a fellow out. All in all, an all-around nice gent," he said, stepping back to get a good look at her. "God, lassie, but ya are beautiful!" he said as his eyes roamed her body. She was wearing the light rose silk gown, and her hair hung loose in great cascades of raven curls down her back. In the glow of the fire, her hair took on a deeper shade, enhancing the fairness of her skin.

"I'm not going to be able ta keep that on ya very long," he said, looking at the deep neckline of her gown.

"I hope not," she said seductively, reaching out and undoing the buttons of his shirt. His passions flared as she slid his shirt off his shoulders, leaving it tucked into his pants and hanging around his thighs.

"Sean?" she said quietly, nipping at his shoulders and licking her tongue along the middle of his chest, sending new waves of sweet touches up his spine.

"Hmmm . . ." He finally managed in a small groan.

"Tonight, I want to show you how much you mean to me in every way," she said as her fingers made quick work of his belt and pants zipper.

"But . . ." he protested. Still, he did not move his hands from his shoulders.

"No *buts*," she said, sliding his pants to the floor, her hands gliding slowly down the back of his legs, gently squeezing at the hardness of his buttocks.

"Nay, Caroline, I'll not have ya at my feet on the floor," he said, lifting her up to meet him face to face. "I love ya enough ta never see ya knelt before me."

She looked into his eyes, his pride filling her own. This man would see her only as an equal, fifty-fifty in all matters. Her love nearly took her breath away as he pulled her toward the bed, sitting her down in front of him, his hands on her shoulders.

She started to reach for his waist when he grabbed both her hands in his, lifting them above her head. He held her hands captive with one of his while pulling her gown up and over her head with the other. He then let her hands go as he slid his hands slowly down her body, feeling every curve and valley until they rested on her thighs and he was on his knees in front of her.

She reached out and pulled his head to her breasts, separating her legs to bring his body closer as his arms hugged her waist. "Caroline," he whispered, taking a hardened nipple into his mouth.

Caroline thought her body was on fire as she threw her head back and moaned at his touch. She brought her legs around his waist, urging him closer still, wanting him inside her, filling her with his own need. She lay back on the bed, grabbing his hair and frantically trying to pull him up to her mouth.

He lifted from her.

"Sean," she begged, as his hands sought out her body with great intensity, feeling their way in the glowing light of the fire. She had her own fire burning a trail along her secret parts. She opened her eyes, looking right into his as he sought entrance into her. He thrust hard as he threw his head back and groaned with the force. Hot liquid surrounded him, and soft velvet stroked him into frenzy as he buried his head into her hair, lifting her hips and speaking soft words of love.

She slept peacefully beside him. His hand rested across her breast, feeling the steady drum of her heartbeat beneath his palm. His life would be forever changed by her; all he would know would change, and all he would hold dear would disappear as his love for her overtook him.

Sean closed his heavy eyes and drifted off in the embrace of something with so great a hold on him that he found himself surrounded by its beauty. For the first time in his life, he also felt fear from the enemy who had always been his friend.

30.

FRIEND OR FOE

Caroline woke slowly, feeling for him across the span of the bed in the darkness beside her. She knew instantly he was not there. Her hand smoothed over the sheet, feeling its soft wrinkles. It was cool against her palm. She rolled on her side and rested her hand on his pillow.

A sudden billowing of the curtains brought a gush of cool air into the room, sweetly reminding her of the love she and Sean made a short time ago and the need to open the window for some much-needed cool air to fill the room and soothe their fiery passions, which had left them soaked in mingled sweat.

Reaching for his pillow, she hugged it closely to her, inhaling the masculine smell of him and feeling the waves of intense, warm emotions beginning to spread through her being. He had become a part of her soul, and now he dwelt within the confines of her heart. She never imagined a man could mean so much to her, not even Patrick in all the real love she had felt for him. This was different, edgier.

She closed her eyes tightly. She had been so in need of this that she could not in a million years fathom how she had survived so long without it.

Fear gripped her as she fought back the urge to scream his name; its icy fingers squeezed her throat as she imagined the worst. *What if he were killed on some night mission? What if he were imprisoned? What if his strong arms that held her safe in the night were shackled and handcuffed? He was, by all rights, a terrorist and a criminal.* She rolled the words over her tongue. If he were caught, he would be imprisoned—or worse. She couldn't even let herself think about what the worst would be. She unconsciously gripped his pillow tighter, grounding her thoughts as if in some way she could hold him and keep him safe.

The door opened, and she sat up in bed, modestly clutching the covers around her breasts as the low yellow light from the hallway streamed into the room. Sean's darkened form came quietly into the room.

He closed the door quietly. Trying not to wake her, he stood still and looked toward the windows. The promise of dawn's light had begun to filter into the room, giving him enough light to see her raised form sitting on the bed. "Caroline?" he whispered.

"Sean, I was afraid." Her voice was raspy and low.

"I dinna mean ta frighten ya," he said, coming over to the bed and reaching out to cup her cheek. He was cold.

"Where were you?" she asked.

"Just on a wee bit of an errand tis all, but I'm back with ya now." He stood, dispersed his clothes and shoes, and crawled onto the bed and into her outstretched arms. She was so warm and inviting.

"I woke up, and when you weren't here, I . . ." She snuggled close to his chest, feeling his strong muscles.

Gathering her into him, he stroked the smooth skin along her spine. "I'm here now," he said as he raised her chin and gently kissed her forehead and nose.

"Will you always be here?" she asked, her tone fearful.

"Always."

"Will you always love me as you do now?"

"Always," he said softly, capturing her mouth with a bruising kiss as if he meant to force her to understand. He opened his eyes, and when she finally opened hers, he burned his gaze into her with such ferocity she could only believe whatever he told her. "Always," he said again, and she forgot everything but his touch.

"He wants out, ya know."

"Aye, I know."

"It's for the American?" Michael shifted in his seat. Lifting his drink, he took a mouthful of the dark liquid, feeling it burn slowly down his throat. The meeting with Sean this morning was disappointing, and the early snow chilled him to the bone. "Aye."

"What do ya think they'll say? Do ya think they'll let him out?" Paul studied the entrance to the small pub over Michael's shoulder, mostly from habit. His eyes glanced up at every man who came and went through the door.

"Nay, they never have before," Michael answered. He recalled the determined look on Sean's face as they stood outside the castle where Sean had arranged their meeting. He remembered Sean staring up at a window. The look on Sean's face told Michael he was through with violence, through with the missions, and through being alone for the rest of his life. The compassion Michael had seen in Sean's face told him that Sean would forsake all for the woman. Sean would risk the wrath of wanting out, and knowing his friend the way he did, the look on Sean's face told Michael all he needed to know. Sean was in love for the first time in his life.

"What about Patrick?" Michael asked, looking hard at Paul. He had a certain glimmer of hope in his eyes.

"Nay, Patrick never really belonged," Paul said in a matter-of-fact tone.

"But they let him go, didn't they?" Michael asked, even though he already knew the answer.

"Did they?"

Michael felt a blood-curdling chill run down his body as he raised his glass to the barkeep, motioning for another.

The food was the best she had ever tasted. Everything was bursting with rich flavors, taking on a whole new texture and consistency with every bite. She was ravenous.

"We should be heading home, ya know," Sean said as Caroline took a sip from her heavy water glass.

Staring at him over the rim, she put it on the table and reached for his hand. "Oh, Sean, do we really have to?"

"Aye, me ma will be worried, and Claire will begin to run amuck if I'm not there ta keep her in line. She's a wild one, full of shenanigans." He leaned in and smiled at her, giving her hand a gentle squeeze of reassurance.

Claire. Caroline's mind raced with imagining all sorts of things that would occur when his sister found out about her and Sean.

"What do you think she will say about you and me?" Caroline asked, chewing on her lower lip.

He looked into her eyes, fierce determination glowing bright green within them. "There's nothin for her ta say. Don't worry, lass, it makes no difference what she or anybody else has ta say. I love ya; ya know that, don't ya?"

She smiled, believing there was nothing Sean McNally wasn't capable of or willing to try. He was right; it didn't matter. "Will we be heading back today?" she asked.

"Aye, but I've another small errand ta see to first tonight. And Caroline . . ." He paused.

"Yes?" she asked, dropping her eyes.

"You will stay put this time, 'ey?"

She looked up at him, feeling the grip of fear take hold of her heart once again; she tried not to let her face betray her growing panic. It would be pointless to try to talk him out of it. A man like Sean would never have his business dictated to him by a woman, even if this was the new millennium. After all, she was in Ireland, and for all its beauty, the men still were used to living in the overly male-dominated ways of their ancestors.

For now, she thought, but didn't dare say.

The roof was cold against his back. Even with his sweater and coat on, he could feel its chill deep within him, biting his flesh.

It was a starry night, clear and without promise of snow. He turned to her. "Are ya all right, lass?" He knew he never should have let her come, and the sick feeling in his stomach told him so with increasing uneasiness. How had he ever allowed her to talk him into this? It could prove dangerous, yet she had still insisted on coming with him.

She could smile with just the right amount of glint in her eyes to get her point across. "If you swear you won't be in any danger, then what's the harm in my coming along?" He could still hear her goading him, her voice sweet against his chest when he was about to leave, her arms tight around his waist. He was finding it hard to deny her anything.

"I'm fine, Sean; what are we waiting for?" she whispered next to him. She was lying on her stomach, studying him as he stared into the night sky.

"The lads."

"Oh. Then what?" She moved closer to him.

Though they were lying low on the roof, the wind blocked by the two-foot-high wall, it was still freezing up so high. He reached out and pushed a wayward curl out of her face, tucking it under her cap. In truth, he was thankful for her being there and for her body next to his.

"Weel," he whispered, pulling his prepaid cell from his pocket. "I'll make the call ta warn the people inside ta get out and ta safety after Wee Willy sets it into place and gives the signal," he said, studying her expression carefully. He didn't want to frighten her. This was going to be a warning only—no injuries, just a singular military target to get a point across. The pub British soldiers frequented would be destroyed, and the RA would take the credit.

Sooner or later, the Brits were bound to get out of Northern Ireland or face the consequences. His team, however, was not in the habit of senseless killing. It would come down to that now and again, each time leaving Sean with the same unanswered questions.

"You sure there won't be anybody in the pub? No one is going to get hurt?"

"No one is going to get hurt," he reassured her, hoping with all his heart the words he said were true.

"What?" she asked when he pulled her down next to him, his finger to his lips.

"Quiet. They're here," he said, and her heart skipped a beat. "Stay here!" He hissed low. Caroline was taken aback by the force of the command, watching him practically crawl toward the fire escape at the back of the building.

Within moments, she saw two hooded figures coming up and over the top of the building. She was not surprised to see them wearing their familiar black masks and outfits.

Sean whispered quietly with them for a few moments, and with a nod, one of the figures went back down the escape, disappearing over the edge. The other looked toward her, his eyes blue as the Caribbean, and lifted his mask. She caught sight of those wild, red locks of hair, and it brought a smile to her face. Paul. Her heart slowed slightly with his presence. Michael and the others had to be there also, and she felt a wave of relief sweep over her. After the terrible night on the docks, she knew these men could run this mission. Sean was safe for the moment.

He gave her a wide grin and started over the side. Just then, Caroline thought the end of the world had come. The explosion thundered in her ears, followed by a blinding flash of light. Debris went flying through the air, landing all around her, some still on fire. Something sharp bit into her left arm.

"Oh, my God!" Caroline yelled. "Sean!" He was at her side before she got the words out. "What the hell happened?"

His eyes were a mixture of pain and anger, almost glowing green in the darkness. The brightness of the blaze illuminated his features. He was pointing to and motioning at the figures in black.

"Come on, let's get the hell out of here!" Paul yelled at them. His arms were motioning them toward the rear of the building. Caroline turned toward the pub, or what remained of the building. In all her life she had never seen anything like it before. The only thing that came close to describing the destruction of what lay ahead of her was what might remain after a war.

The entire building was ablaze, engulfed in a matter of moments. Bile rose to the back of her throat when she saw the bodies strewn over the ground, some still on fire; most lay still, and no warm breath could be seen rising in the cold night air. A small cry escaped her as she saw the young man crawling toward the body of a woman, her face bloodied, her long hair around her like a halo. Caroline could not distinguish whether her hair was red or just soaked with blood. "We've got to help them!" she screamed.

"Nay, Caroline, there's no helpin any of them now," Sean said, tugging at her arm. She knew he was right and stood her ground a moment longer as the man on the ground crawled over to the woman, collapsing on her chest.

"You said no one would get hurt!" Caroline whirled, screaming and hitting her fists against Sean's chest.

"Caroline! Get hold of yourself! In a few seconds, the whole bloody British army is going to be here! We've got ta go now!"

She knew he was right. He couldn't have had anything to do with this. Not Sean. Not the man she thought she knew and loved. Not Paul, not Michael . . . not Sean . . .

She searched his eyes as if they were his soul. Green met green, and she saw the pain and anger that glowed there. In that instant, when she could have let him go on without her, when he could have stayed and turned her back on him and all he stood for, she made her decision. She would remain with him, at his side, for the rest of her life. She knew within that split second her life was not her own anymore. They were bonded, like it or not.

She grabbed his outstretched hand and ran for her very life.

Sean held his breath. The men passed by, leaving them undetected behind the trash bin. He listened as they made their way around the corner. "They're looking for us?" Sean heard Caroline's soft voice behind him ask. "Aye," he said as he pushed her further back. "Someone tipped them we are still in the area."

"A bloody traitor!" Paul groaned beside him, never giving voice to just who he thought the traitor might be. After the conversation with Michael in the pub, he had been looking over his shoulder more than usual, but no, the RA would never do this. After all, they didn't even know Sean wanted out yet.

"Let's go! Quick!" Sean held tight to Caroline's hand. There had been a second on the roof when Sean thought Caroline might not go with him, but she did, and he knew she had made one of the hardest decisions of her life in doing so.

Coming around the corner, Sean went first, then Caroline, followed by Paul. The way seemed clear. Too clear.

"Halt, or I'll shoot!" a deep voice commanded as a man jumped out of the shadows. Wasp stood before them, and his gun was pointed directly at them. He glowered over the top of the barrel, his eyes cold as death.

Caroline had initially gasped but felt the relief quickly spreading through her body. It was Wasp. One of their own. Then she narrowed her eyes as she caught something glistening in the light. A badge. A British police badge.

"Wasp?" Caroline pleaded. His eyes never left Sean. He had known who they all were, slept in warehouses and gone on missions with them, and now he stood with a loaded gun pointing at them.

"Ya bloody bastard!" Paul hissed, and Sean put out his hand to stop Paul from advancing toward the man with the gun.

"Shut up, ya Finnien bastard," Wasp—or whatever his real name was—sneered at him. "You're through here!"

Caroline felt Sean's hand squeeze tighter. He was inching her behind him.

"Wasp? You've got to let us go. Please?" Caroline pleaded.

He owed her—after all, it was she who saved his life on the docks. "Wasp, I didn't save your life on the docks to have you forfeit ours now." She felt Sean's eyes on her. He hadn't known.

"What the hell?" Sean hissed. "What's this?"

"And I'm grateful to ya, Miss, but this 'ers my job, and we are at war with these bastards." Caroline noticed immediately how distinctively British his accent had become.

"You owe me!" she said firmly. Neither Sean nor Paul moved a muscle as they watched the man with a gun contemplate her words.

"Agreed. You, Miss, can go free, but these here stay with me."

Caroline watched as the police officer waved his gun at Sean and Paul. "No!" she cried. She would never leave Sean!

"Caroline!" Sean whirled her around to face him. "Ya must go, lass. He's a fair man in letting ya go!"

"No! I'll never leave you!" Tears began rolling down her face, their hotness burning her wind-chapped skin.

"Caroline! Ya must obey me in this! Its yer life we're talkin about!"

"No!" Her legs felt weak.

"Go!" Sean gave her a hard shove toward the street and freedom. "Go!" he yelled again. She turned, knowing he was right, and staggered, eyes blinded with tears, toward the street, her heart breaking with each step.

Caroline collapsed a few blocks away. Her heart was ripping from her chest, unable to stop the flow of tears that fell onto the hard concrete where she was sitting. *Where am I? What town am I in?* "Sean." She placed her face in her palms as the sobs wracked her body.

"A pretty lass like you shouldn't be crying when there's so much ta be happy for."

"What?" She looked up from her palms and into the smiling face of Michael.

"Come on!" Caroline heard Wee Willy's voice yelling from the van. She had been so distraught she hadn't even heard them pull up alongside the street.

"Sean! They've got Sean!" Caroline cried as Michael bent to give her a hand up.

"Aye, we know." Michael's voice was calm, matter-of-fact.

"We know all about it. That bloody bastard Wasp tried ta kill us all. He triggered the bomb ta go off before the people were out. A bloody shame it was." Her eyes remained fixed on him as he recounted the whole story—how they found out in time to get away from the blast, how they hit him on the head from behind and escaped looking for the rest of the team, and how they had already called for additional help.

She shivered, and he handed her a blanket from the back of the van. "Do no worry, lass, we'll get 'em back to ya before your head hits the pillow tonight." She wanted to smile, but the pain in her heart remained, as she knew it would until Sean was safe and back in her arms.

"Listen!" Willy stopped the van. He had some sort of headset on attached to a portable radio. "They've got the van with McNally and Finners! It's on the bridge!" He stepped on the gas, and Caroline's head hit the back of the seat as he took off in a fury, leaving black skid marks on the road.

Caroline's heart sank as they drove up to the bridge. She looked in horror as she saw a gutted police car burning and the police van's back door blown off its hinges. Her horror intensified as she saw a pair of unmoving figures on the ground.

As the van stopped, she flung open the door and was out, racing the wind to get to Sean. *Where is he? Did he survive the blast to the back of the van? He had to be all right. He had to be.*

She suddenly stopped in her tracks as two figures emerged from the back of the van. "Wasp!" She gasped as the man exited the van, his hands held high on his head, Paul close on his heels and holding a gun to his back. *Where was Sean?* She felt sick.

Sean then emerged quietly from the back of the van behind Paul. His strong form stopped as he caught sight of her standing in the rolling fog off the bridge. The ghostlike swirling of the fog made her look as if she merely floated without legs, a magical beauty waiting in the silence and beckoning him, like a fae princess.

Her breath caught in her throat. He was alive! She couldn't move; her legs were frozen in fear. It was too good to believe. Suddenly and without warning, Sean started running toward her. "Get down!" he yelled at her. She was quickly blinded by the light coming from overhead. A police helicopter lowered above them and hovered alongside the bridge.

Without warning, shots rang out as bullets rained down around them. She remembered Sean telling her of the Brits' "shoot first" policy. She looked down from the sky in time to see Sean reaching her, his hard chest slamming into her with the force of a train, knocking her over the railing and into the ice-cold, wet darkness.

Blackness was everywhere, surrounding her, engulfing her in a graveyard of ice such as she had never felt. She wanted to let out the scream that tore at her insides. Her chest burned as her lungs demanded air. She gave in to the darkness, opening her mouth, when a strong hand grasped her arm, pulling her upward with such speed she felt as if she were flying without time or space. The next thing Caroline knew was that she was sitting, choking, coughing, and feeling the pain in her sides gouge her like a knife with each spasm.

His embrace was too wondrous to believe. Those strong, warm arms she had come to depend on had saved her once again. She did not need to look at him to realize it was him. She felt it. His hair was wet in her face, hers wet in his hands as they held each other, gripping onto the life within them.

They embraced without words, the heat of their bodies forcing away the chill. Caroline opened her eyes when she felt his hold on her lessen. His head slacked against her shoulder, and his weight forced her backward to the ground.

"Sean!" Panic gripped her as she realized there was something wrong. He was losing consciousness. He fell against her, and it was all she could manage to let him down gently. With his head in her lap, she placed a loving hand on his cheek. Blood dripped from her fingers. He had been shot! She frantically began to search for the source of blood. She screamed in agony when his eyes closed, and a thousand flashbacks of Patrick whirled before her. She knew she would never survive this.

31.

TO SCREAM WITHOUT RAISING YOUR VOICE

Thanksgiving. Caroline felt a slight chill looking out the large picture window of the small cottage. The grey overcast seemed to stretch on for eternity, looming low over the sea. The waves that were crashing against the rocks below were sending high splashes up the sides of the cliffs. Tiny drops of rain streaked the windows, blurring the scenery and giving her an eerily faded view of the world beyond.

She hugged her arms around herself; despite the warmth of the fire, she had held on to the chill of the freezing water she had barely escaped more than a week ago. Only one week; it seemed like at least a year to her. So many things had happened to her in the last few months, and she felt drastically changed because of them.

She lifted her chin and straightened her back in an unconscious move brought about by her circumstances. No longer was she the weepy, scared little creature from America. A new sense of being surrounded her, and she was stronger for it. She had to be for him. He needed her, and she stayed. He needed her to be strong at this time when he was weak, and she was stronger than she ever thought she could be. Still, deep inside, she was weak when it came to him—with her heart, but not her spirit.

"Caroline?"

Her heart melted at the sound of her name coming across his lips, his voice deep and liquid.

"How are you feeling?" she asked, turning from the window and walking toward him. He leaned heavily against the doorframe, his large body still weakened from the pain medication Doc McFinny gave him after he removed the bullet the first night they arrived. She was so frightened that night. She hadn't even known where she was, but thinking of the only person who might help, she placed a desperate phone call to the doctor, who was more than willing to come to her and Sean's rescue. They were staying now at the doctor's holiday cottage.

"Are you sure you shouldn't stay in bed a little longer? That shoulder took a pretty bad hit," she said, sliding herself under his good arm to support his weight as they walked over and sat down on the couch in front of the fire. Its warmth was nothing in comparison to his.

"I'll not lie in that bed a moment longer. Unless you're willin ta stay in it with me?" He placed his large hand on her thigh, giving it a gentle squeeze.

"Sean, you can't be serious." She playfully slapped his hand away. "You're a sick man, for Pete's sake."

"Who's Pete?" he asked, frowning.

"I, I don't know, it's just a saying. I guess I never really thought about it," she shrugged.

"Weel, just as long as there's no other man in yer life." He moved closer, pulling her into the crook of his arm, her head against his chest.

"No other man, Sean. You are the only man in my life. Besides, when would I find the time to see him between keeping you alive and running around in the middle of the night in strange cities, falling into rivers, being shot at, and . . ."

His lips were on hers, tasting and tempting her beyond common sense. She held fast to him as if he might disappear when it was over. "Do ya regret it, Caroline? Do ya regret gettin involved with me?" His voice was soft as he held her tight against him.

"No," she said, kissing his neck. "No, no, no." She trailed her lips down his chest, whispering each word after a tenderly placed kiss.

"Caroline, look at me," he said, his voice stronger.

She lifted her eyes to his and was startled by the look she found in them. "What is it, Sean?"

"I never meant for the bomb ta hurt anyone. It had been planned ta get the people out ahead of the explosion."

"I know, Sean. I know all about Wasp and him being undercover British and all." She was beginning to worry from the seriousness on his face.

"Blowin up a Brit's business is one thing; not getting the people out is another. Caroline, if Wasp made daily contact with his people or if he survived on the river . . ."

She laid her head on his lap. His hand stroked the tangle of curls cascading over his knees. She knew what he was saying. The British would never give up in their hunt for them if they knew who they were.

"Not too many can stand up ta the Brit's interrogation, lass. I've heard they can reduce a man to a cryin babe." He was still stroking her hair but staring into the fire.

"That can't be legal," she said, feeling the fear she had managed to quell over the last week begin to rear its ugly head again.

"This is not America, Caroline; they still wear wigs in court, for Christ's sake. They'll use a man's family ta get him ta do or sign whatever they want him to. There is so much hate on both sides, each thinkin their way is the right way."

She closed her eyes, not wanting to see the anguish she heard in his voice. "What drives the forces here, Sean? What makes them take up arms against each other?"

"Food, hunger, pride, hope, desperation. They all drive in equal measure. All motivate the masses, propelling their actions, feeding the fire in their souls." His hand moved from her hair to stroke her shoulder and arm. "I'm thinkin Patrick was right ta get out when he did."

A closed-over wound in her heart began to ache.

"I can't go ta jail, Caroline," he said, barely choking out the words.

She sat up then, placing her hand on his strong forearm. The muscles were thick and hard beneath her fingers.

"We'll find a way to make them understand, Sean." She wanted to protect him, ease his fear.

"It's not for the loss of my freedom," he said, leaning close to her so that their lips almost touched. "It's that I'd never be able ta live without you. Without you lying next ta me in the night. Your heartbeat under me when we are making love, the touch of your silky hair tangled around my hands wen I kiss ya."

She couldn't hold the tears back. The raw honesty in his words ripped at her, and his eyes glistened in the fire glow that touched every hidden recess of her heart.

"They might as well kill me, for I be dead already."

"No!" she cried, almost lunging at him. They lay along the length of the couch with her on top of him, smothering him in an unstoppable fury of kisses, inflaming him to a painful point of desire. Her hands raked his hair; his good arm stroked her face. He was overly hot from a still-elevated body temperature. Raising above him, she straddled him, feeling the hardness of him under her, begging for freedom as she undid his pants and pulled her skirt up around her waist. She lifted herself and, in one slow, fluid movement, took him inside her. He groaned with passion as his hands grabbed and kneaded her breast that he freed from her blouse, buttons flying across the room and landing with little clanks on the wooden floor as he ripped her blouse in his haste.

They took each other then in a fury, quick and unrestrained, not only from desire, but from sheer need. The need to escape reality and to feel freedom for just a little while.

Afterward, they moved to the bedroom and made love again, this time slowly and gently, exploring and lingering in the presence of each other. When they at last were spent, they lay tangled in each other's arms and slept to the sweet lullaby of the beat of their hearts, unaware of the storm raging outside.

Mary stood at the stove, her hand slowly stirring the stew, her thoughts adrift as she turned the mix of vegetables, meat, and rich gravy over and over again, folding their contents into each other, absently noting the degree of thickness and the flavorful aroma drifting around the kitchen.

Sean and Caroline would be coming home any time now, and she couldn't help the nagging questions that had plagued her ever since Sean's phone call last night. It had been a little more than a week since Doc McFinny informed her of Sean's shooting. How her mind had whirled that night. The pain of knowing her son might have died sent her heart ripping from her chest. She had already lost one son to senseless violence; she didn't think she'd be able to survive the loss of another.

Turning the burner off, she placed a cover over the stew. Her mind returned to the frightful questions at hand. Involvement with the IRA was a given, but how had Sean's accident come about, and what of his relationship with Caroline? She shook her head, clicking her tongue in frustration. The biggest question of all still clouded her mind, refusing to leave: was Sean still in danger?

Her heart tugged at the thought of him forever on the run from the Brits. How could she possibly protect him from this? Her mind was searching for some answers when Robbie's sweet voice boomed as he came running breathlessly into the room, his wild, red curls almost ablaze around his fair face. "They're back, Ma! They just pulled round the front." His eyes grew big as he added, "An Ma, Sean's wearin a sling on his arm."

She rinsed her hands and dried them on her apron. She hadn't told Robbie or Claire of Sean's injury, thinking it was best for him to say what he thought best about the whole matter. In truth, she didn't want them reminding her of it during his healing. Such good as it did.

"Ma." Mary closed her eyes as Sean gave her a hug with his good arm, his strength still taking her breath away. She fought to keep a single tear from escaping.

"It's so nice to be back; I missed you so much," Sean said, releasing his hold on her and stepping aside to reveal Caroline waiting closely behind him.

"Caroline, come here and give me a hug, girl," Mary said, opening her arms wide to receive her. "I missed you both so much. I'm glad ya come home." Mary thought that Caroline and Sean both looked a little worse for wear, but she noticed something different about them too. Something she had never seen on Sean's face and something similar on Caroline's; she almost appeared to have a faint glow about her, and Mary knew instantly that the strangeness wasn't that strange at all if you thought about it. Well, love could be strange sometimes.

"I'll not sleep a wink for missing ya next ta me tonight," Sean held her in his embrace, placing a sweet kiss on her forehead.

"I'll miss you too," she said as her body melted into his. Standing at the door to her room, they were feeling like each had been given a jail sentence. For their crimes, they would spend each night under his mother's roof apart. A grave sentence indeed, but one worthy of respect.

"I'll love ya with all me heart, lass," Sean said, lifting her chin to meet his eyes. She felt her strength leaving her as he placed a lingering, passionate kiss on her already-swollen lips. "I'd better go 'fore me ma brains me for keepin ya from your rest. I don't know why she thinks ya need ta rest. I'm the one who was shot, for Pete's sake." Caroline laughed into his chest as he used her very American saying. "Weel, it's true, ya know," he said in his Irish brogue, which was decidedly thicker.

"Well, I wouldn't want you to get brained over me," she said, looking lovingly into his eyes and stepping out of his embrace.

"Oh, Caroline, I'd walk through fire for ya; ya know that, 'ey?" He pulled her back to him for a last kiss.

"I know, and Sean, you know I'd do the same for you, 'ey?" With a grin, she pulled her door closed and listened to him linger a moment outside it.

When at last he walked slowly away, she glanced around the room she had grown to love as her own. Despite all its comforts, abundant charms, and warmth, she still felt a slight chill at realizing this was going to be one of the coldest nights of her life as she heard the howling wind outside. She also knew it was going to be one of the loneliest.

She did survive. The night was almost endless. The wind whistled out her windows, shadows took on the shapes of British soldiers, and the trees pretended to be lurking monsters, but survive she did, and now her heart picked up speed again. Not from fear, but in anticipation of being with him again, seeing his handsome face and hearing his deep voice. She soon found herself rushing around the room and feeling like a silly schoolgirl.

Rushing down the stairs, she was assaulted by a familiar smell—baked apples and cinnamon! It was indeed good to be back again. She inhaled deeply and headed straight for the kitchen.

"Weel, sleepin beauty finally awakens!"

"Claire!" Mary snapped. "Mind ya manners, girl, or you'll find yourself muckin out the barn with Robbie and Sean." She smiled and winked at Caroline, who was still standing surprised in the doorway. "Sit yourself, lass, I made ya yer favorite." Mary smiled wider toward the basket full of oversized muffins steaming on the table. It was clear to Caroline she had been up baking for some time.

"Tea or milk?" Claire asked with an upturned eyebrow.

"Both, please." She knew Claire was deliberately goading her.

Claire stepped forward and placed a delicate teacup in front of Caroline and reached for the hot teapot with her mittened hand. Over Clare's shoulder, Caroline saw Mary holding her breath. Looking up at Claire, Caroline saw her staring directly into her eyes with a mischievous grin. She held the steaming pot of tea, pouring it into Caroline's cup and never letting her eyes leave Caroline once. The thought of being scalded didn't sit well with Caroline, but she never let Claire see her fear as she held her gaze and continued to stare her down until she rose without spilling a drop. "Thank you, Claire," she said, noting Mary slump and let her breath out, rolling her eyes heavenward.

"Thank you for the muffins, Mary; you shouldn't have gone to so much trouble," Caroline said after Claire left to go back to her room with a sudden headache.

"Oh, it's no trouble!"

"You will wake me next time to help, though, won't you." It was a statement, not a question.

"We'll see, we'll see," Mary said, laughing and taking another muffin herself.

"Is Sean really mucking out the stalls?"

"Oh, aye, he hasn't had his share of breakfast yet. If you don't mind ta go out ta the old smelly barn ya could take this out to him. A man can work up a powerfully dangerous appetite with such hard work and all." She handed a warm plate covered with a kitchen towel to Caroline.

Walking out to the barn, Caroline smiled to herself. It occurred to her that what had just taken place was more than the mere talk of how hungry Sean was.

"Hello?" Caroline asked, looking around the barn and seeing no one. "Is anybody here? Sean? Robbie?" She called again; there was still no answer.

Setting the plate down on a bench, Caroline closed the massive, wooden door to keep the heat in. Turning, she heard Sean's great, black stallion give out a loud whinny.

"What's the matter, boy?" she asked, walking slowly toward the horse's stall.

"He missed ya, lass."

Caroline nearly jumped out of her boots at the sound of Sean's voice. His arms came around her, pulling her close to him. He smelled like fresh hay and horses. "And so did I," he whispered into her hair as she felt herself being walked backward into an empty stall.

"Where's Robbie?" she asked as Sean lowered her to the soft hay on the stall's floor. A soft horse blanket was already there.

"I sent him on an errand when I saw ya coming," he said, taking off his shirt.

She looked at him above her. She ran her fingers along the length of him from neck to bellybutton. "Errand?" she asked.

"Aye, a long errand," he said as he nuzzled her breast, taking a nipple in his mouth through the fabric. "I'm burnin for ya, Caroline," he said as she helped him pull off her boots and jeans. He rose and removed his own pants, throwing them across the stall in his haste.

The heat of him as he lay along the length of her was searing. His mouth covered her in warm kisses up and down her neck and chest. She writhed beneath him as his hands searched and stroked her until she felt the warm rush of hot liquid between her legs. "I love ya," he said over and over as his mouth brushed over her flat stomach. He lifted, spreading her legs as his soft tongue stroked her beyond reason, entering her only to tease and taste.

Caroline grabbed great handfuls of hay in her attempt to remain grounded as he sought to take her soaring with desire. Feeling her readiness, he raised, and in one motion found her lips with his tongue and her entrance with his aching manhood, throbbing painfully for release. She wrapped her long, silky legs around him as he sat up on his knees, bringing her onto his lap. She cried at the depth he attained as she clung to him, his hands on her waist guiding her movements. As he lay her back again, their peaks came together in a fury of unabashed movements, soaring higher and higher as they held tight to each other, the two becoming one.

They lay together, each gently stroking the moistened skin of the other. Arms, back, chests were all fair game in this playful end to their joining.

"We best be gettin dressed before Robbie gets back, 'ey."

Caroline merely nodded, too exhausted to speak.

"See, sleepin apart doesn't have ta be all bad. It can have its rewards."

Caroline laughed as he threw her pants to her. He leaned against the door to watch her dress while buttoning up his own shirt.

He liked the way she blushed at finding him watching her, when just moments before she had been a wildcat in his arms. Leaning against the hard wood, he could still feel the effects of her stretches on his backside. His devilish grin soon turned into a wide smile as he continued to take pleasure in her movements.

Her hair was loose and wild around her shoulders, with little bits of hay in it here and there. Her lips were full and swollen from his hard kisses; her fair, creamy skin seemed aglow. He felt like the luckiest man alive, and it took every ounce of strength he had not to take her in his arms again and ask her his question. He wouldn't, though. He thought long and hard about the right time to ask her to marry him. It would need to be perfect for her, and he would make it so.

He had known all along she would be his; getting her to realize it was definitely worth the effort. She would say yes; he would bet his life on it. The only question now was how much his life was worth for her right now. He wanted her to marry him free of that, and he loved her enough to wait to make sure he came to her on his knee just that way, without the warrant of arrest haunting them for the rest of their lives.

He smiled as she knelt before him, giving him a sweet kiss and pulling bits and pieces of yellow hay out of his own hair. "Thank you," she said, stroking his hair.

"Nay, Caroline, it's I who thank God every day for you," he said, standing and bringing her up with him.

"Is it still painful?" she asked, tenderly placing her fingers along the white, gauze bandage. He was struck by the look of concern on her face.

"Weel, only when I'm doin some strenuous work," he grinned, but quickly spoke up when he saw her look turn to fear. "It's almost good as new, really."

Just then, the barn door opened, and a red-faced Robbie stood looking at his big brother and Caroline in each other's arms. Each had the most guilty look on their faces he'd ever seen.

Caroline emerged from the barn red-faced and slightly rumpled. She smiled and shook her head from side to side. *Poor Robbie*, she thought. *The look on his face was priceless. If I only had a camera, we could have won America's Funniest Home Videos.*

"What's so funny?"

Caroline looked up, startled to see Claire walking toward her. "Oh, nothing."

"Hmm," Claire snorted and brushed right past her toward the barn. Caroline wondered where all the hate came from. She had tried hard to remember a single incident that might make Claire dislike her so much, but failed each time to come up with anything solid.

The girl just didn't like her, and try as she might, there seemed nothing she could do or say to change that.

The air was biting at Caroline's skin through her sweater. Looking up at the gray sky, she found herself somewhat surprised to realize she didn't really miss the sun. Here in Ireland, she had gone days without feeling its warm touch on her face, but the continual gray that hovered threateningly above seemed almost a comfort, beautiful and inspiring. At home in Arizona, she'd pray for winter to come; though the temperatures stayed warm in the valley, she could always look up at snow-capped mountains and dream she was in a real place with changing seasons. There was just something morbid about seeing Christmas lights and decorated trees among the cactus and desert terrain.

Here, Caroline thought, Christmas would be a dream, celebrated with such quaintness it would seem taken from a picture in a Charles Dickens book. She could see it all clearly in her mind's eye. The team of horses adorned with jingle bells would be hitched to a sleigh, and she and Sean would be snuggled under the red, plaid blanket from her room, sipping hot chocolate and making their way over snow-covered hills.

"Our first Christmas together," she thought, and the warmth spreading into her caused a slight flush to color her cheeks.

Almost to the back door, she suddenly stopped, remembering the plate of breakfast food she had taken out to Sean. It would be ice cold by now. Turning around, she quickly made her way back toward the barn. *I'll bring him a new one if he hasn't gone and eaten the cold food already,* she thought, remembering the way he could eat almost anything.

Within earshot of the barn, she heard Claire's voice. Reaching the large, wooden door, her hand went to pull open the latch, but she stopped midway, hanging it in midair as she heard her name.

"Caroline can be good for us both if you'll just give her a chance." Caroline heard the deep tone of Sean's voice. "She can help us, I know it," he continued.

"Maybe so, big brother, but what's ta say she's willin?" Claire asked, and Caroline leaned against the side of the door, her head leaning back against the cold, rough wood. Sean must be trying somehow to persuade Claire to accept their relationship.

Sighing, she realized how hard it must be on Claire; after all, Caroline was an outsider here. Claire must certainly feel jealous of all the attention Sean was giving her, attention Claire was probably used to having all for herself. Still, she had hoped to eventually gain Claire's trust.

"But then again . . ." Caroline heard Claire continuing. "If it all works out well, then you can be married and take over things in the States. It will be the same as when Patrick was alive; you can run his little shop and continue your work for the cause just like before. You're right, big brother—she can be good for the both of us after all, and your marrying her will get ya the green, 'ey? Ya big oaf, that's what ya been planning all along. I never should have doubted ya knew what ya were doing. It was a great stroke of genius gettin her involved with the team and all. I never would have guessed ya had it in ya, Sean."

Caroline's mind whirled. She felt sick, dizzy, and hurt all at the same time, all attacking her with equal forces threatening to consume her on the spot. Her hand flew to her mouth to hold back the scream, tears racing down her cheeks. She felt like she was on fire, and the anger quickly equaled the pain of betrayal now eating at her very soul.

Sean! He had tricked her! Used her! She felt as if she were dying. How could he do that? *How could he say the things he did to me and make love to me, all the time lying? Lying!*

She had to get away and now! *Run!* Her mind screamed. *Run and don't look back!* Like a person possessed, she ran for the house. Within feet of the back door, she felt a tidal wave of nausea overtaking her, forcing her to grab hold of the nearest tree in agony. She could still feel the creamy stickiness left from Sean between her legs—a painful reminder of the love she thought they felt only moments ago.

Sitting with her knees drawn up, she cried hard into her hands. The cold wind whipped her hair into her face, sticking to her wet, salty tears. She hated him. Hated him like no other. And for the first time in a long while, she cried again, mourning the loss of Patrick and the honest love they had known for such a short time.

Sean stretched in his bed, the sunlight streaming into his room. *How long has it been since I've seen the sun? It must be a sign. A sign from heaven to finally make Caroline realize exactly how much she has come to mean to me.*

After his talk with Claire in the barn a day earlier, he'd gone back to the house to find Caroline asleep in her room. She had retired early, claiming an intense headache. He wanted to go in, to hold her and comfort her, but on his mother's advice, he had let her be to rest it out. When she did not come down for dinner, he finally opened the door to check on her.

She looked like an angel. Her thick lashes lay against her pale skin as she slept. Little sounds escaped her parted lips. Sean took in a deep breath, remembering the sight of her with her curls strewn about her pillow and wisping on her face.

His decision to ask Caroline to marry him today was not only attributed to the sun this fine morning, but he also had to give credit to his little fireball of a sister. She had goaded him in the barn. Angered him beyond reason with her ridiculous accusations and stories. Imagine—she thought he was only using Caroline to gain a green card! Her ideas were so horrible that they ignited his anger, just remembering them.

He couldn't believe Claire would suggest such a thing in the first place. He loved Caroline. Loved her so much it took his breath away just to think about her, to picture her image in his mind. He would never let her go back to America. Patrick had warned him of possible danger there for her. No, he would face the consequences of his actions here in Ireland. They would wed, and he would keep her safe here, no matter what the cost to him. He curled his lip with the thought of his large, strong hands around Claire's creamy, little, lying neck.

Sighing and regaining some of his composure, he looked out the window. It was a perfect day. The snow shimmered like a million tiny diamonds in the sunlight. "Today, Caroline, today," he whispered aloud as his breath clouded the frosted glass.

A bang on the door brought him from his thoughts.

"Sean!" It was Robbie, his voice urgent and demanding as he banged on the door. "Sean! She's gone!"

"What?" Sean flung open the door, his heart in his throat.

"Caroline, she's, she's packed her things and left in the night. Sean, she's left ta go back ta America!"

Sean's heart sank. She must have heard Claire talking to him in the barn!

He threw back his head and roared in pain, "Caroline!" His heart ripped in two. She hadn't stayed long enough to ask him about what she might have overheard or to hear his response, and now, she not only had forsaken him, but she was headed straight back to the unknown danger that awaited her in America.

PART THREE

OUTSIDE IN

AMERICA

“Oft in my waking dreams do I live o’er again that happy hour.”
—Samuel Taylor Coleridge, *Love*, 1772–1834

32.

DREAMSPINNER

It should have felt good to be home, to feel the warmth of the desert sun, to see the clear blue of a cloudless sky, and to relish in all things familiar, but for Caroline, it all seemed empty and desolate. The days stretched ahead bleak and without form, leaving the void in her heart a great black hole full of despair, without hope—or so it would have been, had it not been for the doctor's visit last week.

She was pregnant. Alone and far from him and all he stood for. At first, she could not believe it possible, but knew it to be true deep within her. She could feel it. The tiny life force grew inside her. Sean's blood and hers flowed through its body, a product of forsaken love. A lie.

Running her palm slowly over her flat stomach, tracing loving circles over the babe, she leaned back against the pillows and dreamed. She was safe here in her own bed, safe in America, and far from him. Her mind evaded her dreams; she wanted his baby. Wanted it with all her heart. Something of them. Something of the love she had so fervently felt for him. A tangible piece of that love to hold on to and to cherish, letting herself feel she could feel those things despite the beginnings of that love. She still couldn't bring herself to remember him, and yet she saw him everywhere; her own will was still not her own. She couldn't help it, and now, with his babe growing to the beat of the lullaby, her heart drummed; she still loved him. She knew she always would.

Her mind floated high and far. The soft echoing sounds of pipes filled her ears as endless rolling green hills with clear, sparkling streams rose to meet the raging tides of bluer-than-blue seas. The faded smell of leather, straw, and damp, moist earth filled her senses with a faint longing. Ireland would always be a part of her. She smiled sleepily. Despite the hurt, despite the pain in her heart, she found herself secretly wishing for a raven-haired son with deep green eyes.

Vince was elated. She had finally come home. Home and back to him. He couldn't will the wide smile from his face. His cheeks hurt, and his heart felt like it was trying to escape the confines of his chest.

She had been gone for so long. He hadn't let her down, though, keeping up his constant vigil of waiting. Even when he found it hard to concentrate at work, he still kept her in his mind, and when those nurses tried to make him forget her, he just got rid of them and the distractions they flaunted before him. He wasn't about to let anyone take his Caroline from him. She would never have screamed when he tried to kiss her, anyway, not like they did. Their shrill voices never stopped in his ears. He had to make them be quiet; he had to. Quiet was good. Quiet was nice. They were quiet now; he had seen to that. Now, his mind was clear again, his thoughts focused on his ultimate goal, Caroline. She was the one and only, *his* one and only, and now that she was back, nothing would separate them again. Nothing.

This loneliness was more than she could bear. It surrounded her, engulfed her, divided her, and took her soul to uncharted and deserted places. Why did Sean still have his arms around her in her dreams? Why did she still long for them every minute of her waking existence?

Trying desperately to shake him from her mind, she reached for a photo album. The cover of soft-blue bonded leather felt velvety under her fingers. Opening it instantly brought a slight smile, strained as it was, but nevertheless, still a smile. Her eyes relished in the soft appearance of the photos, which had started to fade, leaving soft yellow and brown hues to the skin tones and an overall mystical quality lingering in the moments of the past.

Caroline let her fingertips gently trace the outlines of the faces of her youth, the slickness of the plastic covers smooth and cool beneath her feather-light touch. An ache in her heart brought a lump to her throat as she glanced over at the sweet, young, bright-eyed smiles of friends she had long ago lost contact with, but ones who were forever a part of her memory. She sighed at wondering how many people had passed through her life, in one door one day and out another the next. "What has become of them?" she asked aloud, receiving a quick response in the form of a sleepy "Meow" from Sam.

"You old thing, you," she said, placing a long stroke down his back. "Still, I do wonder."

If she saw them today, would they appear young or old? Unrecognizable? Would she still see the boys in the faces of the men? Sighing again, she closed the book of the past and decided she'd better get out of the house before she totally drowned in the depression that was beginning to pull her down.

She hadn't meant to come here, to this place, to *his* place, but the pull was too great to resist. With a gentle tug on her heart, she found herself in the parking lot of Patrick's store.

The windows were dirty and smudged, making it hard to see inside. Caroline pulled the key from her pocket and held it in the palm of her hand. The landlord was kind enough to give it to her after a bit of explanation of who she was—a little too kind, she was beginning to think. Patrick had paid months in advance on his rent, and the landlord was a bit anxious to get the stock out of the store to make room for an operating business, as the other merchants were complaining about the appearance of the store and the way it was discouraging customers from patronizing their own businesses.

Caroline placed the key in the lock and listened for the click. She swallowed hard, summoning courage for herself as she pushed open the door and stepped inside. *Hey, you're letting all me cold air out!* Caroline leaned back against the door for support, her mind summoning Patrick from the past. She could see him clearly walking toward her, his dark hair loose and flowing about his shoulders, his green eyes warm and comforting as they raked over her body. "Oh, Patrick," she whispered as he faded into thin air.

There was dust everywhere, thick and gray on the glass of the countertop where she placed her purse. *Here's the new CD of that group ya were interested in*, his voice echoed as her memory served him up again. She smiled, turning towards the tapes and CDs. Walking toward the rack, she saw the door to the stockroom standing open. Her heart sank as she felt her body, driven by a mind of its own, walking toward the room. This was it. This was the reason for her coming. She had to face the past once and for all. She had to rid herself of the guilt and make some sort of closure with him for herself.

Tears streamed down her cheeks as she pushed open the door, an annoying squeak reminding her of reality. Before she knew it, she was on the floor on her knees, her hands open and gliding over the red blood stain on the floor. She was loudly crying now, her sobs uncontrollable as she saw him there before her. She lay on her stomach, face to one side, trying in some vain attempt to feel him beneath her. Her cheek swam in the pool of tears she was creating. "I loved you, Patrick!" she cried, "Why did you have to leave me?"

Caroline finally drifted from the storeroom, taking Patrick's hand as he brought her to Ireland and the farm. She saw Sean then, his face welcoming her in love as Patrick smiled at her. She looked down at her hand he held as she felt him nudging her to lean toward Sean. The brothers hugged and pulled apart with similar grins. She looked at them, confused, her mind not wanting to contemplate the meaning of this, but she quickly understood when Patrick took her hand and laid it into Sean's outstretched one. She looked up at him then, her eyes full of tears. *I loved ya too, lass*, Patrick said as he took a step backward and away from her.

"No!" she cried. He was leaving.

Know that I loved ya like no other, Caroline. His voice was becoming fainter as were his features.

"No!" she cried again and turned to look in Sean's face when Patrick finally disappeared. She tried to pull away, but Sean held fast, his large hand not letting hers go.

"No!"

"Caroline, open your eyes, girl. Look at me; you're having a nightmare."

"What?" she asked.

"It's me, Mr. Thompson, the landlord. Are you all right? What are you doing here on the floor? Did you fall?"

"No," she said, opening her eyes and seeing his round face and shiny bald head. As he lifted her off the floor, she said, "I must have fainted or something."

"I never should have let you come in here alone, seeing how close you and McNally were and all," he said, brushing off her shoulders. "You sure you're all right?"

"Yes, yes, thank you," she said as she wiped the dampness of the remaining tears from the side of her face. She didn't really understand the dream, but one thing was for sure: Patrick still wanted her to be with Sean. Her heart sank at the thought as she placed an unconscious hand protectively over her abdomen. She realized that he might come if he really loved her—and then her heart sank even lower as she realized he hadn't come in the two weeks since she'd left Ireland.

33.

NIGHT AND DAY

The waiting had been torture. Sean couldn't sleep, eat, or think. He spent the last two weeks in a zombie-like existence, going through the motions but feeling nothing. Nothing except the constant longing for Caroline. A longing so powerful it was all-consuming and ever-present.

He sat in front of the fire, his mood dark and unapproachable. He'd snapped the heads off his entire family today and said a hundred apologies; he groaned inwardly, knowing he'd probably say another hundred tomorrow if the mail did not bring the necessary documents for him to travel to America.

He lifted the glass to his lips and took another mouthful of the liquid, squeezing his eyes tight to the run of the alcohol down the back of his throat. "Oh, Caroline," he moaned, feeling the pain of missing her and letting his head fall back against the high back of the chair. If only he could just speak to her on the phone, to hear her voice, to know she was safe, but he had no way of reaching her. He didn't have her phone number or address in the States, and all his failed attempts to reach her through the operator were met with the same results: her number was unlisted.

He raised the glass again, swallowed the last of the liquid in one gulp, and threw the glass into the fire, making a great crash from the force and sending little sparks and pieces of broken glass onto the floor.

"I'll not have ya burnin the house down, lad," Mary said in a soft, understanding tone.

She placed her hand gently on his shoulder when he did not respond. "I know it's been hard on ya, Sean; we all miss her, ya know."

Sean groaned and shifted in his seat. He hadn't slept well, and his eyes ached in his skull, the liquor doing little to numb his pain. "I don't know how much longer I can stand it, Ma. I need ta know. I need ta know she's all right."

"Don't worry; the papers will come tomorrow," she said, trying to reassure herself as much as she was her son. She missed Caroline too. The lass was so funny and kindhearted, but more than that, she knew her son was in pain from worry about her. *If only she'd call, or write*, she thought, but she didn't voice her concern because she knew Sean would think only the worst.

Claire has really done it this time. It's a good thing she's off in Dublin with her aunt until Christmas. Mary's mood suddenly turned sour with that thought. As glad as she was that Claire was away, Sean would be away in America for Christmas if his passport came through. She turned from the fire and let her eyes linger over him sitting in the chair next to her, his face a little thinner from not eating, the dark circles around his eyes from lack of sleep making him seem less a man and more the boy she once held so long ago.

She reached over and ran her fingers lightly through the thick hair on his forehead, savoring the silkiness and enjoying the peaceful look on his face that sleep had finally brought him. She wished him small again for that moment, as mothers often do with their grown children, especially if they are suffering in some way as this one was. She pulled her chair closer to his and sat back down next to him; leaning over, she placed her head gently against his shoulder, feeling the hardness of the muscles against her face. "So old, and yet still so young," she whispered, closing her own eyes and listening to his slow, even breathing. At that moment, he was the child she once carried next to her heart—and she was feeling old beyond her years.

"Sean! They've come!" Mary yelled, pulling the packet full of papers out of the mailbox. She'd seen the mailman pass and went out herself to retrieve the contents, hoping to spare her son another disappointed look and allow him a few more moments of some much-needed rest.

She turned to look up at his window but found him instead bounding toward her with no shirt on and bare feet, his hair loose and waving like a banner behind him. He looked like a huge Viking berserker on a coastal ride. "Calm down, lad, did I not tell ya it would come today?" She smiled as she handed him the packet. "Weel, what does it say, son?" She held her breath while he ripped the packet open and read its contents.

After a moment, he looked up from the papers to her. "It says I'm nearby granted leave ta travel out of Ireland for a period of not more than ninety days."

"Weel, at least that's somethin, 'ey?" She put on a strained smile for him, not wanting him to see her fear.

"Aye, it's somethin," he said and headed back toward the door.

Mary watched him walk slowly away, his head lowered as he continued to read. Stopping at the front door, he turned, letting their eyes meet. "Ya best be comin 'for the wind gives ya a chill."

She didn't move for a second; instead, she stood on the cold ground and felt the wind whirling through her skirts and against her skin. She pulled her shawl closer around her shoulders, choosing for just a moment longer to let her gaze linger on his features.

He smiled and cocked his head in some understanding way, his mouth turned up in his familiar devilish grin. "I promise ta take care, Ma. I'm just going long enough ta get her and bring her safe back here." When she still didn't move, he added, "Three months, Ma—not a lifetime, 'ey?"

She smiled then and walked toward him and the warmth of her home, thinking to herself it was going to be a bleak holiday indeed.

Sean looked at the ticket in his hand. In a few hours, he'd be on his way to America. The excitement inside him was dampened only by his lack of knowledge about Caroline's safety. In the endless days since she'd left Ireland, he'd thought long and hard of little else. She clouded his mind every waking minute and tortured him in his dreams with her presence.

He glanced around the crowded Shannon Airport; it was busier than usual with all the holiday travelers and tourists. He quickly found a seat and hoisted his carry-on bag over one shoulder when a hand reached out and grabbed his arm. Startled, he turned quickly and came face to face with a rather large fellow with dirty-blonde hair and wearing a black leather jacket.

"Ya best be comin wh' us, lad, and no trouble, 'ey." Sean jerked his arm out of the man's grasp and nodded at seeing him place his free hand on the inside of his jacket, indicating a weapon. "That's a good boy, now. No trouble; we just want a wee bit of a talk is all."

Sean looked at another man, who now stood on his other side. He straightened his shoulders to show defiance, gaining height and stature in the process. He gave a quick, devilish grin and raised an eyebrow in question.

"I've a plane ta catch, boys," he said.

"You'll not miss yer plane, lad. Now, if you'll be good enough ta follow us, there's a bloke who'd like a quick word with ya." He nudged Sean with his shoulder toward the exit for emphasis.

"What's this about, boys?" he asked, his voice deep.

"We're just ta bring ya, no explanations 'er given," the dirty blonde one said, giving Sean a wide smile of rotted yellow-and-black teeth and patting the bulge in his jacket, appearing to be a bit nervous at Sean's apparent size and strength.

Sean nodded again, wanting to get this over with and be on his way to Caroline. He followed one man while the other stayed close by his side. "I fear lives will be lost if I miss me plane, lads," Sean stated matter-of-factly, wondering all the while if he was being summoned by the Brits or the IRA.

Sean narrowed his eyes at the black car with tinted windows sitting in front of the airport. The man in front of him stepped off the curb and opened the door, gesturing for him to get in first. Sean hesitated, and the man standing beside him gave him a small push.

He turned then, not moving an inch, and grabbed him by the front of his jacket so quickly and firmly that he barely had time to blink. "If ya touch me again, I'll kill ya where ya stand," he growled.

A man's voice came from inside the car. "There's no need for killing, lads. Get in, Sean; I want a word with ya, son."

Sean dropped the man whose jacket he had grabbed, noting the pulsing vein throbbing in his neck, gave him a quick wink, and got into the car, leaving the man more than a bit shaken.

"Michael! You bloody fool! What's the meaning of this?" Sean bellowed at the sight of his friend sitting across from him in the car, laughing.

"Sean, ya should have seen yer face, man; I couldn't resist. When I heard from yer ma you were on yer way ta America, I rushed right here ta see ya off."

"Michael, why all this?" Sean motioned at the car and the men outside.

"It's me grandpa's," Michael snorted.

"The one who runs the bloody funeral home?"

"Aye, that's the one!"

Sean laughed. "And those two?" he said, gesturing at the men waiting outside.

"Grave diggers!" Michael was laughing so hard that he barely got the words out.

Sean just shook his head at his friend and said, "Verra funny, vera funny."

Sean waited for his friend to calm down, then, with a solemn look on his face, he asked, "Michael, have ya heard from Paul or Willy?"

Michael's face went pale. "No, I was hopin you've heard somethin by now. Maybe they're just laying low like we were."

"Maybe." Sean's thoughts returned to the night on the bridge, bringing a phantom ache to his healed shoulder.

"What do ya remember of that night, Michael?" Sean asked, hoping his friend might offer some new clues.

"I remember seein you and Caroline go over the railin, I remember the bloody Brits rainin bullets like hail all around me, and I remember how bloody freezing that water was when I jumped in on the other side of the railing. I never said anythin after that. Just remember barely gettin to the edge and a nice lass pulling me from the water downriver a bit."

They both unconsciously shivered at the mention of the river. "A nice lass, 'ey?" Sean smiled at his friend.

Michael always had an abundant supply of women, and it appeared his good looks attracted them even when he looked like a drowned rat in the middle of the night. "What about that Wasp bastard?" Sean asked.

"Oh, aye, I did see his bloody arse go down before I jumped. A shot through the head, his brains were all over the bridge. A might fittin if ya ask me, seein what he did to the pub and all." Michael closed his eyes then, and Sean knew it was not that bastard he was grieving for, but for the innocent people in the pub.

"Do ya think he got the chance ta spill about us—I mean, do ya think the Brits know who exactly we are?" Michael asked suddenly.

"I'm thinkin they would have come for us by now if they knew. I've been home for two weeks now and nit a sign," Sean answered.

"They could just be followin us, waiting," Michael said, his nervousness becoming apparent.

"Aye, but I don't think me passport woulda gone through and all." Sean was secretly hoping that was indeed the case, and he glanced out the window in a quick survey of the area.

"So, ya ma says yer off ta find her; she left ya, huh?" Michael said, trying to lighten the mood.

"A wee bit of a misunderstandin is all," Sean answered.

"Ya ma told me all about it. Sean, ya go and find that lass. She's quite a sport; a real looker too." He reached over and smacked Sean on the knee.

"I'll have ta. I can't bloody well live without her." Sean was taken aback by the words that freely flowed from his mouth, but they felt right. It was true: he didn't want to live another second without her. "I've a plane ta catch, friend," he said, reaching for the door handle and opening the door. He stopped, one leg outside the car, and turned to his friend. "When I get ta where I'm going, I'll send word to me ma of the address and phone. Let me know when ya hear of the others, 'ey?" He was trying to relieve some of the fear they both felt for their friends. They had both heard of teams who'd lain low for months, but this situation still felt odd.

He closed the door with a nod to Michael, then turned and walked up to the man he had threatened earlier. "Hope I didn't frighten ya, lad?" Sean asked with a grin.

"Oh, no . . . no, Sir!" He stammered, his eyes still too large as he stared blankly at Sean.

"Good day to ya, then," Sean said and left the man staring after him as he went back into the airport.

"Passengers may now board Flight 320 bound for New York at Gate 6."

"Finally," Sean grumbled under his breath. His heart was pounding, and he was surprised to notice he was shaking a bit from just the thought of seeing her again. Holding her again, smelling her sweetness again. He groaned, lifting up his bag to take his place in line to board the plane.

"Sean McNally?" a voice behind him asked.

"Verra funny, Michael, but I've a plane ta ca—" He stopped when he turned to see three men standing around him, dressed in full British police attire.

"Mr. Sean James Eric McNally?" the one flanking his right asked, a stony expression on his face.

"Aye." Sean swallowed hard, his left eye starting to twitch as he clenched his jaw.

"You best be coming with us, Sir," he said, placing his hand under the inside of Sean's upper arm. Sean managed to jerk free of the man's grasp with little effort.

"I've a plane ta catch, as ya can clearly see," Sean said, but barely got the words out when a blow to the back of his head knocked him into total darkness as the word *Caroline* escaped his lips.

34.

UNSEEN EVIL

He could see her through the trees. Her beautiful hair bound up in a girlish ponytail, her long legs made longer by the little, white shorts she wore. She was sweating, her face flushed as she swung her tennis racket, making contact with the ball and sending her opponent running for the far side of the court.

Vince licked his lips as the little moisture droplets beaded on his upper lip. *She is perfection*, he thought, and he narrowed his eyes on her, watching as she held up her hand for a time out and went for her water bottle. He swallowed hard as he watched her from behind the large tree. He moaned in the back of his throat as he watched her full, sensuous mouth drink from the bottle.

"Hey, you!" Vince whirled around to see a police car stopped along the road close to him. A policeman was yelling at him. "Yea, you. What are you doing over there?" he demanded.

"Ah, nothin'," Vince groaned, kicking the grass with his black tennis shoe and looking at the ground, careful not to make eye contact with the man in the car.

"Hope you ain't pissin' in the park, buddy; hate to have to drag you in," the policeman yelled.

"I ain't pissing," Vince called out—adding "you bastard" under his breath—annoyed at being interrupted from watching her.

"You move along now, you hear? Move along; this is a family park, and we don't want the likes of you hanging around." Vince watched the policeman motion him on his way.

"Son of a bitch!" Her red Jeep was pulling out of the parking lot.

"Hey, girl, you really gave me a run for my money back there. I think you were visualizing that ball with someone's face on it!"

Caroline turned to look at Vanessa. Her blonde hair was in a single French braid, and she was wearing her usual happy-go-lucky grin. Waiting at the light with her fingers tapping out the beat to the barely audible music on the stereo, Caroline stopped and grasped the steering wheel so tightly her knuckles turned white. She'd have to tell her sooner or later; after all, she was supposed to be her best friend, so she had a right to know about the baby. "Vanessa, there's something I've got to tell you," she said, looking at her friend and giving her a forced smile.

"Oh, God!" Vanessa's face went pale. "Caroline, what is it?" She looked concerned and scared.

"It's just that, well . . ." Caroline sighed, thankful for the light that just turned green. "It can wait," she said. "How about lunch?" She looked over again at her friend, who was still pale.

"Is that the best you can do? Man, I'm famished!"

Caroline looked down at her friend's plate overflowing with delicious meats, potatoes, and vegetables, then looked at her own, which contained a small salad and some fruit. She shrugged and headed back to their table. Caroline had always liked buffets. *Sean would really like this one*, she thought, quickly frowning as she reached for her iced tea. She chastened herself for the thought. It had been almost three weeks, and still there was no word from him. She had to let it go. She had to move on with her life and forget about him; he wasn't coming, and that was that. Claire had been right—he had used her, and the realization of it hit her like a ton of bricks. Caroline could feel the tears threatening to come.

"Hey, why the grim look? This place isn't so bad." Vanessa plopped down in the seat across from Caroline.

"It's not the place, Nessy. I'm going to tell you something, and I don't want you to scream, okay?" She knew her friend was a bit high-strung and didn't know exactly how she would take the news of her pregnancy. "Okay?" she repeated.

"Okay, okay!" Vanessa said, putting her fork down.

"Well . . ." Caroline began. "I'll tell you right off that I brought something else besides the plaids and postcards back from Ireland with me." She smiled at her friend, who was staring at her a lot like Bambi caught in the headlights. Caroline went on.

Caroline was not disappointed in her friend's reaction to her news—it was just as she predicted. She sat perfectly still and managed to listen intently to the whole long story—that is, all the way until she mentioned the baby. Caroline looked innocently around the restaurant at the surprised stares of the other diners. She smiled sweetly and raised her eyebrows, shrugging as if her friend had gone temporarily mad.

"Baby! Caroline, my God! A baby! What are you going to do? You have to tell him."

"No! Not just yet."

Vanessa shot her a concerned look.

Caroline put her fork down and grabbed her friend's hand from the table. "I'm not ready to talk to him yet. I don't think I can manage to hear his voice yet." It was a lie. She had lain awake nights wanting nothing more than just that. His voice. His touch. *Oh, God!*

"Caroline, maybe that sister of his was lying. Maybe he really does love you. From all you've said about how the two of you were, of how he was with you . . ." Vanessa squeezed her hand for support.

"No," Caroline whispered through a lump in her throat.

"Why not? Anything is possible."

"Because he hasn't even called—and look at how long I've been back." Caroline was staring at her plate, realizing she'd lost her appetite. "Maybe," she finally said. *Please, oh please, God! Let that be the truth.*

She'll be back tomorrow, Vince thought, shuffling through his small spiral notepad. *She's been coming here every morning at ten for the past week.* He flipped through the pages of the notepad, looking at all the pictures of her he had glued in the book. Smiling, he stifled a chuckle. "I'll keep you so busy you'll never want to play tennis again," he said aloud to himself. "Busy, all right—busy with me!"

"Hey, you!" Vince looked up from the book, dropping it in his lap as he saw that damned policeman again. "I thought I told you to move on!"

"I'm going, I'm going," Vince mumbled, starting the car.

"Hey, Bob, I don't like the looks of that guy," Mac's partner said as they both watched the blue car pull out of the lot. "Wasn't that the same guy who was here yesterday?"

"Yup, and the day before. I think he's some low-life perv. I've seen him watching the tennis courts in the mornings."

"Maybe he's got a thing for sweat or something," his partner joked.

"Or something," Mac said, making a mental note to have a chat with the two women on the court if they came back tomorrow.

"Hey, darlin', you going to play today?"

"Not today, Mrs. Winters, I'm not feeling up to it this morning," Caroline said, reaching for her paper off her doorstep. It was true; she had woken this morning with the worst case of morning sickness so far.

"Hope you didn't bring some foreign germs back with you from that heathen place you went to a few weeks back," Mrs. Winters said, lifting the collar of her house robe up to her mouth and nose.

"No, Mrs. Winters, nothing like that, I assure you." Caroline could feel her temperature rising. Mrs. Winters was probably the most prejudiced person Caroline had ever had the misfortune to meet, let alone live by.

"You know what they say about those Irish? A lot of lushes, the whole lot. Not a sober one in the whole filthy country!"

Caroline straightened her back and stared at the little woman before her. The deep age lines in her dark, tanned face left her looking a little like a troll, especially with her back beginning to hump slightly. *The early signs of osteoporosis*, Caroline thought to herself.

"Really, Mrs. Winters, how can you . . ." Caroline stopped when the irritating little woman went back into her house, muttering about leprechauns and fairies, oblivious to Caroline and her opinion.

Caroline gritted her teeth when Mrs. Winters closed the door. Leaning against it, she tightened her grip on her paper. *The nerve of some people.* Closing her eyes, she visualized the soft, green meadows around the McNally farm. She could see the family's smiling faces and open arms. *How very unfair*, she thought to herself. Ireland was a wonderful country, its people the most friendly and hospitable she'd ever known. They were always ready to lend a hand or help out a stranger in need. Oh, they had their problems in the northern areas, but all in all, the Irish were just like any other people, proud and fiercely protective.

She felt a strange pull at all the thoughts clamoring in her mind, a pull toward something she couldn't quite make out. Something strong and energizing at the thought of that tiny, wonderful green isle. Something stirring inside her. She laughed then, and a great, wide smile broke out on her face as she realized the baby inside her must just "be getting his Irish up." She knew it was still too soon for the baby to be moving yet, but she felt the power nevertheless.

She placed a tender palm to her still-flat belly, patting it gently. No matter what happened between her and Sean, the baby would always be a link for her to that beautiful place and those wonderful people.

"Vince, honey, where are you going, dear?"

"Out, Mother," he answered dryly, opening the back door.

"When will you be back, sweetie?" she called after him.

He didn't answer but kept walking out to his car. Getting inside, he closed the door. Grabbing the steering wheel, he began to bang his forehead against it.

"I hate her, I hate her!" he said over and over again until he finally let his head rest against the back of the seat.

"Why don't you just go to your room and redress some of those dolls you like so much again and leave me the fuck alone!" he yelled into the night air. He saw her do that. Play with the porcelain dolls she kept in her room. She had to have at least fifty of the blasted things. She kept each one in a protective glass case to shield it from the dust. He'd often seen her take three or four out at a time and sit with them on her bed, talking to them much like a small child would when playing tea time.

He shook his head, regaining his thoughts. *She is okay, just a little weird, is all. I'll leave her be as long as she leaves me alone. She seemed harmless enough most of the time, and the school doctors had the nerve to say I am the one with a few problems!* He chuckled and pulled out of the driveway.

Driving out to the desert, he had put music by his favorite group—ACDC—in the car's cassette player. As he drove through the night, the loud rantings of "bang your head" thundered through the cool night air.

Pulling up to his trailer in the deserted area, he stopped and gathered up the brown paper sack that had been sitting on the seat next to him. He smiled as he lifted it from its spot and pulled it with him out the door. He had stopped earlier in the day at a local hardware store to pick up a few of the necessary things he would need for Caroline, for when the time was right. It would be soon. He wanted her so bad he didn't think he'd be able to keep his love for her in check very much longer. *She will make a wonderful Christmas gift to me*, he thought. *Like on those commercials for the Humane Society. I'll open up a large box, and out will pop my new pet, complete with a big, red bow around her neck!*

He laughed as he pulled the long, red ribbon from the bag and put it next to the rope and duct tape. "Perfect!" he said. "But if you're going to be my Christmas present, then I'd better get the tree up." He went back out to the car, where he proceeded to pull a large, brown, cardboard carton out of his trunk marked *Artificial Christmas Tree.*

Caroline put her journal down in her lap. She was so tired these days, and it seemed an effort to even write. She had at least tried to put into words some of the million or two thoughts she had racing through her mind over the last few weeks. She wanted to record all her feelings and fears, especially during pregnancy, but once again she ended her entry with the same line: *Still he does not come.*

She sighed. Maybe if she tried to eat more, or if she could only sleep well at night, she wouldn't be so tired all the time. Maybe, maybe if his arms were around her in the night, maybe if she could feel his hard chest behind her as he held her tight and she could feel the heat of his body keeping her warm, maybe. She closed her eyes and laid her head on the desk. *I wish I had a picture of you to show the baby*. He'd be so proud if only he would call. If only . . .

She drifted then, her head cradled on her arms atop her desk. The soft sounds of Irish pipes flowed from the CD player, and Vince watched her through the window from his hiding place behind the trees.

35.

BEYOND THESE WALLS

"He still refuses to speak?"

"Yes, Captain, still sittin there staring at the walls, not makin a sound. If ya ask me, the bastard's guilty."

"Well, we've no proof of that, and since he won't utter a bloody word, we're hard pressed ta get a confession out of this one, I'd say," Captain John Scott said in a disappointed tone. He'd been at this prisoner for five days now, and he had to admit that this was one tough bastard. Most of the others usually cracked in three, four days at the most, and most of them were ready to sign anything you placed in front of them. It would seem this particular one had as much mental stamina as he did physical.

"What did the surveillance camera pick up last night?" he asked while studying Sean through the two-way mirror of his cell. He was sitting up on his bunk with his elbows at rest on his knees, supporting his hands that were fisted under his chin. Given his tall stature, the Captain was sure his feet must hang over the bottom of the bunk by at least a foot.

"More of the same, Captain. He just lies there starin and thinkin to himself. When he finally does sleep, it's restless, and he speaks of that woman again."

"Aye, Caroline, is it?"

"Yes, he calls out to her in his sleep."

"Must be his girl, 'ey?" the officer said, putting both hands into his pants pockets and rattling some loose change.

"That would be my guess, lad." John leaned closer to the glass to get a better look at the man they were holding. Seeing fresh bruises and marks on Sean's face, he said, "Looks as though the boys got a bit rough this morning."

"Oh, yes, well, it seems as though one of them made a crack about this Caroline he calls out to at night." The young policeman chuckled. "Got him pretty rowled, I guess. Took six men ta calm the bloke down."

"See to it that sort of thing doesn't happen again, officer! You forget, this man is innocent till proven guilty." John was angry at the men who had provoked this prisoner. He knew well the kinds of mind torture they inflicted on prisoners. It made him shudder to be associated with those Nazi-like techniques left over from the war. He also knew he'd have withstood the same kind of blows to protect the honor of his wife. It left him with a deep admiration for the man who sat so still in his cell. It seemed to strengthen the weird bond the two of them had forged over the last few days. Any man who'd still protect the honor of a lady's name in this day and age deserved some amount of respect.

"Should I bring him out to ya now, Sir?"

"No, I think this time I'll try it in his cell for a change," he replied, thinking maybe in his cell he might be more willing to at least talk to him, but at the same time, he doubted it.

"Sean, will ya at least acknowledge my presence, man?" John asked, hoping to gain his attention for once. He was suddenly surprised to see the man lift his eyes to meet his own. *Maybe this might work after all.*

"Sean, you've been here for five days now, and still you refuse to even speak a single word to me, lad." He swallowed as the man's green eyes bore a hole through him, making him a bit nervous to be so close to him in such a small setting without guards flanking him on both sides, ready to assist should the need arise. He gave a quick glance at the two-way mirror, subconsciously reminding himself that he was at least being watched. "Sean, will you at least tell us if you're innocent of the charges brought against you?"

Still no reply. He decided to try another approach. "Sean, does this Caroline lass like men who hold their tongue? Maybe she likes strong, silent types, 'ey?" With the mention of her name, the green eyes narrowed. At least he was on the right track. "My own wife, Mary, well, she can talk a man's ear off. I barely get a word in otherwise, half the time."

John began looking around the cell, trying to avoid the man's eyes. "She's a real looker, though. Pretty as a spring day. We're trying to have a baby. We've been married for three years and no luck yet, but she keeps riding me about it, so to speak." He glanced up at the tiny window high off the ground. The sky was gray, as usual. He wished it were spring, wished the sky was blue again. But most of all, he wished he were anywhere but in this cell with this prisoner. The man's rugged appearance, with his bulging muscles and long hair, made John feel like he was questioning some great Viking warlord from a thousand years ago. It also made him look small, doing this small man's job he hated so much.

"Will you bairns know what ya do to your countrymen for a livin?"

John was surprised from his thoughts. The man had spoken at last. He envisioned the men behind the glass cheering.

"What?" he asked, trying to get him to speak again.

"I said, are ya proud of the fine Job ya go to every day?" Sean's voice was low and raspy from lack of anything to drink for the last five days.

John's face went pale at hearing him speak so painfully. He walked over to the door and banged for the guard outside.

"When was the last time this prisoner had anything to drink?" he demanded.

"Why, uh, he never asked for anything, Sir," the officer replied with a smirk.

"Bloody hell! Get this man some water immediately!" John roared.

"Sean, I know the IRA trains their men to withstand intense interrogation, lad, but do they also train you to die from dehydration?"

There was no answer, only that same old stare again.

John knew he was off track and quickly switched the conversation back to his babes, if he should ever be so lucky to have any. "No, Sean, I hope to be out of this Stalin place by the time my kids are born. Contrary to what you might think, I probably hate it here as much as you do." He knew it was going well when Sean lifted an eyebrow in surprise at him. "It's true. I put in for a transfer to a desk job in Parliament weeks ago."

"I'm innocent of the charges," Sean said after downing the glass of water in one gulp. The cool, soothing water was heaven to his dry, parched throat.

"We have a witness—an officer—who placed you at the scene, Sean." He was going out on a limb; Wasp was dead and unable to testify.

"You've no witness, and you and I both know it," Sean stated, leaning back on his bunk against the wall, lifting one leg up onto the side railing and staring at the thick, yellow stripe down his blue jail uniform. A matching stripe adorned his left arm, indicating to the guards that he was the most dangerous of prisoners. He smirked at seeing the Captain's jaw clench from his statement.

"I'm still keeping you the full seven days I'm allowed under the law."

"Aye, I'd expect nothin less." Sean smiled his famous devilish grin at the Captain.

"Sean, when ya do get out, lad, take my advice and leave this place. There's a whole world awaiting a young lad like you. Maybe take that Caroline with you, 'ey?" And with that last remark, he left the cell, thinking to himself that he'd pick up some flowers and surprise Mary for lunch.

The air, cool and crisp, smelled of winter and moisture. Sean inhaled deeply, filling his lungs with its freshness and expelling the stifling stench of the jail. He was free. Free to finally leave and be on his way to Caroline.

He hailed a taxi. Michael had volunteered to pick him up and drive him to the airport, but they both agreed it was for the best that they not be seen in each other's company for a while. He sat in the back of the taxi and called out to the driver, "Shannon Airport."

He peered out the windows at the passing buildings, a blur of brownstones and gray bricks. This was one of the lucky neighborhoods; it had been refurbished to retain some of its yesteryear elegance, unlike so many of the ones that were quickly leveled to make room for more modern, cheaply built structures. Ireland was indeed trying to keep up with the rest of the world, and it pained his heart to know that the cost of economic prosperity was also the death sentence to a culture rich in history and customs. That was one of the main reasons he and Patrick committed to never succumbing to the hairstyles society dictated. Small thing as it was, leaving the length like so many of their ancient clansmen before them gave them a small sense of victory in a changing world.

He reached up and ran his fingers through his mane. It did indeed seem appropriate—and besides, Caroline seemed to like it. Whatever pleased her, he would do; whatever she wanted, he would get for her; and no matter where she went, he would find her. Find her and make her understand his love for her. His overwhelming need to be with her, to hear her soft voice from those sweet lips, to feel her in the night beside him as he lay with her silky hair under his cheek.

He closed his eyes and concentrated on her face. He would find her and make her understand his passion. Passion that made him scream for her in the darkness of the night.

36.

CAPTIVE OF MY HEART

"Today is the day!" Vince yelled at his reflection in the mirror. The face staring back at him was slightly unfamiliar in its appearance. He smiled and ran his fingers over his freshly shaven chin, feeling the smoothness. He narrowed his eyes as he looked at the new length of his yellow hair, shaking his head slightly back and forth to get the feel of the shortness against his collar. "You'll never know what hit you, girl!" he said to his reflection.

"Vince? Are you all right, dear? You've been in there a long time. Is everything all right?"

He squeezed his eyes shut, holding his palms over his ears. *That infernal screeching of hers has got to stop!*

He opened his eyes and stared at the scissors lying in the sink, partially covered with the long strands of hair he had just cut off. His mind whirled at the thought of sinking the shiny, long tips of those scissors into his mother's wagging tongue. He quickly shook his head to clear it of the tempting scene. No, he would never harm her. She loved him, and so did Caroline.

He opened the door to find his mother staring at him blankly, like one of her dolls with its marble, glass eyes.

"Vince! I love it! I absolutely love it!" she raved.

"Yea, yea, Ma, let me pass, okay?" He felt five years old again.

"It must be a girl! I knew it! Oh, honey, I'm so happy for you!"

Vince held his temper in check all the way down the stairs and out to his car. *Finally, some peace*, he thought, getting into the car. Once inside, he reached over and unzipped the black bag containing the necessary stuff he needed to get Caroline today, double-checking to make sure everything was there. He glanced at his watch. Eight-thirty. *Good*, he thought, *I have plenty of time to get to her before she meets that friend of hers at the park.*

"I'm coming, my love," he whispered, backing out of the driveway and driving off down the road.

It was risky, taking her in broad daylight, but he knew if he was going to do it, it had to be today. Christmas was only four days away, and she might be planning to go out of town to visit relatives or have them over. Either way, if he wanted his plan to work and for her to be his for Christmas, this was probably his only chance.

Vince waited in his car in Caroline's parking lot. It was a stroke of luck, his managing to park next to her Jeep; with all the people out holiday shopping or already gone to work, it seemed to be fate somehow. He watched for her door to open, periodically glancing at his watch to note the time. *She must be running late*, he thought as he tapped nervously on the tiny glass to make sure it was still working. He heard her then, and his heart jumped in his chest, his blood racing through his veins, and the sudden jolt of adrenaline giving his system a shock.

She was beautiful. Her long, thick hair was bound up again in a ponytail, swaying as she walked toward him, its dark, rich color making her skin seem fairer than usual. He swelled inside with a feeling of desire. He couldn't wait to touch that skin, to feel for himself if it was as creamy and soft as he'd imagined.

He waited behind her car in a crouched position where he was sure he would go unnoticed, waiting for her to come nearer. He could hear her soft humming as she walked in the sunshine and saw the gentle way she walked with a slight sway—not a vulgar display of her womanhood, like he'd seen so many other women do, but a sway that gave an air of confidence to her, a natural easiness in her femininity. He suddenly felt hot all over, his palms sweaty and itchy. He turned the white piece of cloth over in his hand, careful not to touch the wet area he'd soaked in chloroform a moment ago. He had to remain in control. If he were going to get the job done, he would have to keep it together!

He bit the inside of his cheek to take his mind off his bodily functions threatening to release, which would ruin everything. She was so close now. He watched until she was bending inside the back of her Jeep to put her gym bag away when he finally summoned up the courage to make his move.

Quick as lightning, he leapt from behind the safety of his car and lunged at her from behind. She jumped and startled as one arm came around beside her. He smashed the white cloth, smashed against her mouth and nose; his other hand grabbed her flailing arm in a vice grip, his fingers biting into the soft flesh. She was indeed as soft as she looked. His face was buried in her hair, his nostrils filled with the scent of her shampoo.

Vince held the cloth tightly against her mouth as he felt her struggling beneath him. She was a bit stronger than he'd imagined, but he knew instantly he'd win in the end, and he chuckled at the thought of her futile attempts. "Easy, Caroline; it's going to be all right," he whispered in her ear. Suddenly, he felt her body going limp against him. He held her up, feeling the fight drain from her body as she leaned heavier into him, her head falling back against his chest as she finally lost consciousness. "That's the way, my beauty," he said, lifting her up in his arms and carrying her over to his car.

He balanced her on one knee as he opened the back door and placed her on the wool blanket he had laid across the seat in preparation. She was like an angel. He kissed his fingers and placed them against her cheek, lightly brushing them along her lips before he abruptly jerked the blanket over her face and body to hide her presence.

Closing the door, he hastily ran around to the driver's side of the car and slid behind the wheel. He adjusted the rearview mirror to hone in on his new pet, who was motionless beneath the blanket. Smiling, he started the car and backed out, pulled ahead, and drove off into the morning light as Mrs. Winters stood open-mouthed at her window.

"Hey, Mac, did the old lady tell you anything new?"

"No, I was just putting together some pieces. Did you get anything new from the blonde?" he asked, motioning toward the pretty girl who was leaning against the victim's Jeep, crying.

"Naw, she's too upset to recall anything right now. I'll have a go at her again in a few when she calms down."

Mac looked over at the young girl, who was talking with some other officers. Something familiar came to mind about her and that red Jeep. He searched his mind for the reason he kept feeling there was something important about it—why it all looked so familiar to him. "Where did she say she was supposed to meet the victim—Caroline, is it?" he asked.

"The tennis courts at the park, uh, at about nine o'clock, I guess. When Miss Blackwell didn't show up, she got worried and came here looking for her. The rest is, well, you know." He glanced up from his notepad and squinted his eyes at his partner, trying to read his mind. "You think you got something, Mac?" he finally asked.

"I do have something, all right, and it ain't good, son. It ain't good," he stated as the full force of the implications came to mind. The park, the tennis courts, two pretty girls, and one son of a bitch! He brushed his holster with the inside of his arm, knowing that before this was over, he'd need it once again.

The sunset was the most beautiful Sean had ever seen. Violet and blue streaked the sky, lit up from underneath by the vivid orange of the setting sun glowing bright against the outlines of the mountains. He held his face up to the sky. Despite it being dusk, he was filled with the warmth of it all the way to his soul.

While he was in custody, he had thought hard on where to begin his search for Caroline, and he couldn't wait to get started. Hailing an airport taxi, he pulled the address of Patrick's shop from his pocket, handed it to the driver, and leaned wearily into the seat. It had been a long and boring flight.

"How far?" he asked the driver impatiently.

"Just a hop, skip, and a jump, Sir. Have you there in two shakes. Hey, you're a foreigner, huh?"

"Aye, just in from Ireland," Sean said dryly. He was not really in the mood to talk to the man, but thought it might be in his best interest to be polite. He glanced at the man from behind and wondered, *Do all men here wear nothing but cowboy hats and boots? Would Caroline like me in those things?* It really didn't seem to fit her personality; she had seemed to fit right in at his home, surrounded by all his family's dated furniture and antiques. She seemed softer somehow, and compared with what he'd seen so far, this was an arid climate, with little use for tapestries and plaids.

"You come to visit relatives?" the driver asked him with a quick look in the rearview mirror.

"Aye, more or less." Sean's mouth curled slightly. Caroline wasn't a relative yet, but she soon would be. He glanced out the window, amazed at the desert terrain with its prickly little bushes and tall palm trees. Imagine, palm trees in the middle of the desert! He had thought them only to be along the coasts where it was tropical, or at least where some small amount of water abounded. He shook his head, trying to understand why Patrick would choose this dry place to live in after the lushness of Ireland. It would truly seem he didn't want any reminders of home. Perhaps reminders of Ireland might have made him homesick, or maybe he was just punishing himself for what he'd left behind in his native country.

"Here we are," the driver said, pulling up to the curb of the deserted parking lot. "It looks like it's all closed up. Do you want me to wait?"

"If ye don't mind, please wait while I have a quick look," Sean said, opening the door and stepping out. The sun had fallen behind the mountains, leaving the parking lot in total darkness except for the glowing signs of the shops. Sean felt a wave of grief take hold when he glanced up and found the sign to his brother's store darkened, lifeless between two brightly lit signs of the shops on either side.

He stepped up to the shop windows and peered inside the darkened shop, then saw a note on the door indicating the mall manager's phone number in case of emergency.

After locating a pay phone and speaking with the manager, he walked back over to the taxi driver and leaned on his door, handing him the address the manager had given him over the phone. His heart was beating wildly in his chest. "Do ya know it?" he asked the driver.

"Sure, it's just a hop, skip—"

"Well, then, let's not waste time chatting, 'ey! Move, man, move!" He jumped in the back of the taxi and again said, "Move!" He was so excited. Finally, he was just moments away from her. After a bit of explaining, the manager told him that a beautiful young woman had been in the shop just a few days ago, and she had left her number and address for him to get in touch with when the time came to clear out the store. Sean knew it had to be her, but when the man said her name, it was too good to believe that he had found her so easily.

"Caroline," he mouthed, but no sound came forth, just the feel of letters across his lips and the memory of her spinning in his thoughts.

Sean swallowed hard, a sudden lump forming in his throat, making it difficult to breathe. He'd sent the taxi driver on when he saw lights on in her apartment. She was home, and he had felt a great wave of relief at realizing she must also be safe. His palms were sweaty, leaving him feeling like a sixteen-year-old lad on his first date. After wiping them on his pants, he raised a shaky hand to knock on her door.

In all his imagining of this moment, he never once pictured the pretty blonde who opened the door to greet him. She stood in the doorway, staring at him like he was an alien from outer space. "Might Caroline Blackwell be at home, lass?" he asked hesitantly. Perhaps the store manager had given him the wrong address.

"Oh, my God," the pretty girl said softly, and he noticed that she looked as if she had been crying. "Are ya all right?" he asked, suddenly getting a bad feeling in the pit of his stomach—the same kind he always got before a bad mission with the team back home.

"You're him, aren't you? You're Sean?" She raised her hand to her mouth and stepped back, eyes wide.

"Aye, that would be me, Sean McNally at yer service. Is Caroline here, then? I must speak to her; it's very important." He was at once relieved to know he had at least found someone who knew her and who even seemed to know him. His heart felt joy at knowing she had at some point mentioned him to this girl, but why was she still staring at him so? "Is she here, then?" He was looking over her shoulder to try to get a peek inside in case Caroline was there but didn't want to speak to him or see him. He wouldn't blame her, but there was no way in hell she'd get by with that.

"No, oh, God, you're too late!" She was starting to openly cry now. He stepped forward and pushed her out of the way a bit more roughly than he'd intended to.

"I must see her!" he roared. "There was a misunderstanding, is all. I must make her realize that!" He looked around the room; it was Caroline's apartment, all right. Dark, wood furniture and rich colors abounded. Thick rugs and crystal lamps were tastefully arranged with a Victorian hand. It smelled of her, too—soft and sweet.

His attention was yanked from his surroundings by the girl's soft whimpers. "I'm sorry, Miss, I dinna mean ta hurt ya, it's just that I've come a long way and I—"

"I told you, you are too late!" She raised her fists to him and started to pound on his chest.

"No, lass, it's never too late. Here now, stop that!" he said, easily grabbing her wrists and holding her still.

"No! You don't understand!" she yelled. "She's gone because some bastard in an old, blue car kidnapped her this morning!" She looked up at him, her blue eyes liquid with tears.

"What?" Oh, my God! His heart screamed. He was too late! Damn the IRA and damn the bloody Brits for holding him so long! If only he'd been one day sooner, if only he'd caught an earlier flight, he would have been here this morning! "Calm down and tell me exactly what happened to her!" he said, lowering his voice, making it deeper and more masculine. It was a tactic he often used on Claire to get her attention. It was working. The girl was staring at him with a fair amount of fear in her eyes. "No need to be scared; just start with your name and tell me what happened so I can find her." He was speaking softer now to gain her trust. She surprised him by throwing herself into his arms. "There, there," he soothed.

"She's pregnant, you know, with your baby," she said in a timid voice against his chest.

His world collapsed in an apocalyptic explosion.

37.

WISHES

Vince stared at Caroline lying on the bed, her eyes closed in a forced sleep, her hair dark against her fair skin. He just couldn't get over how incredibly beautiful she was. His eyes lingered on her facial structure, delicate high cheekbones, perfect nose, dark lashes, and full lips. She moaned in her sleep. *It won't be long till she wakes up*. He let his gaze follow the graceful curve of her neck and shoulders, down further still to the swell of her breast. She was breathing slowly and evenly, and he watched the rise and fall of her white T-shirt, smiling. His eyes continued over her hips and down her thighs. Her legs were long and sleek; he liked that in a woman. He had removed her shoes when he first brought her here this morning; he didn't want her to be uncomfortable. An owner must take care of his pet, after all, and he would be a responsible owner of this one—that was for sure.

She moved her feet in her sleep, like he'd seen dogs do when they were dreaming. Was she dreaming of running away from him? Would she try to run away when she woke up? He frowned at the thought. He could never allow that. Touching his leather belt that held his jeans at his waist, he knew he wouldn't hesitate to discipline her just as any new master would.

He left her in the room alone on the bed after double-checking the rope that bound her hands and feet. She would awaken soon, and he needed to prepare something for the two of them to eat. They had both worked up their appetites.

Caroline's entire body ached, and her head swam round and round in a deep pool of thick haze; even her eyelids hurt. She tried to move, to stretch, but there was something binding her hands and feet together. She opened her eyes with a start, causing the pain to shoot straight into the center of her skull. She struggled harder at her restraints, to no avail. As her memory became clear, she realized what had happened to her.

She looked around the room. It was dark, other than for a faint, yellow glow coming from under the door. *How long have I been asleep? What time is it?* She had her watch on but had no way of seeing it with her hands tied behind her back. She grimaced with every move; the rope was too tight, and it burned her skin, bringing fresh pain to her wrists.

She tried to relax, to gather her thoughts and assess the situation. *Okay*, she thought, *get a grip, Caroline. You must stay calm and think of a way out of this.* She thought of the baby then; was he all right? Did the drug or whatever that bastard had used to make her unconscious harm the baby? As she thought it through, she figured it was just some form of chloroform, probably harmless if she didn't count the massive headache she had. It felt every bit like the migraines she used to get in college before a stressful test.

She tried to remember who had brought her here. Her thoughts were fuzzy, but she was sure it was a man, given the still-painful, tender flesh of her arm where his fingers had gripped her tightly as she struggled under the drug he used. She took a few deep, cleansing breaths to try to clear her head so she could think more lucidly.

Why had the man taken her, and what did he intend to do with her now that he had her? Wait—he knew her name; she heard him call her by name just before she lost consciousness. How did he know her? Was it an old boyfriend? No, she couldn't place his voice. Maybe a disgruntled customer from the bookstore? She didn't think so, and yet there did seem something strangely familiar about him. She couldn't quite put her finger on it. She was brought out of her thoughts when the door opened slowly, and a thin figure came toward the bed.

She narrowed her eyes to try to see his face, but the light was behind him, leaving him nothing but an outline in black looming over her bed.

"So, I see you finally decided to join the living?" he said in a low voice that sent shivers down her spine.

"Who are you and why have you brought me here?" she asked.

"I've wanted you from the first night I saw you in the club," he answered quickly. "Now I've finally got you, and you're mine," he added as he reached toward her face. She sank into the mattress to avoid his touch. He placed a tentative finger on her cheek and laughed when she tried to turn her head away from him. "Now, now, my little pet, that's no way to treat your new master."

"Master? Pet?" She was beginning to get angry now.

"What do you want from me?" she asked defiantly.

"From you?" he asked, tilting his head like a confused puppy. "I want nothing from you, little one. It's *you* I want; just you."

Her mind whirled. "You can't mean to keep me here! People will be looking for me! I've a life, and—" She broke off before she let it slip that she was having a baby. *Who knows what kind of maniac I'm dealing with? I will protect the life inside me as best I can for now.*

"Don't worry, you will like it here, Caroline. I've gotten all your favorite foods, and I've made up the place real nice for you. Yes, I know that once you get used to it, you'll like it here better than that place of yours."

Caroline stared at him in disbelief. *He intends to keep me here with him indefinitely! Who is this lunatic?*

"Hungry?" he asked, sitting on the bed beside her, his weight causing a slope in the mattress and her face to come in contact with his thigh. He smelled of old clothes, like those stores where people donate discarded items and the store sells them. She felt his hands move to her ankles and begin to fiddle with the rope bindings.

She was relieved he would at least allow her legs to go free. "My wrists hurt," she said softly. "The rope is too tight."

He came close to her and leaned over her side, checking the tension around her hands.

"Will you untie me, please?" she asked hesitantly, not wanting him to become suspicious.

"I think not; you'll have to earn that privilege, my sweet," he said sarcastically as he leaned back in front of her slowly, allowing his chest to come in contact with her breasts. "I think we will begin working on trust after you've eaten; you're a bit skinny, don't you think?" he asked, running a light finger along her hip and thigh.

She thought she might scream. His breath was rancid, and his touch repulsed her, making her weak stomach lurch.

"I guess I *am* hungry; what time is it?" she asked innocently. Better to keep him talking than let that mind of his dwell too long on her physical appearance.

"About eight o'clock or so," he said, lifting her up under his arms.

Her head swam. She was extremely dizzy, and without her arms to use as support, she quickly fell into him.

"Easy now; not so fast," he told her as she leaned against his stomach for a few seconds to gain control of her nausea.

She did need to eat, she realized, and the sooner the better. His hands came to her hair, and she felt the barrette give way as he pulled her hair out of the ponytail.

His fingers gently raked through her hair as he arranged it around her face and shoulders. "You'll wear it down, like this," he said, letting his fingers feel the length of it down her back.

She squeezed her eyes shut, denying the instinct to slap his hands away. She must remain in control if she were to have any chance to escape. She would need to gain his trust so he would untie her, and for that she needed to let him think he was in control and she submissive.

"A little grub, and you'll be good as new," he said, lifting her up off the bed. With one arm around her shoulders, he steered her toward the open door.

"God, a baby!" Sean roared, pushing Vanessa back from him and grabbing at her shoulders. "Did she not mean ta tell me?" he yelled, shaking the woman.

"I don't know; I think so. Hey!" she yelled, jerking out of his grasp. "You used her!" She was angry now.

"No!" he countered.

"Caroline said she heard you in the barn with that sister of yours. She said she heard you say—"

"No!" he interrupted sternly. "It was a mistake. Caroline heard only me sister; she didn't stay ta hear me tell my sister she was wrong. She never heard me say that I love her. I love her more than life itself," he said with his voice getting lower. He turned and raked his hands through his hair. Why did his head hurt so much?

"I believe you," she said, placing her hand on his shoulder. "I don't know why I do, but I do."

"That son of a bitch has me bairn now too," he said, his eyes becoming darker. The anger was boiling over in him, red and hot. He squeezed his eyes shut as the muscles in his jaw clenched. *Should I be angry at Caroline? Did she ever intend to tell me about our child? No, I can't dwell on that now; I have to find them. Find them both and bring them back home safe.*

"I need ta know everything ya know about the bloody bastard who took her!" They had wasted enough time, and it was now time to get moving so they could locate her. His thoughts were clear through the pounding in his head as he once again faced the task of trying to find Caroline. He would not come this far to lose her —now—to lose *them* now.

Mac held his cup of coffee with both hands, fingers wrapped around the outside, savoring the heat from the liquid inside. The coffee itself was too dark and too bitter to enjoy, but it made an excellent hand warmer just the same.

The girl was taken almost twenty-four hours ago, and there was no word on the possible whereabouts of that damned light-blue car. He leaned his head to one side, feeling the pull of the tight muscles in his neck and shoulders. What was so familiar about this case, and why couldn't he get the fact that she drove a red Jeep out of his mind? He was thinking hard on the subject when he saw the pretty blonde friend of the missing girl coming toward his desk with a large, fierce-looking man following close at her heels. "What can I do for you, Miss…" he asked, putting his cup on the desk.

"Vanessa, and this is Sean McNally, Caroline's, ah, fiancé," she said, stepping aside to give him a clear view of the man. He was immediately taken aback by the man's presence. He was overly tall and thickly muscled with long black hair and glowing green eyes. *This is one hulk I would not like to meet in a dark alley, even with my trusty gun at my side.*

"Hello, I'm Mac Forester, the officer in charge of the case," he said, standing and offering his hand to the man.

"Have ya found them yet?" the man asked in a thickly accented Irish brogue.

Mac raised his eyebrows at the man, who nearly broke his hand with his powerful grip. "Well, we haven't gotten any leads yet, but rest assured, the police are on top of matters here. Now, why don't the two of you just go on ho—"

Before he could finish, the man reached over and grabbed him by his shirt collar, pulling him across the desk with ease—not an easy task, since Mac weighed close to two hundred pounds.

"Hey! What do you think you're doing?" Mac yelled at the man.

"I want them found, ya hear me! I want her and me baby found!" the man growled at him. Mac could see the racing pulse in the veins that throbbed in his thick neck.

"Hold on just a minute! You unhand me this minute, or I'll have you arrested and thrown in jail! I don't know where you come from, son, but here we don't take it too lightly when someone threatens a police officer, do we, boys?" He raised his eyebrows in the direction of the three officers behind the man with their weapons aimed at his back. The man turned his head, catching sight of the policemen out of the corner of his eye. Mac felt the man let go of him. "There, now, if you promise not to do that again, I think we can sit down like civilized men and discuss this matter without the need of violence." He sat back in his own chair as the large man sat in the one facing him. The girl also sat down, rolling her eyes toward the ceiling and giving a slight huff.

"I'm sorry, Officer Forester, he's just in from a long flight, and he had no idea until I told him that Caroline was, well, kidnapped." She patted the man on the shoulder. "He is taking it very hard, as you can see."

"Yes . . . well, now that we've all calmed down . . ." He gave the policeman behind them a dismissive gesture with a wave of his hand. "Sean, is it?" he asked the man, who was rubbing his temples with his fingers. "Would you care for some aspirin?" He pulled open his side drawer and located the economy-sized jar he kept there for himself.

"Just in from where?" he asked, handing Sean three of the small, white pills.

"Aye, thank ya," Sean said, taking them and swallowing them without water. "Ireland."

"Ireland, of course—the accent. I should have known." Mac handed him a small paper cup of water from the dispenser behind his desk.

"I thank ya," he said, swallowing the water in one gulp. "Please accept me apologies, Sir. I've no business in takin it out on ya, but if ya could tell me all ya've found out so far, I'd be grateful."

Caroline's stomach pitched, sending waves of nausea cascading through her body. She swallowed hard, sucked in a great gulp of air, and closed her eyes tight. She knew it was coming; it was just a matter of will as to how long she could hang on before her body gave in to the ancient, instinctive ritual of vomiting at dawn. She held her breath and kept swallowing. She knew he would come soon, and she took advantage of her aloneness.

She glanced around the room in an attempt to distract her thoughts from the inevitable. Lying on her side, she could see only half of the room. A nightstand held a plastic pitcher of water and a cup; a small window was high off the ground and glazed over with a white substance that didn't allow anyone to see in or out. There was also a small trash can. She curled her lip at that; seeing its bright yellow and orange daisies reminded her of her predicament. If the man,

Vince, didn't come soon, he was going to have one hell of a mess to clean up, especially considering the green, shag carpet on the floor. She scooted over as close to the edge of the bed as possible—not an easy task with her hands and feet still bound. At least she wouldn't have to lie in her vomit if he didn't come quickly.

Her arms ached, her muscles burning from being restrained in one position too long. Her stomach threatened again. She thought how much she would appreciate one of the soda crackers she kept in her bedside table in her own room. She thought also of how much she wished she were in her own bed right now. She closed her eyes and fought the fear of the unknown. *What will happen to me now? What will happen to the baby?* She found herself wishing for Sean. Wishing for his strength now. She had called him her knight in shining armor on more than one occasion, and she felt a grip on her heart that came with the knowledge that he wouldn't be here for her this time. *How could he when he is thousands of miles away? He might as well be a million more miles away, since he doesn't care anyway.* She shook her head to rid her thoughts of him. *I have to maintain a hold on reality, especially now, when I have no one to depend on except myself. I have to survive. I have to, for the baby.*

"What the hell happened here?" Vince was livid when he opened the door. The smell nearly knocked him out.

"I tried to wait till you came, but—"

"Are you all right? Are you sick or something?" *This pet is a bit more work than I first thought.*

"No. It must have been something I ate," she said quietly.

He narrowed his eyes at her. He wasn't sure, but she didn't sound too convincing. He almost got the impression she was lying.

"Can I have some water, please?" Her voice was low and shaky. It was probably just all the commotion from yesterday. She was going to need time to readjust to her new life and to him.

Last night, when he put her back into bed, she tried to distance herself from him. When he went to retie her ankles, she nearly came off the bed when he let his hands linger over the smooth skin of her calves, his fingers feeling the silkiness of her skin. She would need time, all right; the problem was, he didn't know how much longer he could continue being so accommodating to her. He wanted her. He wanted her with a desire so great it was all he thought about.

He poured some water into the cup on the nightstand and sat down beside her on the bed. He had to lift her head to help her drink. "I'll get you a cold washrag," he said, feeling the moisture on her forehead. "What's this from?" he asked as he lightly touched a tiny scar under her bangs above her eye. It was pale pink in color and probably hadn't been there very long.

"I don't remember," she lied, remembering the incident with Robbie and the colt in the freezing pond. She didn't like this man being so close to her. The smell of mothballs radiated from his clothes, and his icy touch sent chills down her spine. She could feel his eyes on her, feel the desire in his touch. Last night had been a close call, and she didn't know how much longer she'd be able to bide her time with him before she could make her escape.

"Caroline?" he asked in a low voice.

"Yes." His hands were stroking her hair, and she could feel his arousal as he held her. She wanted to scream.

"I'm glad you're here," he said, trying to hide the strain in his voice. He was just inches from touching her. He reached down and tentatively cupped one of her breasts.

"No!" She yelled and tried to squirm out of his hold. His grip tightly held her still. She was moving against him and could feel him already swollen for her, the movement driving his need for more.

"No, please!" she cried as his hand shifted to the other breast. He could feel the hardness of her nipple through the fabric of her shirt. He leaned closer and smelled the rich fragrance of her hair, letting his tongue find her earlobe. "God, you're beautiful," he groaned.

"Please! No, oh, God, this can't be happening!" she yelled. She could feel his hands all over her. Though she was fighting, she knew she could do little to stop him—a feeling similar to the panic she'd felt in the dark alley in Belfast with her would-be assailants. She knew this time there would not be anyone to save her at the last moment. The sheer panic from her total helplessness took hold, and she did the only thing her body could do at this point. She threw up on him.

"Christ! What did you do that for!" he screamed, jumping up from the bed and throwing his hands dramatically out to his sides.

"I couldn't help it," she lied again. If the situation had not been so serious, she could have almost found it funny. He jumped around the room, his shirt wet and clinging to his thin body. She thought him a great stand-in for the Charles Dickens character of Ichabod Crain. He was a puny excuse for a man—but then again, after being in Ireland, most men seemed that way to her.

"What's the matter with you?" he demanded.

She didn't know what to say. *Maybe I should tell him I'm pregnant. Maybe he will take pity on me and let me go. It's obvious he doesn't like the way I react to his advances. If I can convince him it might only get worse; he might give up this insane notion of holding me prisoner. He might lose all interest in me altogether.* She gathered all her courage and proudly said, "I'm pregnant."

"What did you say?" he asked, his voice low.

She knew immediately it was not the right time to tell him, and as she felt the burning sting of his blow to her face, she also realized that he packed one hell of a punch for such a small man.

"You bitch! You rutting bitch in heat!" he screamed. "I thought you were different! I thought you were special, but you're not! You're just like all the other sleazy, easy women out there."

She sank against the pillow, wishing it were a rock she could hide under. The warm trickle from her nose seeped into her mouth, and she tasted her own blood. She instinctively tried to curl up, wanting to protect her abdomen should he hit her again.

"After all the work. All the time and energy!" He was pacing now, holding his hand out and banging his other fist into it violently. She was glad it was his hand he was hitting and not her.

"I can't keep you now. Not after this. I thought you were pure, untouched, but you're not! You're just like all the others!" He glared at her. His eyes became cold and lifeless. She wanted to feel happy that he said he couldn't keep her now, but something about his look made her think he wasn't through with her yet.

She was right.

"I wanted so much more for you, Caroline. I wanted so much more for *us*. Was it that Irish piece of shit from the store?" he asked coldly.

She couldn't have heard him correctly. She must have taken a harder blow than she thought. "What?" she asked, feeling the pain mix with red-hot anger.

"I said, are you knocked up with that Irish bastard's brat?"

At first, she thought he might really mean Sean, but at once the reality of his statement left her out of control. He had known Patrick! She couldn't contain the scream that burst from her soul.

"Yeah, just what I thought. I guess I should have killed him a night or two sooner," he stated smugly.

"You killed him? You son of a bitch!"

"Yeah, I guess I am that, and you know what else?" he asked, bending down close to her face. She winced as he reached out and grabbed a handful of her hair, twisting it into his fist as he lifted her by it and brought her closer to him. She could smell her vomit on him and relished in that small triumph.

"Now I'm going to have to kill you too," he whispered like a snake in her ear.

She closed her eyes, fighting the tears that didn't matter now. She knew it was over. The fight drained out of her body, and the only thing she wanted now was the sweet peace of death that Patrick had come to know before her.

"Be done with it then, and get on your way," she hissed back at him, going limp in his hands, closing her eyes, and listening to the demonic chuckle that flowed from his smiling lips.

38.

THEN CAME A KNIGHT

"You really do love her," Vanessa said quietly. It was a statement, not a question.

"Aye," he said with his back to her. "More than life itself," he added, whispering so low she didn't hear him. His fingers trailed along the wood shelving about the fireplace. *Why would anybody need a fireplace in this country?* From the moment he arrived, it felt damned hot to him. He supposed that after living in Ireland his whole life, he must have become accustomed to the coolness of the weather. Here, his blood seemed to boil, but he couldn't decide if it was the situation or the climate.

He liked looking at her things. It felt right being in her home, surrounded by all the little treasures she lovingly picked and cared for. He knew why Caroline sat in front of the fire so often back at his home in Ireland. She loved the whole romance of it. He could feel that here, too, her romantic spirit was everywhere. He looked at all the polished, dark woods and deep colors that made her home. Gold-trimmed pictures hung in antique frames holding soft Elizabethan art and portraits. His mouth curled slightly at what she could do with a real home of her own, what she would do with their home if given the chance.

"You sure you'll be all right here?" Vanessa asked, bringing him back to reality.

"Aye, and I thank ya for all yer help, lass," he said, turning to face her. She looked a little worse for wear, but still very pretty in a way he was sure his friend Michael would find enchanting. "You'll call me if ya hear anything new, 'ey?" he asked as she gathered up her jacket and headed for the door.

"Yes. She's very lucky, you know."

"And why is that, lass?" he asked. It seemed strange to him that she would think her friend was lucky at this particular time.

"She's found a real knight in shining armor," she said with a smile, leaving him standing alone with his heart breaking into little pieces. Caroline had called him that same thing, and he shook from the fear that came with the tribute.

Mac was just about to bite into his dinner when his partner came running over to his desk, waving a piece of paper and shouting his name. He groaned as he put the foot-long Italian sub down in front of him. "What is it?" he asked, looking up at his young partner, whose face looked a little flushed.

"They spotted the car!" he exclaimed, throwing the paper down on the desk in front of Mac and directly on his dinner.

"What?"

"Oh, sorry, Mac," the officer said, watching him pick up the paper and hold it by its corner, Italian dressing dripping steadily off the soaked paper.

"Now slow down and tell me what the paper said, since I can't very well read it now, son," he asked, frowning.

"It said they just spotted the car, Mac."

"The light-blue one?" he asked, jumping to his feet. "Where?" he demanded when his partner nodded.

"On the old highway. Just about six miles out of town heading south."

"Do they have him?" his heart was racing. It was nothing short of a miracle to spot him so soon.

"No, but the border patrol said he was still heading south when they lost him on some deserted desert strip."

Mac knew the implications of that statement. If the kidnapper was heading south, that meant he might be trying to make a run for the border, or worse, he might be heading out into remote areas of the desert to kill her—if he hadn't already. His heart sank with the very real possibility that the killer might be trying to dump her body.

"Let's go!" his impatient partner was yelling.

Mac picked up the phone. "There's someone I have to call first," he said, hoping he was doing the right thing.

Sean had just stepped out of the shower when he heard the phone ringing. He knew there was no way he'd be able to sleep, and with a few days' dirt on him, he decided he might as well clean up in case something should happen. In fact, he was hoping that if he did take a shower, something would happen. "Don't hang up! I'm bloody well coming!" he yelled at the phone, grabbing a towel and running to find it.

"Mr. McNally?" the voice on the other end asked.

"Aye," he said. His hand was still wet, his hair dripping into his face.

"I'm coming to get you; be ready in ten minutes."

Sean felt the blood rushing in his veins, his adrenaline making his hands shake. "You found them, then?" He wanted to ask if they found her alive, but he didn't want to hear the worst.

"Yes, I'll tell you all about it on the way. Sean?"

"Aye?" He felt a panic at the officer's hesitation.

"It could prove dangerous; are you sure you want to come?"

Sean grinned. "Have ya an extra gun by chance?" he asked and heard the man hesitate, but he knew the officer on the other end was grinning too.

Caroline was in total darkness. It was cold, and she was shaking. Her teeth were chattering, and her muscles screamed in agony with every bump the car hit.

She had her eyes open even though she couldn't see. Being in the trunk wasn't something she looked forward to, but the same space held some comfort in the form of safeness. The tight space provided adequate support, so she wasn't thrown around so much. Besides, for the moment, she was safely out of his reach.

She figured they must be driving through the desert. The road was no longer smooth, and she could hear sagebrush and other things scratching the underbelly of the car. She felt a small amount of panic. He must mean to kill her in the desert and dump her body where only the coyotes would find it.

She wasn't afraid, really. As a matter of fact, once she accepted the fact she was going to die, it didn't scare her so much. In some small way, she almost welcomed it. Welcomed the possibility of seeing Patrick again. She felt a tear escape as she thought of the baby. Thought of the coyotes ripping her up and stealing the baby out of her womb and carrying it home like some prize to their own young.

"Oh, God," she cried, realizing how selfish she was being. All she wanted to do was be free. Free of the pain of missing Patrick and free of the pain of loving Sean. But she hadn't really considered the baby in the last few hours.

The tears were rolling fast and hot down her face. She wanted the baby to live. Wanted him to have a chance at a life. To know his mother's arms, to hear her singing him to sleep. She also wanted him to know his father. "Sean," she whispered, wishing with all her heart that she could feel the warmth of his arms around her one last time. Wished she could tell him that no matter what he had wanted from her, she would gladly give it, if only she could hear his voice one more time.

The car came to a sudden and abrupt stop, causing her face to slam against the back of the trunk and sending pain echoing from the swollen site of the blow she received from Vince. She cried out in pain as the trunk suddenly opened and the man yanked her out. She looked up at the star-studded sky. It was probably the most beautiful, clear sky she'd seen in a long time. How strange for her to be noticing beauty amidst the darkness of this night.

"Come on, let's get this over with!" He pulled her along after placing her feet under her. She stumbled, almost falling as the muscles in her legs tried to remember how to work. She looked ahead at where he was dragging her. Her heart sank when she saw the entrance to a mine. Old boards were nailed over the opening, and a large *Keep Out* sign was plastered there as a warning to would-be intruders. She slowed her pace, forcing him to practically drag her along. No one would find her here. She needed to make her move and make it fast.

As he let go of her to pull down the barriers of the entrance, she ran. "Stop!" he yelled after her. She didn't even turn to look how close he might be behind her; she just ran the race of her life. If she could just get far enough into the darkness, she could crouch down behind some brush, and he might not be able to find her.

She soon realized that wouldn't work. With her hands free and her athletic ability, she might have been able to outrun him. But having been through so much, having so little food and sleep, and having her hands bound behind her, she didn't really have a chance.

"You stupid bitch!" he screamed when he caught hold of her arm. His fist slammed into her face. She was thrown to the ground with the force of the blow, and without her hands to break the fall, she fell face-first into the dry, desert sand.

"Get up, slut!" he yelled.

"I, I can't, you little prick!" she said, trying not to eat any more dirt. She felt him lifting her to her feet and saw the look on his face when his eyes met hers.

"What?" she demanded when he didn't move.

"I just . . . nothing!" he said and roughly pulled her along behind him. Caroline thought she might have seen something different in his eyes just then, but it was probably just his mind racing with the thought of how much he was going to enjoy killing her.

"What the . . . shit!" he screamed as they were both suddenly engulfed in a bright light. A helicopter thundered directly overhead. Caroline cried out with relief. She was going to make it.

Vince yelled a few obscenities at her flying saviors and took off in a run, dragging her behind him toward the mine entrance.

"No!" she screamed.

"Stop and release the woman!" She heard the voice over the speaker ordering him from above. Vince grunted something incomprehensible and pulled her into the pitch blackness of the mine.

"There!" Sean yelled, reaching for the door handle and finding none. "Let me out! I must get to her!" he roared.

"Slow down, son. It looks as though he's taken her into the shaft with him," Mac said. They heard reports of what was happening all the way there, and they knew she was still alive for the moment. Now, with the man ducking into the mine, it was just a matter of negotiation.

"I'm going to let you out only if you promise not to go running in there after her. We have specially trained men for that, and I won't be held responsible for another civilian. Do you understand?"

Sean frowned at being talked to like a child. He knew he probably had more training and more experience than anyone here when it came to urban warfare. Hell, it had been his life for as long as he could remember.

"Promise?" Mac asked him again.

"Aye. I promise," Sean said grudgingly.

As soon as Mac came around and opened the cruiser's door for Sean, he leapt out like a cat and, in one fluid, quick-as-lightning motion, grabbed his gun and ran for the mine entrance.

"Hold your fire!" he heard Mac yell behind him as he jumped into the darkness of the pit.

Sean wasn't prepared for the total darkness of the mine. How was he ever going to find her or his way in this blackness? He put his hands out in front of him, trying to feel his way along the edge of a wall. Bits of dirt and rocks crumbled at his touch, and he knew immediately they were in for more danger than just that from a madman. They were in very real danger of the mine itself collapsing.

The air was thick with old dust and something else that Sean couldn't quite make out. A rancid, putrid odor weighed heavy in his lungs. He pinched his nose from the burn, feeling a little queasy all of a sudden and thinking to himself that something large must have crawled into the abandoned mine to die recently.

He turned as he heard footsteps approaching from behind and the low voices of the policemen. Their whispers echoed through the shaft past him. He shook his head at their infantile procedures. How in the world were they supposed to surprise the kidnapper, making all that noise?

"There you are." Sean squinted at the brightness of the flashlight that threatened to blind him.

"I'll have my gun back now, if you don't mind," Mac said in a whisper, and Sean looked at him after he lowered his light and shone it in his own face to reveal who he was. Sean gave him a lifted eyebrow, asking without words if he might keep it a bit longer. The man shook his head slowly, taking Sean's obvious hint to remain silent and held out his hand for the weapon.

Mac patted him on the back and whispered in his ear, "Did you see which way they went?"

Sean rolled his eyes at the man; this was going to be impossible. If he had any chance at all to save Caroline, he was going to have to distance himself from the awkward motions of these men. He shook his head, indicating no, and then lifted a finger to his mouth to remind them again to be silent.

Pressing forward, they quickly came to a fork in the mine. Two long, narrow passageways stretched for an eternity into unending darkness. Sean let his instincts take over. Crouching low to the ground, he placed his hand onto the dirt floor. Clearing his mind, he tried to focus on the kidnapper's thoughts. If he were the man, which way would he go? He held his breath and waited.

The officers behind him stood and looked down at him with wonder, pointing and shrugging to themselves. He had to focus, but it was hard given the disturbance behind him. He clenched his jaw and tried again. There it was! He had them, and he knew which way they went. He jumped up and pointed to the tunnel on the left. He knew the kidnapper and Caroline went into the right tunnel, but he did not want to be dissuaded from getting to her because of a few undertrained men.

They bought it. The five officers, including Mac, went ahead into the tunnel to the left. *Sweet Mary,* Sean thought to himself as he slipped further back from the others and re-entered the right tunnel alone.

His heart was thundering in his ears. *She's got to still be alive*, he thought. *She has to be*. He pushed further ahead, still feeling his way and moving with surprising speed, considering how quiet he was. He smelled it then. The odor was more pronounced. His nostrils were filled with death; he must be close to the dead thing now.

His hands slipped off the wall into nothingness. A hole, perhaps? No, it was much too big. It must be another tunnel, some sort of alcove. He tilted his head into the blackness. *The smell! God, what is it?* he mouthed to himself. Instead of turning, he walked straight ahead in the same direction he had been going, his hands at arm's length in front of him.

He found what he was looking for. The wall continued on, and as he walked a few feet away, he also noticed the smell lessened. Whatever died in here was certainly in the room or tunnel he just passed.

Continuing on for a few more feet, he suddenly became aware of the darkness fading ahead of him. There was a faint light coming from ahead, and as he walked further, his heart sank. He must have gone full circle and was about to run into the very officers he had just ducked out on. He almost forgot his composure and started to yell at them not to shoot him when he heard her. *Oh, my God! Her voice!* It was weak and a bit hoarse, but he knew it to be hers instantly.

He slammed his body against the wall, careful still of any noise he might make. Her voice! He could barely contain the joy that swept over him with the relief that she was still alive. He did keep silent as he remembered she was still in the hands of that bastard. He stilled his breath when he heard the man speaking, giving a slight grin at noticing he was only a few hundred yards behind them and that he was apparently still unnoticed.

"This is all your fault!" he heard the man yell. "All I ever wanted was a nice pet, something I could love. Something that would love me back. But nooo! You had to go and fuck things up with that piece of shit Irish trash."

Sean curled his lips and calmed himself with the thought of what he was going to do with the man when he got the chance.

"Stop it! Stop it!" he heard her yell back.

Good girl! Sean thought. She still had some spirit. He grinned again and moved a few feet ahead.

"Why should I stop?" the man asked. "You and I both know you rutted like a dog in heat with that Irish store owner, and now you're ruined! Everything is ruined!"

"No!" she yelled back. Sean kept moving toward them, a few steps at a time. He was close. So close.

"I won't have you talk about him like that! Patrick was a decent man! Why did you do it? Why did you have to kill him?" she cried.

Sean sucked in his breath. Patrick? What was she saying? He had just assumed that when the man had said *Irish*, he was referring to Sean. God! The realization struck him like a ton of bricks. Caroline was in the hands of the murderer! Patrick's murderer! He closed his eyes, his blood boiling in his veins. He started to shake with the sheer force of the vengeance surging through his body. His jaw was clenched so hard he was sure he was going to need major dental work by the time this was over.

"I did it for you! I did it for us," the man said. "That Irishman was in the way. Oh, he looked the part, tall and handsome—and that hair. What was up with all that hair? He looked like a girl to me." Sean could tell the man was being sarcastic now.

"Shut up!" she yelled at him.

"Oh, I know. Did you hang on to his hair when he was on top of you? Is that it? Is that what you liked?"

Sean couldn't think of enough appropriate ways to make this man suffer for all he had done.

"Stop it!" he heard her yell.

Sean's heart was breaking at what she must be feeling right now. He knew she had really loved his brother, and it gripped his heart to have her subjected to this. "Hang on, lass," he said under his breath. He was only a few feet away now.

"Yeah, yeah, yeah," he heard the scum continue on with his badgering. "Well, you'll be glad to know he screamed like a stuffed pig when I shot him. A coward. Oh, he was big, all right, and it took another shot to bring him down, but I did. And you know what, Caroline? He didn't even try to get up. No, he just lay there and bled like the gutted pig he was."

Sean would kill him for that. His thoughts focused again on Caroline. She was sobbing now, and Sean couldn't hold himself back any longer. He looked down at his hands that held nothing. No gun, no flashlight, nothing he could use as a weapon. It didn't matter. He knew at that point he would kill this man who had caused him and his family so much grief, killed his brother, and kidnapped his only love. He knew he would need only his hands to exact his vengeance this fateful night. He lowered his hands at his sides and fisted them once again so tightly his knuckles turned white. He was about to jump when the man spoke again, catching his attention. He stilled. He had already heard enough, but he had to think clearly if he was going to get Caroline safely out. He had to think first.

"Caroline? Look at me." There was a sudden change in the man's voice. It was softer, almost compassionate. "Caroline, I never meant for this to happen. I never meant to have to do this to you. You were all I wanted in life. All any man could want. I'm sorry, but at least you will be with him now. I give you to him."

Before Sean could blink, he heard the shot ring out, and pieces of loose rock slammed into his head from above. His heart pounded in his chest as he jumped out of his hiding place and saw Caroline on the ground, hands and feet bound. There was so much blood—more blood than he'd ever seen before, soaking the ground around her head.

He stood for what seemed like an eternity, his mind reeling while he stared at her lying so deathly still on the ground, unable to move. Sean's trance was broken when he heard the man yell at him, bringing him back to reality.

"Who the fuck are you?" the man snarled, his hand shaking like he'd just seen a ghost. He pointed the gun directly at Sean's heart.

"I'm Sean McNally. The man who's come to deliver ya ta Satan, lad," he said without emotion as he walked directly toward the man.

39.

LOVE UNENDING

Sean stood motionless, staring out at the sea with his hands folded across his chest and the breeze blowing through his loose hair, causing it to flap gently in the freshness of his country. The salt from the mist sprayed cold seawater against the sides of the cliffs. It was warm for so late in September in Ireland, and he closed his eyes to the sun hanging low and orange in the western sky. His thoughts floated with the sounds of the seagulls flapping and wailing in the distance, the restless ocean waves crashing against the stillness of the land.

He sighed, opening his eyes and looking at the setting sun. It reminded him painfully of his time in America with its violet and pink streaks trailing across the sky. He swallowed hard and felt in his mind a slight pang of the pain he had felt that horrible night. It had been more than nine months, and he could still feel it as though it were yesterday. Somehow, he knew he always would. It somehow served a purpose in his life, and it was a part of him. A gentle reminder of all he lost and of all he still had.

"Sean, are ya going ta stand there all day starin at the ocean like a statue?" He groaned low at his sister's voice. He had long ago forgiven her, but sometimes she still felt like a thorn in his side.

"Claire, leave me be, lass." *God, but she could rile a man's nerves.*

"Me, Ma, and young Robbie have packed up the picnic and are headed home now. Don't ya even have the manners ta come and say yer goodbyes then?"

She had made her point loud and clear, and he opened his eyes to her standing with her hands on her hips as she always did when riled up. He grinned at her long, red hair blowing about her face. It looked three shades darker when she had her temper up, as did her eyes.

He reached out and tickled her, and she slapped his hands away, turning for the house, but not before he thumped her bottom good. She hated that, and he knew well enough to run fast past her before she got in a good punch. She had quite a hit for being such a scrawny little thing.

He laughed with her in hot pursuit all the way back to the cottage.

"Sean, you're the devil's own, ya are!" she said breathlessly when they reached the door.

"Aye, but ya love me still, 'ey?" he said, grabbing her and hugging the remainder of her breath away.

"Aye, and a curse it is, I'll tell ya that!" she said, pulling away and landing a good punch in his upper arm.

"Go on then, be off with ya before me wife has ta see me beatin yer bare behind!" he said, waving her off toward the car in the driveway. Robbie was leaning against the side, shaking his head at them and their childish behavior.

"Ya wouldn't dare, ya big oaf!" she yelled back at him, and he took a menacing step toward her. It was enough. She ran and practically jumped in the car to escape him.

He roared with laughter. Through all they had been through, she still remained his little sister, even if she was still a little hellion at times.

He turned to go inside and was suddenly in the way. His mother pushed him off to the side and batted him out of the way. "Let me help ya with that, Ma," he said, reaching for the bag she was carrying.

"No, no. I can manage just fine. I'm not so old ya need ta be treating me like an invalid yet, lad," she said in a no-nonsense tone. "I've come ta depend on myself now that ya moved up here ta the cottage and all," she added over her shoulder.

He stood for a moment and watched them pile into the car. Mary rolled down her window for a last wave goodbye and blew him a kiss. "You'll be sure to give yer old ma a call now and then, 'ey?" she yelled as Claire drove off down the long drive.

"Aye. That's a promise, Ma!" he yelled back and watched their car disappear over the hill. He liked it when his family came for an outing, but if the truth be told, he couldn't wait for them to leave. He looked through the porch glass into the house, a devilish grin breaking over his mouth. Alone at last. He turned and went inside.

Rounding the corner to the kitchen, he saw her. She had her back to him and wasn't aware of him watching her. She was humming softly while putting away the few remaining dishes left out to dry.

His breath caught in his throat. She was so beautiful, even with that old, white apron and those silly, bright-fuchsia slippers on she loved so well, he couldn't imagine anything lovelier than his wife.

He stood a moment longer in the doorway, letting his eyes soak up her image a while longer. He crossed his arms over his chest and leaned against the wood frame. His grin became wider as he watched her in the throes of domesticity. Her long, dark curls swayed around her slim hips as she moved, and he felt his want for her beginning to grow with each movement she made. When she reached high to put a bowl away, and he caught a fair glimpse of her long, shapely legs under the hike of her long skirt, it was nearly his undoing.

"Sean McNally, I know exactly what you're thinking with that devilish grin on your face, you bad boy!" She had caught him unaware. He actually felt his face become warm, and he looked at her with his head slightly bowed. "Aye, tis the truth, lass. I couldn't think of nothing else but for wanting ya all day," he said huskily.

"Well, well, husband of mine. Go and get your shower, and I'll see what I can do to relieve this burden you've been carrying around with you all day," she said seductively while walking toward him, untying her apron in a mini strip tease. He nearly lost it at that and almost took her there in the kitchen but forced himself to settle on the gentle kiss she offered before he ran for the bath.

Coming out of the bathroom, he noticed the faint smell of vanilla; with the lights dimmed low, he knew she had lit some candles. Walking to the bedroom, he frowned at not finding her waiting on the bed for him. He let the towel he had placed modestly around his waist drop to the floor as he continued on into the living room in search of her.

"Caroline?" he said softly. His eyes were drawn to the fireplace that was now glowing softly and the pillows that had been placed close to the hearth. He smiled as he realized how much effort she put into the tiniest of things for him. He started to call for her again when he heard the water from the shower start up again. She knew him. Knew he wouldn't want to wait if he saw her again, so she slipped by him to get to the bath.

He sat on the thick carpet in front of the fire. The warmth dried his body and took the chill out of the night air. He leaned back on one arm and watched the vivid flames gently lapping the sides of the wood. *I have to be the luckiest man alive.* No, *blessed* was more the word for how he felt these last months. He had finally found love in his life, only to nearly lose it. It was a mistake he would never again make.

Sean's eyes grew dark as he pulled the memory of that awful night so easily into his thoughts. He had thought her dead then. Thought his life was over that night in the mine shaft. Rage had taken complete control of his actions when he saw that bastard standing over her still body, the gun still smoking from the bullet that had nearly taken her from him. He was crazed with anger, sheer and uncontrollable anger, as he pounced with lightning speed on the man, knocking him down and beating him senseless. Only when the man stopped fighting back and lay motionless in his hands did he turn to Caroline on the ground.

He picked her up and started walking toward the opening when the man he thought was dead yelled out to him. Sean stopped, turned with her in his arms, and stood face to face with the man as he took aim and fired. Sean closed his eyes, fully expecting to feel the sting of the bullet with the noise of the shot, but he didn't. Slowly opening his eyes, he realized the man was dead on the floor from a single, clean shot to the forehead. Mac stood smiling at him.

Sean shook his head, and tiny droplets of water shook off the ends of his hair. He could see the scene that night in the mine shaft so clearly it made his heart ache as though he were still there.

He remembered taking Caroline outside to a waiting ambulance and placing her lovingly on the bed they had set up. He remembered being reluctant to let her go; the paramedics had to drag him off her. Then he remembered the words he never could have imagined hearing: "She's alive, man! She's breathing!"

Sean believed in God that night. Believed in a higher power looking over his life. He believed again later when they let him near her, explaining it had been only a flesh wound, and she and the baby were going to be all right. He dropped to his knees then, and in the middle of the desert night, he fell flat to his face and promised God a thousand promises.

"Hey, why such a dark look?" Caroline asked, reaching out and softly placing her fingers on his chin, forcing him to look at her. He was so engrossed in memories that he didn't hear her enter the room.

"Oh, Caroline," he whispered, pulling her close to him. She had seen this look before and knew what clouded his thoughts while he lay gazing at the fire.

"I love you, Sean," she said into his chest. He smelled so wonderful to her, especially after a shower, and she loved to just lie against him and inhale his fresh, masculine scent. She ran her fingers through the thick mass of crispy hair on his chest and felt the strength under her touch when he shifted to pull her tighter to him.

"How's the lad?" he asked, grabbing her hand and bringing it to his lips for a kiss.

"Asleep; your mom wanted to put him down before she left. Something about his dad not knowing such wee bairns shouldn't be played with so much."

"Aye, I tend ta want ta do that. It's just that he's so wonderful, is all. Is it a bad thing, me wantin ta be with little Jamie so much?"

She looked into his eyes, finding it difficult to be so near her husband and keep her thoughts from floating toward the pleasure he could so easily bring her. "No. I think we're both the luckiest people on earth to have such a wonderful father and husband," she managed to say, her mind being reeled into his intoxicating presence.

His eyes caught and held hers for a long gaze that left her to taste his lips.

"I'm glad ya thought of the name. James Patrick Robert McNally—now there's a mouthful. It does seem to fit the lad, though, 'ey?" he asked. He was purposely goading her on. He wanted her so badly it was killing him not to rip off that silly nightgown she put on and show her exactly what she was putting him through, but the knowledge she was feeling as much as he was at this very minute made it worth the fun.

"Yes," she whispered, biting his neck playfully, trying to get him to stop rambling.

"And it's nice that Michael and Vanessa have taken ta callin each other on the phone. Michael told Paul and Willy she was flying over for Christmas. Said he intends ta wed with her."

He made up the last sentence. Caroline's friend really *was* coming to Ireland over Christmas, but Michael didn't ask her to marry him yet. Sean grinned as she continued with her quest to make him notice her. She wasn't paying any attention to what he was saying. He reached over and lifted her face up to meet his.

Her eyes were smoldering with desire. She laced her arms around his neck as he pulled her to him, bringing his mouth down on hers, his tongue sliding into her awaiting lips to stroke and duel with hers. He rolled over and pushed her down under him, pulling her thin gown off her shoulders and exposing her breasts. She looked up into his eyes and begged without words for his touch. He had her full attention now.

"Caroline?"

She put her fingers to his mouth, not wanting him to talk. She smelled so sweet. He took them into his mouth and sucked them softly. She moaned and arched under him. The playfulness he had started suddenly lost all its fun, and he nuzzled his face against her breast, warm and swollen with nourishment for his son. He kneaded them, and she nearly came up off the floor, crying out at the sensation his touch brought her.

She couldn't believe how much fire his touch held. He could bring her to the brink of ecstasy over and over again, letting her ride the waves her body felt until she thought she couldn't take any more. Until she thought she would surely die if he didn't come with her to the heaven they could both create on earth. She felt him cup her face in his hands. Felt the hotness of his body covering hers. She opened her eyes and looked into his loving eyes.

"Never change, Caroline. Never stop loving me just as ya do now. I need ya, for ya are the very heart of me. In all me life, I could never replace what we have right now. Do ya understand?"

She understood.

"Love is the only thing we search our whole lives for, and it's the only thing worth finding. Sean, I'll never leave ya, no matter what," she whispered. She knew he was still frightened after almost losing her in the mine, and the thought of her great giant of a husband with all his strength and muscle hanging on to her next statement, she said it with all her heart. "No one ever told me about the fire, Sean. The fire that burns in my soul for you. No one ever told me it would consume my whole being and that I couldn't stop it no matter what I did. I . . . just . . . can't stop loving . . . you, wanting you, loving only you. Sean, we are a part of each other now, and with little Jamie, we're a real family. Bonded together with a lifetime of love ahead of us." She spoke softly, and as she watched the tears form in his eyes, she also felt her own sliding down her cheeks and into her hair.

"I love ya, lass," he said, choked with emotion, bending down and kissing her with a lifetime of love in his heart. Both tasted the saltiness of each other's passion and love, both knowing the sweetness of the safety in each other's arms.

EPILOGUE

The night winds were blowing hard outside. She could hear them through the walls, their blowing seemingly dark. With the thickness of the stone walls to protect her and him, life seemed safe and sure, untouchable. Sean stirred next to her, pulling her closer to him in his sleep and wrapping his legs around hers, trapping her close.

She smiled at feeling his warmth invading her. Dreamily, she breathed to match his, inhaling him inside her as he exhaled. He was her life, and her life was safe for the moment.

Caroline's dreams took her to the familiar stage of the deserted theatre one last time. She could feel herself guided along in the dance by her husband's strong arms, the music soft and somehow echoing her life.

She saw him the moment she sensed him. He was still strong in her memory, and her heart knew him well. He was standing in the darkness, alone against the curtains, where he had been reluctant to start from before. She caught glimpses of him over Sean's broad shoulder as he danced her across the stage. He was smiling with twinkling eyes, and she heard him speak to her in her soul, though no words passed between them.

"Ya did good, lass," Patrick said as his form started to fade. This time, unlike before, she did not feel the immediate panic that threatened to seize her heart. She did not feel a loss at his leaving. There was no need to flee, to hold onto him. Instead, she stayed in her husband's sure arms as they floated across the stage together, bathed in the haunting blueness of the dimmed lights.

She felt only peace at Patrick's leaving, and in her heart, she knew he would always be there watching over them. Best of all, in her heart, she knew that was where he belonged.

AUTHOR'S NOTE

On August 30, 1994, the IRA's Catholic political wing, Sinn Féin, under the direction of its leader, Jerry Adams, declared a ceasefire. It was the first in more than twenty-five years of bloodshed and a monumental event for the people of Northern Ireland.

On October 15, 1994, six weeks after the IRA's ground-breaking announcements, the militant Protestants declared their own ceasefire to the bloodshed.

Britain, however, still refuses their leader's acceptance of the negotiations at the peace talks until both sides turn in their arms.

It is the wish of this author that the end of the violence that has plagued Ireland is finally over and that both sides can put an end to the hatred and begin anew, both forgiving each other's past sins and coming together finally in a lasting peace.

Slán go fóill

Born in Columbus, Ohio, in 1962, Melody lived a life defined by resilience, curiosity, and an enduring love of storytelling. She never knew her father and grew up in a non-traditional household; her mother was a professional wrestler in the 1950s, and she was raised alongside her sister Patty. She had a baby sister, Crystal, who was given up for adoption in 1966, and she never stopped searching for her, keeping a bond alive through hope and determination.

After her divorce in 1995, she traveled alone to Ireland, Scotland, and England—a journey that reignited her sense of self and inspired her to write her romance novel, *Across the Sea of Desire*. She returned home with a newfound love of Celtic culture, music, and history, and a determination to share stories that celebrated passion, roots, and connection. She also instilled a love of travel in her two daughters, showing them that the world was full of wonder and adventure.

Professionally, she dedicated herself to the care of others, working in the NICU at University Medical Center in Tucson, Arizona, supporting premature babies and their families with compassion and skill.

She passed away in 2012 from cancer, leaving behind her beloved novel. Her oldest daughter, Amanda, fulfilled her mother's final wish by publishing *Across the Sea of Desire*, preserving her mother's voice and her story for readers to enjoy.

Her life was one of searching, loving, and creating—qualities that shine through every page of her novel.

www.ingramcontent.com/pod-product-compliance
Lightning Source LLC
LaVergne TN
LVHW100504110826
845146LV00002B/513

* 9 7 9 8 9 9 4 9 3 7 7 1 6 *